BOOKS BY EDMUND GILLIGAN

VOYAGE OF THE GOLDEN HIND

THE RINGED HORIZON

THE GAUNT WOMAN

BOUNDARY AGAINST NIGHT

STRANGERS IN THE VLY

WHITE SAILS CROWDING

CHARLES SCRIBNER'S SONS

VOYAGE OF
THE GOLDEN HIND

Voyage of the Golden Hind

by
Edmund Gilligan

NEW YORK

Charles Scribner's Sons

1945

To

GERTRUDE RITTENHOUSE

VOYAGE OF
THE GOLDEN HIND

1

JOHN BANNON is my name. Gloucester is my nation. I am the captain of the *Golden Hind*, a schooner long employed in the Grand Banks fisheries, and I shall remain her captain as long as there is life in me and fish in the Atlantic.

Now the name of that vessel has become well known to many people, in and out of the fisheries, because of certain events on the Grand Banks in which she played her part, as I played mine. These happenings were hard enough to bear at the time and there would seem to be little good and much pain in living through them again, especially when I call to mind that I am no quill-pusher, but a man with cod to kill and a vessel and a woman to care for, as best I may. Nevertheless, I put my fist to it, tonight in the cabin of the *Golden Hind* while she lies snug on Sable Bank, for the good reason that a darkness of shame has been cast upon vessel and woman and upon my own name. This is a matter I will not let rest. Grief and anger and manhood speak out against it.

I had thought my deeds had been clearly the deeds of a faithful doryman (which was my circumstance at the time); and that I clearly showed myself to be the better of Captain LeNotre. Time and humanity have taught me otherwise. Even the courts of inquiry, in the Dominion and at Gloucester, failed to make clear all that happened. Yet the courts are not to be blamed for such harsh things as sidelong glances and words said slyly. Among the words, I know, is this one: murderer. It is not said openly to me or to her; and I do not intend that it shall ever be said to our son when the day comes for him to steer the *Golden Hind* on her voyages. No! Such a word is whispered only when I am at sea. I say, at the outset, that I did not leave Captain LeNotre to his dreadful and deserved fate. That accusation I do deny. Yet I also say: I would have killed him with my own hand, if no other hand had been ready nigh.

Let there be no mistake about it. When I have done, there'll be two caps fitted to crafty 'longshore heads: the dunce's cap and the liar's. Yet there is more to this matter than the lives and happiness of a man and a woman and the good name of a famous vessel. Such wrongs can be borne, especially when I consider that justice will be done in the end. There is a greater wrong being done, a wrong to an entire people, which is something not to be borne without protest.

* * *

I had been a full season without steady work before the voyage of the *Golden Hind* began. This idleness was of my own choosing, although I had hardly enough money to keep soul in body. The choice between idleness and a comfortable site on a dragger was a matter of conscience with me. Since that decision was the chief cause of all that befell us, I should make it plain why I could not go fishing as my father had and his father before him.

These two men were high-liners of Gloucester in their day, which is to say that they always found the fish and always made the Boston market on a Wednesday when a hundred thousand pounds of cod were worth a lot more dollars than a day later. They were captains of old-fashioned dory trawlers, the topsail schooners of Cape Ann. In fact, both went skipper of the same vessel: our own *Pennypacker*, which was destroyed in the wars while fishing on Emerald Bank. A dory trawler is a schooner that catches fish by hook-and-line; that is, by thousands of hooks fastened to a long line called the trawl. This is a natural way of fishing. Grandfather Sebastian, who once caused a considerable stir by writing an account of his adventures on the Grand Banks, used to say that the cod's mouth was expressly designed to take a cod-hook. And it is a fact that only a fair-sized fish will take a baited hook. Nature provides that a young fish, which has not spawned and multiplied its kind, cannot take a hook. I speak generally, of course. The rule applies to well-cut bait. I have seen young fish taken when the bait was cut too fine, a harmful practice followed by careless dorymen.

Thus briefly, I give you the way of fishing in the old days.

That day has passed. It is over and gone; and with it has gone the pitiless labor of the dories in fog and blizzard, the hard task of hauling trawl, ripping and gutting fish, icing them down, and, at the same time, making sail and handling it. There are some men who profess a rather romantic sadness at the displacement of sail in the fisheries by power. I am not one of them. Such terrible labor was a harsh price to pay for life, a life that was never sweet and rarely easy. Yes, I could always understand why an old doryman took death calmly, whether it came to him in a warm bed ashore or on an icy deck. He had enough of life.

Well, it's over. There isn't one vessel carrying a mainsail out of Gloucester today. More than that, there isn't a vessel carrying working dories to sea from our wharves. And the truth of it is that I myself wouldn't know a main-sheet from a table-cloth if the Doonan family hadn't clung to their *Golden Hind* and her dories and sails. Long after all the other families had taken off main-booms and mainsails and had put engines below the beautiful decks, the Doonans, a stiff-necked generation, remained steadfast to a way of fishing that had made them rich and famous. Aye! and, in the end, poor and driven to harsh measures. When I was only twenty years old, I went skipper of the *Golden Hind* for two voyages, simply because I was the only trained sailing-master in the port who preferred the meagre earnings of the *Hind* to the abundant earnings of the draggers.

Here, by the word "dragger," we come to the true meaning of these matters and to the reason for my chosen idleness. I would not kill fish with dragger gear. It is against nature to do so; and it has always seemed to me that an act against nature, whether at sea or 'longshore, will ruin a man of conscience, a man of good will. Such fishing is against nature because the dragger cannot select her fish. Her enormous net, towed along the bottom by a powered vessel, sweeps up all that swims in her path: cod, haddock, halibut (small ones, of course), sharks —everything! And, as you will learn, the net can sweep up things that are strangers to the sea.

The most grievous fault of the dragger is that the net will catch and kill multitudes of small fish. They cannot escape. I have seen fifty thousand young and healthy cod poured out of a cod-end onto the deck of a dragger. Such fish were no good to man. Most of them were killed by the pressure of the net and of the catch itself. The others died on deck. All of them were shovelled over the side to feed the gulls and sharks. Had the fish been left to flourish for another season, the gain in marketable fish would have been great; for it is known that a healthy cod, if it finds fair feeding, will double its weight in a year.

It will be plain to some people that the vessel which caught the fifty thousand had been dragging in a nursery ground. Such a haul of young fish couldn't have been made elsewhere. And it may be asked: What were you doing aboard such a vessel? The answer is: I made the voyage (to Georges Bank) for the express purpose of seeing for myself the extent and meaning of this slaughter. At the time, I was doing what I could to help the government in its examination of the fisheries. I was taking cod from the bags and measuring them. To my way of thinking, these men of the civil service were doing a great and necessary benefit to the people, who must have cheap food. The government men wished to prove to the fishermen and to the owners that there was a danger in the dragger fishing, a danger that their livelihood might be lost and the fisheries ruined.

'Twas an unholy greed that drove men to this destruction of nature's gift. The destruction was accomplished by means of a net made with a small mesh, which, at the best, was no larger than two and a half inches wide. This was the very net which made such havoc in the North Sea fisheries, where I once spent a season at my father's request and expense in order to study this matter and bring back the true gospel. The Scottish Board of Fisheries showed me great courtesy and sent me to the Dogger Banks as a passenger aboard an experimental trawler so that I might see for myself the reasons why a five-inch mesh should be used. The Scots asserted (and proved to my satisfaction) that the larger mesh would eventually catch just as many pounds of fish as the smaller mesh. Best of all, the large mesh permitted the small fish to escape. The use of that larger mesh was, in the end, required by Scottish law; and the other governments concerned (the English and the Danes) joined in the task of saving their fisheries. Fish had become so scarce in their waters that a first-class British trawler on which I sailed (two hundred and fifty tons, I mean) caught only eighty pounds of fish in an hour's dragging! This was ruin, indeed, and I doubt if the North Sea fisheries will ever afford the abundance of the days when fish were killed by hook-and-line and by nets made in an honest way.

Now, in our own time and waters, the story is the same. It is a bitter thing to know and it has been a great unhappiness to me and to other men of my way of thinking. I can put it all into a nutshell by saying these things: first, that a market was found for small slices of fish prepared by the filetting process, by which baby fish could be profitably killed. Second, that in the year I first fished on Georges Bank the fleets took a grand total stock of two hundred and fifty million pounds. Last year, as the market for baby fish increased, the catch was less than sixty million pounds. And this was so, despite harder work by vessels using the latest thing in dragger gear.

By this I know, and I fear, that the day will come when it will no longer be possible to fish and make a living on the Yankee Banks or on the Grand Banks. It is a fear called childish and false by some men, who are fond of saying that I will know more when I grow up and that there will always be fish in the sea. I take it that these men are the direct descendants of the travellers who saw our vast herds of buffalo on the plains of the old West and could not imagine, when they dined on buffalo tongue, that the day would come when nothing would be left of those millions except a few heads wagging behind bars.

They are the men to whom I have said: When did you last kill a big halibut? They have no answer; for the truth of it is that the great halibut fishery of the Grand Banks, where my people earned a good livelihood for generations, has been destroyed by the French draggers. The scoffers say that the halibut have merely moved off to a secret bank beyond the Gulf Stream and that they will come back some day. I declare that it is not so. I declare that the time is not far off when the haddock and cod will vanish, too, and that there will be an end to the first and greatest of all the Republic's trades.

There is proof of it on every hand. Last night, when we hove to on Sable, we spoke the Columbia. She had gone all the way to the Grand Bank itself in her search for ground-fish. She had found none. And now she will fill her pens with redfish and go home, with nary a cod in her pens, as all our Gloucester vessels are doing today.

This is what I meant by saying at the beginning that there is more in the voyage of the *Hind* than the lives and destiny of a man and a woman and a vessel. There is a great disaster to be prevented and, if I say so as shouldn't, I am one of the men who can and will prevent it. It is my desire and my duty. That is why I made a fair net with my own hands and, at last, resolved that the *Golden Hind* should take that net to sea and do so well that all other vessels would follow her example. This was the reason why I locked the door of my sail-loft on the Doonan Wharf one October evening and solemnly determined that I should become captain of the *Golden Hind* and that I should make my mark with her. The hour had come because on that day I heard harsh news. Captain Matthew Doonan, owner of the *Hind*, lay dying in his mansion on the hill that overlooks the harbor of Gloucester. And the *Golden Hind*, still dependent on sail and wind, was many days overdue.

2

I ENTERED the great room softly and stood by the flickering hearth, where I had been welcome these many years. Captain Doonan did not hear me. He paid me no heed. I watched in silence until the old man's eyelids slid down again. Once or twice, the lids lifted halfway, like the lids of a baby's eyes when he fights off drowsiness in the midst of play. He slept, at last, and then, deep in his dream, he sang out cheerfully: "Tumble out, chums!" and, a moment later: "Oh, lively now!"

He laughed in his dream. I couldn't help laughing with him because I knew well enough the beautiful and lively images that leaped and spun in that grey man's memory. Those images were mine, too. I could tell that for him, in the evening of this frosty day which was the evening of his life, a blue wind kicked up whitecaps far away by bleak Sable, by black Miquelon. And the glass fell four tenths in an hour of foreboding, while he, young and resolute again, roared out that the *Hind's* topsails should be clewed up and dories summoned from the hauling. Brisk Gloucester skippers and mighty dorymen strode by him in the salty chronicle of his remembrance; and my father and my grandfather laughed amongst them. He saw them lean out of cranky dories to gaff the halibut, heard them repeat the old, old order: "All hands! All hands!"

Once again, there in his last reclining, he saw men live for fish and die for them, die the death of gales, the death of cold in dories wandering in the winter vapor. He groaned deep in his dream and stirred under his blanket. He cracked his scarred hands weakly together, turned his closed eyes eagerly to hearth and coals, as if he sought assurance that he was here in the beautiful room and not there on the Banks steering the *Golden Hind* in the hopeless circle of search, her horn crying for her children, and poor cook beating his dishpan loudly in a hissing waste of water.

I flung my cap down and went to the bay window, where I had watched many an hour for our returning vessels, either from the risky voyages through Newfoundland ice or from the winter quarter down Virginia way. Far to sea, a squadron of destroyers steamed on an eastward course. The evening light pierced the aisles and colonnades of vapor that stood off and on the shore. Now and then a beam glanced on a plunging bow. Nearer, two little gill-netters struck through the heavier seas beyond the Point and ran toward the harbor. A searchlight at the Point laid a beam on each one, held it long enough for recognition and went dark. Farther down the coast, an orange-colored hand lamp began to blink on a vessel lying close to Norman's Woe.

I searched the darkening sea beyond old Thatcher's, striving to make out the lights and gleaming topsails of the *Golden Hind*. A tide of rose-colored light ran from the back of the world, dyed the blue, and splashed into the darkness beyond the twin towers of the lighthouse.

Beneath the window, and between the house and outermost wall of the high garden, there stood another watcher, dimly seen in the shadows that poured along the flagstone path and gathered under the bare boughs of the mock-orange tree. I could just make out the familiar straddle of the long legs in doryman's dark trousers and doryman's boots; and the turned-up collar of a pea-jacket. A sou'wester (that wind which was to mean so much to us) began rising. It struck down the hill-side and whooped among the boughs, making the dead leaves fall. The watcher moved closer to the wall and stood against it in a sea-going slouch, half ease, half alertness, like one who expected the prowlike jut of the garden to crash into a boarding sea.

I rapped at the window. The watcher did not turn. I rapped again. She looked over her shoulder and gazed briefly at the window. Some trick of twilight and mist made the sharp plane of her cheek gleam in an almost ghastly hue against the dark cloth of her jacket. She swung her arm toward the sea and turned her head that way again.

The old man stirred uneasily in his chair and cried: "Whoosh!" He opened his eyes carefully, as if he dreaded what he might encounter. Eagerly his eyes sought and found the fire, so that he lay secure, and thus drove away all the blinding fog from the Banks of yesterday, where he had been in his dream. He made the floes of winter and bergs of spring drift by and melt away. He let the wind of blue summer pour into his spirit until the loveliest of all his sea-images swam smoothly into his ken: the image of his *Golden Hind*, dear to him beyond all saying. He sent his eyes a-roving through the autumnal shadows of the room and fixed them with tenderness upon her real image, painted on canvas, framed above the fire. Under a whole mainsail, and under topsails, too, she leaped before the no'theaster, fair for her in the passage home.

He whispered an old Gloucester compliment to her beauty and usefulness: "Good dog! Follow you anywhere!" He gave some consideration to her gay coloring: the old-fashioned bottle-green from waist to waterline, buff decks, blue waterways, and white mastheads. And, in a gesture of despair, he raised his withered hand to her and cried out: "Lord! Lord! Where is she now—the *Golden Hind?*"

I replied: "We're watching for her, Captain."

It took some time for him to find my voice in his memory, though days only had passed since he had listened to it keenly. After a time so long that it filled my heart with stir and fright, he whispered: "Ah, 'tis you, Captain John?"

" 'Tis I, sir."

He waited for his breath. He said: "No one has spoken her?"

"No one."

A log on the hearth sent out a tiny rocket and began to burn fiercely. In that rush of light, his face became clearer to my eyes, and I marked with sadness the inroad that had been made in the days since I had last stood in that room. His massive head, erect for a moment in new attention, caught the fresh light and gave it off brightly and made his greyness change to silverness. His thick sweep of hair, too long uncut, shone like the metal. Hitherto, the changing shadows had partly hidden the signs of his age and of his passing. Now the light revealed, clearer than ever before, the wreck of a once mighty man. His cheeks were gaunt, were sucked in by the deliberate breathing of a man who knows his time is running out. The wind whistled in his thinned nostrils. Nevertheless, he lived hard in his eyes, in which green of shoal water and blue of deep were mixed. They shone like gems in a waxen face. Yet their strength and fire showed what he had once been: a free captain on a free ship.

The garden door opened. The squall slipped over the threshold and struck boisterously at the fire. The heir of the *Golden Hind* and of all the *Hind's* woes came into the room. He turned quickly toward her. His anxiety made his eyes

beam; and their beseechment drew her toward him in a vigorous stride, so much like a doryman rolling across a slanted
deck that the old captain cracked out a laugh. She passed me
by, gave me less than half a smile, which had been her way
with me for some time now. For my part, I gave her the tenth
of a smile in return.

Captain Doonan took strength from her, as he always did.
To her woolen shirt and patched trousers he gave a mocking
look; and to the leather boots, halfway to her knees, he gave
a look of more than mockery. He whispered: "Nora!" and
then, in a firmer voice: "More like a man every day!"

"Ah, no, Grandfather! Not that!" Yet she looked down at
her boots in the same disapproving way and struck at a wisp
of rope yarn clinging to her trousers. She took another step
forward and stood between him and the firelight in such a
way that I could see she was becoming a tall girl, a Juno, long-
limbed, and hard-handed. She carried the marks of waterfront
toil. Her hands, spread on her hips, grasped belt and cloth in
a manlike grasp. The nails of her hands were broken and
grimy; and the left hand bore a white scar, deep-cut and
shaped like a cod-hook. And I well remembered the day that
she suffered that scar aloft on the *Golden Hind;* and how glad
she was to have a certain party on hand to bind the wound.

It wasn't hard to find his image in her. She had his sea-
colored eyes, his big forehead, from which her black hair was
swept plainly backward and caught up in heavy braids. As
we used to say of her, she was nothing to write home about,
except that her mouth had always been a good thing to look
at. Her lips had life and flesh to them, whereas his mouth held
only scantiness. Her lips seemed unused; seemed, to me at least,
like verses of a fine song not yet sung too often.

She came closer to him, her right hand outstretched, and said: "'Tis her longest voyage yet—by three days."

"I was never so long!" He spoke quickly in his old pride, taking the words out of her mouth. "But why? Why, Nora darling?"

"You were never so long, Grandfather. Even that time you were hove down on the Middle Ground. And I lay there"— she pointed toward the window—"for two whole nights and couldn't close my eyes."

I knew that she had readily called up his past to keep him away from the present fear. Just the same, I took it unkindly of her not to remember that I had sat there in the window seat during all that fearful vigil when we were children.

Captain Doonan spoke with growing vigor. "You remember! Ah, you're sweet to me, Nora. A sweet girl! Aye! you did look out for me. And me hove down. Hove down, indeed, and with a hundred thousand pounds of halibut in my pens. Sixty cents a pound! Sixty, Nora! And 'tis all gone, poor dear. None for you, none for you. As I meant there should be." He gave a lick to his dry lips and whispered the grand price over again: "One hundred thousand at sixty. Sold her right through, I did. And bought her a new suit." He groaned again in misery. "She's taken back all she ever gave!" And: "Where is she now? What's he keeping her out there for?"

She tried to soothe him. "The *Lark* spoke her on Western Bank a week ago today. So they say in Boston. I was sure, Grandfather, that by now—"

" 'Tisn't good luck that's keeping her, Nora. Mind what I say! Remember I said that now!"

She sat upon the arm of the broad chair and touched his forehead gently. "I'll remember. And if you're wrong—if

Captain LeNotre brings her home all pens full—why! I'll forget what you said. Is that it, sir?" She spoke the "sir" in the joking vein that always made him smile.

"Proper thing. Proper thing." He bent his head in childish pleasure to meet her caress and he whispered a word that she couldn't hear. When she lowered her head to listen, he said: "And where were you working today? And to what good, Miss?"

"I went aboard the *Silver Stream*—"

"I don't know her!"

"She's lying at the machine-shop wharf. From Newfoundland, she is. Tom Macklin's her skipper."

"Macklin? Macklin?"

"Aye! Grandfather, 'tis that man. Under sail yet. Like us. So I sold him the old mainsail. He had need of it. Bad need of it. And we'll have no use for it."

"How much?"

"Three hundred dollars."

"Whoosh!" Her chandler's skill delighted him, yet there was something in her story that sharpened his mouth, made him search anew in the fog of his mind. He cried "hem!" and "ha!" until he found his hove-down thought. "What's his need of a mainsail, Nora? Who else carries a mainsail out of Gloucester these days, I want to know?"

"Newfoundland, I said. Or didn't I, Grandfather?" She looked up at me in dismay at his forgetfulness.

He said in a vexed tone: "You did not." He considered the new fact for a time and nodded sagely over it. "From Newfoundland he comes. To Newfoundland he goes. He's a trader and finds that wind is cheap for him there as it is for us here. No engine, no oil for him. Well, he's a wise man, that Macklin. I—I remember his father. Yes, I do! He was also a wise man and a good man aboard a vessel. What's Macklin doing here with his schooner? Salt fish?"

"Yes. He came down from Miquelon and Fortune Bay. They gave him a charter yesterday. Salt to Trepassey Bay. That's why I went aboard her. I knew he had money to spend. And his mainsail—why! Grandfather, 'twas nothing but one big patch—"

In the midst of her pleasant chatter, the old man let his head fall back slowly. He slid at once into his deep dream and breathed easily.

She left him and came to me, her hand held out, and the question for his well-being unspoken in her widened eyes. I took her hand and said: "'Tis natural. Be content with it, Nora. He has lived his life."

We went into the garden and took up our watch for the *Golden Hind*. Full dark had come on. There was no moon. We stood in the shelter of the wall and scanned the sea. The searchlight at the Point again pierced spray and gloom. The beam struck on two incoming vessels, then settled on the first, a big dragger.

She said quickly: "The *Doubloon!* And Captain Parren."

"Aye! Parren." I could not keep the bitterness out of my voice, although I wished to; for he was a good friend of the Doonans and I feared also that she had heard enough from me on that score. Parren was a Boston skipper, one of those whose style of fishing I hated and feared. I said: "Another one of them!"

Nora made no reply.

The *Doubloon* was a handsome, broad-beamed ship, built not long since for dragging. She was shining with new paint. The searchlight revealed her starboard net hoisted against her mainmast to dry. Her port net lay in a dark fold between the gallows. I could see her crew, already dressed in shore-going togs, gathered near the main hatch.

The dragger rode deep.

Nora said: "Two hundred thousand more pounds for him."

I answered: "He can have it! He can have his nursery stock."

The light drew away from the *Doubloon* and dallied upon the second vessel. I saw that she was the *Mary and Martha*, a schooner of the old time that had been launched in Essex a year after the *Golden Hind* slipped down the ways. Like the *Hind*, she had killed fish for many years by hook-and-line, handled by dories. She had been converted into a dragger two summers ago. The nests where her dories had once lain were empty now. Two of her dories were cradled on her new pilot-house. Her towing gear was braced against her empty main-mast.

Her foresail, which was the only canvas she carried, came down while we watched. The old schooner also showed by her deep and sluggish approach that her pens were full, that the long nets had been dragged across the ocean bottom to good purpose.

The vessels moved slowly toward the wharves, where arc lights flashed on to greet them. Throngs of men moved under the lights. They were owners waiting for news of a rich haul, and lumpers ready to empty the pens.

I lifted my eyes from the glare and looked beyond the Point again. A green running-light glimmered there. The shadow of a plunging hull moved steadily shoreward. Above that shadow, I made out a spread of sail; and from the canvas came beams of light. I flung up my hand and cried: "There she is! There's your *Golden Hind*, Nora." I knew that my voice had changed from gentleness to sharpness, thus making my meaning one of mockery, instead of joy, that the *Hind* had returned. It was a mockery touched with sorrow for the watcher at my side. I really meant to say: "And much good may she do you!"

Her arm trembled against mine. As if she did not wish to face that new failure, she whispered: " 'Tis too far, John. Too dark to say what yonder vessel may be." She moved away from me and peered through the night. "And yet there's no other one carrying topsails into this harbor. And those are topsails that I see."

"Topsails, indeed!" I saw the green light vanish in a heavy sea. I said: "She's been taking her time. She wouldn't come in with the draggers. She's ashamed to come home, she is. And I don't blame her. She's empty again."

The *Hind's* green light vanished behind the towers. Soon the port light swung around into plain view as she steered inward. The searchlight found her and I saw her mainsail come down. I saw the dories piled in their nests, the tubs of trawl that carried her thousands of hooks to the bottom; and I saw her graceful buoyancy, untouched by the weight of tons of fish in her pens.

All our hope for the *Hind's* success blew away.

Nora said: "You're right, John. She's failed again." She, too, could see now that the *Golden Hind* had returned as light as she had gone. Lighter, in fact, because her tons of costly ice and stores had been consumed.

She said sadly: "We'll go down to meet her."

I said: "Wait! We've plenty of time." I stepped into her path and took her by the arm. "I've news for you, Nora. For you and your *Hind*."

"What is your news, Captain?"

"All this—all this work and worry and poverty—well! you can put an end to it easily enough."

"How?"

I asked: "The *Hind* is yours, isn't she? He has given you title to her already?"

"Yes."

I had kept my secret overnight; that's all. Now that the time had come to tell it to her, as I had been asked to do, I couldn't help pausing at a step that might take her schooner from her. With the words ready on my lips, I gazed at her in that gloomy place; and the thought came to me that, by speaking the words I had to say, I might also put a barrier between me and the *Hind* forever. My heart was set on steering her to sea some day, fitted and changed to take her place in a new world. Yet that hope was far off; might, indeed, never be realized; because such a change, from dory trawler to dragger, required an immense amount of money. And there was none to be had. I stared in silence at Nora; and, as my luck would have it, a beam of light blew down from above the bending trees and gave me such a clear look into her eyes and into her heart that I determined to speak. In that swift glance, I saw that, within the room, she had hidden her full thought and fear from the old man and me. Now I plainly saw that she had suffered more than I knew. She had grown years older in the few steps she had taken from the door to the garden wall. I said to myself: "This is really how she looks when she goes about the Doonan Wharf seeking some odds and ends to sell."

To her I said: "I can get you one hundred and ten thousand dollars for the *Hind*."

I saw her catch her breath in surprise. Yet she answered calmly enough. She repeated: "One hundred and ten thousand, John?"

"Aye! All of it. In cash. Pushed across a desk at the bank tomorrow morning."

She startled me then by the fierceness of her question. "Whose money? Parren's?"

I shouted in astonishment. "Parren's! I wouldn't touch a dollar of that man's money if I was starving! You're on his books already, aren't you?"

"I am. But not the *Hind*." She lifted her hand to turn the words back to the purchase, but I cried out: "You can't draw a line between yourself and your vessel!"

She answered: "I've drawn it. Grandfather did, too. It's our word. Not the *Hind's* that's been pledged." She asked her question again: "Whose money then?"

"The same syndicate, Nora, that bought the *Laura* for the West Indies trade."

"Ah!" The strength of her sigh and the quick turn of her head away told me at once that I had not brought good news to her. She kept her silence for a moment and then said: "The men that bought the *Laura!*" She said the name over again: "The *Laura!*" and I knew that her sea-wise thought was calling up the image of that great sailer, against whom we had raced in palmy days. And then she said to me with a curiously tender change of her voice: "Where is she now, John? Tell me where the *Laura* is!"

She knew well enough that I could tell her. Indeed, there wasn't a boy in Gloucester who didn't know all that there was to know about the *Laura*. I made the answer she expected. I replied: "Broken on a coral reef."

"So I hear, John. So I hear. I saw her old skipper today on Ben Pine's wharf. Rather a puzzled look in his eyes, I should say. Forty years on the *Laura!* And now she's breaking up on an Indies reef." She shook her head in sadness and looked away into the squally night through which her *Hind* must come. She kept her silence a little while and then said: "You know my answer, John. It would be the old captain's, too. I want no hundred thousand dollars. None of it! None of it! Do you hear me? What is going on in the West Indies that makes a hundred Yankee tons worth so much? My grandfather wanted to know that, too. Do you know what he said when I read him the piece in the Gloucester *Times?* About the *Laura* going to the Indies? 'Queer!' he said, 'queer! 'Tis like sending a fine woman out to walk the streets!' That's what he said, John. No! the *Hind's* mine now and mine she remains!"

I said: "Have done with it."

Arm-in-arm, we hurried through Gloucester's Saturday night. The lights of the old town were dimmed. Sailors and soldiers thronged the pavements. Shore patrols passed up and down the cobbled lanes. The saloons and eating-places were crowded with fishermen and skippers, flush with the big money paid by draggers. Here and there stood groups of dorymen, relics of the old trawling days. These were the men who had filled the old Yankee till by hook-and-line for centuries past. Now they were on the beach for good. Brash draggermen sometimes spoke of them as "pick-up bums." The dorymen greeted her and tugged at their caps; for they held her in high esteem because she clung to their way of fishing and, at times, made use of their skills.

We came to the Doonan Wharf, which was like all the others: a long story-and-a-half shed and a plank roadway running out into the harbor. On either side, there were other wharves and sail-lofts, all cluttered with spars and dories off ancient schooners and the hulks of abandoned vessels. A hundred masts stood against the sky. There were many vessels on the move, in and out. I could hear the uproar from the fish companies' wharves, where the lumpers were taking the fish out of draggers' pens.

Nora and I took up our stations at the far end of the wharf, where we had waited many a night since our childhood for the *Hind* to come in. Now, as before, the schooner came on in silence, shooting to the wharf and growing in our eyes as she came. They had taken off some sail on her way up the harbor. Mainsail first, then jib and jumbo. Her spars moved steadily against rain-clouds, grey and dappled; and, as always, her white mastheads made me think of huge candles on an unlighted altar. Her cross-trees glistened with dew.

Nora said: "She seems all right, Captain."

I don't know what it was that put a harsh answer onto my tongue, but I at once replied: "Aye! she seems all right. But she is not."

Captain LeNotre had the helm. I saw the sleeve of his yellow slicker gleam when he lifted his arm and sang out: "Away! Away with it, boys!"

Her foresail came smoothly down.

Her masts, the tallest ever set in Essex, seemed taller now; because the *Hind* had a way of showing herself off, even under ordinary circumstances, such as shooting to a wharf. The night magnified her beauty and made her seem powerful, immense. And, once again, she made it easy for me to understand how the wisest men might become enthralled by her famous grace and strive to keep her so, no matter what the cost in lives and dollars. Yes, I can remember clearly, even while I set it down, the strength of the appeal she made to me that night, as if in her woman's heart she understood that I was a plotter against her.

The *Hind's* lively pace slowed into a glide. The cook, still in his blowing apron, took down the green lantern out of her rigging. He puffed his cheeks and blew against the wick, but before he blew his eyes shot out two green rays; and that made Nora laugh a little, in remembrance, and she whispered to me: "Green-Eye is home again!"

I picked up the line that fell in a thumping curl at my feet, gave it a turn and made ready to check her way. The men forward heaved another line on. Nora seized it and gave it a turn.

Bear in mind that not a word had been spoken to us from any man aboard that vessel.

Captain LeNotre left the wheel and walked swiftly forward, where there was a stronger light. He stood at the rail, watching her last easy movement with much care. He did not look up at us. I wished to speak to him; that is, in the natural course of things, I wished to greet him and to receive his greeting. Just the same, I didn't hail him. I turned a little so that I could watch Nora and I said to myself: "How has this struck her?"

It seems a little thing—this break from the natural course— yet in the fisheries such items often have deep meaning; and are not to be slighted by us. By the stiffness of her pose, there on the stringpiece, I perceived that she had not been far behind me in judging the vessel's temper. Yet she didn't speak at once, which was even stranger than my own reluctance, because, added to all things else, she had a woman's desire to hear the captain's voice and to know that he was well. The other reason—the woman's reason—was this: amongst us, these two were accepted lovers, in the old-fashioned Cape Ann way of speaking.

Once upon a time it had not been so, but the old gave place to the new on the Christmas Day that the *Hind* returned with her captain dead and this young LeNotre, a yellow-headed wanderer on the Banks, in command. Until that day, he had been only a skilled doryman, noticed by few and not at all by Grandfather Doonan and Nora. Yet he had shown himself to be a great man in a time of peril. He had saved the vessel when her spars were flat on the water, and had driven her home with a wind largely made up of strange French oaths off Miquelon, where he had lived as a boy in the cod-fleet. The old captain admired and respected this stranger. He gave him the command. As for Nora Doonan, nothing need be said, except that Captain LeNotre possessed something that was rarely found in the Gloucester fleet; or in Gloucester itself, for that matter. It's an odd thing to tell and, in a way, a hard one, but the shortest word is the best. This man had beauty. By that I mean physical beauty in his Breton blondness, his big head, which was thickly covered with golden hair that—I give you my word!—I have seen gleaming like a helmet of gold three miles across a blue sea. For the rest, he was a creature molded and strengthened by the Banks, by rowing dories, by hauling trawls, by handling sail. And now by the heavy task of keeping the *Golden Hind* at work. Therein he had failed of late. He had not found the fish.

He had failed again. I knew that, of course. Nevertheless, his failure was not a good cause for the silence aboard the *Hind*, which now seemed strained and unnatural, even under these circumstances. Nothing marred that silence, except the rattle of the tide, until the old schooner at last settled in her place and gave out a sigh, profound and sad, as if she wished to say: "Here I am! Home again—and a shame it is that in my old age I come home to you empty."

Captain LeNotre stepped down from the break and stood near the port dory-nest. There he took off his sou'wester and wiped the dew from his forehead. He struck his hand twice against his matted yellow hair. He then looked directly up at Nora. Yet he didn't speak. He didn't have to speak. His eyes spoke for him. They were dark with weariness and toil, failure and anger.

"And something else!" I said to myself.

I came a stride nearer to him.

He made a slight change in his straddled stand, there amidst the neat rows of trawl tubs. In a way too subtle for naming, this change shook off a part of his weariness. I knew him well enough to mark this down as an assertion of his physical strength, a display of his powerful, tall body. More than that, he thus revealed an inner determination, a hint of arrogance, which had this meaning to me: "Bear in mind that I am captain!" He became dominant.

He also became alone; that is, he set himself off from the others. This was a new thing to me, as it was to Nora Doonan. No man stood near him. We dimly saw their faces, their unstirring figures. I perceived that they had left their captain alone to face her.

Now her desire to speak became so strong that it broke down her desire to learn no more that night. The disaster of empty pens was enough for a day. Aye! and for more than a day, since empty pens meant empty pockets and new danger for her beloved vessel.

I saw her step forward a little distance. She bent a little over the edge of the wharf and sang out cheerfully enough: "Welcome home, the *Golden Hind!*"

The squall caught up her words and tossed them across the crowded deck, where twenty faces gleamed in the dew and mist. The gaiety of her greeting made the silence even deeper. She stood that silence for a moment and then cried out again: "Hey, chums! Are you all ghosts that sail her?"

After that, a man answered from the darkness amidships. He said: "No, Miss." His words ceased, then began again in a strange sort of voice, a voice that had anger and sorrow in it. His words struck me hard.

They were: "There be only one ghost aboard the *Hind!*"

3

THE DORYMAN'S words were spoken sadly. They gaffed Nora Doonan in a hard way. She flung up her head and let her mouth suck in the rainy wind so roughly that it seemed to me she had hidden a sob or a cry of despair. Her hands had been flung out in a welcome. She now joined them over her heart. I heard her repeat a part of those words; and then she did cry out. She cried out like a frightened child suddenly bereft of something dear.

I took her arm and closed my fingers on it.

A man among them cursed. His words, too, were terrible to hear; because they were solemn words, spoken from a man's sorrowful heart. Yet they were of such a nature that I cannot repeat them. I remember them, each and every word; for his curses were laid upon the *Golden Hind*, upon her captain, and upon all those who sent her dory-trawling over stormy seas with fish to haul and rip and gut, and sail to handle night and day.

This was more than I could bear.

I took a stride closer along the stringpiece and I gazed at the silent, unstirring captain. I waited for him to speak; as, by rights, he should have spoken in such a matter. Nevertheless, Captain LeNotre did not break his pose; neither did he turn his head toward the curser. No rebuke for the blasphemy came from his lips. It was plain to me that he intended to make none. I bent my head so that I might judge the meaning of his expression. I was astonished. I found nothing new there, found no change in the angry set of his jaw or in the haughty air.

Thereupon, I raised my head and shouted: "You there! You in the lee of the jib!"

That man replied: "Yes, Captain Bannon."

I cried out to him: "You pipe down! Do you hear, chum? Stop up that jaw of yours or—by the Lord Harry!—I'll stop it for you!" I took a step sideways to be nearer that man; and I cried out again: "Are you a blasted greenhorn? To curse aboard a vessel now? Isn't she bad enough off yet?"

I had chosen my words. I had made an appeal to that ancient taboo which holds strong sway on sailing-vessels. I heard the dorymen murmur.

The curser walked out of the shadows. Indeed, he moved like a shadow; so much like one that a man might have imagined he was up to some deviltry, that he was actually trying to be ghostlike.

He stopped and said: "Aye, Captain! I curse!" I made out the gleam of his eyes and teeth flashing over his words. He drifted aft toward the port dory-nest. He halted a dory-length away from Captain LeNotre; and it was clear to me that he wished to be near him for some further purpose, yet not too near to mar the hatred that lay between them.

I had done all a man in my circumstances could rightfully do. I fell back a pace.

Nora Doonan stepped forward. She could see her men standing there, looking up at her, waiting for word or action, waiting for something to break the spell that had been cast upon them all, upon them and the *Golden Hind*. Knowing, as I did, that custom required the captain of the *Hind* to speak that word, or to take that action, she, too, gazed hesitantly' down at him. She was a strong young woman, vigorous in heart and body, yet the times had placed her in circumstances that would have been harsh enough for a hard-minded man to bear. She had never faltered; and when I saw her hesitate, and give a quick glance toward me, I came nearer to her in my heart than I had long been. I pitied her greatly; and even more when the man, from whom she must expect all things, bore her scrutiny without wavering.

She then called out to the doryman who had cursed. She matched her voice, in loudness and authority, to her position as owner of the *Hind*, which demanded such qualities.

She said: "Is it you, Daniel Corkery, who stands there on my deck and curses captain and vessel and owner?"

The man answered: "'Tis Daniel Corkery, Miss, and no other."

By a twist in his voice, the doryman put a second meaning into his words. I was accustomed to Irish skill in talk. So was she. Thus she knew, as I did, that he had given significance to that word "Daniel." In her despair, she murmured the name over and over. Yet the man's meaning fled from her; and I could not catch it, though I pursued it eagerly.

She told me of her trouble by a glance. I said nothing. Nevertheless, I had to give a captain's answer to her look, which was a beseechment in the gloom. I nodded my head sternly to show what she must do in the honorable course of things. I meant: "If you are fighting for the *Golden Hind* and your life, you must fight now. You know what to do."

She lifted her voice and sent her words, even louder, down to the deck. "Then, Daniel Corkery, take your gear off my vessel! Heaving-stick and gaff and pipe! All off, Daniel, and stand ashore. Your brother will take your settlement for you. If any there be!"

These were exactly the words that I expected from her. Their effect on the dorymen below was extraordinary. I heard, distinctly above the flow of the tide, a sound of many breaths taken sharply and a sighing; and certain faces turned up a little more to stare at her with eyes that had grown even wider and gleamed brighter in the gloom of the *Hind's* deck. It was then that Captain LeNotre gave heed. He merely let his head bend so that his bright face vanished under the brim of his sou'wester.

A lashed bundle rose through the darkness, tossed by Dan Corkery's hands. Before it ceased to roll at Nora's feet, the man himself stood before her; and he seemed enormous. The eye under the ledge of his skull pierced her. The gear in his right hand rattled. In this fierce, silent exchange, the true meaning of his words became clearer; and that meaning struck her a harsh blow, if it be borne in mind that the Corkerys, skilled and famous dorymates, were as much a part of the *Golden Hind* as was her mainmast.

Nora asked: "Where is your brother? Where is James?"

His bare left hand raised slowly and pointed beyond. Beyond Gloucester, beyond the Yankee Banks, beyond bleak Sable.

"He feeds the salt!"

Our ancient idiom of the Grand Banks death came out of his mouth in a voice rusty with his agony.

A man below gave a groan; and the *Golden Hind*, finding her place in the tide and in the timbers yielding to the tide, groaned also.

The doryman bent over and picked up his bundle. He took

one step away and then, with his back turned, spoke gently to her over his shoulder; and I can't tell how he spoke gently because his lips were drawn back over his teeth as if the taking of breath racked him. He said: "I don't curse you, Cap'n Nora. Ah, no! Nor the old man. Nor the poor *Hind*. I don't curse her. But him!—him that goes skipper of her—LeNotre! —him I do curse! He is a murderer!" His gear rattled loudly. "May the curse of Christ rest on his four bones!"

A voice below murmured: "Ah, no! Ah, no, chum!" I knew that voice. It was the Lisbon, old Terrio; and I saw his right hand flash back and forth across his face in the sign of the cross to fend off the evil of a curse from his young captain.

Doryman Corkery walked away.

No one stirred or spoke while the bereaved man strode up the Doonan Wharf. Once he stopped and, again without turning toward us, he seemed to consider some matter. Dim against the glimmer of the upper street, he stood bowed over his gear. A moment later he threw his bundle over his shoulder and, at a slower, grieving pace, trudged out of sight.

The new burden of woe in Dan Corkery's words kept her stock-still, her bare head bowed in sorrowful reflection. A briny rain blew against her crown of braids and glistened there. A briny taste made her mouth downcast, made it poor instead of rich. My pity for her became so strong that I could hardly keep from touching her cheek or her hand in order to tell her, with the authority of a man who knew, that this would pass. My pity grew because I was aware that my own grief for the lost Corkery, who had sailed with my father in the old days, was no less than hers. She and I could recall, times without number, the returns of Corkery from the Banks and how he never forgot to bring home to her in her childhood a gift from the Provinces, or a jewel from the shells undersea or an odd-shaped fruit that he brought up in his trawls when the hooks caught in the Atlantic orchards.

'Twas true, also, that Nora Doonan understood the return of the *Golden Hind* without a good stock of fish was an evil almost fatal to her hopes. She could not help recalling that I, and others, had warned her: dories and hook-and-line will be the death of the *Hind*. The schooner had failed too often. She was not earning her keep. Yet that evil might be borne. Besides, it had been foreseen; and I was soon to learn that she had a desperate venture at hand which might gain for the vessel one last chance to fill her pens and keep herself alive and useful.

The death of a good and faithful doryman was another matter. He could not be replaced. There were no capable hands at ready call in Gloucester. The winter voyages to the Banks required more than skill. Such fishing required great hardihood and endless stores of courage and strength. Even more was needed on the *Golden Hind*, where sail must be handled and storms defeated. These skills, but not the strength, were to be found among the old men, who might be willing to go for a Doonan. Yet she couldn't rightly ask them to do so. Younger men must be found; else the *Hind*, if ever she went to sea at all, must go short-handed, short a hard-working, money-making dory.

Count it all up, and there's a poor prospect. Yet there was more for her to bear. It was this: the loss of Corkery was even more saddening because it cast the first dishonor upon her vessel, her family, and upon the man she loved.

* * *

Captain LeNotre did not say a clear word until he faced Nora in the family's establishment at the head of the wharf, where the business of the *Golden Hind* was done by her. It was a beautiful room, richly furnished in leather and walnut panels and great desks, all earned by the *Hind* in her happier days. A fire of cannel coal burned in a Franklin stove set in the old hearth; and by the stove lay Ambrose, the striped cat, who had general charge of the storerooms beyond the office. Even poor Ambrose had a loss to take that night; for it was to him that James Corkery never failed to bring a steak of choice halibut when the *Hind* returned. Ambrose lifted his head, looked sleepily for the gone man, and fell to drowsing again.

When Captain LeNotre spoke, he at once showed his confidence in his hold over her, in the strength of her passionate and faithful nature. Instead of relating at once the tragedy aboard the schooner, he asked: "Have you any money, Nora?"

This made me jump.

Before she could reply, he made up a smile so close to wheedling that I stirred uneasily. I must confess that it was hard for me to be comfortable in their presence; and I should add that, not long after, I remembered this talk of theirs and could not deny that there was a fine flavor—a French flavor—of intrigue in it. By that I mean that it was daring of him not to come straight to the point and tell us at once how James Corkery met his death. I could say nothing of such matters at the time. I had a strong desire for Nora's happiness, wherever it might be, and I had my own wish to be fair to men. And I was wise enough to see that I could never speak to her as freely as I once could; for I had it in mind that anything I might say could be laid to my old attachment to her. All I did, then, was to come out of the corner by the streaming window and turn up the wick of the brass lamp that swung from the middle beam.

I said: "A little light on the subject, Captain."

Captain LeNotre repeated his question: "Have you, Nora? I don't need any for myself. It's for them." He nodded toward the window and the rain. "For the men. A little for them to take home to their women. They've got to be back aboard tomorrow."

She kept her hand thrust into her jacket pocket. I knew what she had there: the last of the money that she had earned that very morning by selling the spare mainsail. Her captain's question added to her distress. He had said nothing about the fish that might be in the *Hind's* pens. This meant that he had none for the market; and I later found out that the few thousand pounds he had killed were, in the end, thrown away because he had stayed out too long in the hope of filling up.

I knew what that money meant to her. Out of it flowed the strength she needed. It would buy coal for the galley stove, grub to cook on it, and a little fresh gear for parted trawls. And that wasn't all. Her new venture depended on that money. In short, it was the very life of the *Hind* that the captain was asking for in so careless a manner.

She took her eyes away from his and repeated aloud a grim saying that had been often heard from her grandfather of late: "If it isn't one thing—it's another!"

To him, she said: "How much, Paul dear?"

He replied: "Twenty-three men. Ten dollars apiece, if you can spare it."

"Two hundred and thirty dollars." She actually trembled when she did the sum and spoke it aloud; for it was precisely the sum that she had left in her pocket. Perhaps it wouldn't have been so bad if he had asked for even more than she had. But to hit on the exact sum, down to the dollar, was unbearable; because it bewildered her, sharpened her queer notion that she was trapped and could never escape.

Captain LeNotre misunderstood her. He took her troubled expression as a sign that she was penniless again. He said: "If you haven't got it, Nora, I can get it for you."

My temper had shortened up a bit; and my sorrow hadn't made me any wiser. These were, I suppose, the reasons why I asked at once: "Where? Where can you get it?"

The *Hind's* skipper gave me no answer. He kept the angry look off his face. He couldn't keep it out of the glance he gave to me. By this he meant, of course, to indicate that the business was between owner and captain. He made no reply until Nora repeated my words: "Where will you find that money, Paul?"

He replied: "Parren. Captain Parren will give it to us."

I at once repeated what I had said earlier about Captain Parren. "I'd go to sea hungry before I took a dollar of that man's money!"

This was going pretty far. I spoke hastily and in poor temper because I didn't like old Parren's way of fishing. I should have kept in mind the fact that he had been helpful to Nora and to her grandfather and that he and Captain LeNotre were chums. Both of them had been born down Newfoundland way; and they had been much together in the provincial ports and on the islands. Of course, my words were a slur to LeNotre. He let some of his anger boil over.

He said harshly: "Parren's a friend of mine."

"You've got better things to boast about." I passed the words over in rather a light fashion, but before I could put a check on my tongue I flung harder words after them. I added: "At least, I hope so."

Nora shut off the quarrel by raising her hand in a weary

gesture. "I've heard enough of Captain Parren lately to last me some time. He's been a friend of ours. Perhaps too good a friend—"

Captain LeNotre asked her at once: "What's the meaning of that remark? 'Too good a friend'?"

She replied: "I've learned today that my grandfather borrowed more money from Captain Parren than I knew. Friend or not, he's got to be paid back sooner or later. We'll leave him out of it for the time being." She then drew the money out of her pocket and flung it down on her desk. "Two hundred and thirty! There it is! Call them in."

Neither of us missed the trick. Two hundred and thirty needed; two hundred and thirty slapped down before us. I saw that there had been a close call here—and an unexpected one.

Captain LeNotre looked at the money and said: "Two hundred and thirty? Just two hundred and thirty, Nora?"

"Just that, Paul. No more. No less."

I mark this hour as the one in which I began to watch all men with even greater care than when I had a vessel. Perhaps I had grown suddenly older under the burden of hard times, though I had many a taste of poverty before. Or it may have been the working of an instinct not easily named, which is more likely, because I have often found that a man may make good judgments without knowing exactly why. I told this to a Boston greenhorn once, when he was on the *Thebaud* with us, and he told me, in the most serious way, that a man is often guided, unbeknownst to him, by nothing else than his sense of smell. By that he meant that one man can actually snuff up something off another man which creeps into his brain, in a most mysterious, primitive way, and warns him off. I'm not rightly sure this would work out at all in the Gloucester fleet, because we all have one common, universal fragrance and that's the same fragrance that you find on a fresh-killed cod. Faint, but distinct, just the same. Well, whether it was my nose or my jealous heart, I began to find some satisfaction, then and there, in watching Captain LeNotre.

He flicked his forefinger against the pile of money and then pulled away from it. He gave Nora that close look that he used to make up his mind when a thought wasn't quite balanced. Like the rest of us, he was a good man at reading a face. I had seen him do it often enough. And, as I say, I had some skill of that kind myself. I perceived that Paul wished to ask: "Where did you get the money?"

He kept the question to himself. Oddly enough, there came into his bearing a poorly hidden show of disappointment.

This didn't escape Nora. It baffled her. Even in the midst of her anxieties, she was proud of the bargain that had brought in the money. I suppose she wanted to hear a word of praise from him. She didn't get it. In her bewilderment, she said to him in a tone far from gentle: "What's biting you now, Captain? It's honest money. It's schooner money."

He answered: " 'Tis nothing, Nora dear. I thought"—here he stumbled over his words a little and then spun them out. "I don't get much of a chance to help you. And I want one. I want one."

She took quick comfort in his good intention and shed a smile that was all warmth and full of a new contentment, as if things had suddenly taken a turn for the better. I understood part of the swift change. Captain LeNotre could make a woman's eyes grow moist and bright merely by standing around; and that's more than a grim, black-browed party of my acquaintance could ever do. No, I couldn't even keep a civil tongue in my head.

I said: "Your men are waiting outside, Nora. In the rain. For a little cold charity."

She was as anxious as I to get this business over and go on to the story of the *Hind's* voyage, but she took time enough to give me a portion of her ready scorn. She said: "Call them in, Captain Bannon, and see if you can be civil to them. If not to us."

I opened the door and peered into the squall. I called out a name and cried: "Come aboard, chums! Settlement's on." Before the first man struck his boot on the outer step, I turned to her and said: "You hand it out to them and get rid of that pout of yours. Do you know what I mean?"

She understood my hint that there might be a rift between captain and crew, so great a bitterness that they might refuse money from his hands, especially because it wasn't the usual thing. On the contrary, they owed the vessel money for their grub, which was an expense the dorymen had to bear ever since the first schooner set out for the Banks.

She nodded and picked up the money.

The dorymen came thronging in. One by one, two by two —a sight to behold, and one not to be seen in any other shop in Gloucester. These were men of the old, old school, the school bred to sail, and taught to handle it long before we had blinked the light of day. They had been taught in Norway and Ireland, Portugal and the Labrador, in Newfoundland and in Nova Scotia, on all the islands of the Western Approaches. The whole Atlantic world, blue-eyed and bristly, brown-eyed and gaunt, stood before her, crowding the ancient room, filling it to the beams with their shoulders, bowed a little and widened much by years upon the Banks. Even the least of them carried himself in such a way that you could tell he'd break the back of a gale. And each man showed his courtesy by taking off his cap and giving her the salute of rope-hardened, blackish fingers. Each one broke apart his lips to make a smile for her; because they remembered her as a child aboard the *Hind*.

I was a friend, yet they greeted me coldly. Some ignored me. There was hardly a man among them who wasn't twice my age and all of them had known me since I first played on Ben Pine's wharf. Yet I wasn't hurt by their action. I knew that it was not meant for me. It was meant for Captain LeNotre, to whom they did not give even a sideways glance.

She gave them their ten-dollar bills. It made me furious to see such honorable and well-scarred hands reach out for a new debt, to be added to the old. How long, O Lord? I took my oath that the time would come when their pitiless labor should cease and they would take a new *Hind* to the Banks.

Only one of them spoke to me when they began to jostle away, stuffing their bills into little pocketbooks. This one was the Lisbon, a man who had always been kind to me and to Nora. He nodded his greying head and asked: "You got a site, young John?"

I shook my head and replied: "Terry, I haven't worked this season."

He replied: "One day you work all right." He then went out.

Nora closed the door, drew its curtain and brought the blaze of the lamp down to a glow, so that she might be undisturbed in the grave business that now had to be done.

She began it in the stern fashion that she had taken from her grandfather. She stood square under the lamp and said to Captain LeNotre: "Tell me now, Paul. How did James Corkery meet his death? And why do the men hold it against you?"

The captain of the *Golden Hind* answered her in his forth-right fashion. He began: "Dan Corkery curses me before my men and before you, Nora, and lays the blame on me for the death of his brother when he knows well enough that I'd never send a man anywhere I wouldn't go myself. Aloft or below. And that I never drowned a man in my life by putting over dories when they should be kept on deck. 'Tis a lie, Nora, that I should have such a thing said of me!"

"Go on."

He ran headlong into his story—and he was the boy who could spin one. His voice, deep-toned and clanky, beat like a bell-buoy. He reeled the yarn off with such spirit, such desperate talk of sweeping searches from Bank to Bank, that I couldn't help but become aware of the passionate drive he had thrust into vessel and men. Night and day, from the hope-ful hour when he made the first set on La Have Bank, he had searched for fish. He hadn't killed a cod, not a doryload, on that first set before the dogfish struck in by the thousands. They had swept against his trawls with a ferocity that he had never seen before; and my heart, rapt in the telling, echoed the oaths he must have sworn when he saw the flashing bellies of the dogfish slacked off against the sideboards. He then picked up his dories and sailed eastward to the outer edge, hoping that there he would be free of them. Yet the luck had run against him there, too. This time his gear had parted. The tide had been strong, as it always is there, but he found no reason for not making a set. They baited up by torchlight and he sent the dories over, even before there was day to see by.

"The dories lay out until I gave the fishing signal," he said, "and it wasn't twenty minutes before I saw Number One Dory—the Corkerys'—with an oar raised and I knew they had got hung up on the bottom. So I sailed over and took their painter, meaning to go down to their leeward buoy and let them haul from that end. Well, I'd no sooner dropped them off again than cook sings out that two more have parted gear and I sailed back, thinking this was hard luck and no mistake.

"I picked up Number Three—that's the Lisbon and his chum—and I looked down into it and saw no fish. But I saw something else and that was a box—a wooden case—lying on the bottom boards. Lard! And then I knew what had happened. I'd picked out the best bottom on the eastern edge and now there was a freighter or two breaking up there after the torpedoes. The trawls were getting hung up on the wrecks.

"Well! I could hear the other dories yelling and blowing horns. So I picked them all up and got our gear and cleared out. I had to go, Nora. I couldn't have stayed, even if there was fish. Not after dropping all that gear. And there wasn't any fish. You see, Nora?"

She nodded and made an impatient sign for him to go on.

He halted his story and cried out: "Gear! Gear! That's the size of it all the time. Always wanting to save a bit of gear. Save a dollar to keep her going."

And with that pitiful protest against the poverty that always pressed him and struck at his judgment, he told us how he let the *Hind* fly eastward again under a whole mainsail until he had swept beyond Sable Island and was running along the southern edge of Banquereau in fifty fathom of water, where he had killed fish before and now hoped to kill again.

"I brought up the bottom," he said, "there being some question among the older men as to exactly where we were on 'Quereau, but the gravel told the story good enough for me and I said: 'Bait up, boys, and let's try our luck.' So we baited up and made the set and they came aboard for dinner with the trawls in slack water. When I dropped the dories off again, I was sure we were all right, but before I had the last one over, the wind suddenly hauled around to the northeast and I knew we were in for it. I didn't wait for the glass to fall a tenth. I just came around and picked them up as fast as I could.

"But by the time I got the Corkerys aboard, they had hauled a string or two and they were crazy mad to keep on fishing because there was some fish there, the finest cod I'd laid eyes on for years. The sea was kicking up and there was some snow blowing over. A squall now and then. Well, I was just an anxious as any man aboard to fill up a pen or two, but that was no time to let a dory go live by itself. So I made them come in.

"And that's the time both the Corkerys came to me and I listened to them. Which was the right thing to do because they were the best. They said: 'Let you rig a mark-buoy and we'll heave to by it and fish here in the morning when the blow's over.' I didn't have one aboard, of course. So I took a dory mast and made an anchor fast to it and lashed a few old preservers halfway up and put a few batteries over the cork. I used a bulb from a flashlight—"

"That was going some, Paul," I said quickly. It hadn't really been such a tremendous feat, but he had stirred me with his story and I wanted to say something at the time.

He smiled gravely and went on: "It wasn't the best buoy on the Banks, but I figured it would make do. And the men said so, too. We threw it over and heaved to for the night. Or whatever we had before us."

At the words "heaved to," Captain LeNotre's voice changed to a duller tone; and, by his glance from Nora's sombre face to mine, he seemed to be taking our measure as seamen, seemed to be seeking a sign that we had really sailed those hundreds of miles with him and had made sail and taken it off, fought for the fish and rested to fight again. He grew weary before our eyes. The dullness in his voice was matched by a new dullness in his green and glowing eyes, as if he meant to show how nearly his own fires had been put out by the labor he had undergone.

"It was the mark-buoy," he murmured.

By his desperate, half-seeing stare into the past, he made us peer with him across the heaving waters of 'Quereau, hour after hour, to watch that star-point of light drift and jerk violently over the wealth of fish below. And he told us how the *Golden Hind*, in the beginning, blew sluggishly toward the mark in the lee drift and came back, ever striving to keep close to the signal that might yet make all the difference between failure and success, between full pens and pens washing with unused ice. Twice the mark vanished altogether, overwhelmed by enormous seas or hidden by snow squalls that kept ramming in. The night turned pitch-black and the rain stiffened with sleet. During one of those anxious times when the mark-buoy had vanished, ice began to make on the *Hind* and her deck became too dangerous for a watch forward. The wind rose almost to gale force and it became a question whether the *Hind* could ride it out or should run before it.

I said to myself: "I should have skipped out of it."

Captain LeNotre said: "I had the helm, Nora. I went below only once. I went down for a kink. But I was too worried and couldn't sleep. So I said I'd come on deck. When I rolled out of my bunk, I took a look at the glass and I found her working toward 'Fair.' That did me good. I would have turned in again right then, but I thought I'd go up, just the same. By the time I got on deck, the wind had let up considerable and I went to the wheel to relieve Corkery. James, it was. It was him that took over from me. The watch was an hour."

Captain LeNotre struck his hands together in a gesture of amazement. "Upon my word! you could have knocked me over with a feather! I hardly looked at the man who had the wheel. It was still pretty dark, you know. Terrible dark, though there was some light showing where the moon was. I said something. I forget what. But it was the Lisbon who answered me!"

An extraordinary expression came over the captain's face when he said that last sentence. It seemed to me that he grew pale under some secret stress, as if he still had doubts whether we were really listening with all our knowledge, all our hearts. He paused for a moment, his lids half-way down over his eyes in an almost sleepy way; but the eyes themselves burned like coals in the dim glow from the lamp, and his teeth pressed down on his lip with such force that I thought the flesh would give way.

"The Lisbon!" He repeated the word, again in a low key. "I tell you, John—I tell you, Nora—I almost jumped out of my boots. 'What the hell!' I said. 'I leave a man at the helm and tell him to keep it until I come up and off he goes! Where is he? Where's Corkery?'

"And that damned Lisbon—he says quite easy, just as if the *Hind* was sailing on a duck pond: 'Why, he and his brother put their dory over and are rigging that mark-buoy. The light went out on us, just as we almost runs her down.' I yelled at him. 'Good God!' I said, 'you damned and double-damned Lisbon, you are on watch and you let a dory out of the nest without sending for me? An old man like you?' And he said to me: ' 'Tis the last gear aboard for a mark-buoy, Captain, and we don't aim to lose it.' "

It was my turn to be amazed. I could hardly believe that I'd heard aright. I took a step toward the captain and asked: "The Lisbon? He said that? He did that?"

"Yes!" LeNotre turned to Nora and stopped in front of her. He had been striding up and down, striking at his yellow thatch with that nervous hand of his. Now he beat his fists together, knuckle against knuckle, and stood before her, intently watching the changes in her face. She knew a dory-man's duty as well as I; and the Lisbon's break from it baffled her understanding. There was a little dent in her forehead between her brows. In the months past, I had watched it grow with the heaviness of her thought. Now, at this moment, her wonderment deepened that line before my eyes.

She said nothing.

Captain LeNotre whispered: "So the upshot was—" Here, for the first time, he faltered, either before the deathly image he was about to draw for us; or in a swift realization that Nora Doonan could keep him off that beautiful deck forever, if her temper broke.

She repeated: " 'The upshot'—" and she let her voice rise on the word, making it a keen question.

"The upshot of it was that I found Number One Dory bottom up and Dan Corkery clinging to the plug. His brother was dead. Under the dory, caught in a thwart. Drowned. The first man of mine that ever met his death that way, Nora. And he had the mark-buoy gear—the wire of it—in his hand."

She asked calmly: "How did it happen? The drowning, I mean."

" 'Twas nothing! He was grappling with the mast, meaning

to secure the batteries, which had worked loose, when a sea knocked the mast out of his hand and dragged him over. I figure the wire looped over him. Over his arms." He laughed miserably. "James Corkery was the man who always said to me: 'No! I'll not learn to swim a stroke. 'Twill only take me that much longer to drown.' A stroke might have saved him. Brought him out from under."

He strode away from the stove, passed out of the circle of light cast down by the lamp and stood outside, where I also stood and waited. Both of us waited for her verdict, quite as if she were a judge seated on a bench. Which, indeed, she was. While he waited, Captain LeNotre took a turn on his heel and, coming closer to me, whispered: "I lost the fish, anyway. When we hauled in the morning, there wasn't a thousand pounds on the hooks. Not a thousand. The buoy had drifted off."

Nora asked: "You buried him at sea?"

"His brother did."

"Did the brother speak in a hard way to you?"

"Never spoke at all."

"Sullen?"

"Yes!"

She then gave her judgment: "You should never have left the deck, Paul. If a man like you was tired, then your men were too tired to think properly."

He opened his mouth to protest, but she implored him, by her sad eyes, not to speak. He flinched under her gaze because he was tormented by his desire to justify himself and to fix his story strongly in our memories. This desire twisted him around again to me, and again in his hoarse whisper, he said: "Captain, can you imagine a man going off watch like that? Why! he had the helm!"

I hesitated over my answer. I wished to do good with my words; that is, I saw clearly that Captain LeNotre was in a bad way and I had no doubt that his story had not lightened Nora's burden. If you bear in mind that the Lisbon was one of the greatest dorymen in the fleet, you will understand why I was confused; more than that, I was mystified. However, I had no trouble in seeing that the slate had to be washed clean at once before further harm was done. So I said: "There's an end to it, Captain. Think no more of it. You did your best and when you do that—why! you're the equal of any man and the better of most. As for me, I don't care to use a mark-buoy. My father always said 'twas better to depend on the lead and your heart. But there's an end to it. You lost a good man. Now you've lost his brother. I don't know where you're going to get two new hands to take their dory." Here I laughed rather loudly (and on purpose): "Unless you can get Nora to sign on. And take me as her dorymate."

This pleasantry was the required signal, made by a captain of some experience, that the saddening talk must be ended; that life and work were to go on again. One more name had been added to the roll of ten thousand dorymen who had died upon the Banks since the beginning of the fisheries. He had been given his due; now the tune had to be changed in the way required by nature.

Nora understood my other meaning. She lifted her head, grinned, and said with a doryman swagger: "I could do it, you know, if the worst comes to the worst."

I made fun of her with my eyes.

She went on: "Three summers ago, on the Grand Bank itself, I gaffed a halibut that opened somebody's eyes."

"Me! Me!" Captain LeNotre rejoiced in this sudden grace of Grand Banks talk. He pushed Corkery's ghost away with a swing of his hand, threw back his head and laughed. "Three hundred pounds, John. Oh, Lord! what a beautiful day it was!"

I took my measure of their bright eyes again; and, having found something annoying to me there, I made ready to take my leave. It was about time. Nevertheless, I looked beyond the yellow head and the black one; and, as was my frequent pleasure, gazed briefly at a noble, high-colored painting of the *Golden Hind* that filled the western wall. A bit the worse for Grand Banks wear, she lay slanted and poised for her plunge into the trough of a great sea which had raced to meet her off Sable West Bar. The dorymen were clinging to the lifelines in careless straddles. Her dories were well lashed down under double gripes. And Nora herself, in white duck and pigtails, stood at the wheel, giving childish aid to no other man than the drowned Corkery himself. He stood at a high angle, his eyes turned in the most lifelike manner toward the main topsail. I had always known the thought that the artist had painted into those eyes. 'Twas this: " 'Tis best to clew up now."

You will kindly excuse an Irish fancy; because I wish to say that as I gazed this night, dwelling with inner sadness upon the man (who fed the salt), the eyes in the painting left off their shrewd appraisal of the topsail and grandly turned to me a heart-stirring look, which gave the following: faithfulness, pride, love, and a denial.

Said I: "Good-night, all."

4

I RAN THROUGH the rain toward my sail-loft, where I meant to work an hour on my nets. Or my folly, which was the better name given to the venture by Captain Parren and, no doubt, by others, who were fond of asking one another: Where will the young fool find a vessel to take his cod-end to sea? I jumped over a pool of water and half-stumbled to the doorway; and then I brought myself up quickly, my heart aback and the nape of my neck tingling, because there were four tall men standing in the doorway, where they had no easy right to be at such a dark hour. You'll judge well of the queer state I was in at that time when I say that anger took hold of me because I feared for my work at the hands of strangers. And I was on the point of harassing them in lumper style when the nearest man laughed and sang out:

"Good evening, Captain Bannon! Salubrious, is it not, for a post-prandial stroll? The shank of the evening, as the vulgar say. What?" I saw his hand go up and give a dandy's twist to his white moustache, gleaming there in the dark.

"Hey!" I shouted. " 'Tis you, Ambrose Cameron! You and your talk! You had me buffaloed there a while, I can tell you."

He let out another peal of laughter and, in the midst of it, took a step nearer and asked in the gravest way: "Captain, what's the news about the race?"

"What race?" I asked innocently, knowing he had to have his way.

"Why! Captain, the human race!" He banged out the old saw in his usual manner, but, just the same, I had enough knowledge of him to figure out that he had a little concern with the race that night or he'd never be standing in my doorway.

"No news!" I replied. "But come aboard, come aboard! And we'll try to make up some."

They tramped up the stairs after me. I turned on the light and bowed them into my workshop.

This Ambrose Cameron was no shack of a man. His head was like the crest of a wave. He stood three inches over me. He was three times my age; and he had a wonderful history, a history written by scars and wrinkles on his venerable face. Yes, his history was the history of the world, scar for scar, line for line. He had a great gift of the gab; and on the Banks had been rated a linguist of note; for he could speak hog-Latin, Yarmouth French, two Fortune Bay dialects, and both kinds of English—Boston and American. Half a century ago, he had hauled his first trawl; and now, like the three old campaigners who stood behind him, he had been on the beach these many years, making a dollar now and then by chipping rust and such poor work ashore.

In the first little while of greetings and of their respectful and wondering glances at my great nets, I asked myself: "Have these men heard of the loss of Corkery and have they come to offer themselves as hands to the owner of the *Golden Hind*?" Such a hope in them would have been a pity; because, despite their famous skills as dorymen and sailing-masters, and despite the strength of their long arms and legs, such work was not for them. They'd have been judged too old. Not by me, but by Captain LeNotre. I was sure of that.

So I asked Ambrose: "What brings you here at this hour of the night?"

He replied: "We are sent for by the owner of the *Hind*."

"By Nora Doonan?"

"By the same, Captain."

I asked: "If it is no secret, then tell me what's going forward."

" 'Tis, indeed, a secret," answered Ambrose. "We know no more of it than you do. I had only this word from her: 'The night that the *Hind* comes home—that night you and your chums come to the wharf.' And here we are, Captain."

"The *Hind's* in," I said, "and her pens are empty and one of her bunks has no man to sleep in it. James Corkery was drowned. Did you know that?"

"We did."

Now the shortness of this old man's answer, especially when it came from a talkative and eloquent veteran of the Banks, gives me leave to speak of a custom in the Gloucester fleet that has a keen bearing on all that is to follow. 'Tis a thing worth marking. Here it is: there was a barrier between me and those dorymen. It is the same that you will find in all men of the sea: the immemorial barrier between captain and forecastle. There is nothing of an unfriendly nature in it. On the contrary, it is friendship and respect for the rank of captain that causes good dorymen to leave him to his work and his thinking; because it is his constant and deep thought, his endless observation of winds and tides and stars, which guides a schooner to the fish. Therefore, the men keep their own council. They speak up only when they're asked to give advice on the whereabouts of the cod; and a wise captain will seek their help in time of doubt.

For the rest, talk as they will among themselves, they will keep their thought and talk secret from the captain. And this deference includes all other captains and especially all owners. In the case of the *Hind*, the tradition applied in the strictest way to Nora Doonan, which was the reason why she was kept in the dark concerning certain matters until it was too late to mend them except in the manner that caused such a commotion.

All this is meant to show why I, a captain, did not press Ambrose Cameron and his chums for a word or two concerning the loss of Corkery. They had heard the news from the *Hind's* dorymen. I had heard it from the *Hind's* captain. Only an extraordinary circumstance could give me their story; and that circumstance could be brought about only by an event that would force the dorymen to step out of their characters to save themselves.

I said to Ambrose: "She's talking with the captain of the *Hind* now. Is the business to be kept from him, too?"

He replied: "From all men. 'Twas plain to me, while she talked, that nobody was to learn of our coming here to see her and I make bold to say, Captain, that I'm sorry now we chose your doorway for a shelter."

"There's no help for it now," I said. "I know you're here and that's all there is to it. You know me well enough to depend on my keeping my mouth shut, which is all that she had in mind when she told you to keep it cozy."

At that moment, Nora Doonan pushed open the door and stood on the threshold, awaiting my word of welcome, which I gave to her at once. She came in and closed the door. She gave her greetings to the men and took a step toward me. I couldn't make out the meaning of her expression, but I was at once struck by its seriousness and I judged that she had not been made much easier in her mind by her last words with Captain LeNotre. I thought that the least I could do was to leave her alone with the old dorymen in order to let her mysterious business go forward, but when I said something to this effect, she raised her hand in that commanding way of hers and said:

"Captain, stay here. What I have to say can be said in your presence without any danger to my plan."

Thereupon, she turned to them and said: "To all of you! And to one other you must find, a man that knows a mainsheet from a tablecloth!" She again flung up her right hand. "This is what I have to say to you. If you've a mind for a little hard sailing to help the old *Hind* and me, then get your gear aboard her before sun-up. Get down aft of the pens, where the old sail-locker is, and don't stir or smoke until she's away."

Her words startled them, as they startled me. None of us could help asking himself: What manner of hard sailing is this to be? What's the queer gain in it for her? What is it that the men of the *Golden Hind* can't do for themselves?

Of course, with hindsight and foresight, a man can say: It's plain another vessel is to be sailed by these men! But, at that time, our minds being fixed entirely on the *Hind*, we could see no farther than the ends of our noses.

Nevertheless, the order gave much joy to her old men. They greeted the adventure with uplifted heads and bright glances, one to the other. Nora, watching them shrewdly, measured their hardiness and knew they were the men who could go with her the difficult way she had to go. Her own sombre look changed to a happier one when old Ambrose turned in pride to the others and said: "Do ye cotton to that, my good friends? Neither stir nor smoke nor make a mousey noise until she's away. Are ye for it?"

"Aye!" Their grey heads jerked up and down and they threw out their wonderful, big hands, as if they meant to show her what those hands had done on the Grand Banks and what they could do again.

Nora said: "There'll be a good piece of change in this for us all. If it goes well. If it doesn't, there'll be nothing but your grub. And always"—here she held up her words in a passing fear and then slowly let them go—"always a chance of dying."

Ambrose gave her their answer. "Grub's enough!" he cried. "A piece of change if all goes well, Captain Nora. But grub's enough!" He gave consideration to her hint of danger and he sang out against the image of death. "As for the chance of losing all—why! 'tis what life is for and we're the ones who've done a chancy thing before and are ready to do so again."

His chums growled in their agreement; and I found in their ready anger a scorn for death and a wonder as to how death could take a new shape to men who had faced death on the Banks a thousand times.

Nora said: "And nary a word abroad or at home! Or we'll spoil all."

By a wave of his lordly hand, old Ambrose gave her his assurance before he led them away. " 'Tis us, Miss Nora—'tis us that can talk when talk's needed and can give naught but silence when that's required."

When they had gone, she stood by the door, the knob of it in her hand. I could read much in the fine doryman swagger that she took on, her legs straddled in her rough, stained boots, her other hand thrust deep into her jacket pocket. She meant to carry her mystery off in a dare-devil flourish, but I had seen the desperate look in those eyes before. Thus she had mocked me years ago when I had foolishly dared her to the dizzy climb above the *Hind's* cross-trees; and she had stood upon them in half a gale, the same bravado showing in eyes that didn't fear to look above or below.

I said: "It's clear to me, Nora Doonan, that you're sailing on the *Hind* tomorrow."

"How is it clear, Captain?"

"Who else will give the orders to these men for their sailing? Whatever the sailing is to be."

She stood in silence.

I asked: "Is it to Yarmouth or Shelburne that the *Hind* is going?"

She replied: "Where bait's the cheapest."

I'd have given something to have kept my next words to myself, tho' they were strong in my heart, which dwelt somewhat hotly on her secret recruits, enlisted in my very presence, and no call made upon me, who had the right to be called before all others. I said: "And life, too? Where life is cheapest, Nora Doonan?"

She was not deceived by my taunt. She took my measure calmly, as she had taken theirs, and she replied: "It's because their lives will not be sold cheaply, nor bought like herring, that I ask for them. And receive them."

*   *   *

I was not always on hand to see with my own eyes certain events that came just before the departure of the *Golden Hind*. My account of such happenings is drawn from the best of all possible sources a man can find: the pillow next to his.

So:

Half the sun was out of the black Atlantic when Nora carried her gear toward the *Hind*. In doryman's togs again, her cowhide boots clattering in the frosty stillness, she swung down the upper streets, empty now except for the black-robed Portuguese women hurrying to Mass at Our Lady of Good Voyage. Nearer the Doonan Wharf, the murmur of the tide against keels and under wharves became part of a grander harmony, a roaring far away. By this she knew that the seas were breaking over Norman's Woe and that there would be hard sailing if the sou'wester stayed on. This wind was always exciting to her, and she became even gayer when, at last, the sun left the water and a blue day filled south and east. She marked the whitecaps this side of the sun. Through them, a big dragger sailed shoreward. While she watched, the vessel abruptly changed to an eastward course. This puzzled her, until another swift change in course showed her that they were adjusting a compass out there.

It was then that she saw her five secret recruits marching briskly down to the wharf, their bedding and gear on their shoulders. They were a little tardy, the sun being well up, but this arrival was true enough to their word. She waited, there by the sail-loft steps, until they had flung their bundles aboard the schooner. By the time she came to where the *Hind* lay, they had gone below to their hiding-place, leaving no trace except a footmark in the rime of her deck. The sun scoffed up the frost.

Nora gave the *Hind* a hail. "Anybody aboard?"

No answer came. She climbed down to the deck and took a turn or two there, passing her hands in pleasure over the furled mainsail, creaky in its crotch, and stopping now and then to look into the tubs of trawl in their neat rows. Some of the trawl lines had already been overhauled for the new voyage. These tubs, she knew, belonged to the Portuguese, who were best of all at the trade and always did their work on the homeward voyage. She smiled in satisfaction at the hooks amidst the coils. They were already straightened by the hook-sets, were ready for the next baiting up, five hundred miles away.

She went down into the galley, opened the draft of the stove and pumped water into a great coffee kettle. She poured a bag of coffee into it and returned to the deck.

The dragger had turned shoreward again, had come so much nearer that she could make it out. It was the *Doubloon* of Boston. On its bridge, she knew, was the friend she must see before the *Hind's* voyage could begin. "Parren!" She spoke his name so loudly that a gull on the *Hind's* cross-trees lifted itself off and floated with the wind.

Money had to be found within the hour. And there was no place to get it, except where it had been borrowed before: from the skipper of the *Doubloon*. She had ordered ice for the pens and fresh stores for the ice-chest: beef, lamb, butter by the tub, and crates of fruit. The stores and the galley coal had been put aboard during the night because the *Hind* was to sail as soon as the tide served and her bills were paid. Had she been able to keep the money she had made by selling the spare gear, she would have been happier. She became disconsolate at the thought of making a new debt, one to be added to the old. Yet there was no help for it.

She flung her bag into the gone man's bunk, with never a look for poor Corkery's ghost, trudging after her among familiar things. She went back to the galley, put the kettle of coffee over her arm by its long handle and slung a brace of mugs onto a long spoon. She carried these to the cabin and knocked against the after bulkhead, behind which her men were hiding.

Ambrose Cameron came out to greet her.

"All clear, Ambrose," she said. "Here you are. To stay you until she sails."

"I thank you kindly, Cap'n Nora." He turned back to the sail locker and set the coffee down for his chums. He filled his own mug and drained it and sighed in satisfaction over it.

She asked him to step up into the cabin. There she said: "Ambrose, there's no reason on earth why I shouldn't tell you what I'm trying to do. No reason, except this: only my grandfather knows what it is and he made me promise that I'd not tell another soul until we were away. I tell you this because, after thinking it over in the night, I said to myself: ' 'Tis hardly fair to ask such men to go on a wild goose chase without even naming the goose.' "

He raised his hand to stop her. "Think nothing of it, Miss Nora. A bargain's made and it's agreeable to us. I've only one question to ask and that has nothing to do with where we're going and what we're bound to do."

"What is it, Ambrose?"

"Are we signed on regular so nobody can stop the vessel and take us off? Or make trouble for her?"

"Yes. The names are on the Coast Guard list. All except the new man you were to find for me."

"That's Peter Lord."

Nora said that she'd give the name to the Coast Guard before the schooner sailed and asked: "He's a good man aboard a vessel, isn't he, Ambrose?" to which he replied that Peter Lord had sailed many times with her father and added: "He was dorymates with me on the *Mary and Martha.*"

Nora lifted her eyes to the cabin skylight, which now glittered with sun rays. One of the smaller panes had been cracked since she last stood there. She frowned.

At once, the old doryman said: " 'Tis easy fixed, Miss Nora. She found some weather last trip."

She understood his allusion to the *Hind's* fruitless voyage. He had heard much talk of it during the night, which was natural; for, in these days, it wasn't often that a man was lost on the Banks. Few fishermen were exposed to the dangers of dories and of making sail in rough weather. The draggers gave them shelter on deck and kept them there, with only the nets to handle. No doubt, all Gloucester had waggled its head over the story of Corkery's death, as it was related by his shipmates and his grieving brother. It was her place, as owner of the *Hind*, to know such things, if she could find them out. Yet, as I have said, there was a barrier between her and the dorymen. She had seen it rise, in a natural way, since her grandfather deeded the *Golden Hind* to her. Before that time, the dorymen were free with their chatter and jokes and sound advice to a girl who had a hard row to hoe. Now things had changed. It wasn't that they liked her less. No, they were even more devoted to her. But there was a new dignity in the ownership of a famous schooner and custom had thrust an aloofness upon her.

Yet the sight of that beautiful old face above, seared and dyed as it was by the Grand Bank years, filled her this day with a mysterious comfort. And his words concerning the *Hind* proved to her that the barrier was not too high between them yet. He was thinking kindly of her; and she knew that all his skill and courage were on her side.

Therefore, she sought him out. She said: "A bad blow on 'Quereau it was, Ambrose." And then, without taking much thought of her words, she suddenly exclaimed: "We'll be needing a compass for the work in hand!" Thus she showed to him that, indeed, another vessel was to be sailed by him and his chums.

He nodded his silvered head. "I thought as much, Miss Nora. I took the liberty of thinking that far." He then waved his hand toward the bulkhead. "I brought the old one off the *Mary and Martha*. It could do with some adjusting, but it'll make do." He thrust his hand into his jacket and brought out a pocket compass. "I brought this gadget along, too. Just in case."

Please to remember the old man's words: "Just in case."

Now Nora clearly saw how right I had been in warning her to keep the venture a secret. Any shrewd man could figure out the meaning of her preparations. Not in the exact sense, perhaps, but nearly enough to excite an interest that might cause bold action on the part of enterprising men, especially if they had also learned that she hoped to win freedom for herself and her *Hind* by the venture to the eastward. Remembering my words, her gratitude to an absent friend made her say earnestly: "I'm thankful to Captain Bannon for his friendship."

He had been seeking such a turn of talk. He said at once: "I'm a very old man, Miss Nora. The last leaf on the bough, as the song says. And I wish to tell you that John Bannon, young as he is, is the skipper to be listened to, as you say. 'Tis your rightful duty now, as the owner of the *Hind*, to keep the vessel's welfare uppermost. I mean in your mind. Your thinking. Now I've seen Captain Bannon working on the draggers with the government men. Men of science and knowledge, they be. And he measuring cod and weighing them and trying out a big-mesh net. When he might have been making twenty thousand a year on a dragger. Like Parren yonder on the *Doubloon*. And why? Because John knows. As his father knew before him. The small mesh must go.

" 'Tis your duty, Miss Nora, to help him and the others like him—for there are a few—and show them all that a big mesh will catch more pounds an hour and let the nurseries thrive. So there'll be spawning in plenty and billions of haddock again."

He patted her cheek fondly. "I know what pride is, Miss Nora. You've got your father's and your good old grandfather's. I had my pride. When I was skipper of the *Mary and Martha*, I kept my pride. A stiff-necked generation, as the Good Book says. I would stay by trawl and hook-and-line!" He flung up his hands in a wave of sorrow. "You see me now! Grateful for your coffee, grateful for a chance to earn a piece of change."

She said: "Ambrose, do you know how much it costs to do such a thing? To make the *Hind* over? If I decided to do it, after all?"

"Not exactly. No, Miss."

"Just thirty thousand dollars. Engine and winch and towing gear and a pilot-house for her deck."

He sighed over the image of so many dollars to be earned or won. " 'Tis a lot of money, Miss Nora." He took a step toward the bulkhead, then turned to her and whispered: "Let's you and I go get it!"

He went back to his hiding-place and Nora climbed to the deck at the very time that I came around the corner of the wharf with two of her dorymen, all of us laden with coils of new manila. I waved to her and pulled open the door of the sail-loft. I let the dorymen climb up the stairs and I sang out to her that I should like some breakfast aboard the *Hind*. She told me to come aboard when I was ready.

I had seen the *Doubloon* on her way in; and I had half a mind to have another word with old Parren on the matter of my nets. I really didn't care who used them as long as I brought on the change in fishing that I desired. By the time I had paid the dorymen off and had flung open the loft window, the *Doubloon* had found a berth aft of the *Hind*, where Captain Parren often tied up when the other wharves were crowded.

There were only a few men aboard the *Doubloon*. Just enough to handle her for the compass work. There were several men in the pilot-house. Presently one came out, a little, bowed man in a grey ulster. He carried a black box under his right arm and a leather bag of tools in his left hand. This was the compass man from Boston. He climbed over the rail to the wharf. Captain Parren followed him. The captain, as usual, bloomed like a piece of the sky. He was a dandy of the Boston waterfront, where a good tailor commands much respect and high prices. Old Parren was a tailor's joy. Today he had on one of his blue 'longshore outfits: blue hat, blue topcoat, blue suit, blue tie. Yes, and I give you my word that he'd have worn blue shoes had he been able to find them. He wasn't the man to let one thing swear at another.

I watched with pleasure while he paid off the compass man; and I saw that Nora, leaning over the *Hind*'s rail, was enjoying the performance. Captain Parren's blackish jowls shook in laughter while he pulled the bills out of his wallet. He passed an extra one to the little man and laughed even louder when he shook his head in refusal. Parren shouted: "Ah, go on! Buy yourself a blue coat like mine. Blue's very nice. Don't like grey."

There were two men left in the *Doubloon's* pilot-house. I gave only a casual glance at the spray-marked window. It interested me, in a mild way, that one of them should open the portside door and make something more than a careless scrutiny of the *Hind*. That is, he was not merely admiring her salty good looks. I knew that extraordinary face, a cross between a dead haddock and a grinning fox. No, I should amend my words. The face had none of that righteousness which I have often marked in the expression of a mature haddock.

This was Billy Atkins, a man whose past held more shadow than light. He had once been a top-notch doryman. Long ago, he had given up the dories for the easier, better-paid work on the draggers. There was queer blood in that man. Some people said that it was an odd strain off the Canaries. He had been Parren's chum for many years, even before they sailed together. They were cronies ashore and were often seen in the Nova Scotian fishing ports. And I had heard that they had turned a few neat tricks in their time. In one case (so 'twas sworn by certain Newfoundlanders) they had saved their lives on St. Pierre Bank at the cost of three fishermen. By some men with long memories, Atkins was regarded as a criminal.

That's why I gave him a second glance. But not a third. Neither did Nora Doonan care to speak to him.

I waited for the second man to come out. Atkins, however, said something over his shoulder and closed the door. He had seen Nora. The second man did not come out.

Nora hailed Captain Parren as soon as the compass man was out of earshot. She said bluntly: "Good morning, Captain. Have you any of those bills to spare for a time?"

The captain jerked gallantly at his blue brim and gave his

usual boom. The laughter suited him. It was big. So was his mouth; and the teeth that flashed there were good big ones, too, adorned with new gold. His big, black eyes became wet with good feeling. "For you, Cap'n Nora? For her?" He bent his head toward the *Hind*. "Always! Yes! Sure! Why not?" He thrust out his wallet.

She answered: "For me, Captain. And for her." She inclined her head toward the schooner as he had. "Come aboard for breakfast, Captain, and I'll sign my life away. Collateral— an immortal soul."

"Ho! Ho!" He laid a hand over his blue corporation to hold its jolly shaking down. "Breakfast—yes! Why not? But you don't sign your life away, Miss Nora. You sign nothing. Take what you need, eh? For as long as you like."

"One thousand. Ninety-day note and six and a half cents on the dollar. That's the story, Captain."

"No cents on the dollar. This is not business, Miss Nora. This is—"

"What?" said she.

"This is love. I love"—here he let his sky-piece bend *Hind*-wards again in a fancy manner—"I love her. Very much! Why not? I sailed on her when I was wing-high to a duck!" He bellowed at the thought of big Captain Parren ever having been such a mite.

Nora said: "I do, too. I love her." Since a share of her inner desperation had come into her voice and thinned it, put an edge on it, he at once became solemn. He followed her down into the galley. She broke a dozen eggs into a pan and put bread over the coals to toast. She pulled down the table and hung it, pushed a dish of oranges toward him and let him rip a few apart. She poured coffee and sat down beside him on the locker. When he had eaten a little, he took out his wallet and counted a thousand dollars before her. She stuffed the money into her trouser pocket and asked for his pen. She scribbled the note and slipped it into his wallet.

"If you say so," said he.

"I do," she replied. The signing made her tremble a little because she had an image in her mind of other notes of the same kind at home. Her heritage. She thanked him earnestly. "No one else in Gloucester would lend money to the owner of a vessel still under sail. And earning so little. You are very kind."

"Ah, the *Golden Hind!*" He held up his coffee mug, drank from it, and began a genial account of the day he first stepped aboard the schooner.

It was I who saw that second man come out of the *Doubloon's* pilot-house; and I think it a shrewd, worldly thing that a man's life and much more may turn upon a glance that was next to idleness. Had I been keen in purpose at that moment, I would not speak so, but at certain hours in my thought it seems ironic that a chance opening of the eyes may do as much good in a man's work as all his thought, known and unknown.

After Nora and Captain Parren had gone below, I again examined the manila that the dorymen had carried up. My first glance at it, the night before, had caused me some anxiety. Good manila twine had become scarce. The Navy had built up a great stockpile for ropes; and the intensity of fishing had taken more than the ordinary amount. There had been some talk of a new cotton twine coming into use for dragger nets. I didn't want to make a change. All my work on the big-meshed cod-end had been done with manila. And I was pleased now to find that this last shipment was as good as the old. I rubbed the strands between my fingers and snuffed it.

This satisfaction made me think of my breakfast and I went to the loft window to see if Parren might be leaving the *Hind;* for I had no wish to interfere with their business, the nature of which I had figured out. While I was watching, Atkins stuck his head out of the pilot-house again. To me, this action became important; because it had been twice repeated; and because I really disliked Atkins. In time, I came to hate him, which is my way with men. Candor requires me to confess that, apart from natural causes, my vague distrust of Captain LeNotre was partly due—perhaps wholly—to his long-standing friendship with Atkins. Of course, since Captain LeNotre and Captain Parren were chums, it stood to reason that Atkins would be in the fellowship, too, since he was Parren's follower. Yet I had chosen, in days and nights when I was lonely or down-hearted, to think ill of LeNotre because of his comrades.

I watched Atkins while he looked up and down the wharf. It was deserted. He then spoke to the man behind him. The man came out at once and jumped to the *Doubloon's* rail. I saw him plain. I swore aloud. The man was Captain LeNotre.

To save my soul, I didn't know what to make of his strange appearance on the old man's vessel; and his actions seemed stranger yet. To one way of thinking, the skipper of the *Hind* had a right to go out on a compass run with his chum. Both men were Newfoundland-born and their friendship had never been denied by Captain LeNotre. Indeed, he never had reason to deny it. Moreover, since Nora Doonan was, at the very moment, borrowing money from Captain Parren, the decent thing was to suppose that LeNotre had gone on the *Doubloon* to arrange the matter. Just the same, the visit seemed hardly a proper action on that very day when the *Hind* herself was making ready to sail.

I said a surprising thing to myself: "They must have needed a talk rather badly to get up in the middle of the night for it!"

Captain LeNotre's next action surprised me even more. I submit that it was not the action of an innocent man.

He hurried across the wharf and ran through the open door of the last dory-shed. He closed the door behind him. At that moment, when he turned to reach for the knob, I saw his face distinctly. It bore an expression that I had never seen on it before. There was a queer sort of anxiety showing in his mouth and eyes, the mouth pinched up, the eyes half-closed. It was clear to me that he didn't wish to be seen by any of the *Hind's* people. The reason for such a wish was more than I could learn by staring at him. I could tell what he was going to do: he'd go through the sheds, by passing from one to another, until he came to the head of the wharf, where he would be hidden from the *Hind*.

I waited in my place. Presently I heard a door open to seaward and I heard it close softly. Another door soon opened directly beneath me. He left it open. I heard the scuffle of his boots. I edged a little nearer to the window and looked toward the head of the wharf. The last door in the row opened and Captain LeNotre hurried out. He crossed the upper street and turned into a seamen's bar.

(To those who wish to know, or have professed such a wish, I offer that account as an exact narrative of the beginning of our peril.)

I at once boarded the *Hind* and went down into the galley. Rather, to the forecastle, where the table was set up. There I greeted Captain Parren in the same genial way that I always used toward him and I called out to Nora, who was at the stove. She replied: "Aye, sir! Breakfast coming along."

I poured a mug of coffee. Before I could sip it, a familiar voice hailed the *Hind*. I quaked at the cheerfulness in that voice. It said: "Anybody aboard?"

"Why!" said Nora, " 'tis Captain LeNotre come for breakfast, too. What luck! Three men—and all devoted to me!"

Captain Parren's laughter rumbled behind the blue front and he heaved to and fro under the strength of it. He screwed up his eye in a prodigious wink at me and bellowed: "Captain LeNotre? Good!" He pushed his coffee mug toward Nora and he then said something that nearly sent me to the deck because it frightened me so. He said: "Fill up, Miss Nora. I'll stand by a bit. I haven't seen the captain in a long time. I must tell him where to kill some fish."

I had my mug at my lips, and this saved me from a betrayal of my quick thought. Aye! a thought more than quick. 'Twas forty fathom deep, a true halibut of a thought—strong, and cold, and brutal—that swam (as I sat in the cheerful forecastle) into the sea-slime of men's secret minds and flashed in vast tail-strokes onward through undersea gloom. Blind search for food; blind search for light. As the halibut breaks a cod to pieces, I broke his sentence: "I haven't seen the captain in a long time." I broke it up, fed on it, tasted each part; and found no nourishment for an old innocence. Ah! if I had only leaned across the galley table and cursed him out then and there!

I didn't speak. I didn't bat an eye. I proved to myself my own depths of duplicity and evil. I drank and I smiled, but in my heart I took an oath that nothing—nothing that walked!—would keep me off the *Golden Hind* for that voyage.

I greeted Captain LeNotre, made way for him. I stood up and I went away with something rolling in my heart, something like the long, easy swell which is left by the gale. Something new; which is to say, something old.

*   *   *

Before noon the bills were paid, the dorymen were on hand, and the topmastmen were working aloft. Yet the *Golden Hind* could not stir. No men had been found to take the places of drowned Corkery and his sullen, wretched brother. Their shipmates were already breaking out new hooks and gangins for the trawls. The smoke of burning gangin tips thickened the salty air. But there was a dory out of action and new hands had to be found for it.

Captain LeNotre had gone ashore twice in his search for Daniel Corkery. He hadn't found him. Worse than that, he could find no one who had seen him. Every man young enough to haul a trawl had been roundly beseeched to make the voyage. None would go on such a long and chancy cruise. Some of them laughed in LeNotre's face at the odd notion of standing by a mainsheet on freezing nights; and I heard later that one Irishman said to him in scorn: "I'll go with you, frog, if you won't ask me to rig a mark-buoy!"

When I was asked by Nora, I joined the search for a doryman and I almost laid hands on a man. I came upon a middle-aged fisherman idly chipping rust at Mellon's Yard (as a sort of Sunday penance for old sins, I guess) and, by a brisk use of blarney, I persuaded him to come to the Doonan Wharf. The fisherman, hearing the loud hails from dorymen at work on the *Hind's* deck, brightened up considerably. He became less eager when he learned that there was, as yet, no dorymate for him. He balked altogether when he was told that Nora had to be taken along as passenger to Nova Scotia.

"Not a chance!" said he shrewdly. " 'Tis the worst of luck

to have a woman aboard a fishing vessel. I'm surprised at ye, I am that. A man would have to have an awful jag on to do such a thing.

"Besides," he added piously, "sailing on a Sunday ain't to my liking."

He hurried away.

During this uneasy hour, there was a grand lot of talk aboard the *Hind* and on the wharf, where we were having the benefit of advice from a number of piazza sailors. Too much talk, indeed, for Nora Doonan. She was at her wit's end. Captain LeNotre had fallen abruptly into the black and listless mood that had marked his forthcoming. I thought that he had taken whiskey. He stalked up and down by himself and would not meet her glance. This had always been one of his faults. She, of course, laid it now to the endless anxiety caused by the *Hind's* failure to earn money, and by the present prospect that her dories would be short-handed. She was, by this time, accustomed to his moodiness. Today it made her more eager than ever to get the schooner away; because she saw that her dorymen were in no mood to take any of his short temper or sullenness. The breach between men and captain hadn't been closed much. Long talks in the night past, talks with anxious wives and cronies, had added a mysterious quality to their behavior, which made us all fear that more of them might take their gear ashore. Some of them were angry enough for that; poor enough for it. Nora didn't like the way certain men gathered in groups and held themselves aloof. Nor did she care for the over-the-shoulder glances that they gave, now and then, to Captain LeNotre. Even the best of them— the Lisbon—had been affected by the bad feeling. He stood apart.

Then, quite suddenly, Dan Corkery appeared. No one had

seen him come down the wharf. No one had heard him speak. He was in poor shape; seemed, in fact, to be a little on the mad side. In a way, this was to be expected because he had really loved his brother, not only as a brother, but also as a skilled and courageous dorymate, which is a bond equal in strength to the blood bond. Grief had made some inroads on him during the night. Grief hadn't sent him to the bottle, as I had feared it might. It had taken away his sleep, had made him gaunter and had deepened the black pits in which his eyes lived out their misery.

Captain LeNotre was the first to spy the doryman. He hurried toward him and said roughly: "Where the hell you been?"

Corkery held up his reply briefly to let the people understand that nobody could swear at him without rebuke. Having made this point, he answered: "I've been in church all night, Captain. Praying for him. Where you should have been." He then came forward an inch or two, making his way by a shuffling step, his eyes looking downward.

Wise heads among the staring throng shook in warning at his answer. Not because they disbelieved him. On the contrary, it was because they knew he spoke the truth. The truth alarmed them. Corkery was no church-goer, in the common course of life; nor was the myth particularly strong among the others. The chief effect of his stealthy arrival and of his words was a fear that he had actually gone mad, a fear that had been whispered on the *Hind* after the terrifying hour when he, by himself, had tipped the death-board for his brother's burial and, for the first time, had cursed LeNotre.

Nobody seemed lively enough to crack the deathly silence that he now created and drew over them, just as he had kept them spellbound on the night before when the schooner came home. In truth, Corkery looked a little like old John Deth himself, standing there with a pocketful of blighting curses for all on deck and wharf. Those stanch legs and arms, now clad in black shoddy, seemed to have thinned out in the night. He kept his hands clasped behind his back as he bent forward. He changed his gaze and kept it unwaveringly on LeNotre's ruddy face. It was uncanny the way he kept them enthralled; and even managed to gain another inch or two in his advance without further alarming them. For my own part, I could not summon up enough brightness to watch him for long. I had my heart set on another trouble.

The *Hind's* cook was the man who saw what the others couldn't see: Corkery's hands. The cook had just come up with a hod and was about to dump ashes over the rail. The queer silence made him look up. Reddened by the galley fire, his face, for that moment, beamed like a moon all filled up; then something more than the sou'wester cooled it off, opened it up. He howled.

Nora had been standing almost between Roades and Corkery. At the warning from below, she had just time enough to turn toward Corkery as he leaped forward. His right hand swept around. It held his bait-knife. He, too, let out a howl and closed in on Captain LeNotre.

Nora cried: "For God's sake—no!"

She struck savagely at Corkery's rising arm.

Captain LeNotre was not the man to let her—or anybody else—stand in the way of such a fight. He had obviously been watching Corkery out of the corner of his eyes and had perceived his murderous intention. And LeNotre was ready. He jerked back his reefer. He made a fancy, twisting step to the right and thrust Nora away so violently that she fell headlong.

Captain LeNotre jerked out his own knife. It was an extraordinary weapon, a French trick that he had picked up after a brawl in the cod fleet at Miquelon years before when some bloody scrape had kept him off the mainland for a time. That knife had taken a proper drink before now. The ivory handle was quite as long as the wonderful blade; and the ivory was carved into a gargoyle shape, a Breton death's-head. He could handle it, too. He was no fist-fighter. That style meant broken hands and spoiled livelihoods. It hadn't been in favor among his Miquelon cronies.

He shouted: "Stand away, all!"

He jumped backward a good stride to baffle Corkery's headlong charge. He laughed wickedly at Corkery to taunt him into carelessness and again shouted. "I'll make bait of you, you crazy mick! Come on again!"

Corkery lunged forward. They grappled and each man lifted a hand to seize the other's knife-hand. They were strong and well-matched, one by coolness and hate, the other by the desperation of madness. Their lithe bodies clashed gracefully. Both the knives glittered aloft against the blue. And the little, carved eye in LeNotre's hilt stared down over his knuckles into Corkery's distorted face.

It had taken only the split of a second for the fighters to move into this lock.

It took something less for me to settle their hash for them. I drove my knee right between them, rammed it against their straining bellies. And in the same upward movement, I struck each man hard on the jaw with a fist that knew well enough how to strike a blow. They groaned and fell apart. The knives came down. The ivory weapon turned skillfully into the Miquelon twist at the hip.

I had no fear of them after that, knowing that I had shaken them. A crack on the jaw for a maddened man is as good as cold water for a mad dog. And I may say that I showed the others how a captain handles men; because, instead of striking another blow, or threatening them, I turned my back on them and said to Nora: "Get up, you goose!"

I stretched out my hand to her and helped her.

At once, an uproar started among the men. I gave them a deserved portion of my scorn by saying: "Oh, you talk now, do you? Shut up, greenhorns!" And I took a step toward Corkery and the captain, so that it was plain to them that, should they join the quarrel again, there would be a worse cracking of jaws and no mistake about it.

It became plain to me that there was no easy way for either Nora or Captain LeNotre to do the business which had to be done hastily. Therefore, I did it, by saying to Corkery: "Dan, will you take the hell out of that heart of yours and go aboard the vessel?"

He replied: "I will not!"

I said: "I ask you again: will you go aboard your vessel and let her make a trip? One good trip is needed by us all." I knew my voice trembled in earnestness, in a passionate desire to smooth the way for Nora and the *Golden Hind*. Yet I made no stir in the Corkery depths.

I then did something which made the others murmur even louder. Quite as if I hadn't this very action in mind all the time (one way or another), I said: "Dan Corkery, you know me and I know you. You go aboard your vessel and I'll go dory-mates with you."

Even Corkery, in the dullness of his waning fury, jerked up his head at this sentence. A skilled captain's offer to go back into a dory is a rare event. Of course, there had been captains who had drunk themselves back into a dory. A sound skipper takes such a step down—or, rather, backwards—only under extraordinary compulsion. I did it because of my old attachment to Nora and because of my fear for her welfare and the welfare of her vessel. None of them, of course, could possibly understand the force that was working in me. There were others who became aware, by the working of their instincts, that something of a desperate meaning was going on.

Captain LeNotre was one of these. He must have sent a signal across to Captain Parren, who stood apart, backed by his crew. That wary twitch of the eyeballs, or a jerk of the head, whipped Parren into action. He stepped forward in the grand manner and opened his mouth to speak a few words. However, his inner agility couldn't do double duty. He couldn't drum up some scheme to keep me off the *Hind* and, at the same time, keep his mind on the mystery of which he was a part. The result of his brain-storm was, for once, a sudden splash of frankness all over his wide face. This left what seemed to me a loutish look.

His expression set me ablaze again. I almost made him jump out of his 'longshore shoes by stepping forward and shouting in a crazy manner: "What are you going to say? Hey?"

Nora gasped in dismay and cried out my name.

Now this man Parren was twice my age and more; and he exceeded me in stature. For that matter, he outranked me in authority and prestige, since he, at least, had a vessel to command. Nevertheless, he couldn't get under way. My question, in itself, was enough to make a man laugh. For why should a man be gaffed for words he hadn't even spit out?

I suppose that Parren, too, now had an inkling of what had taken place in my mind. He must have figured that I had worked out some pattern of thought and action and that there was no longer geniality between us. He withstood the force of this knowledge rather awkwardly. It seemed to me that he warily avoided a two-sided exchange; because he spoke to Nora as follows:

"Miss Nora! Under the circumstances—that is—why! sure! Why not? Oh, I ain't going to follow Captain Bannon's example and go dorymates with anybody"—here he roared and his own men had the grace to laugh at the thought of his giving up thirty thousand a year for a doryman's pittance. "But here's a man who can bait a trawl and haul and he'll go for you, Captain Nora!"

Without turning his head, he held out his blue arm and let it fall in jovial fashion on the shoulder of the man next to him.

That man was Billy Atkins.

You could tell, in that jumpy moment, that Atkins was ready to drop dead in his tracks. Up to then, he had no more idea of going on the *Hind* than he had of trawling on the moon. His boots slowly keeled together, as if the weight of that beautiful arm was something more than he could bear. Which was true. Yet he had to bear it. In doing so, he made it perfectly clear that he wasn't his own man any more and that he had to go back into a dory at his master's word.

Atkins closed up that fishy thing which, for him, passed as a mouth. It had opened in a haddocky gasp. He grinned bitterly and whispered: "Sure! Sure! Why not?"

Somebody among the *Hind's* people said: "That's one man!" There was impatience in that voice; and there were other sounds from the dorymen which meant: "If we're going —let's go!"

Nora said: "All right."

Captain LeNotre repeated her words.

Captain Parren said: "Good! Now I'll find the other. A dorymate for Billy."

At this, one of his own men said in a cool manner: "And

find another to take Billy's place while you're about it, Captain. Because we don't sail short-handed. Not on the *Doubloon*, we don't."

Others near him nodded vigorously and murmured at this hint concerning the fierceness of labor on the *Doubloon*, once she was on fish.

I turned to the Hind's dorymen. "Have any of you gone dorymates with Billy Atkins?"

There was a natural delay in the answer. Nobody wanted Atkins aboard the *Hind*, yet there was no chance of finding another; and such a skilled hand meant money to take home. There were two or three men who had been in a dory with Atkins. Only one answered. This was the Lisbon, the same Portuguese who had been put in such a bad light by Captain LeNotre's story of the death of James Corkery.

The Lisbon said: "I have, Captain."

"And is he a good man in a dory, Terry?" I asked.

"He was with me. Rigged for halibut, we was. On the *Rachel*."

"And a good man aboard a vessel?"

"He was then, Captain." This was damnation by faint praise, but I didn't falter over it. I'd have gone dorymates with the devil himself. Yes, I was resolved to go with Nora on the *Hind* if I had to steal below and hide with her secret recruits.

I said: "I've got no work and I could use a couple of hundred dollars."

A *Hind* man laughed at my cheerfulness.

I went on: "Billy, if you'll go dorymates with me, I'll go dorymates with you. And we'll set fifty hooks to a string and get rich honestly."

The dorymen laughed at this gibe at lazy men who shirked

a full set of trawl hooks. The draggermen sneered at my sneer for them and their slaughter of baby fish.

Atkins signified his acceptance by cordially running his red tongue out and drawing it in. He raked Corkery with a mean glance and whispered a word that I could not make out.

"Is it agreeable to you, Captain LeNotre?" I asked the necessary question with some coldness. My respectful attitude was more than the traditional bow to the captaincy and to the law of the fleet. It was also a good doryman's way of buttering up a captain whom he had just cracked on the jaw. Thus I showed, one and all, that I had become a doryman again; and that I knew my place.

Captain LeNotre nodded his head.

I turned to Nora and she, too, nodded her head gravely.

I had one last use for my experience in such circumstances and for the lessons my father had taught me. Knowing that the *Hind* had to be sailed by an even-tempered lot of men, I sang out cheerfully: "Well, then, chums! Twelve dories! Twenty-three men and a boy! What more can you ask?"

I scraped the scowl from my face and, by so doing, freshened up all the others.

All save one. Corkery's. His listless stand, by Nora's side, made it clear that he was once more in perilous communion with a new-made ghost. Nevertheless, he, too, had to be swept up in the embrace of good feeling, had to be made happy and resolute again. It might have been my work, but I had taken on my new rôle and my instinct for what was proper had already made me drift a step or two toward my new shipmates.

Nora raised herself out of the gloom that had beset her. She left off gazing at LeNotre and took a step toward Corkery so that her hand could touch his arm. She said: "There's more mouths for you to feed now, Dan Corkery, and the *Hind's* not done too well."

The doryman made no reply.

Nora spoke again in an even gentler tone. "Come back from where you are, chum!"

Corkery lifted his head and came alive. "Aye, Cap'n Nora!"

"Then, Dan, where's your gear?"

Corkery took up her gaze in the growing strength of his own and answered: " 'Tisn't far away. No!"

"Well," said Nora, without a by-your-leave to Parren, "you go aboard the *Doubloon*, Dan, and take Billy Atkins' place."

"Why!" cried a *Doubloon* man quickly, "Dan Corkery's a good hand with a needle and fine at a winch brake!"

"Why not?" shouted Parren. "Yes! Sure! Come aboard, Dan, and help us make a big trip."

Corkery swung on his heel and, in a livelier measure, strode to the wharf sheds. He reached within the very door that Captain LeNotre had used and pulled his gear out of the dark.

"I'm obliged to you, Captain Parren," he said. "I can do the work fine. I did it on the *Esmeralda* till she burned in Tor Bay that time." He then made his farewells to Nora and to me; and to me he sent a signal with his eyes: "You have a chum aboard the *Doubloon*, where you may need one."

At this, Captain Parren gave the nod and his crew began to drop aboard the dragger.

Captain Parren said: "We'll be dragging on the Middle Ground in a few days." He tugged at the blue brim and said to Nora: "Maybe we'll be meeting you thereabouts. Good luck to you and the *Hind*, Miss."

The *Doubloon's* engine, which had been idling, opened up and the dragger turned out into the stream.

Soon after, like a dancer gliding in her first, free carelessness toward the center, the *Golden Hind* began her departure, quite concealing in the gentle drawing of her headsails the fury of strength and beauty that I had known of old. She slid away from the Doonan Wharf in a waltzing turn; and took along her attendant gulls, soaring and crying among her lovely spars, where the topmastmen lay at ease. In an idle motion, the schooner swung her bow out of the lane between the wharves, where Gloucester citizens, in Sunday best, shouted across the widening space and told their children to wave their hands.

The *Hind's* forefoot touched a strong whirl in the tide. She curtsied gravely to the tune of sou'wester music in her shrouds. Jib and jumbo filled and pointed her toward the open sea, which changed from blue to green as she went on. A shout rang down her deck; and her foresail, flashing like the white-caps far away, ran up boisterously. It had been swayed up so suddenly and smoothly that the *Hind* seemed surprised, seemed to have missed her cue. She tarried a while in a foolish way and I, for all my heavy heart, exulted in her qualities; for I had been long away from her and from the sweet rattle of gear and canvas.

She careened to the east, splashed, and then began shooting for the passage. A new shout, louder than the seas which sprang to meet her, pealed away from the main-boom; and the mainsail's enormous shadow darkened her blue waterways. The mainsail roared and filled. Rainbowed spray arched over her. A boarding sea struck at her lee dory-nest. She cleared herself; and, in a last furious plunge onward and upward, she leaped into the Atlantic.

5

CONCERNING THE famed waters to which the *Golden Hind*
now sped to seek her fortune, it seems to me that some un-
scholared words on the general subject cannot be amiss; because the true meaning of the cod fishery is not the plainest
thing in the world. Nor the true meaning of the *Hind*, for
that matter.

I have read in an English book (taken by my grandfather
from the ribs of an ancient frigate tossed up, from centuries
past, by the sands of Sable) this saying: "It is a certain maxim
that all states are powerful at sea as they flourish in the fishing
trade." Witness: 'twas by the dry-cured cod that old England
won from Spain a share of the golden treasure dug up in the
New World before the Queen took to outright robbery on
the Main. And why were the Portuguese skilled in the long
voyage and able to sail up to the back door of Prester John?
Because the Newfoundland cod, which they had in their stores,
was the only fish in the world that could be carried below
the Line and come to the galley table, in the heat of Oriental
day, without taint and loss of savor. Again, to the failure of
the French to make a good hard cure of the cod may be laid
all of their troubles in the New World and much of their woe
in the Old, then and now. A green cure, like certain wines,
doesn't travel well or far. And there's even more to it: the

power at home flows from the same natural storehouse, a truth that bears prime meaning to all men who have a mind to greatness in peace. To my way of thinking, such greatness can be won and kept only by the procurement of good, cheap food. An army marches upon its stomach, says the Great Murderer of Europe. True enough; but note that it's always empty stomachs (or the fear of emptiness) that sets the corporals going. It's a principle easily come by and needs no great expounding: that there was never trouble in a land where a fat cod could be stuffed and baked for a fair part of a man's wage.

Let me, then, put a portion of it down. Here a little, there a little.

It was mighty Denmark (nourished by cod, of course) who drove the West Country English and the Europeans away from her Iceland fisheries; and sent them, emboldened by hunger, across the Atlantic to kill cod along the shores of a new-found land. New-found by the great Cabot and his Bristol seamen in the summer of 1497. Thus the scholars placed the cod-seekers some five years after Father Columbus, who was merely searching the wherewithal to buy a mess of cod for devout Spain. On this score, I have heard the Lisbons of my own time speak with genial laughter; for they hold it to be the truth that their forefathers were filling up pens along the shores of Avalon years before Columbus learned the table of two. And they say more: that he found the clue to all his glory by happen-chance, namely: on a visit to Lisbon he came across a fishing skipper, who listened to him with all respect and, in the end, gave him his star route over a mug of wine, saying: "A new world, Captain? Sim! I've a summer villa there and a red-skinned girl waiting for me and I've seen white whales there and I eat the flesh of great auks when the galley's empty." To this yarn, fancy or not, I can add a near word of

my own: that in 1498 the King of Portugal sent a skipper to
Newfoundland. And, since it is notorious that in those days
kings were slow to make up their minds on matters nautical,
we can judge that the Lisbons may not be wrong in their
declarations.

Yet what does it matter who was first? There's a little pride
to be taken out of it. But not much; because we are to bear in
mind a wise saying which Grandfather Sebastian could reel
off in Greek and I can barely scribble in plain words. He said
it was written by a fisherman named Plutarch, and here's the
salty go of it: " *'Tis a glorious thing to be well-descended,
but the glory, for the most part, belongs to one's ancestors.*"
Spoken like a doryman, I do declare. And to top it, I should
say that, first place being taken by skill or accident, the credit
goes to the man or race that holds on. Which leads to an equal
division of the glory among the races of Europe, saving the
Dutch, the Scandinavians, and the creatures living between
those shores. All others still share the cod fishery: the French,
standing free and hardy on the Islands of Miquelon; the Portuguese, calmly hauling away tho' the world rumbles beneath
their decks; our Canadian cousins, especially in Nova Scotia;
and, last to arrive, our young selves. It is all done in brotherly
fashion. There's no gunpowder being burned because of the
fishery; and no knives drawn, except to rip the bellies of fat
cod. I will end by repeating what has been cannily said: "Let
the statesmen study the cod fishery; there's the way to get
along in our world."

So much is enough (or must suffice) for the cod fishery in
general. A little more will serve for the Grand Banks, which
are the heart of that fishery. And that little is to the point
because we ourselves (that is, the *Golden Hind* and the
Doonans and the Bannons) have a history that bends back-

ward to the first fishing on the Grand Bank itself. It is the best judgment that the Normans (from Dieppe, Honfleur, Bretagne) were the first Europeans to kill cod on the Grand Bank. In support of that history, I cite this truth: that names first given to a sea or place are apt to outlast the names given by second-comers. Thus Banquereau, which is one of the Grand Banks of Newfoundland, was most certainly the French "banque d'eau," or bank of water; and the word clearly shows the old use of the word "bank," meaning a shelf of earth in river or sea. There are some seamen and cartographers who use the words "Great Banks" rather than the French "Grand," but it isn't the most common usage, since it lacks great age. There's a record culled from the mountainous debris of history by a Canadian scholar (a man named Innes) which states that the first account of a fine stock of cod from the Grand Bank was in the log of a French vessel, the *Catherine*. She fished there in 1599. 'Tis a long time since.

By your leave, I now call up the name of Sir Humphrey Gilbert, a good man aboard a vessel, who laid his Queen's hand on Newfoundland in the year 1583, thus giving a certain hint concerning the reasons for the quick recruitment of the Spanish Armada and its defeat five years later. The chief reason for both recruitment and defeat (take a fisherman's word for it) was the same: cod. For the wise Elizabeth had declared the cod fishery to be the prime nursery for her seamen; and she had also ruled that there be two fish days a week, which plainly required a doubling of the supply, chiefly acquired by robbing the Iberian fleets on the way home from the Banks.

The Doonans will declare that in Sir Humphrey's glorious expedition there was a *Golden Hind*. I, and far better historians with me, have another admiral in mind, but I've made a compromise there. So—there she sailed and there she lies. I'd give a pen of cod to know her fate. I've often thought as I lay hove to on the Grand Bank: "Perhaps the old *Hind* lies below me now—her anchor and her chains, at least. All that the salt cannot feed upon." And I had this notion, staring down into the beauty of the green, because Sir Humphrey was the first man (so far as my grandfather's books show) who ever put down, or gave out to the press, a charting of the Grand Bank. His account says it lay, under clouds of sea fowl, about fifty sea miles off Newfoundland, ran north to 52' and 53' in a bank ten miles wide, and ran south for an unsettled distance, there being always between twenty-five and thirty fathoms of water. So Sir Humphrey marked it down; so let us all.

It's the Doonans, in their pride, who'll tell you that an ancestor was pilot aboard that first *Hind;* and that he had the good fortune to be left behind by Sir Humphrey when the fleet sailed to encounter the fateful no'theaster. Knowing the Doonans somewhat better than they know themselves, I take it that this first of the North American clan was thrown off the *Hind* for not keeping a civil tongue in his head. They (the Doonans, I mean) will assert that their ancestor came out of Newfoundland in a hogshead that had been full of New England rum and sold to the fishermen of Newfoundland for their stomachs' sake. Join with me in the pious hope that there was a noggin or two left in the bottom for the young man's dear sake. His discomfort must have been a powerful thing. They say that his wonderful device to reach our shores was due to Britain's everlasting need of seamen. I've no doubt that he was an Irish captain who came to a British fishing port to buy cod; and presently found himself arm-in-arm with a press gang. Persuasive lads they must have been. Whatever his case,

England took stern measures to keep her sailors. She'd not leave them behind to winter in black, hungry Newfoundland for fear of sickness; nor would she give them leave to go to Gloucester or Boston, the new ports which were already sending dark looks across the sea. So it was that the Doonan, having lined a Yankee purse with his seaman's pounds, took a queer sort of French leave and tumbled out some days later on Cape Ann. It is in his memory and in the memory of his English admiral that the family keeps the name of the *Golden Hind* alive in gleaming gold on a free ship in a free ocean.

As for my own name: I could wish that it might have been written in bolder fashion on the general log of the New World, but the unalterable truth of it is that the first of us was a slave in iron chains, thrown down on the wharf at Boston by an English captain, who had bought the valiant body (but not the soul) for a few pounds after the Confederate Wars in Ireland. Owen Roe Bannon had fallen in the very courtyard of Dublin Castle with Hugh Og MacMahon, who was bloodily bent on the seizure of English cannon and gunpowder. Nevertheless, this poor slave beat off his chains and, in the time to come, appears on the Grand Bank as a Cape Ann fisherman. He and a hundred other skippers began the great traffic which, in the end, baffled old England and made her give way, peacefully for the most part, until we carried our rum and Indies' molasses and beef and corn to Newfoundland, took back the cod, sold it to the navies and the slave marts of the world, and fed ourselves. On Fridays and in Lent, that is to say. Thus the Grand Bank became the nursery of our own seamen, too, as it had been England's; and, since those seamen have always been the first to meet the enemy, and since the dorymen of Cape Ann saved Washington and his men on more than one perilous occasion, I'll make no bones about saying that you owe your freedom to the cod. Bless him next time he shows himself on a hot platter.

All this (though, in fact, it's only a little of the sum total), I put down to show, as best I may, that the cod fishery is not a matter to be put in second place to any of the abundances with which Nature endows us. And to show further that those who go to the Banks for their livelihood are men and not boys sent on a man's errand. The fishery is a fruitful pasture, a universal common, that must be maintained for the sake of all poor men, for all the poor children of the world, far and near. This I solemnly declare.

Now, scholar, throw me your gear and come aboard the *Golden Hind*.

6

Knot by knot, the *Golden Hind* lifted her pace until her lee rail ran under. A sun shower washed deck and rail clear of town dust, and wetted her sails down, so that she plugged along handsomely until she dropped the land, put all ledges and dunes out of sight, until nothing was left of 'longshore things except sun flashes off old Thatcher's walls. These dwindled soon; and with this final passing of the land, there came over me that old serenity and delight which marks the outward passage of a sailing vessel. Here is a feeling so strong that it is a cause of some puzzlement, especially because years and years of departures do not seem to lessen its pleasant force. I take it to be a subtle signal by Nature herself that she is now in command, that she is to be trusted and will provide the winds and tides for the work to be done, as she has always provided since man first hoisted cloth.

I remember that I said to myself: "It's surely an odd thing that a man can find such joy in a whole mainsail and yet—in his heart—be fully determined to have done with it!"

With this thought already half out of mind, I looked at Nora Doonan, where she stood, braced against the rail. She was strapping a sou'wester over her dark head; for the sea was kicking up a good deal and we had to oil up to keep dry. And I saw that a similar joy had moved her heart; because the spray had washed her face clear of town dust, too, and of town thought, also; and she stood, straddled to the sway, like some young captain bent on a sweep of the Grand Bank itself. There was no counting the number of times she had begun such a voyage, in childhood and womanhood. Yet it was clear to me that the first enchantment had not waned for her.

Not until the shore had vanished in its mist did Captain Le-Notre speak. All this sailing had been done without an order from him, which is usual with a well-trained crew. At least, he had to give nothing more than a nod or wave to me, for I had taken drowned Corkery's place as mate at the captain's order. That is not a distinguished post aboard a Gloucester schooner. The mate does a doryman's work just the same, and becomes first officer only when there are orders to be repeated to men at ropes, or dull work on paper to be done at customs or at settlement time.

As soon as the schooner sailed free of the land, Captain LeNotre made a sign to me that I should take over the wheel. He shouted above the pounding of the spray: "I want to take a look up forward! Put her on the other tack. And tell them" —he jerked his hand toward the waiting topmastmen—"tell them to go ahead, if you want to. She can stand it yet a while."

I had been standing near the main-sheet gang, who were trimming her a bit. I came aft a step and lifted my voice above the din of water and settling sails. I said: "Staysail, too? Will you want it on, Captain?"

Surely there was nothing in my words to stir a man up or cast him down. They were said with the utmost respect and in the proper course of my duties. The staysail was often added after the tack because it saved the shifting of that sail for the new tack, which would leave the vessel on her course for Nova Scotia, whither she must go for her herring bait. Nevertheless, Captain LeNotre didn't answer, even when I slid another step down the slanted deck and repeated my words. At the worst, a man could call it only strange, unmannerly behavior. Yet my surprise grew to something stronger in the next moment because Captain LeNotre actually became listless, which was unaccountable in a skilled sailing-master. He kept his hands on the spokes and, in this curious forgetfulness, failed to hand over. That is, he gave the *Hind* another spoke or two, looked at the sun, and then gazed dully into the binnacle, as if he really didn't care what story the compass told him.

Once the vessel splashed badly. He didn't do anything about it.

In my bewilderment, I turned toward Nora Doonan, thinking I might pass the thing off by a word with her. She hadn't missed any of that exchange, such as it was. Her face had brightened considerably in the excitement of the race for the open sea. Now her face darkened again and she let her shrewd glance go quickly from his face to mine and thence to the turned backs of her dorymen, gathered near the break.

Captain LeNotre then called out in a surprising change of mood: "Nora! What do you say?" By a wave of his hand, he invited her to take the wheel, a courtesy that was part of the *Hind's* famous hospitality, especially to an owner.

She nodded her head toward me. Certainly she herself was eager to have the pleasure of steering the *Hind* again; for she was something of a sailing-master in her own right. But I suppose that she remembered how long it had been since I had laid hands on such a lively wheel.

At this, Captain LeNotre again beckoned to me, quite as if he hadn't done so before. I took the wheel, held it a while to get the feel of it, and then raised my hand to the foresheet gang.

Captain LeNotre began to go forward slowly. In passing the men at the mainsheet, he came face to face with Billy Atkins, who was standing by for the tack. You can judge how keen a man this one was; because it was plain to me that he had noticed the changes in the captain's manner. There was a strong and familiar meaning in it for him, possibly because he had seen something of the kind on other occasions when they were ashore with Captain Parren. Whatever the reason, he sneered openly and said something to the Lisbon, who was standing at his side. The Lisbon rebuked him by a word slipped out of the corner of his mouth and by a quick lowering of his head, which I at once understood as a sign of his shame at being shipmates with such a man.

Certainly this was a harshness not easy to be borne; that, at the very outset of our voyage on which all depended, the necessary good feeling aboard a vessel should be marred by this cursed draggerman. I had a mind to cross the deck and bring him up short, which would have served him well for his impudence, but that impulse was at once overwhelmed by a natural and eager curiosity as to what Billy Atkins had said to the captain. And how dared he? And how dared our captain take that word (whatever it was) without show of offense? Indeed, he didn't even turn his head. I will say this much more of the happening: that it freshened my anxiety for the *Golden Hind* and made me feel, more keenly than before, that she was being drawn into some mystery which, in the end, would bring no good to her or to the Doonans.

As luck would have it, the exchange between the hand off the *Doubloon* and Captain LeNotre did not escape Nora Doonan. It had long been her business to watch dorymen with care; and her particular duty to observe a man who was new to her vessel. Had one of the *Hind's* own people acted in this way, she might have laid his surliness to the events of the last voyage and to the extraordinary behavior of Daniel Corkery on coming ashore. Now I saw how it angered her that the man she loved, and who loved her well, should be exposed to a crafty insult by a stranger on her own vessel.

This anger, which she must hide, took away her brightness and lent her a gloomy air, leaning there against the wake of our vessel or tilting into the blue when the *Hind* hurtled a sea. It seemed to me, inwardly contemplating her and her captain, that such dourness was now a habit with her; and was likely to become habitual with him. Since I had again resolved to think kindly (and, if I could, deeply) of my people, of the human heart and not always of things, such as my nets, I couldn't help sharing her sadness. I knew how eager her affectionate nature could be, how high her hope could rise. By that I especially mean the promise of happiness in the future of a man. Such a future is one of work, by which a man must stand or fall, according to the dignity he enjoys and uses, either with a heaving-stick keenly handled in a dory, or by a skipper's authority coolly mustered in a time of peril. By this reckoning, which I take to be a true one ashore or afloat, she and I had seen Captain LeNotre lose just a little bit of something rather precious; and our hearts went out to him, as the saying is. She, because of his meaning to her as a woman, and I because of his meaning as a human being, who lived in pain and in a growing loneliness.

I saw him make way at the dory-nest for a doryman carrying a tub of finished trawl across the deck. A moment later, a cloud of galley smoke, blown into the downdraft of the foresail, hid him. He stepped forward and, after a long look at the foresail, he paused in the lee of the jumbo, where there was some shelter, and there gazed ahead. He pulled off his sou'wester and roughly ran his hand through his thatch of yellow, matted hair. The schooner sped toward a black comber that came on high and heavy. I gave her a spoke to keep her well into it. In the instant before the breaking of the sea, I clearly saw his head and face against the sheen of water. It seemed sterner and sadder than ever; like a face engraved on a coin, where a man never finds a joyful sign.

Nora drew nearer to the wheel and, marking her state of mind, I called out cheerfully enough: "O. K., chum?"

She replied: "All set, John."

"Here we go then!"

I brought the schooner up into the wind. I shouted. The men hauled. Booms and sails came roaring across the deck; and the *Hind* began to fall gracefully onto the new tack. She stayed in the wind a little longer than was good. Her canvas slatted and then took hold, so that she came around in good order. I waved my hand again. Presently the topsails bloomed against the sky. A little later, the staysail went swaying up and, under all her muslin, the *Golden Hind* sped toward her landfall hundreds of miles away.

Nora took the wheel at my bidding. For her, too, it had been long since she had felt the powerful drive of that hull beneath and had seen the top hamper spread dark against the clouds. She found some joy in this return to familiar and beautiful action. She took the stand that had been taught to her in pigtail days, and she gave the leaning sails a sailing-master's scrutiny, so sharp a one, in fact, that two of the main-sheet gang started toward their stations, thinking they must trim again. She shouted a word to them and they fell back to the rail with fond looks at her and a grin between themselves.

The word passed among the men, who were repairing trawls amidships, and they shouted to her, gave her a wave of their hands. Once she had to lighten the *Hind* up a bit. When the schooner settled again, she saw my pride in her seamanship and she laughed again over the dewy spokes.

I said: "That's the way to drive her, Captain!" She gave me a driver's bold wink as payment; and steered the vessel smoothly onward, watching for the rise of a boarding sea. In so doing, she found something in the fore weather rigging that held her eye and darkened it. She leaned away to take a full look beyond the standing gear. A man was going aloft. Halfway up the shrouds, he hooked his arm in and looked steadily ahead. For a while, he searched the sea, and then he slowly swung his head in a sweep of the empty horizon. She and I saw that the searcher was Billy Atkins. It was plain (to me, at least) what he sought in the pleasant waters: the *Doubloon;* which was natural enough, of course, in a man who had been on the dragger since she was fitted out.

I must confess that I was a little startled by Nora's next words; for I had not yet succeeded in driving from mind the secret nature of Captain LeNotre's visit to the *Doubloon* early on that day.

She said: "John, do you know how the *Doubloon* goes?"

I nodded and she said: "I'd like to overhaul the *Doubloon*. And pass her."

"There's nothing in that," I replied. "She's no match for us today, for all her horsepower."

She cried out some words which were half-lost in the noise of our passage. I heard enough to understand that she wished Captain Parren to know that the *Hind* was going briskly about her business. A sea came in at the break and swirled against our boots. She eased the schooner. When the rattle of her clearing ended, I said: "I'll take you past the *Doubloon* before nightfall."

"Do that!"

I climbed into the main rigging and stopped under the cross-trees. I looked westward. I came down again and made her change the course to the westward. I waited by the wheel for some time and then passed the word along to the bow-watch that he was to sing out if he sighted a dragger on that course. I then went forward myself. When I came coasting by the port dory-nest, I saw Captain LeNotre standing there. At first, I thought he was under the influence. He was gazing in a perplexed way at the top dory; and making such a hard job of it that his gaze seemed like a drunken stare. I soon understood why this was so. The top dory was a stranger. Moreover, there were seven in that nest. Not six, as usual. This was such an odd circumstance that I myself passed beyond perplexity into astonishment. I could hardly believe my eyes. I even stepped forward on tiptoe and tried to touch the strange dory; and I took a stride forward and gave its marred sideboards a close look, as if its secret might lie there.

Captain LeNotre cried out: "What do you know about that?"

I at once replied: "I don't know anything about it! It beats me. Why! it's a stranger. Five seasons old, if it's a day." That was true. The dory had long been out of use; three seasons being about the life of even the best Yankee dories.

The captain said: "Seven dories!" I saw how he counted up the dory-straps until he reached the chafed strap of the stranger; and then he counted down again, his lips parted in a whisper. During that flashing of his troubled eyes, I added some things on my own account: the two and two that were lying fresh in my memory. That is, the secret recruits kept

below the *Hind's* deck by Nora Doonan; and the known fact
that they had been promised some hard sailing. (You will
remember that old Ambrose had used those very words.) I
asked myself: "Is it this dory they are to sail?" and I answered
at once: "No! there's nothing hard about that and no work
at all for so many skilled hands." This adding, and the taking
away, did me no good. All I could be sure of was this: that
Nora Doonan had swung that dory aboard in the night for a
purpose that would be made known at the usual Doonan time:
when she could keep it to herself no longer.

Meanwhile, Captain LeNotre recalled something else that
had obviously startled him as much as I had been in the beginning. He cracked his hands together and shouted a word that
the breeze took away too soon. He swung around between the
dory-nests and went down into the galley.

He wasn't gone long. Yet he had time enough to let his
anger rise. He grasped a foremast hoop to hold himself against
a pitch of the vessel and shouted: "Who in hell's name is captain of this vessel?"

I scarcely caught those words, the downdraft pelted them
away so fast. I worked a bit nearer and shouted: "Hey, Captain? What's that you say?"

He made a trumpet of his hand and shouted: "There's
stores enough aboard this vessel for the Labrador. And an
extra dory! What's going on here, chum?"

Despite his black anger, he was keen enough to see that I
knew as little as he did concerning such a mystery. Stores
enough for the Labrador? And an extra dory? I shook my
head. I must have looked like a dunce to him; and, indeed,
I was being small help to a captain.

He cursed in his harmless Miquelon fashion and hurried
toward the quarter. I kept at his heels and heard him begin

with Nora by asking rather roughly: "You responsible for that stranger dory aboard my vessel?"

She hadn't time to measure the depth of his anger. She nodded her head and shouted her answer. "Yes, Paul! I had it put aboard. I meant—"

He then began to make certain errors; or he showed his ignorance of her kind, because his manner gave no sign at all that he was aware of speaking to the owner of the *Hind*. There he wasn't to be blamed. I suppose he thought that he knew her. Aye! he was vain enough for such nonsense. Foolhardiness for a man to believe a woman will ever permit him to know her.

He said in the same rough way: "What's it for?"

And, quite as roughly in her sudden change, she replied: "Business!"

"The vessel's business?"

"The firm's business, Paul."

Although you can see that this answer was six of one and half a dozen of the other, it served her purpose just then, which, I suppose, was to let him have his say, as long as he didn't blow up and drop the dory over the side, there being a delicate tradition concerning a vessel's gear and its changes and additions.

She said: "What with all our trouble getting away, Paul, and that Corkery business, I didn't have time to explain what I wanted to do. What I had to do."

He listened to her with an air of reserve and a sort of unbecoming impatience.

She went on: "I had to have extra stores put aboard. Didn't cook tell you, Paul?"

"No! I found out for myself."

Her increasing alarm at his anger seemed to satisfy some

need in him. He became calmer and even managed to work up a smile when she laughed again and said: "I've a secret, Paul. I can tell you part of it—maybe all of it—as soon as we drop the *Doubloon*."

"The *Doubloon?*" He repeated the name of his friend's vessel harshly. Now, whether it was plain anger or alarm that harshened him, I couldn't tell. He said again: "The *Doubloon?* Pass the *Doubloon?*"

"Aye! that one, my dear. And all others."

He braced himself against the companionway. I saw that he was now coming close to her secret venture in Nova Scotia; and I saw also that he was baffled and did not like it very much. He gave her a look that really had no open meaning and then, without a word, he pushed back the slide and went below.

The bow-watch sang out and a man aloft sang out, too. A doryman at work on the bait-knives shouted: "Dragger! Dragger!" The man aloft held out his arm stiffly to the west-ward. A dragger lay sparkling under the sun. She was making knots. Her smoke ran off in a flattened stream.

The *Golden Hind* lay on about the same course. I brought the helm up. This made the *Hind* nearer and she began to close up. In half an hour, the *Doubloon* was made out clearly in the long rays. There was no one on her deck, except a man hammering at her winch with a sledge. He was too far away to be made out. A mile or so later, we saw the leeward door of the *Doubloon's* pilot-house swing open. As soon as the door closed, the *Doubloon* changed course abruptly to the north-ward, a change that would bring the vessels rather close together.

The dorymen at the weather rail began loud talk about the *Doubloon*. Nora had hauled herself up into the swifters and was looking at the dragger. She bent down to them and said: "I'll tell you this much. I don't want them looking us over. Or anybody else." This wish to be alone, and to keep out of hailing distance, was caused, in part, by her sudden discovery that sharp eyes could make out the stranger dory and thus set sharp minds a-going.

A doryman replied: "So I say, Miss Nora! We've got his bloody Jonah aboard this vessel and we want no more of the *Doubloon*."

This talk of Billy Atkins and the evil luck that had followed him on the Grand Banks was the first we had heard from the crew on that score. It didn't make us any happier. I, for one, would never make light of the Jonah myth; for it often had a sound basis in the facts of a man's lack of devotion to his duty or to his cowardice, as witness the namesake, who was by no means a good man aboard a vessel, even for a greenhorn. I looked about for Atkins and found him up forward, this time alone by the jib. His stealthy air and the steadiness of his gaze toward Parren's vessel made me glad that Nora Doonan hadn't yet revealed the presence of old Ambrose and his men. Whatever the venture was, I had a notion that Atkins might have figured it out, despite my own failure to do so; and, since there was clearly a lot of money to be made somewhere, I had no doubt that Billy would have tipped the hand to Parren, who was a great lover of the dollar, no matter how he came by it.

The dorymen drifted aft and now dallied by their stations. I gave them the signal: "Hard alee!"

The signal spread fore and aft. "Hard alee! Hard alee!"

The schooner fell over onto the other tack with such force and smoothness that she raced by the *Doubloon* on her weather quarter. No signals passed between the vessels. I saw that Nora was watching for one. In the first minute on the new tack, she was close enough to see the man at work on the winch. It was Daniel Corkery. He ceased his work and looked at the *Hind*; and I have no doubt that the swiftness and beauty of her sailing made him wish he hadn't left her deck. The schooner drew away from the *Doubloon* at such a fast gait that you'd think Parren had his anchor down. The seas began to run high between the vessels.

The wind having increased in force, we clewed up the topsails for the night and hauled down on the staysail also, leaving the *Hind* under a whole mainsail and doing well enough. The cook came up with the lanterns for her running-lights. Soon I saw again the cheerful display that always gave me such pleasure: the ruby gleam beating up and down amongst the seas to windward, the green burning on her leeward froth. A hunter's moon, red as galley coals, came swaying up. The rising of the moon gave such new strength to wind and tide that the *Hind* began fighting her own shadow and shying from it. In the end, she made such a face that a reef was taken in the mainsail; and this understanding of her caprice made her sweeten herself a bit.

Soon after she had found herself and left us alone, the call came for the first gang to go to dinner. This was the captain's table, of course. And mine and Nora's. It was the first set meal of the day. According to the *Hind's* custom when at work, there had been nothing but the traditional mug-up since breakfast. Which is to say, kettles of coffee and tea simmering on the stove and biscuits and cake in the shack locker. The old idea was to let cook have a real chance to show his skill and to display the *Hind's* hospitality, an abundance I had tasted before and was more than ready to taste again.

When we backed down the companionway steps into the forecastle, we found that everything had been done in the true *Hind* style. Poor as she was, she had kept the virtue of the poor: to feed the hungry well. The long table, hung between the lockers that ran alongside the bunks, was set with a new cloth. There was good china, instead of glass, and ivory-handled knives and forks rather than the metal ones that should serve thereafter. At each of the fourteen places, there was the deep white plate that must be used for all the courses, a custom that couldn't be broken for the most honored guest. More than that, the men had made up their bunks neatly. All stray gear had been carefully stowed in the peak; and the smelliest pipes were up there also, where the ventilator blew. This was the proper thing, according to the host laws laid down by Grandfather Doonan generations ago, who was fond of carrying Boston greenhorns to the Banks for their instruction and for his own.

The cook, a venerable man of some seventy years, stood by the foremast butt. He had put on the easy air of a man who had done nothing much in the day past. He failed to deceive us. We all understood that it would have been wrong if he had indicated, in any way, that something impressive had been achieved on the great Shipmate stove behind him. Once or twice he lifted his apron to touch away the beads of sweat that slid down his forehead and red cheeks. Other than that, he made no acknowledgment of labor triumphantly carried on throughout a day that was far from usual, considering its tumultuous beginning.

When the table had filled up, he waited until the chatter and the laughter ceased, waited until we had assumed a respectful and expectant attitude. He then hauled around in regal style and came forward with the first immense tureen of fish chowder. This was a daring opening; for such Gloucester vessels usually ate fish when all other stores were gone, fish being purposely caught for those who didn't have plenty of them. Such a practice, however, was a clear libel against Yankee chowder, especially when made with milk and cream. This serving, at the outset of a voyage, was, therefore, cook's challenge to himself and to the libel.

One glance along the two rows of lifted faces gave him his triumph. He tasted the triumph with all the gusto that we gave to his chowder; and then, by a series of portly turns and advances, he served three yard-square trays of beefsteaks, broiled and fried, to which he added bowls of succotash, green beans, and pan after pan of hot biscuits, all backed up with platters of butter, carved by the half-pound out of tubs. The teapots passed up and down. Nora poured for her captain and for me and passed it along. We emptied our plates of chowder and neatly scoured the dish with biscuits, which we popped into our mouths. A doryman, who had been politely waiting to show his manners, speared a steak on his fork and placed it on her plate.

The *Hind* hadn't sailed two miles before the whole banquet had gone the way it should. The trays appeared again, this time laden with grapes and apples; and after them came six apple pies, nearly half a fathom wide, ranked by loaves of store cheese. The pies ran with cinnamon; their crusts had the lightness of foam.

"What you think, Cap'n Nora?" The Lisbon, seated on the port side, asked the question. For this part of the *Hind's* genial ritual, which I joyfully remembered, he had worked up a black air of dissatisfaction, mixed with famine looks. He gazed in mock despair at the lamps overhead.

Nora shook her head in sadness. She, too, remembered this game of old. "Cook," she said in a mournful way, "is not what he used to be. We must look for a new one. My father always said it would come to that in the end. And Grandfather said the same thing the other day. 'Tis a great shame!"

All the slicked-up heads waggled and the flushed faces grew brighter as they waited for the next cue.

"Why you say that, Cap'n Nora?"

"Because—by the Lord Harry!—we'll all be so fat we can't get into a dory!"

They rolled out their laughter and broke away from their places. The cook bowed solemnly and returned to his stove, where another such abundance was reaching its climax for the second table.

This was the moment when Nora had to surprise them all; and I must say that she couldn't have chosen a better time; for a good dinner enables a man to take a new thing easily.

She called out: "Cook! One moment, if you please."

He lifted a ladle in quick response. "Yes, Miss Nora?"

"There'll be five more men to fill up the second table."

She might just as well have announced that five bull whales were coming aboard for a bite of supper and a mug of tea.

One man shouted: "Hey!"

The cook had tasted fifty years of Grand Banks salt and knew the various flavors of surprise. He was, therefore, man enough to bow and say: "Five more to fill up. Certainly, Miss Nora." He couldn't, however, stop the slight widening of his eyes which was his way of asking: "How in the name of halibut did she get five secret men aboard this vessel? And why?"

I concealed my own knowledge with a proper look of astonishment.

Here's a strange thing: after the first moment of surprise and curiosity, the dorymen became uneasy. One man stood grotesquely with his leg flung into an upper bunk, his head twisted down. The new watch, crowding toward the companionway, paused with their oil clothing on their arms. As I said, they stared at her in surprise; and they exchanged short, quick looks which were really attempts to find out if one of their chums had already figured out the meaning of her words. Their wonderment turned to shrewdness and this, being baffled also, changed into uneasiness. I could tell that by the way all eyes came to one face on which they stayed fixed; and that was the face of their skipper.

Captain LeNotre had slowly lifted himself out of his place at the galley end of the starboard locker. Every man in that forecastle knew at once that their captain hadn't been told about the secret men. This knowledge, added so abruptly to their fresh store of distrust for him, gave such force to their bold glances that he couldn't help answering in kind. He jerked back his head from the full flush of the lamplight so that his face had the shelter of the lesser light flowing down from the deck. The blaze of his yellow hair and flat, high-colored cheeks was thus dimmed. The anger in his eyes made them burn in the half-shadow.

Nora waited for him to speak.

In that anxious moment, I saw certain proof that in the canny, locked hearts of her men there was more hidden than the memory of James Corkery's death. I looked swiftly from face to face along the table and by the companionway and I said to myself: "They don't seem to forget their chum easily." By that I meant, of course, that his loss should have put down deep. At once, I saw that this was a mistake in thinking. Here, once more, I found myself with a difficult sum done before I knew what had to be added and taken away. I knew absolutely that the dorymen would not permit a captain's mistake, even such a fatal one, to stand between them long. Habit was strong amongst them, as it should be. They lived by habit and steered and fished by habit; and the most inflexible habit of all—the prime and ancient rule of the Gloucester fleet—was the habit that forced them to get rid of anything that might hamper them in their search for cod.

Life lay in the cod. Oh, of course, there's no denying that life of some sort could be found elsewhere. They could choke the years away in 'longshore factories or at chipping rust. Yet that was not the savory life they had lived, had become used to, and wished to follow until the end, whatever that end might be. Now, since they endangered this hope of life by their rebellious behavior, it should have become plain to me and to Nora that they were in possession of a secret, too. Had either of us been wise enough to enter their closed hearts and live completely with them, we should have seen that they believed, for one reason or another, that their captain had become a threat to all that was dear to them. Thus their mute rebellion might have been judged by us for what it was: a clumsy effort to save all—the *Hind* and the Doonans and their own way of life. This could not be made plain to us at the time because we were not sufficient in our wisdom; and I can only say so now because of hindsight added to foresight.

Captain LeNotre didn't include Nora in his strong, unflinching gaze. When his eyes, in their slow survey, reached her, he took all meaning out of them and let the lids fall halfway. He then turned on his heel and reached for the companionway rope. The schooner lurched. He waited in a graceful, careless pose. When the vessel came up, he swung onto the steps and climbed away.

The cook's bell clanged. A man on deck shouted: "Dinner! Dinner! Second gang!"

Nora climbed the steps. On deck, she waited until I came out. We heard the relieving watch repeat their orders:

"North-northeast! One hour. One hour." We breathed a noisy frost. The moon, lessened and yellowed, had passed over and was swiftly falling down. It had ceased to beam. Companies of stars burned hard and cold where the moon had been. Black and cold, the following seas poured over the *Hind's* wake. Because of all these things—night and cold, the words below, and the fateful landfall soon to be made—our hearts became chilled again and full of stir. I touched her hand. She went slowly aft through the darkness and I followed. Spray bit at our cheeks. A flurry of snow came whirling down the mainsail. She shivered and struck back the slide of the cabin companionway. In turning to go down, she saw that I had stopped near the helmsman.

She called out: "Come along, John, will you?"

I went below after her.

Captain LeNotre waited in the cabin. He had taken the same position there, that is, beyond the stove and beyond the golden circle of light from the brass lamp which swung stiffly in answer to the swaying of the schooner. His face had grown even harder. It was like a Hallowe'en mask nailed to the dark panels.

She passed him without a word and went down into the hold. She found her old dorymen drowsing in their blankets. She called them up. I heard their cheerful answers when she said night had fallen and that their day in the hiding-place must have been a poor one.

She led them into the cabin. Shaking heads and arms and stamping hard with their boots, they filed past the stove and brought up, somewhat bowed and weary, between the port bunks and the companion steps. Old Ambrose gave their respectful greetings to the young captain and said: "A long kink we've had there below!"

"Long kink!" repeated the man straddled behind him.

Captain LeNotre returned the greeting with an air that did him credit; for their very presence was an attack on the dignity of his office. He said: "Ambrose Cameron!" and, a breath later: "Peter Lord!" He spoke the others' names in a grave tone. He spoke evenly and did not reveal anger or surprise; that is, he carried the extraordinary meeting off in such a manner that Ambrose, for instance, might have taken it for granted that the captain had known of their presence. This was a pretense impossible to carry out for long, if he intended to do so.

I watched the dorymen narrowly to see if their responses might be affected by the talk they had heard in Gloucester concerning the *Hind's* last voyage, a subject to which we had come close the night before. They gave no such sign. They stood in simple, dutiful silence, gazing into the lamp with blinks and yawns. Thus they waited for her revelation of the mystery in which they had been drawn by their need and by their devotion to her family and her vessel.

I soon saw that the revelation was not to be made at this time. More than ever, Nora Doonan was aware that she had made a promise to me that she would not tell a soul about her Nova Scotian venture or tell why she chose to have five old dorymen go aboard hugger-mugger in the secrecy of dawn. She was determined that she would say nothing of it. The secret itself was to remain hers.

She spoke to Captain LeNotre, and sent her words out calmly from under the sagging brim of her sou'wester. "These men are aboard the *Hind*, Paul, as the firm's passengers. Just as I told you concerning the dory—so I tell you concerning them. Their names are on her list and have been given to the Coast Guard. I've work for them to do at a certain place.

Work which I can't reveal to you or to them right now. Although I'd like to tell you, Paul. I'd like to very much. All I can say is this: that the job I have for them is a hard one. A dangerous one. It's something that the *Hind's* crew can't be asked to do. Even these men, who are our old friends, may refuse to do it—"

"We will not!" Old Ambrose jerked his fist up roughly to mark his words.

She spoke on without looking away from Captain LeNotre's impassive face. "I asked them to stay below because the venture is a matter of cold cash. A lot of it, to my way of thinking. If I do what I hope to do, the *Hind* will live and she'll stay mine. For a good time longer, whether she earns her own way or not."

She faced the dorymen and said: "Go to dinner now. Be sure to praise the cook and gain your welcome."

They climbed the steps and closed the slide behind them.

She again spoke to the captain. "I'll tell you this much more. And"—turning to me—"I tell you, John, because you're mate aboard this vessel and have a right to know. I need these men for the job. These—and no others. I need that dory and I may need the extra stores. I hope so. The thing I'm going to pull off, if I can, is a simple one. It's so simple, in fact, that if anybody on the Doonan Wharf had seen extra men and dories aboard the *Hind*—well! they might well figure it out and beat me to it. The same applies to the *Doubloon*. But not now!" Her voice grew louder in the growth of her confidence. "Now I'm in the clear. And I'm still on my own—and there's an end to talk!" She took a step deeper into the light and there, with one scarred hand against her breast and the other curved in an appeal to him, she put off her harsh look and put on an expression so disarming—aye! and so tender—that I turned toward the glass. She said: "Now, Paul, I hope that's all right with you. It is, isn't it?"

How could he help yielding? No, there was nothing for him to do except throw his own mask away, or put on another and a kindlier one. He laughed and stretched out his great hand to her arm, which he lightly touched. "Anything you say goes with me, Nora Doonan. You know that. It must. Don't forget that you're the owner of the *Hind* now! So? You say what you please and we carry out your bidding." He then spoke to me. "Is that it, John?"

That was what I wanted from him. Just the same, the ease of his jump from sullen anger to genial acceptance took me aback. Really, I myself could hardly have fallen onto the new tack as readily as he had. It was against common nature. I am pretty sure that this was the first time, since I had learned of his strange stay aboard the *Doubloon*, that I felt the burn of subtle fear, fear of a man who could do a right-about so quickly. And swallow his pride in doing so. By this same mark, I should have learned to fear myself; because I proved to be as subtle as he. I concealed my thought, grinned amiably and said: "Righto! Her iron word is the iron law!"

Nora Doonan was vastly cheered by our words. She said in bright frankness: "Paul, I must confess that's why I wanted to get clear of the *Doubloon*."

He answered carelessly. "Ah," he said, "I wondered about that. What's the matter there?"

Nora replied: "I know Captain Parren is an old friend of yours. And he's been a good friend to us—to my grandfather and to me. Now and in times past. But he loves money too much for my taste, even if he is generous once he lays hands on it. I hate to say it, Paul, but the truth of it is that I wanted to keep clear of the *Doubloon* so he couldn't possibly learn about this business of Ambrose and the meaning of the dory."

"Good for you!" Captain LeNotre stretched his arms idly and looked down into his bunk. He shook off the whole business by saying in lazy good nature: "The bunk looks good to me, chums. I just can't say how glad I am to be away from that wharf. I thought we'd never make it." He glanced at the glass, which stood at "Fair," and said: "I'll turn in now, friends. Good night."

Nora sat down on the locker near her bunk, stretched out her long legs and said to me: "John, do a tired greenhorn a favor, will you?"

I knelt and pulled off her doryman boots. I hung up her slicker and her oilskin overalls to dry behind the stove and then I turned in. I had taken the drowned Corkery's bunk. It was a double bunk; and another doryman lay sound asleep on the inside, thus leaving no room for any poor ghost that might have come aboard in the passage of the night. Halfway into a dream, I heard the watch come down and speak to the captain. "A big fleet on our course. We'll be in it soon. 'Less they send us home."

I heard the captain say: "Ah, Billy!" and: "Get around it. Shake that reef out of the mainsail. Steer east. Call me if you are challenged."

"How long, Captain?"

"All night. She'll drop them. And then—Seal Island."

"All night. East. Seal Island. Yes, Captain."

"Call me if the wind changes."

"Call you if the wind changes."

I heard the watch climb the steps, and I heard the work go forward on the sails. A little later, the *Hind* lay over to gain her new course. Soon her customary rhythm returned and this gave to us all our exit from troubles and high hopes.

7

THE WIND stayed fair for the *Golden Hind* all the long autumnal night and all the day. I was on bow-watch when the first frosty gleams shot seaward from the Nova Scotian hills. Captain LeNotre had the helm. We had left our topsails clewed up and ran handsomely enough under a whole mainsail into the outer harbor of Shelburne, where our business was to be done. We hove to and tarried there for some time, waiting for the Canadian cutter to give us permission and an entry number for our signal halyard. I reported the cutter as lying within a hook of land to the northward, where she apparently had some business with herring-boats. Before she turned toward us, a Nova Scotian schooner, which was also under a whole mainsail, ran through the Shelburne gate, a barrier of buoys and chains that still guarded the inner harbor and the Roseway River. She hailed, but did not speak us, being too far away.

The cutter gave us leave and Captain LeNotre let the *Hind* shoot smartly through the gate, whereupon Nora stepped to the wheel and by her words gave the true beginning to her venture. She said: "If you'll heave to again, Paul, I'll rid you of the stranger dory now and my men."

I had expected something of the sort because the stranger dory had been swung off and had been loaded with stores and with bundles wrapped in burlap, which I made out to be tools and sledges; because the handle of a pair of blacksmith's tongs had worked its way through the burlap.

The captain told me to carry out her order. He said to her: "And you, Nora? Do you stay with us or go in the dory?"

"I'll stay aboard for the time being, Paul."

He said: "Right you are." He brought the vessel into the wind.

During the night, the five secret recruits had received a part of their orders. These must have been bewildering, yet they kept their mouths shut and went nimbly about the business. And smartly, too. I saw old Ambrose throw a bit of canvas over the tong handles. There was some grinning amongst them, however, and among the *Hind's* people, who watched this curious departure with a general what-do-you-know-about-that? air. The laughter was caused by the comical appearance of tall Ambrose, captain of the five, who was rigged out in his Sunday best, even to a magnificent derby hat that had greened a little in the decades since he had first donned it for a jamboree. In the best of circumstances, a derby is an odd headpiece, especially above a ruddy face; at sea, I'd as soon expect to see a whale with a cape. Ambrose also wore a white shirt—and of all the things to strike on!—a gates-ajar collar with a black silk necktie in which he (or Nora) had stuck a beautiful pearl stickpin. This ornament I recognized as a Doonan heirloom. He had shaved his cheeks and chin to the smarting point and had given his white moustache a dandy's treatment with a little cooking oil from the galley. All in all, what with his grave air and patient eyes, he certainly looked like a rather prosperous greenhorn, like a vice president of the National Bank.

Without a glance at the thronged rail, he took his place in the stern sheets, wrapped his grey ulster neatly around his knees, and uttered his loud "Give way!" The dory, two men to a thwart, steered toward the Roseway's western shore and, in a few minutes, vanished in a twist of vapor sent down from the valleys by the sun.

This was such an extraordinary event, and the cause of so much guessing and conjecture, that a queer, strained silence soon passed over the *Hind's* deck. There were some glances turned toward Nora, of course. I suppose in the hope that she might now reveal her secret. I said to her: "Well, you've fooled a lot of people so far. I only hope you don't fool yourself."

She replied: "It wouldn't be the first time, John. But if I do miss out on this play—it'll be the end of the *Hind*."

Since we were not alone, it was plain that she meant others to know that the gravest part of her canny game had begun. Thus they were to understand that she was in no mood for jesting, which was a trick the older men enjoyed with her because they never could quite make up their minds that the child, who had sailed with them so often, had become this long-legged, solemn-eyed girl in boots, who took a hand in a man's game. Having reeled out this hint for whatever ears were straining for it, she drew me to the rail to talk while the *Hind* ambled onward to Shelburne Wharf, where she was to take bait and leave for her fishing.

Those words, "the end of the *Hind*," had first saddened me, then had made me angry; for I considered it a foolish thing in her that she should dare to risk her vessel in a lost cause. Why! even the Canadians, who had clung to their sails as long as they could, had gone so far by this time that they were ready to build draggers for any man who would do the business for them; and I myself had received a handsome offer from the people at Halifax, who were willing to subsidize the venture for the sake of getting more fish for England. I couldn't sail under another flag, much as I liked theirs. And here stood Nora Doonan, headstrong as ever, with the knowledge growing in her that she must make money on her secret venture, and also make a good stock on the *Hind*, or else give over. I admit that she was bound by certain unchangeable conditions, namely, that she couldn't borrow money on the *Hind* or share ownership, but it was plain to me that she actually considered her grandfather's debts (to Parren and others) and her own debts, which were not small, to be obligations which the *Hind* must make good, either with her earnings or with her hull. This was nothing to be laughed at; or to be put aside lightly. The *Hind* was worth over a hundred thousand dollars as she lay. Converted into a dragger, she could pay for her changes in a few months and earn a hundred thousand a year thereafter. Nora Doonan might have stretched a moral point or, better still, she might have been strictly honest with herself and try to raise the money that would take the mainsail and the dories off the *Hind* and put an engine and my nets aboard her.

I told her so again while we glided into the berth and the herringmen took our lines. "Take my advice," I said, "and buy no bait. She'll lose the cod again and you'll be in the bucket. Take the train back to Boston and be done with dory trawling."

She made no real answer to my thought. We had quarrelled so many times in our young lives that she could always tell when the glass was falling with me. So she was ready. She said sternly: "The *Hind* remains the *Hind* during the life of my grandfather. And, perhaps, during mine. I cannot and will not say." She then took the wind out my sails neatly by asking: "How much is bait here now? Do you know?"

"Four cents."

"And at Yarmouth?"

"Four and a half."

"We did well to come here for it then."

I kept my silence. The price of herring was nothing to get gaffy about.

She read me in a sly, sidewise glance and said: "How long do you think the bait's been in the icehouse?"

"Long enough! Considering that the *Hind's* the only vessel taking bait here in a month o' Sundays."

"July herring maybe. Grandfather always said they're the fattest and the best for the Banks." She looked in a hard way at the herring dealers on the wharf, who were trying to stare at her without her knowing it. "If that's the case—the *Hind* being the only buyer—we ought to beat them down half a cent, don't you think?"

I laughed so loudly that the gulls jumped. "You crook! Give the men their wages, will you?"

She laughed at her success over me; and then watched the baskets of herring swing out from the overturned boxes on the wharf and swing down to the *Hind's* hatch. The Lisbon and Billy Atkins were stowing the bait in the pens. Captain LeNotre stood by the hatch, keeping a close eye on the bait, which seemed to please him mightily. Now and then a plump herring skipped stiffly out of the rattling flow. He'd pick it up, smile in satisfaction at the fat sides, and throw it down into the pen.

Nora said to me: "Go below, John, like a good man, and bring up my suitcase. It's all ready. I'm going to the Loyalist Tavern to dress for my part in this business." She looked down in distaste at her wrinkled trousers and dirty boots. "It'll be a pleasure to get out of this rig, even for an hour."

She wasn't the one to complain about a doryman's rig. Never had before, to my knowledge; and she'd been forced to wear it long enough, the Lord knows. Because of this, her words had more than a casual meaning to me. So had the severeness of her mouth, which had whitened a little at the corners. Thus I knew that she had been waiting for her dorymen to reach a certain place, and that she dreaded an encounter which was now imminent. And I understood, too, that she meant to do some sailing herself, either on the *Hind* or some other vessel. Else why should she speak so plainly of being out of her sea togs for only an hour? Well, I kept my mouth shut for once, went down into the cabin and came back with the suitcase, which I carried to the wharf. I saw her go forward and talk to the captain briefly. She spoke of me in such a way that he raised his eyes toward me and nodded briskly. At the same time, I noticed that the *Hind's* people were staying aboard the vessel or close to it. This was strange; because the men rather liked the town. I spoke to a doryman about it and he said that the captain had given orders for all to stand by until the owner sent back word that her business had been done.

I had received no such order. Presently I found out why this exception had been made.

Nora went down into the cabin and came on deck again, this time wearing a topcoat to make her less noticeable on the streets. She led me away from the wharf and there told me what I expected to hear: that I had been chosen to take part in her venture. She gave me to understand that she had kept her pledge, that neither the captain nor the five dorymen on the river knew the meaning of all these preparations. She was on her own, she repeated, and had no intention of sharing blame or credit, if any there should be. Her knowledge of the chandler's trade had led her directly to the venture, she said, and she would take no advice for or against her plan. She had worked it out to the last possible detail.

Now, while she spoke, I saw the frown of despair come back to her face; and this pained me so much that I said: "Come to the point, Miss. What's my part?"

She answered: "First, John dear, you are to keep a civil tongue in your head whether we win or lose. We're old friends and I don't intend to let our friendship spoil. See that you keep it in repair."

"Agreed," I said with not much grace.

"Then you're to go now to Bannister's stockyard and stand by. Find him—if he's not in Yarmouth—and keep him handy. Ask him the price of beef. Good, marbly beef. He'll not have any. Say that the *Hind's* cook sent you. But, above all, pretend that you don't know me when I come in."

"Bannister!" This was a harsh turn, in my opinion. Bannister was a prime rascal. He had been a small trader in the Labrador, later in Newfoundland, where he was known to Captain Parren and to my father. Father had found him a dishonest dealer and a hard man. Not only with men of the sea, but 'longshore, where he dealt most. His cunning robberies had forced him to drift westward; and for some years he had been handling cattle and meat on an increasing scale in Shelburne and at Yarmouth, where he had an establishment. I knew that only a few years before, when LeNotre had first taken command, Bannister had cheated Grandfather Doonan out of a large sum, earned by the *Hind* in a lucky season and carelessly thrown away in a speculation on government contracts. I could never get the right of it, but I remembered that a large herd, or several herds, of Canadian Angus cattle were involved.

I said: "He's hard to handle—that old wretch. He's beaten the *Hind* before."

The look that came into her eyes was something difficult to bear, it being so close to hatred; and those were eyes in which I had been accustomed to see quite another light. She said in a violent tone: "Bannister is going to be taken today, sure as my name is Doonan! What I'm going to do to him, John, I wouldn't do to my worst enemy."

"He was that very thing!" I said quickly.

"Yes! But we were up his alley on that business. This time the deal's in my line. He can weigh up a steer well enough with his eye, but he doesn't know bilge from pudding."

I said: "There's more truth than poetry in that."

"Go along now," she said; and turned away.

I watched her trudge off toward the town, and she seemed, somehow, to have become a little girl again. I'd have given much to free her from her need and from her fear.

I dallied by the shore a while, and watched two dorymen cutting willow wands for heaving-sticks; and then I went up to the town, where I walked slowly down the main street, stopping now and then to pass the time of day with a Nova Scotian skipper or with a patrol of the Irish Regiment, which was then on provost duty in Shelburne. To one of the sergeants, who used to be a fisherman on the *Bluenose,* I said: "You boys getting any good beef from Bannister lately?"

The sergeant spat.

I strolled down one of the lanes that led to the riverside and turned westward toward Bannister's stockyard. I heard again the squealing of shoats and the lowing of cattle beyond the stys. When I came up to the gate, I saw Bannister taking the sun on a box in front of the shanty which served him as an office. He was blinking at the sun in a crafty manner; and, no doubt, was thinking how nice it would be if he could buy it up and make a slight but universal charge for its use. Special rate for babies. He had a face like a doryman's fist. He was expertly attired, as usual, in patches and broken boots. His right elbow stuck eloquently out of his hand-me-down jacket. The jacket was fastened in front by a rusted horse-blanket pin. You'd hardly think the poor creature had a dime to bless himself with, not to mention a hundred thousand dollars. That was precisely the point he labored to make. And did make.

Up until the moment I hailed him, Mister Bannister had so far forgotten his rôle in life that a look of contentment had brightened his face. When he heard my shout, and saw a Gloucesterman, he switched off his inner lights and began to murmur sadly in the Job vein. "Ah, well! Ah, well!" And: "Good day, Captain, good day! Miserable day, ain't it? Come to look at an old man in the midst of ruin, eh? Well, all right! It's all right. I don't mind." And such gabber, spilt from a mouth that was enough to turn the stomach of a washed man. He rubbed the back of his filthy hand across his eyes, which had at once filled with tears.

I said: "Now, now, Bannister! Don't take on so. Don't! You know what I told you last time. If things don't get worse soon, there's a chance they may get better."

He blew his nose through his fingers and made a sobbing noise. "There's much in what you say, Captain, I do admit. You're a sound young man, Captain Bannon, a sound young man, and that's a thing I've said time and time again at the God-given opportunity and bless us this day."

This was just about the distance Bannister could go without getting a bargain under way. He said: "And what can a poor old man—a very poor one—do for ye this day, Captain Bannon? Some prime quarters of beef, perhaps? Or fair to middling? Lean hams? Canadian bacon which you're all so fond of, perhaps?"

I let my head fall a little in mock despair, which wasn't too difficult for me, considering the circumstances. I flung a hand up in a woeful gesture and said: "I've come down in the world, Bannister, and I make no bones about it. I'm not to be called 'captain.' I'm a doryman again—"

"A doryman!" Disappointment turned his croak into a mean shriek. "A doryman, is it? May the Lord have mercy on us when His snow falls! You were skipper of a fine dragger out of Boston when last I laid eyes on ye! With a big icebox to be filled." He jumped up to take a nearer, shrewder look. He added up the wear and tear in my clothes. "Drunk yourself back into a dory, eh? Drunk yourself out of twenty thousand a year, I take it?" His rage made him dance a bit. The sole of his left boot flapped miserably. "Oh, the world, the world, the drink!"

" 'Tisn't exactly that way, Bannister," said I. "Talked myself back into a dory, I did. That's my story. And now—"

"Talk! Talk!" The old rascal shook his rags to the breeze and hopped frantically up and down. He had already lost imagined hundreds and was apt to lose more, if this kept on. "There's too much bloody talk along this coast!" His eyes had changed into the shape and frost-hue of a dogfish eye. He suddenly gave up in disgust, not being able to hear a jingle in my pocket, no matter how he strained for it. He said roughly: "What do you want, doryman? Out with it?"

"Well, as I told you, I've come down in the world, Mister Bannister"—I leaned ever so slightly on the new "Mister" because I didn't wish to have him drive me away—"and I came in today on the *Golden Hind*—"

"The *Golden Hind!* The *Golden Hind!*" Mister Bannister

smoothly licked his lower lip clear across to the starboard, where the tongue moved reluctantly inboard, quite as if the lip had been smeared with honey. He drew in a good breath of air and blinked thoughtfully.

"And how is that honorable old gentleman—Captain Doonan?" he asked. "A gentleman of the old Gloucester school— he is!" His geniality changed swiftly to a glitter when he added: "And the *Hind's* skipper? You much aware of him?"

I answered shortly that the old gentleman was still alive and I went on with my story, saying: "A doryman again. On the *Golden Hind*. And I need a little gear for the fishing. I remembered you once had a little stuff that you took for a bad debt. I want an old gaff and a gobstick maybe. And boots, perhaps. And have you any old oil clothing? We'll be oiling up on the Banks this time all right, Mister Bannister. And in Gloucester —well! when a man's down and out in Gloucester, where is he? I ask you!"

"He's down and out! Same as here."

The dogfish look was so mean now that I could feel my face flush. I thrust my hand into my pocket and said: "I can pay a little something. I'm not looking for charity."

"That's good, doryman, that's good!" Bannister began scratching the bargain point on his bristly chin. "Let me see! Let me see!" His eyes darted over his domain: barns, sheds, stys and paddocks, all ranged along the tumbledown yard. The horns of bulls flashed in the sun. I heard the clashing of rams' horns from the sheepfolds in the lane.

In order to freshen my eyes a little, I looked over the Roseway. And they were freshened. Widened! The stranger dory from the *Hind* lay there. Even while I watched, a hot speculation bubbling inside me, the port oars gave a stroke or two toward the stockyard. There were only four men in it. Ambrose, in the glory of his 'longshore togs, was not among his chums.

I fixed my eyes on the ground.

Bannister worked over the puzzle. He didn't have much gear to sell to a doryman, especially to a down-and-outer. He didn't seem to be able to remember the things I had mentioned; for the good and sufficient reason that he had never shown them to me. Yet he hated to let go of a chance to turn a dollar, even if it was an honest one and could stand the bite of teeth. He began to inch along in a crab gait and beckoned to me.

We passed the ice-house and turned toward a wharf, where two livestock barges were tied up. And here, a familiar scene to me, we came to a thing that had always filled me with a sailing-master's woe. It was a ruin, yet there was grandness in the ruin. The vessel was a schooner-yacht, a fathom longer than the *Hind*, and yacht-decked; that is, she had no wooden rail, only the vestige of an iron one. Her skylights, well made of maple wood, were broken. Only a few jagged panes remained of her glass. The matched timbers of her deck had resisted snow and frost for many seasons. Everything that could be broken or carried away had gone. Her stays had vanished. Even the ring-bolts were out. She had taken water, too, and lay heavy in the Roseway tide. Nevertheless, enough of her old buoyancy remained so that she leaned ever so slightly in answer to the tugging of the tide. Out of her hold came a sighing and a rhythmic groaning, as if she wished to say: "Aye! there could be some sailing yet!" Nothing—not even old Bannister's ignorance and neglect—could kill her beauty and her strength. Her spars, cracked and peeled, lay along the wharf; and a big-eared mouse played there. The spars, too, gave off a sort of splendor, a hint of gales outworn and glorious races won. She was the *Hind's* own sister.

This vessel was none other than the old contender: the never-to-be-forgotten *Western Star*. Her gallant history was known to all men of the Atlantic; at least, to those who had lain under crowded sails. Her owner, in a time of 'longshore evil, had killed himself aboard her while she lay gleaming in Shelburne Harbor. The sorrowing people, whom he had left behind him, had let her go with a curse into the first pair of willing hands. Those hands, of course, had been Bannister's. Long since, she had been forgotten.

I halted there and laid a hand on the butt of her mighty mainmast and gave her a tender look for the sake of the days when the *Hind* had sailed against her. I remembered her with all her hamper spread under a summer moon; and I remembered her driving before the gale with her decks drowned. Wonderful she was going off the wind, and a gainer thereby.

"Come along, doryman! Come along!" Bannister scratched himself with his claws and urged me on again. Seeing that I lingered above the near-ruin, he said: "Once ye thought you'd take her off my hands before she rots away. Ain't in such funds now, be ye?"

This delicate touch brought no word from me. He murmured: " 'Tisn't a purchase for a poor doryman. No! Tho' cheap she is. Cheap."

I shook my head sadly. I stepped onto the stringpiece and looked through the torn skylights and down into her wrecked, rusted bathrooms, her bursted lockers and cabins filled with murmurs. And with my mind's eye I looked down and down to the great and famous keel that rested ingloriously on the Roseway mud. In the midst of my unhappy remembrance, a terrifying thought shot through me. 'Twas like sudden thunder in the night. I clapped my hand over my mouth to shut off the word that came bursting up.

Bannister capered and drew close. "Don't take on so, laddie. God send the day when ye may take her! Ye raced against her more than once when you were a boy, eh? Aye! I remember, I remember! Beautiful she was. Like a woman. A fine, strapping woman—" His mouth began to lather up.

This was the moment when, arm-in-arm through the gate, there came a portly, handsome man, well-wrapped in a grey ulster, left open to show a beautiful pearl in his necktie. Clinging to his arm, there was a tall young woman in a green suit of woollen stuff, which suited her well. She wore a green felt hat that seemed rather mannish to me; and over her face a wisp of black veil, lightly marked with green dots. The veil was something new to my eyes, but it seemed quite fashionable and fetching. The man looked very much like a vice president of a National Bank. He carried himself stiffly, yet with an easy dignity that spelled worldly success and an inner integrity. His voice boomed beautifully and I clearly heard the words: "Think nothing of it, my dear! Sentiment! Sentiment!"

I knocked Bannister with my elbow and whispered: "Well, isn't that a handsome wench!"

Bannister cackled and tried to crow. "Ain't seen a finer pair of legs since Widow Dumbra skipped jail!" He tried again and, this time, he really crowed in celebration of times past.

"Limbs!" I said, "limbs, if you please."

"Limbs?"

"That's what we say in Boston, where she comes from. Unless I miss my guess. Limbs. Not legs."

"Well, Captain Bannon," replied Bannister with witty good sense, "we ain't in Boston now nor anywheres near it. So legs they is and legs they will remain and a finer set I haven't laid eyes on since Belle Jorkan got knifed!" What other memory shook him suddenly? He groaned and held a hand against his mouth. He found reason to stare at the littered earth. He pulled up at once and said: "What in the name of porridge do you figure such a lot is doing on my old tumbledown?"

I had no interest in these flashes of his nimble, changeful character, except to keep him on his course. I replied: "You've got me, Mister Bannister. Although, to tell the truth, that old gentleman has a familiar look, hasn't he?" Without waiting for an answer, I said: "Don't mind me. Take care of them. Maybe he's a contractor for army beef."

"Could be. Could be." Bannister trembled with the force of revived hopes. "Must be. Must be. I've seen that face somewhere long ago."

I whispered: "Might be in a newspaper somewhere. Looks like important money to me, Mister Bannister."

He squeezed up his eyes to concentrate their fire. The man in the wonderful derby patted the lady's cheek in a fatherly manner. His gloves seemed to cause some difficulty, which he laughed off gently and said: "No, my dear, no! Sentiment! Sentiment!"

Bannister hissed between his charred lips. He closed with me furtively and whispered: "I do believe I've seen him in a picture somewhere." That picture, could he but form it, had been the business end of bait tackle on Shelburne Wharf. His memory couldn't do away with the stiff collar and the pearl, not to mention brilliant gloves.

"Sentiment! Sentiment!" Thus the newcomers drew up. The gentleman said to Bannister: "My good fellow! a dollar for you. Go find Mister Bannister and tell him I am here. There now. Hurry along! No delay. No tarrying, if you understand what I mean."

This beginning was really better than I foresaw; because the speech was delivered in an excellent imitation of the bad imitation which some Bostonians use for English. "Bannister" became "Bahnister." The bubble and flow of words was extremely agreeable and surprising, although I had known there was a gift of the gab there. It was the richness of the gift that pleased me, especially because I perceived that both the gentleman and the lady were far from at ease. I saw the inner strain in his old eyes; and, in her, I saw a stiffened, whitened mouth again.

Mister Bannister raised two of his pretty fingers to the brim of his hat and tugged courteously. This won him such a smile from the veiled eyes that he began to quiver. He was, as they say, rendered helpless. He managed this much: "Wot?"

In order to relieve the actors of any doubt concerning my own cues, I gave my cap a tug and said in a respectful tone: "This here person is poor Mister Bannister. Himself."

The gentleman raised the port brow. He also raised his hand, from which an American dollar blew. With just the proper air of distaste that Mister Bannister loved to create in others, the gentleman released the bill. "Ah, you are Bannister? You may have the dollar just the same." He cleared his throat and said in a louder tone: "Sentiment! Sentiment, my dear Bannister. Do pick it up. Have your boots repaired, my poor man. Do!"

Mister Bannister clawed up the bill in a gullish swoop and went south with it. Into his rags. "Wot?" said he, half paralyzed by this first success. "Wot's wanted, gentleman?"

"A mere nothing, my good man. A mere matter of an old man's sentiment. A family matter, Mister Bannister."

A forward movement by the lady halted his spout of words. He escorted her to the stringpiece, where he gave Bannister a warning glance against interference. There, at last, she looked down upon the ruin of the *Western Star*. In that first, trying moment, she did not lift her head. Wrapped in melancholy, bowed by it, she gazed at the scarred, glass-scattered deck. A moan escaped her tinted lips; then, whispering some passionate phrases to herself, she crossed her elegant arms and gazed into the past.

I took Mister Bannister by the arm and drew him back a step. I whispered: "Listen to me, Bannister. You watch yourself! Here's a pair of the right sort. Part of the old owner's family, unless I miss my guess. They're going to buy her!" I tightened my grasp and peered into the warming eyes. "Grab it! The first offer. Sign them up, right here and now. I know this crowd." I tapped my forehead lightly and leered. "For me—ten per cent!"

"Five!" whispered Bannister. "Five's the best I can do."

"Eight!" I said. "Must have eight. Down and out, you know."

"Split the difference," said Bannister. "That's six and a half."

"Done!"

Bannister advanced. His hands crept together to hide their trembling. Avarice dripped from his mouth like grease from a hot goose. He clutched at his hat again and, faint with longing, questioned the gentleman: "Wot? Wot's wanted, please?"

Thereupon, the gentleman drew a wallet from his ulster pocket and, handing it to me in the grand manner, said: "My boy, take what your employer requires. I make no bones about it, as the vulgar say. It is my intention to purchase the *Western Star*, Mister Bannister. To purchase her, sir, here and now." He drew himself up an inch more and said in a tone of profound sadness: "It's a matter of sentiment, my dear sir. Family sentiment that can be of no concern to you."

I opened the wallet and worked up a bill until the "100" on its face appeared. Mister Bannister gazed in rapture. He took a taste of it with his eyes, swallowed the taste, and, without lifting his gaze, asked: "What was you thinking of paying for her, gentleman?"

The gentleman gave a main-boom sweep of his arm. "Mister Bannister, money is no object! None, sir! We—that is, the family—we are able to indulge in these little sentimentalities, sir." He gave the lady an affectionate glance and took her hand. "It is my intention—yes! my child, yes!—to have this lovely ruin—for such it is, sir—to have her pulled far beyond the surrounding and bordering lands, far to the bounding main, sir, where once she lived and conquered in her glory. And there, Mister Bannister, there, where only the gulls may see and mourn for her departed splendor—there she shall burn!" He swept his gleaming gloves high over Bannister's upturned face. "Burn! Burn!"

"Burn? Burn?" Mister Bannister jerked his glance back toward the magic bill. I gave him a fast, sly wink, extended my hand over the bill and held the fingers out, which meant: "The price is five hundred."

The old gentleman struck hard at his chest and bellowed. "I said 'burn!', sir, and burn it shall be! Aye! let her tattered ensign flame! Long has it waved on high! Burn, Mister Bannister! So that her ashes, sacred to the altars of memory, may settle in peace upon the billows that she loved and ruled in the glory and strength of her youth." He touched his eye gently and coughed behind the glove to hide his undeniable tears.

In my opinion, this was going a little too far. My natural fear of oratory increased my anxiety. However. the money had worked its magic on Bannister. He was almost in a frenzy. His claws twitched.

The young lady apparently had a feeling similar to mine concerning the dangers of eloquence. I saw her fingers close in warning on the arm that embraced her. She whispered: "No, uncle! Let the *Western Star* go as she went long ago in happier days. Let her go down this river, pushed by her own lovely sail, and go into the ocean and there, uncle, let her— let her be—" She halted in charming awkwardness.

"Scuttled?" I suggested.

"Thank you, sir," she said in a prim fashion.

Bannister could stand it no longer. He said briskly: "Five hundred dollars!"

"Sufficient unto the day is the work thereof!" cried the gentleman. "If, Mister Bannister, you say five hundred—five hundred it shall be. A costly whim, no doubt. Costly. But count it out, young man, count it out for your worthy employer."

"Five hundred," I repeated. "American dollars, Mister Bannister?"

Bannister's heart, which he had never heard from before, almost broke. Oddly enough, he giggled. No doubt, he believed I was insane to bring up the matter of exchange. He said hastily: "American, of course. The gentleman means American dollars, I'm sure."

The gentleman nodded and said: "For this—this honorarium, Mister Bannister, let it be our understanding—correct me if I am wrong, young man!—that you will assist us in our sentimental plans. If not—" He looked aloft.

I winked hard at Bannister.

"Yes!" he shouted.

"Sentiment is strong amongst us, Mister Bannister. Nevertheless—well! you will surely assist us to the extent of a pump to remove the water that by now must have seeped into her cellar?"

"Yes!" shouted Bannister. He held out a begging hand to me. I was thumbing over the bills rather clumsily. I drew away.

"And the use of any materials that may be necessary? Such as nails, tacks, strings, and—ah, yes!—sailing cloth? That is, what you men of the sea call—"

"Canvas!" I said. I bowed my head over the bills to hide my eyes.

"Spars and sails are there. Such as they are, you have them!" Bannister bustled up to me and whispered: "Now then! Now then, doryman!"

"And the men we must engage for this venture?" asked the lady. "Have you some workmen, Mister Bannister, who might assist those we may find?"

"Three at five dollars a day, ma'am."

"Ah! you are kind! Kind, Mister Bannister." She glanced at him through the veil and then, in girlish confusion, whispered to the old gentleman, who, turning to me, asked: "Young man, can you write?"

"Can I what?" I shouted.

She gave me a frown and I fell back, having remembered in time that neither Bannister nor old Ambrose could do much more than scrawl their names.

"A plain question, Captain!" shouted Bannister in pitiful anxiety lest one or another of the madmen cheat him at the last moment. "Say 'yes, sir' and that's all there is to it. Oh, the good Lord have mercy on us when His cold winds blow!"

By this time, a great deal of sweat was pouring off his brow and the cleft in his little chin was quite filled up with the foam of desire. He was, in fact, more than half-mad himself. Before he could speak again, I had begun to write the bargain out on a sheet of paper. All present signed it and witnessed it. I thrust the paper into the old gentleman's wallet before Bannister could try to make out the names, if he had the wit; and I explained that the document and the ship's papers must be shown at once to the customs and various others, including the military.

The gentleman and lady bowed and walked away.

Bannister again stretched out his yearning hands. I slowly counted the five hundred, bill by bill, and laid them on the hands. "Now," I said, "my commission, Mister Bannister. For a poor doryman, if you please."

Bannister stuffed the bills into his pocket. After he had them all stowed away, he began pulling them out again, one by one, until he found a five-dollar note. He lingered over it a while, then gave it to me. He added a dollar and a fifty-cent piece from another pocket, saying: "Six and half, you said. And there's my own commission on your part of the deal. But I'll forgive ye that, I'll forgive ye that, poor doryman."

"Thank you," I said. "That's generous of you. Now I won't be needing your old gobstick or your oil clothing, Mister Bannister. I'll buy me new gear. So I will."

I then pointed to the stranger dory. It was coming directly toward the *Western Star*. I said: "The new owners waste no time, Bannister. A businessman all right, I guess. In a hurry to get back to Boston, I suppose."

"Businessman! Business! Ha! Ha!" Bannister rapped his knuckles against the roll of bills under his patches. "Call it business if you like, Captain. I call it something else. I merely sells this floating tumbledown—for which I paid nothing!

nothing!—for five hundred dollars to a set of madmen. They're as mad as the owner was. They're kin all right! And he shot himself. He did! I heard the bang myself as I come aboard with beef that day."

The four old dorymen pulled up to the yacht. They threw hammers and sledges aboard and flung off their jackets. They began to clear the deck of fragments of glass and junk. I heard Peter Lord sing out cheerfully: "Sure, she'll make do! She's buoyant yet."

Bannister said: "Had their men ready all right. Pretty sure of himself, old codger was."

I now perceived that, quite slowly, the cattle dealer was beginning to understand that there might be a fine pig in the poke. He asked: "Where's that dory from, Captain Bannon?"

"Lord only knows! From a shipyard maybe?"

"Must be! Must be!"

I sat by his side, listening to his tales of poor profits and ruin. The day was nearly over. I didn't know what might happen next, although I was sure that Nora Doonan and the dorymen were bound to put in an appearance. Once or twice, old Bannister walked over toward the *Western Star* and watched the dorymen at work there. They gave him neither word nor look. He had returned from such a visit, and was again settling at my side, when I heard him exclaim in surprise.

The *Golden Hind* had sailed into the river. She was under headsails and was steering toward the yard. She towed six dories, all loaded with gear and stores. Such vessels rarely came so far up the Roseway, there being no business for them beyond the herring-house. Her passage caused considerable interest along the shores. I could see men turn from their work, where the herring-nets were stretched to dry. The evening light was glittering beyond her and I couldn't make out who was on her deck. As she drew nearer, I saw that the helmsman wore yellow gloves.

Bannister couldn't see far. He kept squinting under his hand. He spoke against the vessel, as if she had no right to come near his place. Of course, he couldn't tell who she was. Not for a while. At last, he cried out that the vessel was a schooner; and, a minute later, he said: "I'll take my Bible oath that she's a Gloucesterman."

"She is, Bannister," I replied. "There's no doubt in the world about that particular statement."

"And who may she be, laddie?"

"She's the *Golden Hind* of Gloucester. 'Tis my own vessel, Bannister."

"And why in the name of porridge is she coming to my tumbledown?"

"Bannister," says I, "have a taste of wait-and-see pudding."

I was considerably upset by his next words and a change (not for the worse) in his manner; and these proved well enough that a man can keep his manhood and humanity together, despite the drawbacks of living ashore and trading, and will show his mettle under the right circumstances. He had little concern for the *Golden Hind* when she lay downstream, out of his ken. Now her actual appearance, which was unexpected, excited some concern in him. I didn't know its source for a long time to come, but I never miss a trick of the sort, especially when so full of stir as I had been since the voyage began. I knew that Bannister had great knowledge of 'longshore men and towns; and that he was a deposit of evil knowledge and evil tricks. Just the same, there is iron strength in doing evil. It takes a strong heart. It doesn't make a man a weakling, by any means, if he cheats and lies his way through life. (Nora Doonan knew this to be true. That's why she coddled him, instead of doing business in her open and usual way.)

He now began to display both his strength and his peculiar knowledge. He asked: "Does that LeNotre still go skipper of her?" He seemed to have forgotten his earlier remark about our captain.

I said it was so. I looked at him, while he peered at the schooner. I saw his teeth press down on his lower lip. Two distinct expressions followed on his face: first, a look of alarm, and then one of open anger, which, in turn, was bolstered by a dainty piece of cursework.

I spoke again easily. "While I'm not able to say exactly what she's doing here, Bannister, I can tell you that you've nothing to fear from the *Hind*. Bygones are bygones. Especially today."

" 'Tisn't the *Hind* I fear, laddie."

I could make no reply.

He then said in as firm a tone I ever heard from him: "I fear nothing."

Now, of the actions and words which upset me, those were the first. The next thing was even simpler and no less astonishing. Back there a space, I put down the true fact that Bannister's eyes had filled with tears when he played Job to me. 'Twas nothing, merely the art of business, such as are the tears of a woman of the streets. I'm not praising my own sharpness when I say that I can tell the difference. What captain worth his salt can't do it? He sees a variety of both in daily course. Well, a tear or two seeped out of Bannister's eye while he gazed at the men on the schooner's deck. He struck at his eyes. That's all. Even then (without hindsight to aid me) I knew he was hearing from his heart again.

All the dories were dropped. The first one that came over

to the *Western Star* was manned by old Ambrose and the Lisbon. Ambrose had changed into his working clothes. He still wore the handsome yellow gloves. He waved one hand amiably to Bannister and then turned to give the Lisbon a hand in lifting a small anvil to the *Western Star's* deck. This was the Lisbon's gear. There wasn't a bolt or a shackle on the *Hind* that he couldn't forge himself, if need be.

Bannister cried out: "Isn't that—say! Captain, ain't he pretty seamanlike all of a sudden—that old gentleman?"

I gave him no answer. Bad as he was, there was no gainsaying that he was a human being; and I had no wish to add to the woe he was about to suffer, though well he deserved it. And now I come to think of it, he was much the gainer; for in his black ignorance he surely would have let the *Western Star* perish in the slime.

The second dory came alongside. Captain LeNotre and Nora were in it. It was full of stores. Nora, too, had put on her doryman togs again, but there was no mistaking her for a hand. She stood to one side while the other dories came up and put over axes and rolls of canvas and kegs of nails. She waved her hand to me. She made no sign to Bannister.

I said to him: "Yes, that's the *Golden Hind;* and the girl in trousers is the granddaughter of an old friend of yours, Captain Doonan. She's the owner of the *Hind* now. Did you know that, Bannister?"

The wind whistled in his pipe.

Now it came Captain LeNotre's turn. I heard Nora speak rather loudly to him, apparently in countermand of some notion of his. He strode across the deck of the *Western Star* and vaulted to the wharf. Right away, Billy Atkins followed him. I don't know what instinct moved me; however, I jumped to my feet. I had about the time of twenty steps to size the captain up; and I saw that he had the same black dog on his back. Wasn't this a strange thing? Surely, he had learned that something good had happened to the *Hind*. Yet he revealed no pleasure. On the contrary, there was a new and a coarse twist in his face when he set eyes on Bannister. I couldn't tell whether he was trying to hide his contempt for a cheater cheated, or whether there was another emotion disguised there.

He called out: "Bannister!"

Bannister hadn't stirred. He sat there, hunched in the cold twilight, and made a most miserable sight, indeed. Yet I was amazed to see him return the captain's stare with interest added, the interest being an unmistakable scorn. Even his voice had changed when he opened his mouth, at last. I swear it had a fathom or two in it.

He said: "I'll have no truck with you, Captain LeNotre."

The captain appeared not to have heard. He said in a sneer: "You've done a fine stroke of business here today, you son-of-a-whore!"

You can easily tell how far I had gone on a certain course when I say that this dirty Grand Banks epithet was too much for me. I don't like it and I don't like to set it down, but it was the word used and there's no denying it or withholding it. Just imagine such a word passed from a man who was even heftier than I to a little old squeegee of a thing like Bannister. I stepped out of my character and said quite calmly: "Keep a civil tongue in your head, Captain. There's no call for abuse that I know of."

The captain at once switched his sneer from Bannister to me and said: "So you're the broth of a boy who kept the mighty secret all this time?"

Fine words to a doryman! In the presence of a greenhorn! Nevertheless, I took them peacefully; because I was a doryman and I meant to be a good one. I said: "I know nothing of this business, Captain. Nothing! I don't know the mighty secret yet, for that matter. I give you my word."

Old Bannister stood up. He creaked a bit, the cold having reached his works. He said some words in broad Newfoundland that I couldn't clearly understand. It was something like: "Na fash 'isself abaht 'un." I took it to mean that I wasn't to concern myself with his affairs. He then gave a whole and seizing look to the captain and to Billy Atkins, who stood a step behind LeNotre.

Bannister said: "I've no wish to talk to you, Captain LeNotre. Nor to your chum there. Now nor never."

Captain LeNotre paid no heed. He said: "You wouldn't be thinking of giving back the *Hind* any of that money you stole from us, would you? Seasons ago?"

Bannister replied: "A speculation's a speculation. You lost the Doonan money fair and I lost mine fair. But I've no wish to hold talk with the likes of you."

"Bannister—a dirty liar!" The captain put on such a look of hatred that my amazement grew and I said to myself: "If he lifts a hand against the old one, I'll beat his brains out."

At this time, I took note of this fact: that certain of the *Hind*'s people had found their way to the quarter deck of the *Western Star* and stood near us with upturned faces. I cannot tell why, yet it's true that this encounter between the captain and Bannister found a place in my memory alongside a story of the kind too far back to be well remembered. Perhaps it was a story of the old Greek seamen told to me by my grandfather.

Bannister took the new word calmly. I should not have been surprised if he had stepped back in fear; for Captain LeNotre had become wilder with each passing moment. He had pushed his cap back. His hair blew over his face. He struck it back savagely and let his hands play too freely.

I heard Billy Atkins speak. He said: "Always was a liar!" This I took as a sample of their joint knowledge from New-foundland days and Yarmouth nights.

Bannister took a step—half a one—forward. He ran his tongue up and down his lip rapidly; and this gave him a queer sort of calculating look, as if he was actually judging his chances if he struck one of them with his little hands. I began to hope that he would not; because I knew that all would be over then between the captain and me; and I had taken my oath that I would see the voyage of the *Hind* through to the end for the reasons I have recounted.

The captain said: "Anyway, Bannister, you've sold the *Western Star?* That's so, isn't it?"

Bannister nodded.

"You know now that you sold her to Nora Doonan?"

"I do."

Bannister had come under the torment. I saw him bring his hands together. However, he trembled so greatly that he couldn't hide it.

"Nothing held back?"

"Nothing!"

"Keel and all?" asked the captain.

This was the gaffing blow. "Keel!" Bannister, despite his ignorance of our profession, knew that something monstrous was coming his way. He shouted: "Yes! Keel and all. Spars and sails. What's it to you, sir? What you staring at?"

LeNotre's scorn blew his nostrils wide. He said: "I just wanted you to know that the keel's been sold to a party in Boston for sixteen thousand dollars! To be melted down for the Navy Yard."

Mister Bannister had clasped his hands behind him. He held
tight and began to sway. The image of the lost dollars seemed
to be more than he could stand up under. He had stripped his
tumbledown of every nail for the war yards, and the *Western
Star* of every ring-bolt; yet the immense treasure of lead had
lain there unbeknownst to him.

All I have to say is that, in the end, he took it like a man.
He managed to twist his head toward me and say: "All's fair
in trading! Captain Bannon, I'd have never let her have the
hulk if I'd known." He then hit another nail on the head:
"Let her get her buy to Gloucester. 'Twill cost lives, I think."

I heard a chorus of "Aye!" and "Ah!" below me. And these
were sad cries. I echoed them in my heart, which was seawise.
Not for those dorymen of the *Hind*. No! 'Twas for the old,
old men, who had been pledged to the hard sailing. I said to
myself in sorrow: "Now, Ambrose Cameron, see what you
must do for coffee, cakes and a pad!" And in the silence that
now lay over us, I glanced into the tangle on the *Western
Star*'s deck; and I saw his hands fly up in their grasp of a great
sledge.

Mister Bannister had not done. He had turned his head away
from me and had taken up his quarrel with the men who had
chosen to torment him. They hadn't succeeded in doing so.
If there had been a victory, it wasn't theirs. If they had found
satisfaction, he now took a measure to destroy it. He shuffled
nearer to them and gave them a chance to look into his eyes.
What signal burned in them for that time, I cannot say; because I now stood a stride behind him. Yet I could tell well
enough that he held sway over them. Neither the captain nor
Billy Atkins had the will to utter a word or take a step. In the
dusk and cold, Bannister gazed without flinching.

He then spoke his piercing word. It was this: "Murderer!"

He shuffled away into the long shadows of his tumbledown.

A torch blew into flame on the deck of the *Western Star*. I heard a sledge strike heavily and I heard Ambrose Cameron shout: "That does it! Easy now."

The torchlight showed me the faces of those two men standing there; and a rise of the yellow light enabled me to make a cast of the lead into their deeps. Both pairs of eyes glowed an instant and went dark. I perceived the quality of fear in them; and, for a reason that I never could understand, their fear created in me an anger against them. This anger I was careful to divide, keeping one part (the captain's) for another time, and giving Billy Atkins his part by saying an extraordinary thing: "Now, bootlicker, you've got some news for old Parren. He'll be gladder to hear it than you are, I hope."

It wasn't Billy who answered me. It was the captain. And he didn't really answer; that is, he didn't look straight at me. He simply repeated the name: "Parren!" Whether he shuddered or not, I can't tell. But his voice shook; and, even in the faint flashes of light, I saw on his handsome face the same expression which had marked his secret departure from the *Doubloon*'s pilot-house.

I fell back a few paces into the welcome dark. I dropped down to the deck of the *Western Star*. The spectators moved slowly and made way for me in silence. I went forward and saw Nora Doonan take an electric cable from a stranger on the wharf. She passed the end along. I lent a hand and she said: "Old Bannister—what's he been saying to the captain?"

"Why!" I replied, "he was saying something about drowned Corkery. We'll never hear the end of that."

I was wrong there.

8

By MIDNIGHT, there were two pumps (the *Hind's* own and Bannister's) taking water out of the *Western Star;* and it seemed to me, from the quality of the bilge, that most of it was rain which had poured through her skylights and hatches. Good news that; because it gave us sound reason to hope that the hull itself stayed sound; which was a reasonable hope, the *Western Star* being the work of the best Yankees on the Essex River. We knocked off at midnight and slept aboard the *Golden Hind*. In the morning, every man turned to on the *Western Star*. By that time, she had risen high out of her sluggishness and even began to put a strain on her lines, as if she were eager to take the tide that served her.

According to his word, Bannister sent down three good workmen, although he himself kept away. Nora Doonan found two shipwrights, who had been making dories on speculation. They were fine craftsmen. More than that, five men of the Irish Regiment, who were on furlough, joined us for the pleasure of employing their old skills, there being no money left to pay them. These additions gave us a crew of thirty-five able men; so the work of setting up some sort of jury-rig on the yacht went forward far faster than we had hoped. Better still, most of the work, including the stepping of the masts (without topmasts), was to be done under our own eyes; for, at noon of the second day, Captain LeNotre came down from the customs with word that the port had been closed by the military. This was to last five days, at least. Something had happened at sea which required such action. It was a point on which we were told nothing, although there was the usual plenty of guesswork. This delay in the fishing was irksome, yet there was no help for it. For a time, there was some concern amongst us for the pens of bait because the first day of work was warmish. It was feared that the bait might go soft. That afternoon, however, the wind hauled to the eastward and the night's work was done in freezing weather. This left our minds at ease on that score.

I had other reasons for my cheerfulness. The best of them was my old belief that only good things will follow a course laid out according to a man's conscience. And by that I mean good things for all men of good conscience who are part of his life and work, as the dorymen and Ambrose's crew were of mine.

I speak of Ambrose Cameron. I had many images of this man in my memory. When I was a child, I had seen him steer a schooner, heavy with ice and woe, up to Ben Pine's wharf; and I had watched my father unlash him from a wheel to which he had clung alone for three days and nights because of the winter gale and a strange influenza that had laid low every man aboard that vessel. In strength of heart and limbs, that man had never been surpassed. Even the hero, Howard Blackburn, had said to me: "What I have done is nothing to that man's labor." In later years, I had seen him as the top high-liner of our Gloucester captains; which is to say that he always found the most cod, caught them quickly, and drove home to a lively market. And you yourself have seen him, standing idle in a Gloucester lane, on the eve of our voyage. He had lost nothing of his magnificence.

Now, at noon of the fifth day of terrible labor on the *Western Star*, I came upon him in the after cabin of that vessel, which had been cleaned and roughly fitted out. I saw at once that a change had come over him. Outwardly, he was the same: close-cropped silver hair, and grey, spiky moustache; and his thousand seams and wrinkles and the juts of bronzed cheeks and chin that showed the indomitable Yankee heart within. He sat erect, his back against the bunk. By his side lay a pocket compass. In his hands he held a chart on which a course had been laid out. I have said that he and his chums stood to me as a symbol of the Atlantic brotherhood, which maintains boldly a Constitution of one word: Freedom. On this day he became something more: he became the thinker, the symbol of our human genius that calmly drives a hundred tons of wood and sail into an array of elements which has conquered twenty thousand tons of steel and copper. Aye! he was thinking, and my heart went out to him strongly as before; for I knew the wonders of the sea to which he bent his mind. And I knew more! I knew that an old mantle (one he had worn with honor before) had fallen again on his massive shoulders. Had I not been in the presence of a venerable man, I should have laughed aloud with joy. (To the indictment of hero-worship, I now plead guilty in the first degree, and throw myself on the mercy of the court.)

I said: "Captain Cameron!" I gave him the title which I had first spoken to him long ago.

He raised his eyes away from the history of shoals and deeps, of tides and buoys and lights. He gave me, as my quick reward, a blue gleam out of the inner eye and said gently: "Yes, young John. I am a captain again. I am on my own vessel. I am reading her charts."

I murmured something about the cabin and went up the steps, which were eaten by rust.

Nora Doonan had made him captain. In her wisdom, she had found many reasons to do so. First, the law required such an appointment. Second, she took this step in order to break down, if she could, the barrier of which I have spoken. And she became more than ever aware of this barrier because of an inroad she had made on this old man's heart. Faithful to her as that heart had been (even to the laying down of its life), it had been hampered by tradition, by another faithfulness; and that to the forecastle. The change had a most profound meaning to us all. It had taken place that very morning when she had called him from his splicing and had said: "You are captain of the *Western Star*."

The graveness of near departure had brought these two closer together. Knowing that he was deep in friendly thought of her welfare and of the salvation of the *Hind*, she ran the risk that he might be willing to speak of the *Hind* and her people. It hadn't escaped her notice that the dorymen had not restored Captain LeNotre to his old and lawful place. Ambrose had been aboard the *Hind* long enough to have learned much, especially because he had long since won the respect of all Gloucestermen. She, therefore, raised him from the ranks and stood alone before him in the cabin.

He forestalled her opening words by saying: "One thing you must promise me, Miss Nora. Even if it goes against the grain. As well it might, tho' I don't know all your plans yet."

She said: "I promise it, Captain Cameron."

"Beforehand?"

"Aye! Beforehand."

"Why so? 'Tis not your way of doing things."

"Because of your wisdom, Captain, and your old friendship for us."

He then said: "I wish to say that you should leave the *Western Star* to me and my chums. Go home on the *Hind*, Miss Nora. Go with her to the Banks."

"I cannot!"

"Why not?"

She gave him the answer that he must have expected: "I can't ask a man to do anything I will not do myself. No!"

"You are not doing so!" he replied. "We know you would come with us. That point is settled. There's another reason why you should do what I say." With no other preliminary, he then launched into the very subject that she had meant to bring up. He startled her by repeating her own thought: "I've been aboard the *Hind* long enough to know that something's wrong. You must stay aboard to do your duty as her owner. It may not seem the proper thing to do. You'd rather sail on the *Star* and take the chance that we must take. But sailing on the *Hind* is the necessary thing. It's your duty."

She made no answer. He went on: "Your dorymen talked. Of course, they talked. Not as much as they would have talked if I had been signed on regular. I mean, for fishing."

He hesitated again. She knew that he was trying to draw a line between the things he could say and the things that custom and ancient habit must keep hidden. To help him, she asked: "How much of what you heard can you repeat, Captain?"

He said: "I'll give you my knowledge, strange as it will seem to you. And apt, I know, to leave your mind uneasy. But that can't be helped. Not all I know was learned in the forecastle. Part of it comes from the Gloucester *Times*. This is it: the *Lark* came into Boston the day before the *Hind* returned, and sold one hundred thousand pounds. Sold the vessel right through at eighteen cents. She went far for them, I hear. Now, the *Thebaud* stocked eighty thousand pounds. She came into Boston the same day the *Hind* came into Gloucester. The vessels had fished the same banks. Yet the *Hind* had brought nothing much home to you. Please to bear that in mind, Miss Nora."

"I will."

He went on: "A story was told in Gloucester of the death of James Corkery. Captain LeNotre gave you an account of the same thing himself."

"Yes, Captain. And what of this?"

"The two accounts do not agree."

Certainly this declaration stirred her deeply. Just the same, she took it evenly and asked: "How do you know that? Captain Bannon and I were the only ones that heard the captain's story."

He replied: "Young John told the captain's story to me that night. I found him looking for poor Corkery because he feared he might do harm to himself in his grief and madness."

She asked: "Who gave you the crew's account?"

"It was told to me at the Anchor House by the man who was mostly at fault. The Lisbon." He added quickly: "At fault, according to your captain. Not at fault, according to himself."

Nora cried out at this because it seemed a folly to her. "Why does the Lisbon keep this from me? If he thinks that Captain LeNotre is at fault? That there's something wrong aboard my schooner?"

In surprise, he answered her. "You are a child with men, Miss Nora! Don't you know that no doryman could ever speak to you on such a matter, even if he was sure that Captain

LeNotre was led astray? That he has a black reason for not wanting to kill fish for you?"

This was the hardest blow a man could strike. Ambrose knew it; and it speaks well for his courage and his love that he could get the words out of his mouth, which was not used to evil stories.

She repeated in dismay and disbelief the phrases that struck against her mind and heart and hopes: " 'Led astray!' " and " 'Not wanting to kill fish!' "

He offered no explanation, despite the sorrow that marked her face again. And, knowing how careful he was in shipboard matters, she kept her lips pressed tightly together to keep back the other words in her heart, where old, half-formed conjectures were taking clearer shape after long suppression by her devotion to Captain LeNotre.

Captain Cameron then said: "Miss Nora, I can say little of what was told to me in your forecastle. 'Twould be dishonest in me. But I can say what was said to me ashore, now that I am your captain. And if shipboard talk pushes me on—why! I can't help it!"

She appealed to him. "For Heaven's sake, Ambrose, speak!"

He said: "The *Hind's* people know that Dan Corkery— who's on the *Doubloon* now—and his poor, lost brother were hated—aye! hated and feared!—by Captain Parren and Atkins—"

She cried out again at this mention of the *Doubloon's* captain, but old Ambrose hurried on with his revelation. "Yes! And more than that! I'm sorry to say it, Miss Nora, but they were hated and feared by Captain LeNotre, too. There's no doubt about it in the minds of your people."

"But why? Why?"

"That I cannot tell you. I don't know. But there's one man

who does know. He has the true story of James Corkery's death. He knows that he is also hated and feared. And that man loves you like his own daughter."

"Who is that man, Ambrose?"

"The Lisbon."

He would speak no more.

As soon as chance offered, Nora Doonan gave me the gist of the matter. This set me to wondering in a deeper way; because here was a thing against all nature: that a captain should not kill fish when he found them. And it was even more mystifying that he should run the peril of telling falsehoods concerning his men. I had never dreamed that the poor luck of the *Hind* was anything except luck. I made her repeat Ambrose's able comparison of the *Hind's* last stock to the rich stock of another vessel, taken at the same time and in the same waters. I had known of the other trips. Yet I hadn't taken such thought of them; and for that failure I've no excuse, except the same old one: that I was thinking of my nets and working on them.

When she told me the story, in the early morning while I rowed her dory from the *Hind* to the *Western Star*, all my lively speculation ceased and my own hopes lay quiet because my pity for Nora grew greatly. A strange, sweet pity, making up in my heart because I saw that the old man's words had laid waste her heart, or were beginning to do so. Tide and wind beat against the dory so that her dark head and its spray-wet coils lifted against the rim of our sea-world; or sank into the blue. Into light; into darkness. The Doonan pattern: laughter in triumph one season, sadness the next. This was the sea: giving with one hand, taking away with the other. A hope she had of rest from toil and fear. No doubt of that coming true, once the *Western Star* had made her voyage. And yet her greater hope, by which she had bound her future to the future of a man—had it not now come to grief? Since this was unbearable to me, who wished only for her happiness, 'tis plain enough what the quality of her torment must be. There was little of the bell in her voice that morning.

I said: "I don't believe it."

She made no reply and I thought my words had been knocked down in the slap of water and the shouts and hammer strokes blowing off the *Western Star*. I rowed hard to swing the dory into it and I said louder: "I don't believe it, Nora. There's a false reckoning in this somewhere."

Her eyes came in a swoop away from the green rollers bursting beyond the gate and she searched me by a heavy glance in which the green at first was fixed and shot with fire; then went dark, because she had found the kindly falsehood in my own eyes; for I couldn't help but think of her captain on the *Doubloon*. A strange skill she showed. I had never lied to her before.

She asked: "What shall I do, John?" and, since it wasn't her way to seek another's counsel in such matters, she gave her own answer without waiting on mine. "The Lisbon must answer. He has the answer."

"Then," said I, "when we come alongside, call him and we'll take him to the *Hind* and get the answer out of him."

This we did. Another man stepped to the forge; and Terrio, without a glance backward, let himself down into the bow of her dory. Captain LeNotre had been watching the splicing of a wire cable. Our hail to the Lisbon made him turn. He took a step forward, seeming ready to speak. He thought better of it and gave only a moody glance to our parting. I had time for one long look at the Lisbon before he settled down behind my thwart. He was a man of more than middle age. In our fashion, he was called "the Lisbon" because he'd been born in Portugal and had come to the Grand Banks with the Portuguese fleet in his boyhood. He had never ceased to fish, had never stopped talking and thinking as a Portuguese. Nevertheless, he was a thorough Gloucesterman, because much of what we have and do is owed to his race. At this hour, he seemed careworn, and I thought that the unexpected labor on the *Western Star* had set him back. His black hair had long been touched with grey. Indeed, I couldn't remember the time when his hair had been all black. Yet I was sure that he aged even more in the few days of the *Hind's* voyage. The smoke of his forge had blackened his face and hands; and the sparks off his anvil had touched his eyes, so that they were half-closed and weary-looking. There was more to this than plain weariness. Soon I found out why.

We three stood together in the cabin of the *Golden Hind* and Nora said in her forthright fashion: "Terry, the *Western Star* and her keel won't be enough for us, even if we do find her tied up safe when we get home. We must take fifteen thousand dollars' worth of fish home, too. Or the *Hind* will be lost to us. Our debts can go on no longer."

He gave no answer in open words. He looked away from her and sent his gaze a-wandering in his sea-home: that beautiful cabin where the fire shone red as it had shone for him on many a night when the ice was making. Since his expression did not change, I judged that her thought (the one of loss) wasn't a new one to him. He shook his head in a grave fashion.

I said: "I am mate aboard this vessel, Terry, and I've the right to order you to speak freely to the owner, who has come upon hard times and stands in need of faithful men."

Nora Doonan then asked: "Has Ambrose told you to speak openly to me?"

He replied: "He told me you are in trouble, Miss Nora. I know that anyway." He began a solemn consideration of his next words. He didn't think in English; and had to turn his thoughts out of Portuguese. At last, he let them go. "Captain Nora, you dress like a man aboard the *Hind* and in your hard work at home. This I see. You fight like a man for your grandfather, for your schooner and your men. You talk like a man. Yet you are a woman. A young girl to me. So I must ask you this: What say? Do I talk to you like I talk to a man? To young John? Eh?" He thrust out his right hand and let it fall on my shoulder.

She cried: "For Heaven's sake—for all our sakes!—do!"

He spoke in a harsh tone: "All right! What you mean, Miss Nora, by talking to me about full pens and need of money? I am only your doryman."

Nora also roughened her manner. Arms akimbo and thumbs thrust into her belt, she at once swept away the barrier (what remained of it) by an outright accusation of him. "I mean this, doryman! How can we kill fish and save ourselves if you're going to disobey orders aboard this vessel? Disobey your captain and let dories go over as you let the Corkerys' go? And cause men to curse their captain in my hearing? Tell me that!"

This assault set him free, because he learned that his faithfulness and skill, long dear to him, had been called into question. I saw the corners of his mouth whiten, and the dark, ocean-stained cheeks become even darker. He was done with quietness. He roared.

"Madre de Deus!" He swung his hands up to the skylight and held them there, so that he seemed ready to curse his captain as Corkery had cursed him. His eyes glowed, then glittered. He shouted: "Sim! Sim! I speak!"

Wrath in a young and mighty man is terrible. In this old and mighty man it was awful to behold; because it came after a lifetime of patience, labor, and courteous actions. Nora Doonan suffered under it. She had no need of his words. His eyes spoke her doom. Nothing untrue could force that beaming. Only the truth, struggling in a faithful heart, could color him so violently and ruin the melody of his voice.

She thrust out her arms toward him. In what vain appeal, I do not know.

He stepped back and shouted: "It is a lie against me and my chums! Against the dead and the living! I, Terry, never lie. Wine never passes my lips. Nor the lie either. I never disobey. I never make mistake. Never leave the helm until relief. Never let a dory go over when the order is 'no'!"

I cried out into his clamor: "Can you deny that Captain LeNotre told you to keep all in nests?"

He paid me no heed. He held us with his gaze and let loose a spate of words in English, all marked with ringing, pious oaths in Portuguese that we knew well. These he would not dare utter foolishly or lightly for fear of his immortal soul. He denied all that the captain had related on the night of the *Hind's* return. He declared that the captain had sent him below and had himself stood the fatal watch. The Corkerys had never demanded that a mark-buoy be set over the fish. Never! because the Corkerys would have nothing to do with a mark-buoy, which they considered a device for unsure men. They had wished to stay aboard, yet the captain had forced them to put their dory over; and in weather where even the bravest and the best could hardly keep afloat, not to speak of fishing up a drifting buoy.

"I tell you more!" he cried, "and it's this: that the mark-buoy gave mark to nothing. No cod under it. Because the captain rigged it. And did such a job of rigging that the anchor line parts! Aye!"

His first fury waned, he fell upon the captain's pathetic narrative, tore at it, trampled it. In so doing, he made such a proud and passionate defense of his own skill that both Nora and I were overwhelmed, were driven together into unbearable apprehension and despair. I couldn't help recalling the display by Captain LeNotre on that night, not long since, when he explained his empty pens by this: "You damned Lisbon, you are on watch and you let a dory out of the nest without sending for me? An old man like you?"

Now, in our secret hearts, she and I knew which man stood damned and which not.

Yet it must be that Nora and I should boldly try to shut the gates against this troop of images, marauders sent against our hearts. She, for her reason; I, for my secret one. Knowing her heart as I knew my own (because hers had once been mine and mine hers), I came closer to her, so that our hands touched, and she seized my hand and cried out: "Do you say that the Corkerys were sent to death and drowning because the captain feared and hated them? As Parren and Atkins hate and fear? Do you say that, Terry? Is this the word I am to bring to my grandfather? So far gone that I couldn't even tell him: 'James Corkery's drowned from the deck of our *Hind!*'"

This came from the second part of Ambrose's revelation to her.

The Lisbon took no time to measure his words. He said: "It's been told to you once, Miss Nora. I tell it to you again. Hate and fear stand in the captain's heart."

She and I spoke the same word at the same moment: "Why?"

"Corkery—he knew!" He gave the word "knew" the clang of a bell-buoy toppling, put such a strain on it that he frightened us. He filled us with fear of things unknown and clearly to be made known soon. Our fear, which surely touched our staring faces, halted him. In his kindliness and his fatherly love for us (we having no fathers), he had no wish to play this part. I saw pity quench the fury in his eyes, which became dark again and gentler.

I waited for Nora Doonan to speak. I glanced sideways at her and saw her teeth bear down on the untinted lip. Since she couldn't utter the word, I did so. I said: "Corkery knew what?"

The Lisbon replied: "He knew—and his living brother aboard the *Doubloon* knows—that our captain is Parren's little dog. A little dog to be sent on errands!" He lingered reluctantly over the unhappy image he had chosen and then, in cold deliberation, added: "A little yellow dog. To fetch"— he flung out his right hand—"and to carry." He jerked his left hand upward and let it fall.

By this time, so much had been lost to Nora Doonan that she had little left except her sorrow. There was nothing to cry out against, no question of belief or disbelief. She, therefore, put on the Lisbon's air of deliberateness and asked in a voice so clear and calm that she again amazed me: "You are an old man and a wise one, Terry! And you say this to me?"

"I am old and I am wise, Miss Nora. And I say it to you."

"Knowing that I am promised to the captain?"

"Knowing so. Yes!"

She left me and took a step toward him and asked: "Then tell me, if you can and will, what was the little yellow dog to fetch and carry for Captain Parren? Bearing in mind that Captain Parren has always been a friend of ours and has been good to us. Aye! we'd not be here now if it hadn't been for Captain Parren's money!"

He sighed over his thoughts of her and I heard him whisper: "A child! A child!"

I spoke roughly to him. "Out with it! Answer the owner's question! Tell her what the captain was to fetch and carry for Parren!"

He answered: "The *Hind!*"

"The *Hind!*"

"What! my *Golden Hind?*"

For me: clenched silence. For Nora Doonan: another idol gone. For the Lisbon: a victory, and his first bold step toward the declaration of war which he desired above all things else, even above her present happiness. I read in his changeful face these marks: scorn, savagery, and, in the end, the cool mastery of a man who has the upper hand. By this I mean that he scorned us for our blindness, became savage in his hatred of the enemy captains, and then took hold of himself to be our guide in an hour too harsh for us alone.

The *Golden Hind* put a strain on her mooring lines and swung to the tide. I heard birds calling among her furled sails. I heard the cook coming aft and singing loudly the only song that he could pipe:

"Good-bye, my Bluebell, farewell to you!"

He pushed back the companionway slide and came down stern-first, a hod of coals his burden. He swung about and shut his singing mouth. He lowered the hod and, in so doing, looked gravely from face to face. He took his leave without a word.

Nora Doonan retreated. She took a step backward and then sat down on the locker, her head bowed, her hands flat at her sides. I took up the hod and poured the coal into the stove.

The Lisbon began his recital. He had taken a curious stand; that is, he kept his hands locked behind his back. I was used to this in him. He did it to keep his hands out of the argument. Sometimes they said more than his words. He spoke dryly, dispassionately, as if his shrewdness told him we could do with no more of his anger. He declared that he and others had known for a long time that Captain Parren had no greater wish on earth than to capture the *Hind*, by hook or by crook. It was for this that he had displayed his generosity, had given to Grandfather Doonan the thousands and to Nora his open wallet. Captain Parren had been earning between twenty and thirty thousand dollars a year on the *Doubloon*. The vessel herself had been earning five or six times that much; because he drove her harshly, raided the cod nurseries and killed everything that his nets dragged up.

"Aye! he's one of those hated by young John because they slaughter the baby fish with a small mesh. But why does he do it? Why go on? He has much money. More than enough. I tell you, he is crazy for more. That's why he wishes to be an owner and keep the vessel's share, too. He has the money to build. But who can build for him? Nobody! All must go to the wars. The New York people pay one hundred thousand dollars for the *Laura* and take her off to the West Indies. They offer more for the *Hind*. Why? Because she's worth a million—she could earn so much. This is what Parren knows. It's not hard to see. Greed is his curse and greed makes him fool you, Miss Nora, and your grandfather. He takes your hand. Only to crush it. He wants the *Hind* to make her into a dragger as Captain Bannon does. Parren—he cannot buy her. So he means to drive her to ruin and make her debt big and bigger until you, a dear friend, say to him: 'Can't go on! Take her!' "

He had now brought his voice down to a dull, matter-of-fact pitch. He spoke like a man reading a set of figures. He said: "You don't understand him. Because you cannot love money. Young John here—he is the same. I tell you—unless you love money you cannot know men! You are children. I am a man. All my life I fight for a few dollars to feed the mouths at home. So I become a man. So I know, too, that Parren is in danger. He is great today and he swaggers. But he can lose the *Doubloon* and all his money. His owners can say: 'Go!' Something hangs over him. Only the *Hind* can save him from losing all he loves: money. Tomorrow? The day after? Who knows?"

In us there was now no wish to keep his knowledge out of our hearts. We neither spoke nor stirred. Step by step, he drew closer to the key of all his knowledge: the mystery of the captain's treachery. He said that the drowned Corkery had actually heard Parren threaten Captain LeNotre with something worse than death unless he contrived to keep the *Hind*'s pens empty. LeNotre had obeyed, voyage after voyage, by clever means. Yet, in the last few voyages, certain of the *Hind*'s people, perceiving this betrayal of themselves and their vessel, had pushed their thought into dark corners and had come out with the answer.

In my dullness, I said: "Even old Bannister knew. In my presence—and in yours, Terry—he called the captain 'Murderer!' for the death of Corkery."

I heard her groan.

The Lisbon checked me with an upraised hand. Over it, he sent me a glance of warning and he murmured: "Enough! Enough!"

"Aye!" whispered Nora to herself, "enough! More than enough!"

Nevertheless, he had stirred me by his pleading and I cried out: "But there is more! More to be told. Nothing is to be held back. Nothing!"

The Lisbon spoke sternly to me. " 'Twasn't the drowning of poor Corkery he meant. No! How could he know of such a thing?" He bowed his head and whispered: "Not one other word from me in the presence of a woman."

Nora said: "Have done with secrets, once and for all. You're not speaking in a woman's presence, Terry. I am an owner. Not a woman. Go on with what you have to say. And make short work of it. For there's much to do now and much thinking to be done to save us all." At his hesitation, she again spoke harshly: "Something hangs over Captain Parren? I heard you. A disgrace that will drive him off the *Doubloon*. And the same thing hangs over Captain LeNotre and over Billy Atkins? The old chums. Yes! I can see that I'm right. Why was Atkins chosen to fish with us? And on my own vessel, the first day out, I saw him speak in a strange way to Captain LeNotre and sneer at him without rebuke or hindrance. I wondered then! And now—while you speak—I wonder why Parren can compel and threaten a man like Paul LeNotre. Is it money there, too, Terry?"

He answered without further delay. "There be always two troubles with such men. First—money. Second—a woman."

At this, she closed her eyes. I knew the image on which she must then dwell for the last time: a blond Viking of a captain, steering the *Hind* to the Doonan Wharf three years ago and shouting his strange Miquelon oaths to sails and men.

She said: "Go on!"

Terry obeyed. "We dorymen know this. Parren—he gives

money to LeNotre all the time. For rum. For clothes. For debts. You know there isn't so much money earned all this time on the *Hind*. So, the captain—he cannot pay Parren back. Yet he must pay him back some way. Some time. Or suffer."

She cried out again. "The woman!"

His mouth became even grimmer at her urging. He had no wish to speak of such things to a girl. He stayed so long that she repeated her question and added to it: "Speak freely, Terry. Speak your piece. I've not been knocking around these vessels all my life for nothing."

"The woman? Miss Nora, to us woman spells money. And money spells woman. Without money—no woman. Without woman—no money. Why fish?" He caught himself up quickly and said in a lower tone: "For myself, Miss Nora, I have my fun at home. You see, I speak to you like a man." He flung out his hands freely then and said his say. "Many strange things I've heard of them ashore. Parren, Atkins, and your captain. They were friends—good friends—before the captain comes to Gloucester that time. Now, there was a woman in Yarmouth. A beautiful woman. I have seen her in their company. Off the Big Miquelon she is. And bought by the rich Bannister. Bought, but not kept. Next she is Captain LeNotre's woman. Because he knew her when a boy. Then Captain Parren—he buy her. With his money. With his dragger money. She lives in style that time. Then he gives her back to Captain LeNotre. Like that! Generous. Then, Miss Nora, they both have her for a time. And quarrel over her."

I cried: "You mean they shared a woman? Is that what you are trying to say? Paul LeNotre and that old man?"

He shook his head in bewilderment. "She shared them, John. The *Hind* goes out from Yarmouth after taking bait. Woman goes to Boston. The *Doubloon* comes in there and goes out again. Woman comes back to Yarmouth and waits for the *Hind*. *Hind* stays too long." He fumbled over the wooden words and whispered swifter ones in Portuguese. He then looked at her in a strange, fierce way and said: "Now comes death!"

"Ah!"

"Who knows? Who can tell? 'Tis nothing! Many die or are gone and never heard from. One night in Yarmouth they find her. The shore patrol. Gaffed in the snow-drift, she is." He swept his hand upward in a jerky motion that made us shudder. "A knife! Who knows what knife? Even Corkery is not sure and he was ashore. Daniel, I mean, on the *Doubloon* now. Is it a knife with a queer hilt of bone? I don't know. And why must she die? I don't know that either, young John. But some men say they know why. Bannister—he makes no bones about it. Just the same, he knows nothing for sure. But the drowned Corkery knew and it may be yet that even powerful captains can be found out and hanged."

Nora Doonan asked: "When was this?"

"Last winter."

She kept down her cry, but I couldn't keep down my own; for I remembered her winter and the firelit nights passed with her lover in the old house at home.

The Lisbon said: "This I do know; each man has killed before now. On the Banks, or the Miquelons, or 'longshore. They were devils together! One way or the other, they killed."

He was aware of the devastation he had made within Nora Doonan. Her wretched mouth and faded cheeks told him; and half-closed, unseeing eyes. He couldn't face her. Knowing this, she came up to him and said: "Of all those who knew, you alone told me. Told us. I'll not forget. I'll always be thankful, Terry. My life had almost been lost to me. It is—"

Here she held back words of grief, braced up and went on speaking. "The vessel remains. John and I will sail with her. I've given Ambrose my promise to do so. Even before today. The captain will remain the captain for the time being. I'll not speak of such matters to him yet. I must watch and wait. Oh, I believe you! To my sorrow, I must and do. But I must act in disbelief. As if it all had to be proved and—"

He broke into her bewailing: "It will be proved! Wait!" He held up his hand to gain time for his thought. "The last hour has come for them. We have brought it. You have, Miss Nora! The *Western Star* and her keel is our way out. She is ready. Sixteen thousand dollars for her—aye! and more. And a grand stock of fish. Ah, you'll see, Captain Nora, that soon— very soon—someone will come to you from Parren—maybe today—and say: 'Sell the *Golden Hind* for one hundred and twenty thousand dollars!' Watch!"

Nora replied: "We must watch and wait. But you tell the men—those that don't know—all you've told us. Let them be watchful, too."

I said: "All save bloody Atkins."

She flung on her jacket. "We'll all go back to the *Star* now for the last day's work. All will be well."

"All will be well, Nora!"

"All will be well, Captain Nora."

A silence lay on the deck of the *Western Star* when we boarded her. The men were thronged around the mainmast. The men of the Irish Regiment stood at solemn attention, fingers to caps. That mast had no sail; and was stepped only for stays and other standing gear. She was to go under fore-sail only, that being all five men could handle. The men gazed cheerfully at a halyard rigged to the mainmast. I saw the captain amongst them. I saw old Ambrose lift his hand and, in obedience, another hand hauled the colors of our Republic briskly until they unfolded in the westerly breeze. There was no laughter, no cheering. All hands knew what the old dory-men had before them. We said: "So long!" and "See you in Gloucester!" and "Good luck, chums!" We returned to the *Hind*, took in her mooring lines, and sailed down the stream.

The *Western Star* swayed up her little spread and came jauntily after us and passed through the gate. For an hour the *Hind* and the *Star* sailed together in the waning light. When we had put Seal Island Light and the rocks well behind us, the *Star's* people gave us a farewell shout and she fell onto the windward tack heavily, forcefully. The last I saw of her was a blow of sparks out of the galley pipe and a curl of wood smoke. A moment later, she passed into the sunset, where she lingered briefly, black and long, and at her helm a little band of bowed men, their broad backs gleaming. I looked after her with longing. I longed for the day when I should greet the hero.

The *Golden Hind* sped eastward. The captain had the helm. I stood by him and waited for his nod. I took a step forward and shouted the stand-by signal: "Hard alee! Oh, make it lively, boys!"

"Hard alee!"

The cry bowled forward and ran upward through her crowded sails. Captain LeNotre brought her sweetly into the wind. The dorymen shouted, hauled, and shouted. Booms and sails came shouting over and the *Golden Hind*, finding the wind even fairer now, plunged handsomely into the rolling night. Full of foreboding, heavy-hearted with it, I took the helm from him and stood my watch on the passage to the Banks. And I can say that I found little of my old joy in the stars of autumn that rose to guide me.

9

DORYMEN OF Gloucester say: "A sou'wester is never in debt to a no'theaster." Words that smell a little of the counting-house; and I daresay it was an owner who coined it. Yet it's a true saying; for, on the score of fierceness, 'tis six of one and half a dozen of the other, although the no'theaster is more likely to blow a man home. These gales are born far apart; and die so. That is their only difference. One is the land's gift to the sea; the other is the sea's gift to the land. Tit for tat. Riding either out is poor living. The ride's the same: now high, now low, now on beam-ends, and then, perhaps, hove down and fires out. However, it is graciously arranged by Nature that these blows never vary. They come and they go, always sending the same signals before, always hauling them down at departure. Blue water becomes black. Whitecaps vanish. Tide-rips cease their howling. The Atlantic changes to a flat. Sun-rays pierce the greenhorn's heart, make it blithe. It is a mystery to him. None to us. None to the Lisbons, who are kith and kin to the gales; are their beloved children. No change in a far-off hue escapes them, on bow-watch or helm-watch. A darkening sea darkens their eyes. The waning of one harshness in the Atlantic clamor fills their hearts with stir. Before the glass knows, they know. The eternal clock is wound up. Let it unwind. It is only discipline, by which men keep free, that sends them below to read a bill of particulars off the glass, a finite change in infinite weights and pressures, narrated by a column of mercury in a cup of glass, our heir-loom out of the dark.

"She fall two tenth since noon."

The *Golden Hind* was sailing across Emerald Bank when the Lisbon passed this word to Nora Doonan and to me. We two were standing in the sunny shelter between the dory-nests, each bowed in wordless thought, in the only specula-tion that's worth the candle: the one which leads to action. Which thought was apt to make a proper haul out of the fathoms? Man's or woman's? Hard to say, even if we had been left alone. I had my wisdom. She had hers. These were not yet joined. I pondered as a man of the sea; she, as a woman. Not an ordinary woman, content to stand aside and deny all that must be true of womanhood, which cannot differ from manhood in reckless daring. No, she pondered as a free woman, forced by need and by hardy inclination to take a part in men's affairs, to live and work and fight amongst us. She asked no favor because she stood on the distaff side. In-deed, she had now learned to expect less goodness from men than they customarily extend to themselves. No other thought than her own had true value.

Well! whatever clue our minds may have been seeking, all came to naught when the Lisbon said the barometer foretold a storm. Slanting from heights unimaginably above the water world, the universal order shot its changeless signal down to our sea, into our cabin, giving us an hour's notice that a vast bustle was required in those parts. An hour's notice, also, that any little arrangements we might make were to be set aside. And to be forgotten forever! Because this that rises beyond is the sou'wester, the wind of which I earlier spoke and by which our destiny is to be shaped.

The watch came up from the cabin and spoke to the helmsman. A moment later, Captain LeNotre, who had been sleeping, came on deck and turned his bare, golden head this way and that. He scanned the empty sky and snuffed up the spray. He lifted his hand, jerked it downward. At once, the topmastmen jumped into the swifters. The main-sheet gang hauled down on the staysail. Her topsails folded. Soon her pace declined. The watch changed. The man who had the helm turned it over to the new watch. Before the old took his hands off the spokes, he sang out: "East-by-South! One hour!" The new watch chanted: "East-by-South! One hour!" and looked into the binnacle to see that the course was the one he must keep for his hour on duty. The dorymen shoved their tubs of bait back toward the main hatch and they thrust bait-knives down into bulwark sheaths. Tubs of trawl went sliding into their old places along the rail. The washing-tubs were again lashed to the chains.

I went down the ladder into the pens and handled the bait. Not much had gone up. I shovelled herring into Number One pen and threw the ice back. I looked idly into the empty pens, wondering if ever they would be full of fish; and I felt, as often before, how the storm made itself known in those dark bins more strongly than it did on deck. The air was already close below. There was a booming in it. I returned to the deck and the new bow-watch called out to me: "He says: 'Bring up the bottom!'"

"Bring up the bottom! Aye!"

I looked toward the forecastle companionway and met the cook's expectant gaze. He nodded and backed down the steps to his icebox.

I turned to Nora and said: " 'Tis hauling to the south'ard. Bad luck!"

"It is, indeed, John."

No fear for the *Hind* herself drove the little cheerfulness from our faces. We knew which was stronger: schooner or gale, oak or wind, spar or wave. No, it was to the greying west that our hearts turned in sea-wise dismay. There, unless some mishap had already maimed her, the precious *Western Star* must now be creeping down the coast to Cape Ann. Her exact course couldn't be known to us because it had been left to old Ambrose to reckon how he should steer after he dropped Seal Island Light. Two general courses had been open to him. He might drive straight across the Gulf of Maine and take his chances in the open sea. Or he might run from one harbor to the next, ready to take shelter in case of a blow. His job was to save the great keel and bring it to the melting-pot. Yet this storm had already risen in the west and, for all we knew, it might have swept between him and the land.

I lent a hand to the gripes for the double-lashing of the dories.

It was no wonder that she and I became sullen. The anxious faces of the dorymen made us so, though we were bent toward anger. A little while before, the men had been eager for the fishing. On the voyage out of Shelburne, the prospect of getting some hooks down to the bottom had made the men gay. I was aware, too, that they considered our presence aboard as a guarantee that fish would be killed if fish were found. There had been boasts in the forecastle and happy calculations on Boston prices. And their habit of good fellowship had, to a degree, ironed out the 'longshore difficulties and the newness of their plight, being for the first time ever at sea with a captain whom they must look upon as a sort of madman. I did so well that I spoke decently even to Billy Atkins when I had to speak. I found no trouble, either, in working with the captain, who had himself put a good face on it and had driven the *Hind* skillfully to this place for her first set. It was true that both Nora and I found the meal-time meetings a little trying because all hands seemed so openly intent on shaking off the queer forebodings and Jonah talk that had marked the earlier stages of the *Hind's* voyage. These moods persisted in wary glances and shut-off sentences, which became more frequent as the Lisbon's story passed amongst them. Despite the despair and doubt in her heart, Nora, too, soon caught the genial infection and shared their hope of a certain harvest and a quick one. Such a boon seemed sure to them all. Their confidence rested on nothing more than the direness of their need; for it had been explained to them that without a good stock and fair prices at home, the *Golden Hind* couldn't go on.

The cook handed me a round, thick pat of butter, and made his old joke by shaking his head over it and saying: "Bring it back, kid, when you're done with it."

I let out the usual shout of laughter and started aft. A glittering hump of spray slewed us around and I said: "Better oil up, Nora. 'Tis coming along fast, I guess."

She followed me to the break and watched while I jammed the butter into the hollow tip of the lead. I cast the lead far forward and let the line pay out, watching the markers as it ran. I worked aft a bit and presently hauled briskly, hand over hand. Without looking at the armed tip, which would have been a breech of custom aboard the vessel, I handed it to the captain. He turned it upside down, gazed at the tell-tale gravel, then touched it with his forefinger. He rubbed his finger back and forth lightly over the butter. He frowned. The gravel wasn't fine enough. He knew where he was by this touch of the finger. It wasn't where he wanted to be.

"Forty fathom," I said. "Not bank enough?"

"We're almost on it." He gave back the lead and took thought. "Heave her to. We'll have to ride it out here, if we can."

Gale and night met above her topmasts and wrestled there. Out of the last flare in the northwest, a purple cloud spouted and then soared, an immense rocket trailing sun-fire from one rim of the world to the other. The blow fell upon the *Golden Hind* from that arch. She sprang to meet it.

The first boarding sea filled her gangways, forced her down, and kept her so until the following seas piled on her. These came with the usual uproar to silence talk and send uneasy looks around the cabin. She cleared herself and came up to take a breath full of frost and spray. No sooner had she shaken off that first rattling welter than another and larger sea came in over the same quarter and hit her like a thousand of brick. The booming of her pens loudened in the cabin. And there came such a queer noise of rending that Nora, stretched out in her bunk, couldn't help raising her hand; for it seemed to us that some of the gear had parted and had cut across the deck like a scythe. In the next instant, that tearing sound came again. This time it shrieked against the blackened skylight and rattled in such a way that we knew it was hail, driven down like pellets of iron. The wind then began slambanging all around the compass and punished the schooner so harshly that even the dorymen in the cabin bunks became alert and showed some signs that they feared a freakish storm which might suddenly defeat them.

This oddness in the whirl of the gale lasted so long that the vessel couldn't cope with it. She was at her wit's end. She failed to keep her head into it, no matter how the watch labored at her helm. The sea cheated our skill and gave the *Hind* such a hammering that soon it was plain a new thought was running in our minds: is this the one? The seas ran over her bow with such force that it wasn't possibly to keep a watch forward. The captain finally went on deck. A little later, my bunk-mate followed, taking with him a coil of rope to lash himself to the wheel, for the watch was changing and it was his trick again, it being impossible for the men forward to come aft.

When Captain LeNotre came down, I watched him anxiously and saw with relief that he sat down as usual on the locker to pull off his boots. He had only one of them free when the Lisbon, who was lying in the bunk just aft of Nora's, slipped out and stood in his stocking-feet on that slanted and shuddering deck. He stared downward with such intensity that one might think he could pierce hull and keel and thus draw up some secret of the storm from the bottom.

Shouting through the din, the captain asked: "What say, Terry?"

"I hear! You hear?" He lifted his hand and beat time to some far-off resounding music that he had chosen amongst all the other strains and discords. The repeated signals of his arm soon gave us the clue; and my own ear caught the bass note in the west. This grew in grandeur as the music-maker advanced.

The captain put on his boot again and waited.

The Lisbon let his arm fall. The rhythmic succession of loud notes had now merged into one vast clamor. All lesser sounds vanished. The great sea struck and rolled on, taking the *Hind* with it as if she were a chip; which, indeed, she had become, for all her hundred tons. Her lee rail went far down and her stern sank in the same overturning whirl. The swift uptilting pitched Nora halfway out of her bunk; so that she had a hard time of it and clung on only by gripping the side with both her hands. A shower of small gear and boots rattled across the cabin. The Lisbon, who was hanging on to the companionway, glanced sharply at the stove. It was red under the door. The vessel whirled three times in that topsy-turvy style; then slowly, beam by beam, she found herself. Her hold began to boom the old chant again.

Captain LeNotre staggered across the litter and joined us at the companionway. We stared at one another in an unseeing way. We listened for a signal from the men at the wheel. It came soon: three sharp blows against the slide. This meant that the helmsmen, lashed to the wheel in the loose Gloucester style that would save them from strangling, had hung on through the worst blow.

"Old *Hind*—she win!" The Lisbon rolled back into his bunk.

That was the end of freakishness. There was much left: the sou'wester itself. The Lisbon had no fear of it. He called out cheerfully and to signify the further change in his opinions, moved both his hands outward in a flat gesture. He picked up a Sunday hat off the locker and tucked it away. Nora pulled the blankets over her again and lay there all the night while the *Hind* fought out the longer battle.

The rising of the sun (such as it was) brought us a little while of ease. The cook sent down a kettle of coffee and a bag of rolls by the hands of forecastle men, who had rigged lifelines at daybreak. The watches now changed regularly. Weary under the hammering and lack of the big meals which their strength demanded, the men passed into the useful silence by which quarrels are avoided and the work smoothly shared and done. Nevertheless, despite this discipline which we laid upon ourselves, the strength of the storm mauled us when the day waned. The hour came when the heave-to manœuvre had to end; for the *Hind* was living under water.

The cook himself brought down a kettle of tea and a crock of cakes. He said aloud: "I never liked Emerald Bank this time o' year." He had just come from the forecastle, where many wise seamen lay, making up judgments never to be ignored. He himself was one of the best seamen in the fleet; and he always had time to do his thinking and listening. For these reasons, his remark amounted to a suggestion from the crew. This was customary in the fleet, where the day's work had to be directed by joint experience and thought.

I said in a louder tone: "What's that you say, cook?" For I had noticed that the captain, for whom the words were intended, hadn't heard them.

The cook said it over again. Apparently some new move had been making up in Captain LeNotre's mind, his skill being equal to any other in such matters. Between swallows out of his mug, he spoke to me. "Let her go! She'll wind up on the Middle Ground, anyway, and that's where we want to be."

I went on deck and let the *Hind* run before the gale. In her relief and joy, she made such handsome going of it that no sea could catch her hard. She flew up the steep hillsides and toppled down. Two or three times, in the late afternoon, she buried her lee side to the hatches, but she cleared herself without much trouble. At four o'clock or so an airplane carrier and a number of destroyers came up to the eastward. Half an hour later, the vessels changed course and vanished in the vapor.

In the dusk, the *Golden Hind* ran for her life before the gale. It soon came my turn again and I went on deck a little after midnight. I found her driving in toilsome fashion through thick vapor and a rain that kept turning into hail and back again. I leaned against the wheel, my belly roaring for food and my hands taking on the dead set of exhaustion. My chum kept his shoulder against mine so that we could go together on the wheel. I could scarcely see him; for the hail kept my eyes half-shut. Indeed, I shut them altogether at times because the hail swept against us in volleys straight off the water. At times the hail struck the bulwarks and skylight with a clanking sound, like skylights breaking. The *Hind's* eagerness grew with the force of the gale. She pitched badly and then flew up the white seas in a crazy, twisting motion that made me quake; and made my chum twist his mouth against my ear to speak in the din. I felt, even in my numbness, the scrape of his unshaven, iced-up jaw.

He shouted: "John, can you, for—" But at that very moment the *Hind* flung herself across a frosty summit and there leaned almost in a pause, only to start forward violently when the roller surged under and away. She seemed air-borne! I swear her whirling bow thrust out into nothingness. She toppled and dived down into the trough at such a sudden slant that my boots went out from under me and I fell like a green fool face-down into a pour of water deep enough to drown me. A jerky strain on the rope that lashed us to the wheel turned me to my knees. A hand reached out of the dark and pulled. I crawled against the wheel and got my fingers back onto the spokes. At that moment, when I was looking for her to climb out of there, a freakish cross-sea struck her hard at about the main weather rigging—the port—and she passed directly into a black wall which tumbled upon her. But in vain! Her great buoyancy outmatched the tons of water and she bore upwards, shuddering and straining, and flung us into the air again.

About this time, a light pierced the pitch-black near at hand. I let out a yell, not knowing, in my blindness, whence it came; and then I saw the figure of a man, black and bowed, against a dim glow rising from the companionway. He crouched and then, as the slide shot into place behind him, he flung himself boldly into the stream and came up between us; and I felt a new and powerful strain on the wheel, which by now was something that two men could hardly handle. It was the captain. He shouted some word to encourage us and I passed the lashing to him. Thus we three straddled it through the night until the sun came up in a murky dawn. Weak enough was that sun; nevertheless, it scoffed up part of the gale and gave us strength. Soon it cleared a little in the east.

The captain said: "Go forward, John, and get a man or two into the bow. If you think they can stand it."

I left the wheel and went forward on the lines. In a cautious way at first, because I was numbed and harshly beaten; and I kept in mind that a long time had passed since I had undergone such labor. Before I reached the break (which was a matter of minutes) the sun made a good breach through the clouds. I jumped into the shelter of the dory-nests. It was easier there. I kept an eye on the forecastle companionway, for I didn't want to be caught there by a boarding sea. 'Twas my good luck! A doryman fell cautiously back from the lee of the foremast and I saw that the bow-watch had gone up the moment it was possible. This was Ernie Wagner, a Nova Scotian of my long acquaintance, and a better doryman never came out of the Provinces. His present action stayed me where I crouched. He kept raising his head to take a look over the weather rail. Since this didn't satisfy him, he ran to the fore rigging and hauled himself up. I saw him twist arm and leg into the shrouds. He again raised his head to peer into the scud to windward.

I fell back and made my way up the deck between the starboard dory-nest and the rail. By this change, I was nearer and could make him out clearly. A sea buried him. When it ran off between the nests, I saw that he had climbed higher. It was plain to me that he sighted something to windward of us. I wished to see what it was. I could see nothing from my place. Yet I understood that he might want to send word aft in a hurry. So I stayed. It seemed to me that he might hear my voice. I cried out his name. He turned his head and shouted something which I couldn't make out at all. He strained upward and once more looked away. When he twisted toward me again, his face revealed considerable excitement. He thrust him arm directly to windward and shouted; then he drew that arm in and held his other stiffly to leeward, which was a signal. I ran aft and told the captain to take her off a point or two, that the watch had sighted a vessel on our course. Or dangerously near it.

By this time the *Hind* was in such shape that others had come up from the cabin. Among them were Nora Doonan and the Lisbon. She seemed tired, which was natural enough considering the state of things below. The Lisbon kept close to her.

I began making my way forward. I found a doryman clinging to the main rigging. He shouted: "Ernie says there's a vessel on the weather quarter. Coming up fast! Can't make her out. A dungeon of fog!"

This was risky business. Plenty of sea-room was needed in such a blow, especially because the vapor rolled in thick now and then. I wasn't sure the *Hind* had given the stranger a wide enough berth. I sent the doryman aft with his message. He came back soon and gave me the all-right signal. Nora and the Lisbon followed him. They got into the lee of the dory-nest.

I waited until the way was clear. I jumped into the swifters and found a place below Ernie Wagner. There I clung, flying 'twixt night and day, to watch the next act in the drama of the *Golden Hind*. A scene in the ironic vein, written by no mean scribbler, played by no mean hero.

Doryman Wagner struck me on the shoulder. He then held his arm out so that I might look along it. His hand pointed directly into a stream of vapor that was closing in from the northwest. The wind, which was still a gale beyond, kept breaking into that stream, made aisles and frothy vistas in it. Some were shallow, some were caves, some the depth of a mile. Hills of water, black-sided and white-topped, surged across these vistas; or filled them entirely with spouts and falls of foam.

I gazed eagerly. Presently I saw a duller gleam of light shoot across one of the openings.

Wagner shouted.

The dull gleam vanished. I could see no more. I then heard shouts below me. I bent backward and saw four or five dory-men clinging to the gripes and staring into the vapor. Nora and the Lisbon stood amongst them, their eyes fixed on the sea. I saw Billy Atkins raise his hand. They were all able to see a certain distance now; for the *Hind* sailed at a smoother clip, although her speed seemed to be even greater. It was this great speed that kept her in constant danger; because there wasn't much steering that could be done under such circum-stances.

I turned back to the sea again, waiting for a clue to be tossed up in the wilderness. Soon I saw the same dullish light about half a mile nearer. This time I clung to it, followed its pell-mell passage and narrowly judged its speed, so that I could pick it up when it jumped across clear water. In such a way, I looked ahead and far down into an enormous cavern. In its middle, a sea began rising, and seemed to force the ivory walls and dripping arch outward by its force. I saw the bursting of the western wall. I saw the *Western Star* careen into that cavern.

A wail blew over the *Hind*'s deck.

I stared in deepest sorrow at that beautiful hull, caught for an instant on the lifting sea: a bare deck, a mainmast gone by the board, a sail in ribbons, and a black, gleaming mound at her smothered helm. The mound, I knew, could only be her dorymen, lashed to the wheel and driving onward to a fate that I foresaw only too well. Even before this thought could take shape (tho' it had been formed a hundred times in the nights past), the vessel tumbled over that sea and vaulted out of sight.

I let myself down to the deck and made my way to Nora's side. She shrank against the weather nest; indeed, almost cowered there, her face held close to the sideboards. There was nothing I could say to her. It had been made plain to us that we had lost the battle; and this much more: that five old friends were gone, unless all signs failed. Men who had stood by her for the sake of a daring heart. And the precious keel!— it would go sliding into the eternal locker and not into the melting-pots of Boston.

The Lisbon held Nora by the arm and said to me: "You saw? Her deck was under!" He flung his hand out and down in a swooping motion, by which he meant to signify her plunge.

There was new sorrow. But no blame to be taken in grief.

We knew that Ambrose and his chums were fated to die that
way. It was what they were for; what they had been seeking
all their lives. Now it had come. It was not a question of
blame or remorse. There was only pity. I hated, as she hated
with all her great strength, the final image of their descent and
surrender, their capitulation to the gale. I could see them bow
their heads, could hear old Ambrose, jovial to the last, even
in drowning. "*Salubrious, is it not, my good friend?*"

All hands soon had the news of the *Western Star's* passage.
They took it in the accustomed way: calmly and with a word
of affectionate remembrance of the lost. The passage was recounted with poorly hidden satisfaction by Billy Atkins, who
could say, without hurting the truth much: "I told you so!"
Captain LeNotre learned it, no doubt, with a similar emotion,
although he still had enough manhood left in him to keep his
face solemn. He did it with such scant grace, however, that
I said to the Lisbon, as we stood by the wheel that night: "I
wish that man would learn to blush for himself. I'm tired of
doing it for him."

The worst of our toil was over; and the *Hind* went under
a reefed mainsail. I went below once to see Nora. I went in
the hope that the sight of her might stir me to speak words of
comfort. Yet, when I met her eyes, as she lay sleepless on her
blankets, the grief in them left me without words. I reached
out and touched her hand. To this, she paid no heed. So I left
her alone.

10

THE *Golden Hind* lay on the Middle Ground (northwest of
Sable Island) when the gale blew itself out. The Atlantic became blue. Whitecaps filled the east. A blue wind came out
of the west. At once, the schooner took up her work again.
Having given the sou'wester its due, the *Hind* proceeded to
the last and final act: her attempt to save herself. By herself.
All the good habits of the Gloucester fleet came to the vessel's
aid. Cook turned out another feast of beefsteaks and doubled
the strength of the coffee. The icing on the chocolate cakes
lay thick as fudge. The men ate again and the breaking of
our fast gave us some cheer. We spoke well of the gale and
said: "A fair blow! Took us where we wanted to be."

Old hands in the oldest of all the Republic's trades, old in
her oldest sorrow (which is loss at sea), the dorymen now
turned to. The word passed: "Bait up! Bait up! He says: 'Bait
up!'" Those that hadn't gone ahead on their own tucked their
pipes away and came on deck. Once again, the frosty herring
came up by the tubful from the pens. The cutting-boards
were set up between the dory-nests and along the bulwarks.
Long, broad knives—a score of them—began the old play:
down the bait twice and thrice across. Once the heaps of bait
began to pile up, ten men quit cutting and turned to the tubs
of trawl. While their dorymates cut on, these others uncoiled

the trawls and began the rapid baiting of hooks, attached to the trawl line by shorter lines called gangins. They coiled the baited trawls back into the tubs; and those that finished first came to help me and Billy Atkins, who had the rating of greenhorns because our hands were out of practice. Sidewise sweeps of knives sent the herring-heads flying; and golden herring-eyes, full of tardy suspicion, stared from deck and scuppers. Nora turned to with shovel and broom to the green-horn job of cleaning up. She briskly heaved the scraps and heads over the side, where the gulls fed. The knives struck faster and faster until the blunt tattoo rang louder than the gay talk and the shouts to the men in the pens. The talk became gay, as it always does when the fishing draws nigh; so gay, indeed, that at times it became a chant. One of little meaning, except for the hopes of happiness thus repeated. Yet it fell short of song. No man ever sang a song for a Grand Banks harvest; and no man's ever made one. Nor will now.

Within the hour, the first cry of "Enough!" was raised and the trawl-tubs began sliding toward the dory-nests. Number One Dory had been the Corkerys'. To it, Billy Atkins and I dragged our tubs, fresh chunks of herring gleaming on the topmost coils. The other dorymen stood by the lee tackle and swung Number One up and out over the rail and held it sway-ing there while we finished the stowing of our gear: trawl-tubs, buoys, sail, oars, anchors, water-bottle, conch horns, gobsticks and gaffs. And a bag of bread, too, because this was the season when dories might be lost in the vapor and had no choice except the long row to land, with sad failure the usual portion.

Half in the dory, half out, I lay poised on the gunwale with the black key-buoy in my arms, its blackball—a flag marked

"I"—flapping in my face. And there I kept a watchful perch until . . .

"Buoy away!" The captain shouted and jerked his arm.

I tossed the buoy down into the sea. We took our places: Atkins at the oars and I at the first tub of trawl.

"Dory away!"

Number One dropped into the stream and the *Hind*, under foresail only, ambled on against the tide. I dropped over the anchor to hold our buoy in this starting-place and looked up at the captain. He held out his arm to the southward. Our dory moved off in that direction, which he had chosen because it would give us a chance to haul with the tide, a saving of labor and of straining gear.

Once away, I slipped my heaving-stick, a willow wand, into the topmost coil of trawl. I flipped it up and outward. The baited hooks began to fly and soon the first string of the mile-long trawl, with its hundreds of hooks, was slowly drifting to the bottom, fifty fathom down. When I had emptied the first tub of its trawl, I knotted the second tub's line to the heaved one and kept on. By that time, the *Hind* was growing small in the west and all her twelve dories lay at work on the set, the rowers bending back and forth, the heavers up and down. This was the old flying-set, as practiced on the *Golden Hind*. And, since it had been my first work in the fisheries when a boy, I rejoiced in it. So much so, indeed, that I could pull out a grin or two for my dorymate, who had been out of a dory ever since he got a site aboard his first dragger. Some years ago, that was.

"You making out well, Billy?" I asked.

He grunted over the oars, which he found heavy. "She's cranky—this dory is."

I've no understanding at all (even now) of the inner machinery that made me jump at this chance to cast the lead into his shallows. 'Tis a mystery to me. All I know is that, without the grace of hesitation, I shouted: "Corkery never found it so!"

Atkins jumped at my mention of the man who had once sat on that thwart, had tumbled to his death from it. I laughed at his ready fear and anger and I made up my mind that I'd try again as soon as the set was done. It wouldn't be wise to break into that! I grinned and said: "She won't be cranky once we haul a few good cod into her. And I think we will, Billy, I think we will." I paused a split second in my heaving and looked sharply at a hook hanging over my stick. "You cut bait a little fine, Billy, my boy. I'll tell you that for next time."

Atkins chose to ignore this. He said: "Tide's strong here."

"No stronger than a hundred years ago, I guess. You want me to spell you at the oars?"

"Heave away!"

Coming now to the last coil in the last tub, I knotted the trawl to the anchor line, which was fast to another black buoy, and heaved the gear over with a sign to Atkins that he should ship his oars. This done, I set up the little mast and unfurled our leg-o'-mutton sail. I brought the dory around with a steering-oar and she began her homeward run. Atkins lay down on the bottom boards to keep out of the wind, which had a bite in it.

Number One Dory, as usual, was the first to finish the set, by virtue of our head start. The others were not tardy. Soon their little sails appeared at varying distances. It was a pretty sight, long not seen by me, and now enjoyed. A few sails were old and stained yellow by sun and salt. Some were new white; and, farther off, a blue sail and a green shone, making the day a gala one, a regatta off Cape Ann. In the west, her foresail flashing, the *Golden Hind* began her turn toward the first buoy. I also steered to that buoy, which was ours. Long before I could make out Nora Doonan at the helm, I saw my bouncing keg. I tied up to it, there to await the fishing signal from the captain, to whom it was left to judge when the cod had time to finish luncheon.

While I was furling the sail, and again when I made the empty tubs ready to take in trawl, I saw a queer sort of liveliness in Atkins. It was enough! No more was needed to sharpen me than any sort of cheerfulness from Atkins, LeNotre, or Captain Parren of the *Doubloon*. They were all sharks to me; and they livened up only when there was blood in the spray. As soon as the dory was fast to the buoy, Atkins had gone back to his thwart. There he filled his pipe and puffed away. A true draggerman, he was happiest while sitting down. A little later he grunted in a pleasant, shoatish way. This pleasure was too brisk, even for such a pipe as his; and I figured out soon enough that he had seen something that I hadn't made out yet. At first, with a thrill that pierced me harshly, I guessed that the rascal had caught sight of some sign of the *Western Star's* wreck. I tried him out on this score, but I made nothing of his grunting and spitting. In the course of my thought, I struck on Parren and the *Doubloon*, and said at once: "The *Doubloon* must be dragging hereabouts by now. Parren said he'd be here."

This ordinary conjecture must have seemed like magic to the stupid Atkins. He dropped his pipe to the bottom boards and cursed in a wail. He wasn't smart enough to keep his eyes off the sea; that is, if it really was his hope to hide something from me. He shot a sideways glance to the east.

I stood up and looked in that direction. A dragger steamed there, black amidst blue and white.

"Why!" I said, "there's the top Jonah now, I do believe!" I spoke in cautious cheerfulness, lest the draggerman see that I was upset. The coming of the *Doubloon* wasn't good news to me, although I had it much in mind since Parren's farewell to us at the Doonan Wharf. I had my share of seaman's superstition and really considered Atkins as a Jonah, a source of bad luck and sorrow. And, rightly enough, I now considered the *Doubloon's* captain a sort of master Jonah, from whom much evil came. I was more than ready to make a haul on my own account. I judged that the time had come.

I must confess that, under such circumstances, I could be as mean as any man I ever heard of. I had a tongue in my head and bitter thoughts to put an edge on it. More than that, I knew my man and had turned over in my memory the savage hints that lay a-plenty in the yarn spun by the Lisbon. I, therefore, faced Atkins and blandly said: "Ever see a man hanged, Billy?" As I spoke, I ran a finger inside the collar of my sweater. A damnable gesture for a man to make. Worse, I also thrust my tongue far out and let it loll. What possessed me to play such a grim game at such a time is more than I can tell.

Billy Atkins bounced again. "Hanged? Hey? How could I? See a man hanged? Why, no! No!" The picture did some damage to him. He said "No!" again and again.

I put on a rueful look and said with a sigh: "To chuck away a man like that! Dear me!"

"Chuck a man away? Chuck who away? What the hell's wrong here, anyway?"

"Why! nothing's wrong, chum, nothing. Only I had that dream of mine last night again. About Nora Doonan's father.

(This was true.) And he was standing by a gallows—or under a yard-arm. I couldn't make it out, Billy. Not quite. And he was making that old crack of his. You know—'If they hang you, my friend, somebody's going to be hurt!' Ha! Ha!" I peered under my hand and said: "It's the *Doubloon* all right. I only hope that chump doesn't drag his bag over our trawls. If he does—I'll bust him one."

"Hang?" repeated Atkins, "hang?" His own rich stream of superstition had been muddied. He was seeking an omen. "You saw somebody under a yard-arm? That's what you say, is it?"

"Bless my soul!" I pretended surprise that my dream should interest him so much. "Bless my soul, Billy!" I held up my words with some skill, and thus made it clear that, much against my wishes, I was being forced into a revelation I'd rather not make, especially to a man on the anxious seat, where the Lisbon had put him. "Now that you ask me—and I make the effort to recall—why! yes, Billy, there was a face above the noose. Not what you'd call a pretty face. Or a happy face. No! But a face, nevertheless." I had him in a dogfish gape by this time. I put on a graver air. "Of course, a man can't be sure of a face in a dream. But—"

"Whose face in the noose? From a yard-arm? Ah, that's a pretty yarn to tell a man! And you can't remember, eh?"

"I didn't say that, Billy. Oh, I can remember all right. I just said a man can't be sure of a face seen in a dream. Say, you kiss a girl in a dream. Or she cottons up to you. Well—take my advice!—don't act too hasty on it next day." I saw that Atkins was too frightened to repeat his question; so I said in the judicious style: "You know, Billy, there's some truth in dreams after all. Because I happen to know that for crimes at sea you can be hanged."

"Me?" Atkins pushed some spittle out onto his lips with his tongue. His Adam's apple jerked sadly.

"You?" I said. "Excuse me, chum. My mistake. Excuse it, please. I used 'you' in a manner of speaking. A general sort of way. I meant a man can be hanged for crimes at sea. That's all."

"Aye!"

"As for that face, Billy, I'll tell you whose it was. Pass me your word first that you'll never breath it to a living soul."

"Aye!"

"Tell it to a ghost, Billy, if you like. Happen you meet one real soon. But not to a living soul. Hey?"

"As God is my judge—" he began loudly.

I gave him a solemn signal to stop that line. "That face, Billy, a-hanging there under the midday sun, was Parren's or" —I fumbled a bit—"or LeNotre's—or—"

He groaned aloud when I kept slowly on.

"—or, if not one of those two thieves, Billy, then—"

He slapped his hands down to the thwart to keep hold of the world.

"—then 'twas—" I, for once, didn't know what to say. I was stumped. I wished to say: "Your face, Billy boy!" but, by this time, the sweat on that narrow forehead and the patient agony in his eyes had stirred up my pity, of which I still had scanty store. I laid off. I said: "Why! it was Corkery's face! Corkery off the *Doubloon!*"

This blind shot nailed him, gaffed him. He gripped the streaming thwart with both his hands and screamed. His face lost the drawn look that his suffering had put there and it became twisted with fury. "He won't. He won't get me! I'll rip him first! Gut him!—by the God that made me!" I give you my word, his teeth were hidden in foam out of his mouth.

His next words, which were uttered in the same shrill and raspy voice, baffled me entirely. "I had nothing to do with it. I was there—oh! nothing, Captain, nothing! So help me, God!"

It was my turn to be frightened, frightened by his fear, because it was a true token of guilt, if not on his part, then on the part of others. I didn't know which way to turn. I had a notion that if I jumped on him and throttled him a while, I'd have gotten much out of him, but I couldn't resist his pitiful state. I was bent on a good-natured rescue of him, by some light word or other, when two blasts from ships' horns blew by me, the first from the east, the second from the west. Both were fishing signals. The *Doubloon* had finished its dragging and Parren had blown his horn to order his men to the winch and the bag to the top. I saw the *Doubloon* increase speed and steer sharply to leeward, which was the side she was dragging on. The *Doubloon*, having closed the mouth of the net by this twist, began to haul it up. I heard the rasp of wires and winch. I saw how taut the wire cables of the net were at the rail and I knew this meant a good bag.

Since my own captain had also blown the fishing signal, I went into the bow of our dory and put on my horsehide half-mitts, which were to keep the trawl from cutting my palms, by now too tender for the old occupation. I put my gaff handy and brought buoy and anchor in. I began to haul. The first rush of hooks were empty; a few had the bait on. I slatted the softened baits off against the side and kept passing the line back to Atkins, who stood amidships over an empty tub. He took up the line and coiled it into the tub again.

At once, I found that the *Hind's* luck had changed. My first fish was a fat cod, as fine a steaker as you could wish for. In my eagerness, I handled the fish a little roughly and the hook worked out. The cod fought off. I struck out with the gaff and nailed him in the eye. I swung it into the dory and shouted: "Luck's in! Now for full pens!"

I hauled with care and, at last, got the trawl coming up with such smoothness (the tide with me) that I slatted off fish after fish before the dogfish struck in. Like all dorymen, I hated dogfish. They are the curse of the Banks, spoilers of bait and wasters of our sweat. I never could bear just to shake them off and let them live. I kept my knife handy and slashed off nose or tail from each one as it dangled. I killed thirty of them before the run changed and some fine haddock came up.

After a few more bare hooks—and a big cod eaten to the bone by sea-lice—I felt an even harder strain below: the tug of a great halibut. The moment I saw the flat side circling deep in the green and felt again the tug of swimming dollars, I let out another whoop. This was answered from the next dory. The exulting cry swept along the line and by this I knew that all the dories were killing fish fast. I gaffed the halibut, hauled it over the gunwale and sent it thrashing down into the mass of cod and haddock piled in bloody water. I then brought five more halibut to the gurdy.

It now came Atkins' turn to haul. I had already slowed up, because a long time had passed since I had put my beef into that work and the strain was telling on me. My cheeks ran with sweat. My arms ached. Yet I was so glad to be killing fish again and piling up dollars for the *Hind's* account that I couldn't stand Atkins' clumsiness when he took over. I dropped the coiling trawl and gave him a harsh word for his poor work, which was unfair of me, I know, since the poor creature hadn't his heart in it. I drove him out of the bow and finished hauling myself. By the time the dory reached the outer buoy, it was full to overflowing. I took in the buoy and hoisted the sail. Once under way, I scanned the westward sea. Two other sails had been hoisted, but I again had the start on them and came alongside the *Hind* first of all, my sail down, my painter ready.

I flung the painter up to Nora. She gave it a turn. The cook brought our dory around with a hook and the captain handed down the pitchforks. I had kept the biggest halibut on top. I now drove the tines into it and heaved the fish into the checkers that had been set up to make pens on deck. The moment the fish struck aboard, I shouted: "One for the bank!" and then: "See your friend?"

Nora put a strain on the painter to keep the dory in. She gave one sour glance at the *Doubloon*, which was moving off to eastward, and replied: "I see him all right. And I'd rather look at this!" She turned her head toward the load of fish.

From that time on, there was no time for anything but fish. There was time to breathe. That's about all. Dory after dory came up, to one side or the other, and the forks kept the cod flying. I was delighted by the number of halibut, which were running bigger than the men had seen for a long time. Before twilight, the *Hind* had fifteen thousand pounds in the checkers. The dories were back in their nests. Their plugs were out and the pump sent streams of water up to carry off the bloodied water that poured out of the dories. Without a break in the furious rhythm of their labor, the dorymen set up the cutting tables and the keelers to carry off blood and guts and catfish heads. Rippers and gutters took their places. The dressed fish went flying back into big tubs, where the idlers (of which I was one) stirred them in the flowing salt water, washed them clean, and forked them on toward the hatch. Just as the last fish slipped down into the ice, where the Lisbon stowed, the cook called the first gang to dinner.

The *Hind* was certainly much better off, now that there was something more than bait and ice in her pens. The dorymen were in a better temper; because all their hopes for a good stock seemed justified by this rare beginning. Even the presence of the *Doubloon* failed to put them down, although a dragger is the last thing dorymen like to have around their trawls. The nearness of the vessel left its mark on one man: Captain LeNotre. I took care to keep an eye on him during the dressing of the fish, just to see how he took the turn of luck. With his usual skill at wearing masks, he did his part of the work fairly enough. However, he had fallen, bit by bit, into the listless mood that Parren always seemed to create in him. He came down to dinner with the first gang, as usual. He had hardly taken a mouthful of soup before he muttered some words into his spoon and left the forecastle.

This moody action brought on another, which, in its turn, led directly to a crisis aboard the *Hind*. Ordinarily, a captain's moods, and especially his behavior at table, are not open to comment by dorymen, despite the familiarity created by the nature of their work. In the case of LeNotre, this rule had always been followed, the more strictly because the men weren't overly fond of him. This time, the ill feeling among the men broke down the barrier of habit. A doryman seated opposite me put down his spoon and watched the captain's boots drag up the steps of the companionway. This watchful one was the oldest hand on the vessel and had once been mate on the old *Columbia*. He commanded respect, and not only because of his grey hairs. When the slide had closed, he looked about in a deliberate manner until he had forced others to look at him. He then spoke in such a way that it was plain to me that he intended to answer his own question, if no one else did.

He asked in a loud voice: "What's the matter with him now?"

Fully aware of trouble ahead, I lightly touched Nora with my elbow and, in order to make things clear, said: "What's the matter with who?"

The doryman understood this device. He replied: "The captain. Is he off his feed?"

At this, the others stopped eating. The cook paused at the end of the table, a tray aloft. Some of the men bent forward to look at the speaker. Others gazed solemnly into their plates.

The speaker went on: "Here we have a couple of pens full, at least, and it puts him off his feed." So far, his tone might have been taken for one of solicitude for a shipmate. Knowing this and not wanting it, he changed to open insolence. He said: "Maybe he doesn't like the smell of fish."

Of course, this amounted to nothing less than an accusation of the captain. Yet the doryman's words were of such a nature that they could have been laughed off easily enough. No one laughed. Consequently, Nora, as owner of the schooner, had the issue set squarely before her. She knew now that many men in the forecastle believed the captain had betrayed them and her by refusing to do his duty. She and I both understood that the story told to us by the Lisbon had been known to others of the crew. All or part, I couldn't say. Plainly, the rebel amongst them meant to declare that LeNotre had prevented them from killing fish before and was likely to do so again. This was a destruction of their livelihood and they wanted to know why. Also this: was he to be kept as captain?

Nora took up the challenge. She said: "Make your meaning clear, Clem. You're among friends."

"I know that, Cap'n Nora." He paused and then said: "A short and simple answer from a short and simple man. That's what you want and what you'll get. Here it is, Miss. Three times in the last two voyages that captain of yours has hauled up and left good fish behind him. We all know it. No man here will deny the truth of what I say." He waited. No man made a denial. "I don't know anybody who's ever been in a dory with him and I don't know too much about him otherwise. But I do know we could have brought home a hundred thousand pounds last trip. And we didn't! No! Instead of that comfort, we lose a good doryman and come home owing the vessel money again. Now what we want to know is: why?"

Nora answered at once. "I know, Clem. And I'll tell you." She gave them a smile to divide up amongst them and pushed a tray of halibut steaks toward him. "But there's no reason why we shouldn't eat just the same. Scoff it up!" They all fell to again. She said: "What I say can be repeated freely to the other gang and to the men on watch. And should be. Mind that!"

"Except," said I (as I had before), "to that foul Jonah—Billy Atkins."

"Very well." She then told them all that she knew and feared. She told them (in the Lisbon's words) that Captain LeNotre was Parren's dog and why it was so. She told them of the hundred thousand dollars offered to her for the *Hind* by the syndicate at home. She told of her refusal. At this, they murmured and became a little brighter; because they were learning again the kind of wood out of which she was carved. She told them of all the money owed to Parren and (to my surprise) made no bones about declaring that, if the trip failed, he might be able to take the vessel away from her, especially if her grandfather died without new money to settle his affairs. "It's either Parren or the West Indies. Fifteen thousand dollars' worth of fish will hold her for a while. Nothing else! I hoped that the *Western Star* and her keel would turn the trick. She's gone and that leaves it up to us."

She then spoke of the captain, which was a trial to her. She said: "As to how Captain LeNotre falls so low as to take dirty orders from a dragger captain like Parren—and takes whiskey aboard my vessel—well! I'll leave that part to those amongst you who know the Yarmouth story and some others. It's not a tale for me to foul my mouth with!" At this, she gave to the Lisbon a special look which signified that she was leaving that story to him. He nodded.

"I'll tell you this much more," said Nora. "I came along this time chiefly for the *Western Star* venture. I really didn't have the money to pay a railroad fare and I had to get Ambrose and his men here some way. I stayed aboard after we took bait because I figured out something was wrong and I thought it my duty to find out. My duty to you and to the *Hind*. Well, I've found out something and I'm going to find out more! Let's keep this in mind: there's war between us and Parren. Between the *Hind* and the *Doubloon*. And our captain—I hate to say it!—isn't on our side. Neither is Atkins. Just the same, LeNotre will remain as captain for a time, no matter what you say to me now. I want to keep an eye on him. There's more to be found out and I can't do it if he's thrown off the vessel."

Clem said: "That will be all right with us."

Nora went on talking. "I want to tell you that I know the times are changing. The Banks are changing. And markets are, too. Maybe the *Hind* must change. I don't know yet. If she does, you and I will do the changing together. I know why you stay dory fishing. Why you like it. It's your life. The old one. That's why we don't have to be ashamed of what's in our pens tonight. We're not destroying the fisheries. As that fool Parren and others from Boston are. Killing baby fish with drags for the sake of a fillet. The work can be done with a mesh that'll let the small fish go. Some draggers are ready for them now. They'll all come to it, just as the English and the Danes have. John here gave up the draggers and the big money and went back into a dory because he wouldn't destroy what Nature provides for us all. He has his ideas. You know what they are as well as I do. The five-inch mesh he has at home won't kill small fish. And it will keep the big ones. Well, if we get the money—if we beat Parren here—maybe the *Hind* will be a smart dragger, after all. I don't know. I can't tell. I haven't the final say in such matters yet. Money talks."

Old Clem said: "This is fair talk, Cap'n Nora, and useful, good talk. All here will stand by with an eye peeled. But what about the fish that are on the feed now? Do we get them tomorrow or be foxed out of them?"

She cried out: "Get them! We'll kill thirty thousand!"

I said: "On the Middle Ground this time of year—tide and wind being what they are—we'll be needing a mark-buoy, whether we like it or not. Thereby we'll not have to take any man's word as to where the fish are or where the vessel is lying."

"Go tell that to the captain," said Nora, "and see that it's done." She raised her hand then and added: "Or, better still, I'll tell him myself."

I made way for her and she went down to the cabin alone.

The captain had already given the order for the rigging of the mark-buoy. Despite the tragedy which had attended the setting of their last mark-buoy, he had seen that one was required for the Middle Ground tides. When Nora came down into the cabin, he was lying in his bunk, and Atkins was seated on the locker near him, a set of dry-cell batteries in his hands. Either he or LeNotre had picked up a lot of junk at Shelburne for just this purpose. There was a supply of old lifebelts and electric bulbs handy.

Both of them greeted her with cheerful faces. She answered by hoping that LeNotre was feeling better.

He replied: "The truth of it is, Nora, that when I fast—as I did during the blow—it takes me some time to get back on my feed. I'm all right and I'm obliged to you for your kindness." This was said so perfectly that at once she wanted to disbelieve all that she had heard of him and all that she feared now. Yet she had struck on a way that might bring her the truth and she was determined to put the matter to its test. She therefore sat down on the locker opposite them and idly stared at Atkins' clever hands over the gear. She knew he had a good reputation as a rigger of such buoys. It was the only good thing we had ever heard of him. He made them in such a way that they stayed upright and didn't sag. They stayed put over the fish, too.

She watched him, yet she lifted her eyes, now and then, to trace out the changes in the captain's face, which was always a puzzle to her and to me. He seemed to be more than usually interested in Atkins' task, and kept hustling him on with impatient words. His listless mood had departed. Some inner energy, newly stirred, made his eyes shine furiously in the lamplight. He kept running his hand through his matted hair; and, she remembered long afterward, he once laughed aloud for no reason at all.

No question but these actions forced back into her memory certain images of their past, images of which I know little, and would like to know less. Anyway, she instinctively let her eyelids fall halfway and, for a time, kept her gaze on her dirty boots. It was the nearness of a once-loved man, and the knowledge that at any moment she might be alone with him, which brought her suddenly to her feet.

Captain LeNotre delayed her smoothly. "Stay a while, Nora, please. I've something to say to you." He gave to his voice the gentility that often marked his weariness after long, fruitless voyages, a thing I'd marked in him before, especially when he was telling lies. If Nora had kept her wits about her, she might have seen that this was his old blarney. Nevertheless, it suited her needs. The schooner rolled briskly at that very moment. Before Nora could stand straight, Atkins was scurrying up the steps and LeNotre was at her side, his hands raised. In the moment that the slide closed, he put his arm around her in rough fashion and swung her toward him into a close embrace. From what little I know of this happening (there being a plain difficulty involved for me), I judge that the captain mistook her trembling for something else, which is understandable. He tried hard to kiss her mouth. This she denied to him. She thrust against him in silence with her hands. He didn't let her go. Being forewarned, she perceived that his emotion was a fraud and that he had quite another purpose than the old one of courting her. She then learned, too, the depths of her duplicity; that she, too, could pretend certain things if it meant an advantage in the defense of the *Golden Hind*. She lifted her hands to his shoulders and turned her mouth to his.

This was the signal for him. He let her go and said at once: "I'm in trouble, Nora. Awful trouble." He struck his hand against his mouth. "I'm the first skipper of this vessel that ever took whiskey aboard her. I lied to you a minute ago about being off my feed. I'm in trouble."

She backed away from the ring of lamplight in order to

clear the way for her eyes. "What is your trouble? I know you're troubled. What is it, Paul?"

"Parren!" He sent a wild glance toward the dark skylight, as if he could see the glare of the *Doubloon's* deck lamps there. "I didn't want to tell you. But—well! I'm like the *Hind* herself. Like you. I owe him money. Lots of it. And he's been putting the gaff on me for it."

"How come you to owe a man like Parren so much?" She had made a slip there; for, up until then, he had no knowledge of anything but friendliness between her and the dragger captain. He didn't notice that meaning in her words.

He replied: "I haven't earned any money aboard this vessel for a long time. You know that too well, Nora. And I needed it. Badly. Badly."

She said: "You've a reason for saying this to me, Paul. You know I haven't any money. I'd have given you some if I had any. The vessel owes you plenty. You'd have gotten it all if the *Western Star* had worked out. Why do you tell me this?"

He reached for her hands. She gave them to him, knowing well enough why a man believes the male touch can accomplish wonders. He had just such a task set before him; and, indeed, had good reason to judge that he might succeed. For we are to bear in mind that, up to this moment of their meeting, all that had been said of him hadn't been proved. Each turn and step might have been explained away, could have been put aside as accidents and 'longshore lies. He had the power to offer her all that a woman could ask: proof of love, proof that he could deliver her from endless toil and fears. He chose to offer the last thing first. He slipped his hand into his jacket and took out a long, white envelope, which had been carefully kept. He pressed it into her hand and said: "Don't open it yet, Nora. Wait!"

She let her hands fall to her side, without even a glance at the envelope.

Captain LeNotre then cried out: "Nora! There's no beating him! We cannot."

She asked: "No beating who?"

"Parren!"

This took her breath away, made her shudder for the waning of last, fond hopes. She tricked him into giving her time by repeating: "Parren!"

"Aye! that man!" He matched his tone with eyes that filled with hateful fear.

She said: "In what way beat him? Why beat him, Paul? He's my friend and my grandfather's. Tell me, what do your words really mean?"

There's credit for him in his unwillingness to answer her directly. I can't say that I ever understood his character thoroughly. Good and evil fought too even a battle in that man's soul. I believe he would have enjoyed faithfulness to a friend or to a lover. I think that it was just such a feeling for Parren, whom he should have cursed, that made him cry out desperately:

"Parren wants the *Hind*! For his own!" And: "You owe him too much! Sell her to him. He gives more than the syndicate offered." At this, he seized the envelope and tore it open. He drew out a slip of paper, stared at it, and then held it close to her eyes. She read it: Parren's draft for one hundred and twenty thousand dollars. (I am unable to say how the captain came by this draft. By this I mean that it had been made out after our departure from Gloucester and, therefore, hadn't been handed over at the hidden meeting aboard the *Doubloon*. I give the opinion that the two captains had met secretly in Yarmouth during the outfitting of the *Western Star*.)

While she gazed at the fluttering paper, he spoke again, urging her to keep it. He said exactly what the Lisbon had predicted: "Parren can't build a vessel for years and he can't buy one. They're all making too much. He's not sure of staying on the *Doubloon*. He's crazy to get the *Hind*, Nora. Give it to him. And let's clear out." His voice changed to a sweeter, plaintive one, like a small boy pleading. "Let's clear out. To the West Coast. There's halibut fishing there, Nora dear."

"No!" She struck the paper down and shouted: "Never! Do you hear? Never!" And then, having in mind her need of a deeper look into the mind struggling to overcome hers, she cried out against Parren for his deceit, his pretense of friendship.

Perhaps, after all, Captain LeNotre hadn't much hope when he began. In any event, he soon gave up and at once changed his tune. At first, he begged her to say that she would, at least, consider selling the vessel at a later time; and he spoke against me, saying that I had my own plans to capture the vessel. Hereabouts, he became wary of her gaze, which was never an easy thing to bear. Knowing her shrewdness, he hid his desperate eyes from her by turning into the shadow beyond the lamp. There he attacked her with cruel words. He accused her of sending the *Hind's* people to the risk of death in winter fishing under sail in order that she might meet the whim of her grandfather and persuade him to deed the vessel over to her, as he had done. He finished his say (and himself) by: "Worse than that, you killed five good dorymen in that crazy venture with the *Western Star*. You didn't trust me! Had you said one word of it to me—I'd have fixed it for you.

You could have gotten your money right there in Nova Scotia. Yet you told your Bannon. The fanatic!"

She stopped him with a gesture of scorn. "You are calling me the murderer of five good men! Well enough to say so now. But there may yet be something to say about the *Western Star*. Those were men on that hulk." She gave him another portion of her scorn by a stress on the word "men." "As for keeping the *Western Star* in Shelburne a moment longer than was necessary—why! you know well that the old fox would have dragged me through every court in the Dominion! Aye! and clear to the Admiralty in London. Years! Years! Oh, you're wrong there, Captain LeNotre!" She struck her hand harshly against her jacket. "I've got the papers here. And that's all there is to it. All, do you hear? I've lost my friends, the sixteen thousand dollars I hoped to make, and the five hundred I gave that filthy Bannister. But I was right in trying. Right all the time!"

Nora understood by now that her anger had taken her off her course. She got back onto it by saying in a calmer tone: "I stayed below just now because you asked me to. You started to tell me what your trouble is. You give me this news about Parren. I can take it. But the other trouble? It isn't only debt that Parren holds over your head. Is it? After all, he can't do much to you on that score. Even Parren can't get blood out of a stone. What is this other thing? It drives you to the bottle and makes you cry out in your dreams. I've heard you as I lay there without sleep."

His response, by eyes and hands flashing in his Miquelon style, was so genuine in its terror that she became convinced that he had, indeed, been led into a frightful difficulty. She became certain that there was truth in the Yarmouth story; and even believed that there were other matters of life and death which held him bound. Thereupon, she put him down forever as a weak, ruined man who could not help being her enemy. She said to herself bitterly: "He will destroy me to save himself. And he can do so!"

Since he again failed to reply in words, she lied to him once more by saying: "I don't know what the story can be. But tell me this: is that the reason why Dan Corkery hates you and Atkins and Parren? He cursed you for a murderer when he left the *Hind* at Gloucester and we thought it was because he laid the death of his brother to you. It wasn't only that. Bannister had something bad to say to you. And he knew nothing of the drowning of Corkery's brother. What's the meaning of this?"

At the word "Corkery," LeNotre's manner became savage. He shut off the blaze as soon as he could. Before he could manage himself, his hand flashed again, this time to his belt and there his shaky fingers flicked against the ivory hilt that lay there. This dirty habit of keeping a killing knife so handy had always frightened her. She shuddered in a new and piercing cold. She waited a little longer, saying good-bye to him in her heart; and then she left him there, staring at nothing.

11

I saw no great change in Nora Doonan when she came up. A new loss, which was the greatest of all, had been added to the old. Yet she gave no sign of it. Only I do remember that her face seemed colder than the moon to me; and the light beneath her lashes had dwindled to ashiness. She buttoned her reefer, gave a jerk to her cap to pull it down over her braids, then struck her hands together, and looked away from me.

The *Hind* was jogging near her mark-buoy. The month had taken a bite out of the moon. Nevertheless, it shone so brightly that we had trouble, at times, in making out the buoy. It was one star of many shining low. We stood the watch with much anxiety; because something was going on out there. She heard our baffled talk and asked the reason for it.

The other doryman replied: "It's that *Doubloon*. He's out there, dragging over our fish. Couldn't find them for himself, he couldn't."

A little earlier, I had caught a *Doubloon* light directly under the Pole Star; and tried by this to figure out his speed. I now had my reckoning done. I said: "No! He's not dragging. He's just nosing around." I lifted my hand. We saw a star blocked out by a hull. Our mark-buoy vanished. I said: "He drags at three knots. He's making eight or nine. What's he up to? He makes me nervous."

We watched the *Doubloon* sail. Her port light twinkled and then faded into a patch of vapor.

The watch said: "You're right, John. He's bearing on. There! He's coming around!"

A red light gleamed beyond; then the hull went dark. Soon a green light showed.

The doryman said to me: "Know something?"

"What?"

"I hate his guts."

"Ah! not quite that," said I.

We kept that watch for an hour or so. The watch changed again. Nora and I went below and slept several hours. Toward dawn, the *Hind's* horn woke us up. The vapor had thickened and the watch was cranking the horn to keep off passing vessels. The sun scoffed up the vapor for a while. The dories were dropped after breakfast to make the set. All had gone well during the night. The mark-buoy had served; so that the *Hind* now fished where she had such good luck the day before.

Because of the danger that the vapor might close in again and cut a dory off, the schooner picked us up after the set was made, so that we could spend our waiting time in the shelter of the vessel. She kept sailing up and down the line of buoys, now and then letting out a blast or two. We ate dinner two hours before noon. Twice during the meal our fog signals were answered by other vessels. One sounded big.

The second gang had just finished dinner when a horn called to us close at hand. It was the *Doubloon*. She fooled around beyond the hedge a bit, as if she wasn't quite sure of herself; then she came right up and her bow-watch hailed the *Hind*. The dragger slowed down. She stood there, vague in the mist. A flurry of snow slid over her house and darkened up the *Hind*. I had the helm. When I answered the hail, I heard some loud talk on the *Doubloon*. Her engine idled and she came closer. Parren himself spoke up. "That the *Golden Hind* there?"

"Aye! 'tis she!" I said to a doryman: "Tell the captain the *Doubloon* is talking to us."

Captain LeNotre came on deck. He shouted: "You the *Doubloon?*"

"Right you are the first time! Thought I'd never find you." We could hear Parren's laughter. "How you making out, Captain?"

LeNotre gave the customary and wary answer that there wasn't a fish to be had for love or money. "Killed a few here yesterday and marked them."

The sun and wind suddenly cleared up that space. I could now see Parren plain. He filled up the door of his pilot-house. He wore half a beard. He scraped something off his chin and shouted again. "That your mark-buoy I saw last night, Captain?"

"Aye! 'twas ours. We've made a set here just now. Mind you, don't drag over our trawls!"

"What an idea!" Parren showed his teeth in a grin. "I'll clear out. You still got your company aboard, Captain?"

"I have."

At the time (and even now), I could see nothing in this exchange that might be of a secret nature; that is, unless the two had agreed on some second meaning for innocent words. Nevertheless, some sort of intelligence—private, I mean—passed between them. It seemed, at a time considerably after the event, that Parren may have expected good news from his follower. Not getting it then and there, he surely understood that he had lost standing. I know this much for sure: he gave up his pretense of friendship. His next words gave me the hint.

He said: "You'll want the news. Market cod is sixteen cents. Large is eighteen. Nothing much coming into Boston. Redfish at Gloucester. Four hundred thousand pounds yesterday. And your company's kin at home ain't doing so well. So the Gloucester station says." He laughed once more and closed the door. The engine speeded up. The *Doubloon* steered westward and vanished into a new spread of vapor. Her horn began wailing out there.

None of us considered this talk much of a kindness from Parren. He usually spent a good deal of his time listening to the *Doubloon's* radio, now that the Navy had allowed their use. He bored his men to nervousness by trying to repeat the nonsense that the prophets dished up every day. And, as one of the men said, he was such a born liar that it mightn't be true about Grandfather Doonan being in poor shape. However, that was something not to be helped. Nora said nothing at all.

That same vapor now rolled in over the *Hind*. It was so thick that a double watch was set in the bow. More flurries of snow came up. The sea began kicking us around a little. Such conditions were always hard to bear. The news of steady prices at Boston didn't make waiting any easier. The Lisbon held his temper, as usual, and made light of the choppy sea; said it wouldn't come to anything. Just the same, he kept a sharp watch for the trawl buoys. When one rolled by, he brightened up considerably.

This particular action began to get on the captain's nerves. I saw this and I said to myself: "Why should it? He's going balmy on us!"

At last, he shouted to the Lisbon: "What in hell you fidgeting around for? Don't you think I know where my trawls are lying?"

He didn't wait for an answer. He went below and stayed there, after leaving word that he should be called if the weather cleared.

The Lisbon stared after him. He made no reply, of course. He didn't have enough respect for LeNotre to enter into talk with him. None of the captain's words or actions escaped the Lisbon. One thing could be said of this man: he never missed a trick. There were men aboard that vessel who might be misled by a lie or a gesture. Nobody could fool the Lisbon for long. A falter in a sentence, or an eye turned away too soon, was enough to sharpen him. His affection for Nora and her grandfather made him even keener now. He made it clear that he had snuffed up a taint. He said to the men near him: "Me—I'd put dories over now and haul. That's what I'd do!"

He spoke loud enough so all the men—and there were twenty or so on deck—could hear him. Their very presence at such a time of day showed that their rebellious mood hadn't waned much. I understood why they had gathered near the helm. They were, in a way, helpless; for we actually didn't know where our trawls were lying. Had the day been blue, they might have acted on their own. However, in such thick weather, the captain was the only man who would know exactly where the set had been made. It was his part to keep that account in his mind, to add up the miles of jogging, to take away the turns and returns along the line of buoys. He was the man who should have been standing there, ready to point into the vapor and say: "Number One Dory is there!" Other men were expected to take a kink at such idle times in order to store up strength for the labor of hauling. Even I, although acting as first officer, couldn't be expected to watch sailing so closely.

These were circumstances that Nora Doonan had never

heard of, despite all her experience and all the dory talk she had taken in. She was baffled. She kept her silence and watched us stamp up and down to beat off the chill. Often she saw the men put their heads together and say things that brought only new looks of wonderment.

At last, in her need to say something, she asked me: "Has it cleared at all, John?"

"No!"

At this, old Clem turned from the rail. He said: "It'll grow no worse. We can haul all right. We've hauled in worse than this. And for him, too. He's drowned men—he has—in a sea worse than this." He angrily asked me: "You know where them buoys lie?"

I hesitated. Nora saw me falter. She repeated his question. "Do you know, John?"

I flung out my hand. "Number Four lies there!" All their heads changed to follow. Somebody said: "That's what I thought, Johnnie." Another: "That's about it. Four or Five's there."

During this hour, which was later than noon, the *Hind* was sailing back to the beginning of the set. It wasn't long before she came to the place where I had dropped my buoy. She sailed on that course until she came around again for the trip up the line. The tail-end of a squall slapped her. In moving off, the squall breached the thickness beyond. It was another of those remarkable changes that make the Middle Ground a strange place to fish. You might have thought that one powerful ray had been set to work on the mist; because the sun swept after the squall, carved open the upper thickness, and burned a path into the southwest. Flashes of light spun off a black sea there.

I said to the watch: "Will the captain come up?"

Without a word, he turned away and went to the companionway. The slide was open. He thrust his head down, again without speaking. He swung away and shot a word to the helmsman. This was done with a derisive gesture of his hand downward; that is, toward the cabin where LeNotre stayed. He then came back to the rail and said to me: "No!" He also spat, which was his way of signifying that there was something not quite right about the captain. Something new.

I said to myself: "Sucking the bottle again. He's on the merry-go-round." No doubt about it; and full reason he had.

A man forward shouted: "Number One Buoy!"

Before I turned my eyes down, I looked deeper into the opening in the vapor. I saw the *Doubloon* at the far end. Without giving much thought to it, I marked that two of her men were on her pilot-house. They were working on a dory that she carried as a lifeboat. They were either getting ready to put it over or had just hauled up.

The same man let out a startling cry. "Hey!"

Others near me set up a cry. Loudest of all, I heard the Lisbon's voice, uttering some Portuguese phrase in a piercing tone. I couldn't catch the words. Hands went up in gestures of dismay and anger. Out of the jumble, I heard old Clem cry: "It is! It is! Don't tell me, chum!" He struck at my arm furiously. "Your own buoy, Johnnie! Running free!"

I gave the buoy one glance and turned from the rail. I shouted: "Atkins! Atkins!" A doryman pushed him toward me. He half-stumbled. I brought him up with my hand. I meant him no harm. His expression was horrified. His eyes fixed me with a fear that plainly told he expected a blow that would kill him.

I shouted: "To the dory! Over with it!" He gasped, then ran smartly forward.

To myself I said: "To the devil with that captain!" and then aloud: "Dories away! All! All! Get them over!" To Nora I said: "Take the helm until cook gets up!" I shook her roughly because she seemed on the point of imploring me for some word.

She wasn't the one to be handled so freely. She grasped my arm and demanded: "What's wrong, John? What's happened now?"

I had no time for her. I struck her hand away roughly. "You'll find out soon enough, my girl. Get that man to his dory!"

She ran to the wheel. The helmsman stepped away, shouting his question: "What say? What say, Jack?"

Nora put her hands on the spokes and cried out: "Call the captain! Go to your dory!"

The helmsman pushed back the slide and sent the alarm down. In his furious words, which rang fore and aft, he summed up his knowledge that a new disaster had befallen the *Hind* and his belief that the captain was the source of it. He didn't use the word "captain." He shouted: "LeNotre. Tumble up, —— —— you! Lively now!"

The men at the tackle dropped off my dory. Crouched in the bow with my gaff in hand, I bade Atkins put his beef to the oars. The dory jumped across the widening space of clear water and bore down on the buoy. The buoy was acting in an odd way. Its blackball dipped into the sea. The buoy itself whirled freely and tipped. I knew what the story must be, even before I actually saw it. I struck at the buoy with my gaff, brought it up and lunged to seize it. I swung the keg out of the water and held it clear, so that the water from it dripped upon my face. Silent now, I held it aloft, held it in a solemn pose because the buoy had become to me a symbol of all the hard luck and evil that followed the *Golden Hind*. The trawl line had been cut. It hadn't merely parted. Hadn't chafed and worn away. It had been cut.

"Cut!" I tossed the word onto the wind; and the wind blew it back to me, blew it into my mouth again and it knocked me down over that black keg.

"Hey?" cried Atkins from his thwart. "Hey?"

I let the buoy fall and stared at the severed line. I fumbled at the yarn where the knife in an enemy's hand had sliced deftly through. "Cut!" I said.

"Hey?" cried Atkins over his shoulder. "What's that you say?"

I looked at him and then I looked away. The vapor had drifted off. The sea lay clear. I saw the *Hind* sailing up the line. The last dories were dropping off. Soon the clamor of conch horns blew over the water. Horns weeping and raging and cursing. Men's voices mingled with the accents of the horns; and these voices sang out the end of the *Hind*. By these complaining horns and the cries of the dorymen, I knew that every trawl had been cut, that the last of our gear had been ripped from her. All her miles of trawl were gone, all the thousands of Norway hooks, all our hopeful labor. I heard the Lisbon's sweet-toned horn bewailing and the hoarser strain of old Clem's horn, each telling the same tale. I reached for my own conch and blew into it, cupping it in my hands. I filled my cheeks and blew clamorous, grieving notes to tell them that my story was like their own.

It was in vain to try for a rescue. The job had been done thoroughly. By now, the current had washed the trawls far to the southward, where the *Doubloon* lay; and the fish that had taken our baits drifted away to useless death. Yet, for the sake of the *Golden Hind* and the unfortunate girl at her helm,

I turned to my dorymate and said: "You bloody Jonah! row! Let me see your sweat! If you've such a decent thing in you."

I found the outer buoy. It, too, had been severed from the trawl and from its anchor. I drew it into the dory and sat down.

Atkins rowed back into the path of the schooner. Soon the *Hind* turned against the long light of the afternoon and came down the line, picking the dories out of the stream as she came. I stood amongst my shipmates again. I gave one look at Nora Doonan and turned away. No man spoke. There was no need of words. They knew well enough that there was scarcely a full tub of new trawl left on the schooner, and little of the old. They knew, too, the burden of debt that Nora had undertaken to fit out for this last voyage.

Yes, it was the *Hind's* last. All aboard knew it. It was left for the Lisbon to make the gesture of surrender, the signal that our hardy struggle had come to its end, that we could all go below now and sleep, while the *Hind* sailed home to Gloucester, never to come out again as her own self. In his right hand the Lisbon held his gaff, a stout one he had made many years before at his own forge. The barb gleamed in the evening light. His rusty hand shone like bronze where it gripped the wood, yellow and much-scarred. There was no counting the cod it had struck, the halibut hauled from the green. Nor the dollars earned and mouths fed. No other thing could be a better symbol of the pitiless conflict between the new and the old, between the men who killed fish with hooks and the men who swept them into cod-ends.

The Lisbon raised the gaff high above his head. He sent his eyes a-roving among our people. To each pair of eyes, as his encountered them, he gave a glance of pity. To Nora, gazing at him while she swayed to the *Hind's* going, he gave a look of tenderness, mixed with his despair. It was only when his eyes met Atkins' stare that their light changed. And when he looked at Captain LeNotre, sagging half-drunk by the wheel, all tenderness and despair vanished before his anger. His lips moved in a Portuguese phrase. Curse or prayer, I couldn't tell which. He jerked his arm. The gaff whirled, flew over the sea, and vanished into a pool of foam.

12

THE *Doubloon* came on. She sailed at dragging speed, her towing wires cutting the water on this side of her slight wake. At that distance, I could scarcely make out her crew of eight or nine. All of them were on deck, except the old hand off the *Hind*, Daniel Corkery. Two men were standing at the starboard gallows. Two others were at the winch, ready to release the brakes and throw in the clutch when the dragging was finished. The wire-steerers, crowbars in hand, stood by the 'midship gear to guide the heavy cables onto the drums in even windings.

Soon the men in her pilot-house could be made out dimly behind the panes. They steered straight toward us, and made a handsome sight. Yet, despite her glitter and spankiness and the twilight glow in which she brightly moved, that vessel threw a long shadow before her, a shadow to be seen by men's hearts. There was no good in her, one way or the other. There wasn't a man aboard the *Hind* who didn't know that the blow against them had been struck by the men who now came up. No word was uttered on the *Hind's* deck, even when Parren himself came out of his house and lifted his glasses to look at us.

I stirred uneasily in my place. I could feel the impact of those changed eyes, could imagine the thoughts that must now be rolling through that mind. He had accomplished all that he had set out to do; and had done it in so cruel and cunning a manner that he could escape all punishment. Only once in my life had I ever heard of a raid against a schooner's trawls; and that had been long, long ago in my grandfather's youth. A feud between brother and brother, the Barbers of evil memory.

Captain Parren's face became clear. He hung his glasses up. I hated that face; hated, even more, the thought of seeing triumph shine on it. I looked among our own people. I found LeNotre and Atkins together: Atkins whispering, LeNotre trying to listen. The dorymen had now drawn away from the Jonah. It was hard to say what our people were waiting for. Surely they were full of spleen and their hearts wild for the want of something to curse to hell and back again. Every man there, clinging to the rail or to the standing gear, had a new life and a doubtful one before him now. The elders would be on the beach for good; companions to the unwanted. Others must find a strange row to hoe. All had lost their sea-home; a few had lost their only one, there being some men aboard who hadn't slept off the *Hind* for years. Had they all burst into moans, I wouldn't have wondered greatly. Yet there they stood like men of bronze or yellow brass. So she stood in her yellow oil clothing, her long legs straddled, her hands clasped behind her back, her eyes glowering. No need to ponder on her thought!

Even the jeers that now came our way failed to stir us.

Captain Parren came down from the pilot-house step and stood at the rail. He raised a hand to his mouth and brayed across the water: "How things going, boys?"

His men laughed. One clanked his steering-bar. Without facing his Boston rogues, Parren jovially chided them out of the corner of his mouth. To us he again cried: "You boys lost anything? Your tongues maybe?" He roared at this sally and beat both hands gaily against his slicker.

The *Doubloon* surged a length nearer. I could now take note of the slightest changes in their expressions. There was nothing much to hope for there. Birds of a feather flock together and go together to sea. One face among them turned to us with a compassionate look. This was Dan Corkery, the doryman who had once cursed LeNotre solemnly and had made an oath of revenge. Corkery had been sewing on the *Doubloon's* starboard net, laid in thick folds along the rail for use when the port gear ripped. He had kept himself aloof, as if he knew what shame his old shipmates had to undergo. I was shocked by the change that had come over him since the day (not far gone) when, grieving for his lost brother, he had stepped off our own vessel and had boarded her enemy's. He was even gaunter. His cheeks had been thin before. Now they were drawn in. Since he hadn't shaved in that time, he seemed more like a mad creature than ever. Only his eyes showed real life. They burned in sockets the color of coal.

Captain Parren wasn't done with us. "Catfish took your tongue, Cap'n Nora?" He made this inquiry in a lively, boyish tone, surprising from such jowls.

Nora Doonan wasn't man enough to take this. She spat.

Her action delighted Parren. He whispered an aside and, without really breaking off his attention, looked down at his towing wires. They were taut again. The cod-end had taken all that it could. He nodded over his shoulder to his helmsman. The horn blew. Her bow swung sharply toward the *Hind*. The men at the brakes pushed, the winch howled and began to grind the cables in. The dragger leaned a little toward the net, which was rising heavily.

Parren now singled out Billy Atkins. He ignored our captain, pretended he didn't even see him. He said: "How you, Billy? Billy boy, you talked yourself back into a dory, didn't you? You sorry now, chum?"

Atkins wanted to break the silence of the *Hind*. He looked slyly about, wet his lips, opened them a little, and then thought better of it.

This amused Parren. He said in mock aggrievement: "Why, Billy, don't you like us any more? You lose something, too, Billy?" He put his hands together on his front and let his belly shake heartily. "Billy, can't you teach those greenhorns how to fish? Better bring them all aboard and we'll show them how to make some real money."

His men standing forward, ready to take up the doors of the drag, which were emerging, laughed and beat their icy mitts together. Parren glanced at them. "Or better still," he shouted, "maybe we could fix the old *Hind* up a bit and all go aboard her, eh?" At this hint of her fate, his manner changed abruptly to a black one. He spat over his rail.

The doors crashed into the gallows. The space of water between the vessels flattened, grew dark, and began to bubble, as if some monster were rising from the slime. The winch squealed and stopped. A vast stirring took place. This under-sea working caught all eyes. The men of the *Doubloon* put on hungry stares. So did Parren. He chewed at his lips. Our people watched in silence. Atkins even dared, in the growing excitement, to move nearer to the rail. Laced bubbles swam up in circles and burst into reddish froth. And, at last, the *Doubloon's* net sprang loudly out of the sea, a vast hump. Bigger than a bull whale, and wallowing like one, the cod-end came heaving up. Rosy brooks flowed off it. Amidst cries of gulls and a rustling of crushed fins, the bag burst into the twilight. Bound in the long curves of its mesh, thousands of fish, great and small, struggled in a gleaming mass. Blood and foam and guts oozed out of the narrow mesh. Green and beautiful, a shark writhed against the twine, his ivory belly gleaming brightest of all. Hundreds of young cod, too small to take a baited hook, had been swept up in the mesh and now fought, with gasping mouths, to work their way out. A curious squeaking noise, rather kittenish in character, came out of the slaughter. This was a familiar sound to me: the bursting of bladders.

The *Doubloon* men roared with joy for an easy harvest and a big one. They had earned as much in that hour-and-a-half of dragging as we had earned in all our hard sailing. They had done little for it, except to sew up rips and heave the net over. They cheered themselves nobly and bellowed fresh insults to our people, saying: "How you like it, dorymen?" and worse.

The *Hind's* people gave no answer. Half-sprawled over the rail, I kept my mouth shut, too, and closely watched the slaughter of baby fish that took place before my eyes. It was a matter of great meaning to me; that is, I was a student of such matters. I was, after a fashion, still in the employ of scientists who had the fisheries close to heart. I stayed cold enough, yet I hated that dragger as much as ever I hated anything.

The bag heaved higher. Sharks came slanting up out of the green to feed nimbly on fish that twisted out of the mesh. Gulls came down; then rose shrieking at the sight of sharks' bellies flashing white as they curled to bite and swallow.

I saw an odd thing at this moment. A good-sized halibut came up out of the water when the bag heaved. The fish lay on the outside of the mesh. I had hardly taken note of this when the cod-end rolled higher and many other fish—halibut and cod—came into sight, lashing their tails and struggling.

I shouted: "The trawls!"

My chums made the discovery before I had the word well out. They cried out: "Our gear!" and raised their fists and voices against the *Doubloon*. For the *Doubloon's* net, now fully up, bore an extraordinary outer burden. This burden was the *Hind's* own gear and the *Hind's* own harvest. Strung along the edges of the mound, three or four trawls lay tangled and twisted. It was clear to me what had happened. The cod-end, dragging along the bottom, had struck the drifting trawls; and bare hooks had caught in the mesh. Haddock and cod and catfish by the hundreds lay in the long, looped vines of cord. Fish were there by the penful.

Nora Doonan shouted: "The dories! Take the gear away from him!"

The men turned, stared at her, then ran forward in a stumbling rush.

It was no use. Captain Parren laughed louder than ever. He leaned backward against the pilot-house and let his head roll in laughter. He swung his hand in a signal. The winch started and the bag, bearing both harvests, began swimming slowly toward the *Doubloon's* hoisting gear.

Parren made a trumpet of his hands and shouted: "Hey! you boys lose something in the vapor?" His "ha! ha!" drove us into a frenzy; and brought about one of those petty accidents that can drive a mass of men into violent action. Old Clem, turning in despair from the dory-nests, ran full tilt into Billy Atkins. This touching of the Jonah set the old man afire. He clapped both hands on Atkins' shoulders and stared into his face. I've no doubt that Clem meant nothing more than a harsh word. Or, at the worst, a blow; for he knew Atkins' part in earlier events. A second doryman, seeing this, laid hands on Atkins. Thus, for me, a queer tableau to remember long. Such it seemed, because nothing moved. No hand. Nothing. Only the seamed faces stared under brims at the dragger-man; and he, so quickly taken, had no time to change his look. 'Twas empty of fear and of surprise. Yet, before one could speak to another by voice and say: "Do this!" their hearts spoke and they lifted him clear. They staggered aft a step or two away from the fore rigging and, with a loud cry, hurled him into the water.

Atkins screamed in his headlong flight. He screamed again when he struck the sea. He vanished in a welter, rose striking to the top, and, impelled by his terror of icy drowning, flailed with both his hands. He was no swimmer. Nevertheless, he pushed along toward the bag. He clawed against it. His first grasp closed on a fish head, which broke off. He tried again. This time his fingers hooked the mesh. He began to struggle up the mound of writhing cod. His knees sank deep. He lay there for a moment and held his head clear to suck in air. He climbed again, digging his boot-heels into the bulge.

The *Hind's* men shouted curses after him and threats, saying that they'd rip and gut him for a Jonah if ever they laid hands on him.

The draggermen returned both curses and threats. They urged Atkins on. "Hang on, Billy! Take it easy, old-timer!" Parren, raging up and down his deck, shouted to the winch-men. They braked the cable. The bag rode slower, rose higher. Atkins was safe. Stretched out on the hump, hardly daring to move lest he slip down, he lifted his head and spewed forth a good portion of the vile stuff that was in it. He gave Nora a few names that were new to her. For the dorymen, he laid out an astonishing variety of curses. He had travelled considerably in his time. And certain of his jumbled words gave us reason to believe that he had known beforehand of the raids against our trawls.

They took him aboard the *Doubloon;* and tenderly patted his shoulders, looked at his hands. And in silence they hauled the bag up to the rail and made ready to hoist it inboard. It was so big that they had to split it with a rope; that is, take half over at a time. Other men unravelled the *Hind's* trawls. They slatted off all our fine fish and flung them into the pile that now poured out of the net, hoisted high in the gallows.

13

The *Doubloon* turned on her deck lamps for the dressing of fish. She drifted on the tide. So did the *Golden Hind*. It seemed strange to me that Parren didn't put his net over. When I spoke of this to Nora and the Lisbon, they said that Parren had some news now from Atkins. Had much that was puzzling to think about, especially LeNotre's curious position aboard the schooner. I could see that Parren might judge our captain to be an ally of dubious worth.

Nora said: "Parren won't leave us be. Mark my words! Nor am I through with him yet."

There was no wind. The sea became a flat. I could see no reason why the *Hind* shouldn't go home when there was wind enough. There was nothing for her to do. I had overhauled the fishing gear. Even with every odd and end scraped together, there wasn't much that could be rigged.

I gave this opinion to her. She listened to it, then replied harshly: "No! Wind or not, I'll watch this tramp a while. I've my own ideas."

"You're entitled to them," said I. "But what are they?"

She gave me a short answer; something to the effect that when she was ready she'd tell me. She turned to the Lisbon and said: "Tell the men to break out every torch we have. Light them if the *Doubloon* puts her lights out."

The Lisbon went about this business. The *Hind* carried the old-fashioned kerosene torches, which were long handles with reservoirs of oil to supply cloth wicks. These were used for baiting up before dawn and for dressing fish after nightfall. I should have been pleased to know why she was calling for them at this time. However, I had enough of short answers for the day.

The first gang went down to supper. Captain LeNotre kept to his bunk. He was either far gone in drink or pretending so. He made no response to the few words that had to be said to him by the watch. Nor did he take notice when we came down and turned in.

She fell into an uneasy sleep, raided by dreams of her failures and her uncertain fate. I watched her lying there. Once I heard her speak out of her dreams. ("Why, Oh, why, Grandfather?") A little later, she got out of her bunk and turned the lamp wick down to dull its glare. The cabin was hard to breathe in. She closed the stove draft and opened the companionway slide an inch to freshen the air. She closed her eyes again and, at last, fell into a sounder sleep. I also slept.

A while later, a hand reached into my own dreams. I awoke. The watch was standing by my bunk. He had already awakened Nora, who was pulling on her boots and talking to herself.

"What s the story?" I rolled out and he handed me a boot. He jerked his hand toward the captain's bunk. Not long before, LeNotre had been lying there, dead to the world. When I now looked, I saw that the bunk was empty.

I asked: "Where is he?"

The watch replied: "He came on deck and said he was going into the galley for a mug-up. Said he didn't eat any supper. I saw him go forward and below. The next thing I knew he was sneaking aft again. He didn't take a mug-up, Miss Nora. He went to lee side and got to work on a dory. And that's where he is now. Trying to get it over."

"Is he drunk?"

"No, John. Sober as a judge."

We followed him to the deck. I said to the watch: "See if he's off the vessel. Don't lay hands on him." I had a certain knife in mind.

The watch returned and, in considerable excitement, reported that LeNotre had put the dory over and was rowing away from both vessels; that is, to the northward.

We all went forward. At first, nothing could be made out. Soon I caught the gleam of an oar; a moment later, the dory showed up, slowly passing away from the *Hind*. This certainly was a frightening action on the captain's part. Often enough, he had revealed an uncontrollable temper. On one or two occasions, he had been guilty of such deeds of temper that more than one man had declared him fit for the looney-bin. He had the name of a man able to hold his liquor. Just the same, he hadn't carried his load that day with much success.

The doryman said out of the sour corner of his mouth: "He'll wind up in Fortune Bay. At that rate. Or inside an icicle. Well, good riddance to bad rubbish! Better off without him."

"It's not as easy as that, chum," I said.

Nora hauled herself into the swifters. A wash of light out of the moon gave us then a new glimpse of the dory. We saw the blond head turn to look ahead; and the oars strike in good style.

"Bad as he is," she said, "we can't let him do that."

"I can!" The doryman showed his bitterness. But not his wit.

I had other thoughts. "That's not the story."

She asked: "Then what is it? What's he up to now?"

I didn't like the sound of her "now"; it had that toneless-
ness which was part of her when she was actually taken up
with a hard piece of thinking. "Wait a while." I said this and
stood back.

The dory had vanished. I crossed to the windward rail,
where I could see the *Doubloon*. Her deck lamps were blazing.
She had made a short and circling drag and now lay about as
before, not much farther than a cable length. I set my eyes on
the farther rim of the glow in which she lay. I saw LeNotre's
dory pass beyond the *Doubloon's* bow and run in. The *Doubloon* came between me and LeNotre. Soon after I made sure
that it was his yellow hair I saw. It was touched by a frosty
dew.

I noted the stir caused on the *Doubloon* by his arrival. Two
men left their work amidships. One took his painter; the other
gave him a hand. LeNotre fell awkwardly over the rail and
crossed to the pilot-house. Its door opened. A man at the
washing-tubs also went to the pilot-house. I added up the
sum, which gave the following: Atkins and Parren and LeNotre were together again; and urgent need had called them. I
took a while more for my thinking. It was certain that the
hope of gain drew the thieves together. I couldn't figure out
what that gain might be. Slow work on my part, as you will
see. No question but the gain would be the *Hind's* loss. Yet,
what had she to lose? What else was there for the *Hind* to
give over? Nothing! I made up the opinion that LeNotre and
Atkins wished to tell Parren about the loss of the *Western
Star*. He would find satisfaction in the news, just as they had
been satisfied when the hulk drove by. This wasn't the whole
pattern. Something was missing from the picture.

I crossed the deck and said to Nora Doonan: "He's gone aboard the *Doubloon*. I saw him plain."

"Ah, John!"

"That's the story. He's in her pilot-house this minute."

This made the watch jumpy. I said to him: "Best for you to turn out a few more men. Keep a double watch forward and aft. Don't let anybody come aboard this vessel. Not even the captain, unless he comes alone."

The watch went below.

Nora said: "What's your thinking been like?"

"I'm up a tree."

"What more can they do to us?"

Her plaintiveness stirred me. I touched her hand and answered: "That's exactly what I was just asking myself. What have they got to talk about? There's a pattern in it. But I can't work it out." I paused and then added deliberately: "Not from here, I can't."

She took up the hint and added hers: "Parren's got Atkins back. He's still got our Dan Corkery."

I said to myself: "Why beat about the bush?" Aloud: "That's so. Yet it's to be kept in mind that Dan Corkery cursed LeNotre and wouldn't go on the *Hind* with him." This was no obstacle at all to the action she had in mind. It wasn't meant to be. All I wanted was for her to agree and keep her short answers to herself.

"Just the same," she said, "things change. Men change. Maybe Dan Corkery has. He went onto the *Doubloon* because Parren lent us Atkins. Now Corkery's a hated man aboard her. More than ever—now that those two are there. He's got something on them all. Yes! I'm sure of one thing and it's this: if they had a chance—they'd get rid of him! Kill him, if they could frame a likely accident." I heard her take a sharp breath; and I understood that, despite all she had seen and heard, it was a pain for her to speak a thought like that. Naturally, it was. She stuck to it and added: "There's more reason for such a fear now. Because Corkery knows all they've done to us today. And before today."

I struck my hands together. "I tell you, I'd like to get aboard that *Doubloon* for a few minutes. I'm going to knock Parren's head off when I meet him, anyway, and I wouldn't mind busting him up right before his men." This seemed like a leaf out of the boaster's book. Well, I know dog Brag—nobody likes him; and I'd have piped a gentler tune if it was dorymen I meant to face. The fact is that I knew every man aboard the dragger; and there wasn't one who could stand up to it for five minutes.

She said nothing against my notion; and for a good reason, shown by a later action on her part. All she said was: "His men! There's a trouble for you, Captain!"

"Crowd of pick-up bums. They'd think twice before they looked my way."

"Ah!" She came an inch or two nearer and gave me her shrewd look, as if she knew of more than one possible reason for my words, and wished to size me up. "Just the same, it'll do no harm to hold a hard hand over them. Wait here."

I knew what man she had in mind. Little I cared for him.

She went down into the cabin by herself and pulled out a drawer built into the locker under the captain's bunk. Several old charts were there and, under them, a brass-bound box, its key in the lock. She opened it. An old revolver lay there, shining on a fold of cloth. She hadn't seen it for a long time. It had never been used. Her father used to take it out twice a year to touch it with oil. She put it into her pocket and came up. Clem and the Lisbon had been turned out. They had swung over a dory.

She showed the revolver to me. "You take this."

I answered: "I'll have nothing to do with such truck!" I went to the rail and said: "Clem and Terry will put me aboard her and stand by. I'll go into her port gear and they'll never be the wiser. Until I show myself to take Corkery off. He'll come with me, Dan will."

I jumped to the rail. She held up her hand to me; and it seemed to me that she wished to make it a friendly grasp. When my hand closed on her fingers, she gripped hard and pulled herself up. The men murmured against her intention. I wasn't even surprised. She had some curious way of getting a man ready to accept her decisions. I can't tell how. Well, she was cleverer than most people thought.

She swung over the dory gunwale and said: "Let her drop, Clem. It's my business that's being done and I'll be on hand. Or it won't be done at all. I know more of this than all of you put together. Besides, I'm a smoother worker than this lad here. Him and his fists!" She settled on the thwart and there cried out: "And whether you like it or not, I'm going to ask Parren for something!"

"For what?"

"My trawls. The dog's got four of them. Maybe five. We've the makings of another tub. Perhaps more. We've all our bait left. Well, why not? Rig for halibut and take a chance."

"For halibut?" Old Clem looked down at her in astonishment. His reason: there hadn't been a good stock of halibut taken to Gloucester since the *Laura* went away. And she killed hers on the Grand Bank itself, farther than we were ready to go, in my opinion.

"Aye! Where Ambrose last killed them. On Misaine. Now, let's go! And say no more about my not going!"

The dory went down. I knocked the strap away after Clem and the Lisbon had secured the tackle and joined us. We rowed away in the darkness and made a wide sweep of it so that the dory glided up to the *Doubloon's* weather rail without being seen. The lee net was coming in and no man on the *Doubloon* had eyes for anything else.

I crawled over the rail and took shelter in the idle net. Its long folds hid me, but I could see the *Doubloon's* men clearly through the mesh. I was not uneasy. I saw Atkins at work by the main hatch, a pitchfork in his hands, his back turned to me. Dan Corkery stood a jump away from Atkins. The first thing that struck me hard, there in the glare of deck lamps, was the expression on Corkery's face. He seemed like a man standing in a nightmare. He was alive, yet not alive. Parren and LeNotre were in the pilot-house. I could just make them out in the half-light there.

The last bag had been dressed and put down. Now the new set came up. The horn blew, the winch rolled. The net came up and swam gushing to the side. The gallows-men reached out to sway it over. It seemed a good set, although smaller than the one I'd watched from the *Hind*. The men brought it inboard, shouting their signals to the winch. One of them crept under the bulging cod-end to pull the slip-rope. He jerked hard and sprang away. The mottled bullskin (Holstein, I guess) of the cod-end burst open; the avalanche of fish poured upon the deck.

I groaned in the old anger. My word for it! there were fifty thousand fish in that spreading pile. If not more. And they were all baby cod. I couldn't count a score of good-sized fish in the set, except for two or three wonderful halibut that had been feeding on the school, and the usual shark, thrashing with a young cod nabbed in his jaws. Most of the young fish were dead already, crushed by the weight of the catch and the cod-end's great pressure. It was plain that Parren had been deliberately raiding the nursery ground. Yet even he hadn't bargained for a haul like that. The fish were too small for any use. Had they been left to grow a year, they'd have doubled in size and left billions more in spawn behind them. Now they were squandered. I myself had once killed like that by accident on George's. It had made me sick; and the old sickness now tormented my belly.

I heard, above the noises of dying fish and sea, a roar of anger from the pilot-house. A bullish burst that sounded clear above the clatter of gear and oaths from the draggermen. Parren swung down the step and went into his act. He cursed the fish and the Atlantic that made them. He cursed his own luck and aimed a blow at Atkins, who deftly stepped away from it with a yell and a curse that astonished me. A madhouse.

Captain Parren then ordered the men to open the big scuppers. Through these, the dead and dying fish were broomed and forked. This wasn't fast enough for him. He picked up the hose and, still damning what he called his luck, he turned the stream onto the fish. Soon the deck was clear and the bag went down again.

Atkins had some shame left in him. Why it could be, I can't imagine. The blow and abuse left him in a queer, yammering condition. Hysterical is the word. Like his master, he had to take it out on an unfortunate. This was our Corkery. The doryman had slipped on the fish scales and muck while they were pushing the net back over the rail. Atkins may have become excited, in a murderous sort of way, by the physical position that Corkery was in at the time. Corkery had sprawled, just as if he had been struck down. He lay almost on his back, trying to get a purchase with his boot.

He was like that when Atkins screeched some words at him. I don't know what they were. No doubt of their badness. They must have been like barbs, especially to a man who had been taking a lot of abuse aboard that vessel. I saw Corkery twist his head toward Atkins and I could easily tell, by its fierceness (the teeth being bared and the eyes glaring) that he wasn't going to take any more of it.

Corkery uttered one word in reply. I couldn't hear it because of the clattering of the cables grinding forward to the gallows. Yet the shape of his mouth told me the word. It was the old one: "Murderer!" That poor man was obsessed with that awful word, as his heart had been beset by the act.

I did hear Atkins' answer. He repeated Corkery's word in a high-pitched voice that quavered off into another screech. He said this much more: "You pick-up dory bum! Murdered your own brother to save your skin!"

Corkery heaved himself to his feet. He hadn't taken his eyes off Atkins in that rising. His face had now become the face of a man who intends to kill another. Having seen this twice in my life, I'd better not try to say what it's like. His stare was so fierce that Atkins raised his pitchfork and cried out over it, either in warning or in horror. I could never tell afterwards whether Atkins really meant to attack Corkery. It made no difference. The sea and his unset thighs settled the matter. More than once, as the work had gone on, the men near the rail had shouted against freakish seas that rolled out of the dark and came in over the rail. No harm in them if you knew they were coming. Now, at this moment of Atkins' dangerous poise, such a roller hit the *Doubloon*. It shook the vessel and sent Atkins plunging forward, the bloody tines gleaming in front of him. On his face, I saw a look of surprise. An odd thing to say, but it's true. He seemed annoyed at finding himself under way.

My unwise and useless impulse to run between the two men was beaten down by a stronger instinct: to save myself from the boarding sea. It could drown me fast enough. I reached for a stay and clung to it. I bent backward to shout to Nora and her dorymen. The sea buried the deck and struck against my hips. In leaning sideways, my head turned again, and my glance took in the pilot-house. I saw Captain LeNotre and Captain Parren staring through the same pane. Jaw to jaw, they were; their eyes were fixed on Atkins and Corkery.

Such a small measure of time had passed that Atkins' charge had hardly gone forward a stride. He was committed to it. He kicked out his right leg to try for balance. He lost and fell onward, thrusting the fork directly at Corkery's heart.

Corkery had no time to stand aside. He couldn't avoid the blow. He bent his head back and flung up his hands in an awkward, fending motion. A tine pierced the palm of his left hand. He screamed. He then fought for his life. He pressed the pierced hand upward and thus saved his heart from a mortal stab. He closed the pierced hand on the fork and jerked Atkins toward him.

Atkins had to yield. The violence of his plunge carried him into Corkery's grasp. Atkins tried to twist away. He let go of the fork. Yet he couldn't escape. Corkery screamed again, this time not as a man might, but as a bleeding animal. He struck with his right fist, struck a blow so hard that Atkins' jaw broke under it. His body fell halfway in a graceful motion. At this, Corkery struck again. This second blow knocked Atkins onto the grinding cables.

He died in the next instant. Perhaps he may have been dead already from the blows. The cables finished him. His boots became fouled in a link of one cable. His grasping hands or part of his oil clothing were caught by the other cable. Both wires whirled him over and over against a set of steel braces near the main hatch. The cables crushed him there; the steel ate him up.

This happened so quickly that the winch-men, who rarely had occasion to check the cables when they were running out, were unable to act. They weren't anywhere near the winch when the terrible screaming began. As a matter of fact, both of the winch-men said later that they were at the rail watching the lay of the cables as the net sank down. This was their duty; because the doors of the net must fall properly in order to keep the mouth open.

Neither did I have time to think or act. I had hardly pushed the folds of the net to one side before all the deck lamps went out. This blinded me. I blinked hard. At that moment, I felt the net beside me stir heavily. I turned and stretched out my hand and called her name. I said: "I can't see! I can't see!"

She took her place beside me.

I said: "Atkins dead!"

For a time, I was unable to see. It was a passing blindness that made much trouble for me later. But I couldn't see after that bright glare went off.

It wasn't so with Nora Doonan. Having come out of the darkness in which the *Hind's* dory lay, she had full use of her eyes. She saw the opening of the pilot-house door. A cry of anguish came from that door. She cried out, too, cried loudly so that she might be heard above the shouts and oaths of the crew, who, like myself, had been left in darkness, their sight baffled. She said to me: "Parren! He struck the captain!"

Another boarding sea ran its course over the dragger. A man at the gallows shouted: "Lights! Oh, Captain, the lights! A man crushed here!"

My sight returned. The first thing I made out was far away on the *Hind*. A light, as golden and as beautiful as her name, rose on her deck. She bloomed in the night. Bars of golden light shot against her sails and into the dark around her. This was in obedience to the owner's order concerning the torches, yet to me it seemed a curiously timed gesture of defiance, as if the *Hind* were determined to stay in the light, where she had always lived and where her beauty belonged.

The next thing I saw (that Nora saw also) was Captain LeNotre rising out of the whirl of foam amidships. In the dark, his yellow head and yellow slicker marked his steps. He fell across the braked wires and rose again. For an instant, he crouched near the stupefied Corkery, who had jerked the tine out of his hand and stood staring at his own blood. A brook of foam, full of light, shot in a creamy slant from the starboard gallows and spilled against the main hatch, which was open. A brightness came out of that foam, such as phosphorescence might provide. It was this light that showed us clearly (aye! beyond all doubt!) the blow struck against Corkery by Paul LeNotre. I saw the sleeve of his slicker shine in a backward sweep. I saw his bare hand gleam and I saw the glitter of blade and ivory handle. The knife-hand swept over and struck hard.

Corkery leaped into the air, arching his back against the stab. Life ran out of him. Yet he didn't seem able to fall. He danced lamely against the roll and pitch of the *Doubloon*.

LeNotre's hand came away empty. He stepped back, his empty hands held before him in a groping, crazy way. I remember well that he clenched and unclenched his knife-hand;

and once he actually peeked into it, as if something good was held within the curl of fingers.

The same man in the darkness forward: "Lights! Say, Captain, let's have the lights, will you? Man hurt here. Oh, my God!"

At that appeal, one of his chums uttered a warning. An even greater sea had spun up in that same freakish style of the Middle Ground. Its clamor drowned all outcries and stopped all action. I shouted to Nora: "Stay here! Hang on!"

I took a step out of my shelter. The threat of the onrushing sea blocked me again. I moved backward and stretched my hand sideways until it struck against the stay. I'd swiftly judged the force of the fresh sea. It was too much to stand up in.

It was then that I saw the sea pick up Corkery's body, even before it had well fallen, and swing it clear of the tackle. The sea caught Captain LeNotre in the open. Dead man and living man came hurtling toward the main rigging. I braced myself strongly, my hips against the rail and a foot thrust into a gallows plate. I thrust my arms into the pour of water and closed both hands on the first body that I found. A flying boot struck me hard on the jaw. I forced the body down into the scupper and, my own head smothered in foam, waited.

The sea passed. The body that I had saved wrestled with me; then the living man cursed and struggled to his feet. In the gloom, he spewed out salt, and then, with the greatest coolness, he stared into my face and asked:

"What in hell's name are you doing off your vessel?"

I can say that this was certainly the high hand. Here was a man saved from death. Beyond doubt; because that sea would have driven him breathless down into the icy water. Here was a man whose hands had just been washed clean of another's blood. And yet, in these extraordinary circumstances, he didn't step outside his character of captain. I should have given him the boot.

Is it to be wondered at that LeNotre's steadiness of mind frightened me? There's no denying it. My heart grew weak under my ribs; as any decent man's heart may do when he stands in the presence of a calm murderer. This weakness flowed directly from my sudden understanding that a murderer can be stopped only by murder; that you had to kill if you wished to stay in a game like this. A crack on the jaw for a sneak was about the best I'd ever done. Such child's play counted for nothing now. I knew, and Nora also knew, that LeNotre would now hang. We were also aware that he would fight hard and craftily to keep himself free. A hard and crafty opposition was our only course. We both understood this need; and began in time.

I gave her whitened face a quick and warning touch with my hand and began the new game with a show of natural indignation. I said: "Keep a civil tongue in your head, will you, Captain? Are you sick? You must be drunk! Is that the way to talk to a man who's just saved your life?" I didn't wait for him to speak. I gave him time to see Nora plain and then I said: "Nora and I came over to ask you to bring back our trawls. That's all, Captain. The watch said you'd gone over to the *Doubloon* and we came after you soon as we could. What's the matter with you?"

Nora moved in the darkness. LeNotre changed his stand in order to face her. He was, of course, trying to figure out the precise moment of our arrival, so that he might determine what we had seen.

Nora perceived this to be so. Therefore, when he said: "Trawls?" she answered harshly: "Yes, our trawls. All of them. And we've also come for Corkery. Atkins can't come aboard my schooner again. We're thinking of trying to rig for halibut. And if we do, we'll need a doryman. That's Corkery. He'll do what I say."

"Corkery?" This was a thoughtful venture on his part.

"You heard me, Captain! Parren has no need of him. Now that Atkins is back."

"Atkins is dead." He swayed slightly and held his hand toward the place where I had last seen Atkins' body lying entangled and a man bending over it.

Nora hadn't seen that death. Neither had she heard my words concerning it. Therefore, her outcry was thoroughly genuine and convincing. I did the best I could. This helped LeNotre in his course. I could understand the keenness of relief that struck him.

The lights flashed on.

The three of us now stood in the clear. Each could see the other's face. The deceptions that had to be practiced, so swiftly and smoothly, also had to withstand skilled scrutiny, not only from LeNotre, but from Parren, who now came toward us.

Enough time had passed to permit both the captains to recover from the first desperate strain. The result of their recovery was an almost sickening fear of themselves. I saw this clearly in their eyes and by their bitten lips. Actually, there was a flow of blood from LeNotre's mouth. Even if their deeds passed without witness, they had to bear new and old burdens of guilt. And I knew that in each man those burdens were made almost unbearable by other burdens of superstition. It was plain to us that both our enemies had the wind up badly. Their nervousness made them doubly dangerous.

Nora cried out again. "That poor, crazy Atkins! What happened to him?" She stepped away from the rail and once more gave a cry, this time to the three men who were bending over the body. Shrewdly enough, I noticed that they were not touching that broken sack of bones in its ripped oil clothing.

She asked: "Is he really dead?"

The draggermen acted in an odd way. They all faced her. Their mouths were tight with an undeniable terror. I knew it: the Jonah terror. Without saying a word to her, they hurried to the companionway and went down into the forecastle, pushing one another with frantic hands to get out of sight.

It was now Parren's turn to satisfy himself that neither she nor I had witnessed the murder of Corkery. This was an anxiety that LeNotre had already discerned in him. So our captain shook his head in the gloomy style and said: "They—they've come for Corkery, Captain. As I did."

"Corkery!" Captain Parren deftly snatched up the lie. He repeated the name with mournful gentleness. He was keen enough to do that much, yet not quite smart enough to conceal his relief in Nora's apparent ignorance. He drew his hand over his face, as if dazed. "Haven't you told them, Captain?"

I said to myself: "What an actor we have here!"

I then put in my oar again. "Aye! 'Tis Corkery we want. And our trawls." I flung my hand out toward the four deep coils of trawl lying on the deck. One of the draggermen had lashed them to ringbolts.

"Why do you say that, Captain Parren?" asked **Nora**. "What are you up to now? Haven't you done enough to us? What is it that Captain LeNotre has to tell us about Corkery? Where is he? Is he sick? Has—has he killed himself?"

Captain Parren bowed his head in solemn grief. "Corkery is

dead, too." He held his hand to windward. "He killed himself! Yes, Miss Nora. In madness, he did so. He struck poor Billy down and sent him to his death in the towing wires. He yelled out something about his poor brother and—God rest his soul! —he jumped over the rail. He's dead." He struck lightly at his eyes, which were actually bright with tears. "Maybe he's better off!"

Nora let her head droop. She drew closer to me. I sorrowfully repeated: "Poor Dan Corkery! Poor Dan!"

We were aware now that we had only one thing to do: get safely off the *Doubloon* and onto the *Hind's* deck again. This wouldn't be easy. If either of the murderers, standing before us with watchful eyes, caught the slightest hint that the noose might yet be his fate, anything might be expected. It was I who struck upon a likely course. It was, to me, the most reasonable one: that is, to pick a fight with somebody.

I stood away from Nora and said: "Dan Corkery's gone! The same way his brother went. Well, he'd have never been happy on this earth until the day of his death and if a man can't live happy he might as well be dead."

"True! True for you, John." Parren said this in preacher style: eyes upturned to the glowing mist, hands near to joining.

"Too bad," I said, "that a man like that couldn't have Christian burial. But he feeds the salt! Like his brother. And there's an end to him." I took a step that brought me eye to eye with Parren. "Captain Parren!"

"Yes, John?" said the preacher sweetly.

"I make no bones about it! The first time you come ashore at Gloucester or at Boston Fish Pier, I'm going to give you the worst going-over that you ever thought of. And you've thought of plenty!"

Captain LeNotre stepped into it. "Are you mate aboard my vessel? Or what?"

Parren hastily comforted LeNotre with an upraised hand. With his speaking eyes, he quoted a verse from Job, and said: "John's a good boy, Paul. Over-young for his ideas, but a good boy. A good boy. He's been under a bad strain, you know. Losing the *Western Star* and all that money first. And then the trawls and now his chance to use his wonderful big-mesh nets on the *Hind*. Too bad!" He waggled his booming head and said to Nora: "You can see, Miss Doonan, that after what happened today, I can't run the risk any longer. I—well! I must present my bills against the *Hind* when we get home. I'm sure you see why. Plenty of money for you, just the same. Ah, never fear!" He spoke again to LeNotre: "Don't blame poor John. Let him speak his piece."

Nora laughed in his face; and her laugh was a sneer.

"I'm coming to that," said I. "That mate business." I turned again to Parren and tapped him firmly on the top button of his slicker. "Don't you worry about the strain I've been under! 'Tis nothing to the strain you're putting on yourself, Parren. I know you're captain of this vessel and that my own captain is standing here, too. Just the same, those are my owner's trawls and she's told me to get them. Which is her right. Now I'm going to take them to the dory. You make a move against it and you get it right where you're standing!"

"That's a pretty way to talk, Captain Bannon," said Parren in his bland style. "On an unhappy vessel where two good men have died only a little while ago. But if that's the way you want it—you can have it." He faced LeNotre. "Captain, I haven't any idea whose trawls those are. Lots of trawls part this time o' year on the Middle Ground. I saw them first when the bag came up. That I swear. My Bible oath. Do you want those trawls for your own use, Captain LeNotre?"

"I do."

"I give them to you. Gladly." He gave to me a sad, sweet smile. "I'll have my men help you, John, as soon as we get rid of—that is—well! poor Billy can't lie there on deck. I've no room for him in my pens. There's work to be done." He froze the pious mask of his face. "Burial at sea. He'd want it that way, don't you think?"

I answered roughly: "Put the Jonah on ice, if you want to." I grew careless. I saw that we had deceived Parren and LeNotre for the time being. I paid little attention to them. However, I gave them something to think about by saying to Nora: "Tell the Lisbon to come aboard and help with those trawls. Tell Clem to shorten up on that painter."

I walked over to the first coil. I lifted a gangin and its hook to the loop of deck lights. "Norway hooks! 'Tis our gear, all right." I ran my fingers over a gangin knot. "My own trawl."

Captain Parren shouted to the men huddled in the lee of the pilot-house. Without noticing that they made no response, he strode to the forecastle companionway and shouted again: "Below there! Tumble up and lend a hand on this poor man! Cook, a sack of coals! Buck, a blanket off poor Atkins' bunk!" He then spoke to Nora in his mourning style. " 'Tis a doryman's death and a doryman's burial. After all, that's what poor Billy was at heart—a doryman." He waved his hand grandly at the black and heaving sea beyond the *Doubloon's* circle of light. "A sailor's burial, Cap'n Nora! And Christian, too!"

He began to make me sick.

After a delay, during which much talk had gone on in the forecastle and galley, the *Doubloon's* cook and several men came up. They were empty-handed. Other draggermen, five in all, drifted forward. They shied from the body in such a way that Captain Parren was able to read their thought without hearing their words.

He spoke sternly. "Cook, you heard me ask for a sack of coals?"

The cook shivered; because it was cold and for another reason. He was a skinny, little citizen. The chatter of his teeth shook him to his heels. His chums glowered at him, shuffled uneasily. He was obviously their sea lawyer. At last, in a piddling tone, he said: "No coal for a Jonah! 'Twould curse my stove. We ain't called upon to touch no Jonah. Boys here won't sew up no Jonah, Captain." He then consulted his fear of a bully skipper and added meekly: "If you please, Captain."

One of the others spoke up in a bolder strain. "Cook's right, Captain. Besides, he ain't our man, Billy ain't. He's a *Hind* man. Signed on regular, he was. On the *Hind* and must be accounted for by the *Hind*." He nodded his head toward the *Hind*, which was falling behind as the *Doubloon* steamed on with her dragging. "Let them bury him, Captain."

By this time, both Parren and LeNotre were in a new fury, which wasn't to be wondered at, considering the deadly meaning Atkins had for them. Even in death, he was keeper of their secrets and heartily they wished him where Corkery, that other keeper, was: a-rolling in the tide, where the cod-end slid. Yet they themselves were so full of fear and guilt that they couldn't turn their own hands to the job of burial, a task which a decent man would gladly do. They couldn't even bear to look wholesomely at that jumbled face staring at their boots.

Parren soon had enough of this delay and near-mutiny. He shook his head in mock regret and said: "I didn't think of that, boys. Give you my word! Sure he was a *Hind* man and

the *Hind* must care for him. Give him the last honors, so to
speak. Christian burial. Why not? Sure!" He then spoke
directly and suavely to Captain LeNotre. "Paul, you agree
with us, don't you?"

LeNotre pressed back an oath. He glanced wildly from one
set face to another in order to test their firmness. He looked
at Nora, found her flint-hard. He whirled around and shouted
to me and to the Lisbon, who had finished carrying the trawls
to the dory. "Get a move on, you two, and put this into your
dory! Dump it in!"

The Lisbon had figured out what the course of the talk
had been. I myself couldn't strike on a proper action. The
Lisbon knew exactly what he should do; because he had a
profound feeling for decent action. Without paying LeNotre
the slightest heed, he took Nora by the arm and said: "You
come now, dear. We go back to our vessel." This certainly
was wholesome, and natural, too, for a Portuguese, who will
not allow a woman to undergo an unseemly experience if he
can help it; for the reason that he is concerned with the
woman chiefly as a childbearer and, therefore, wishes her to
live in peace and keep her memory unfouled. "You come
now, dear!"

I rejoiced.

Nora obeyed him without hesitation, just as she might have
obeyed her father in his wisdom.

I took a few steps by her side and said: "I'll come back with
the captain, Nora. Keep an eye peeled for us."

She swung her boots over the rail. There she whispered:
"He's captain no more. Get him back on the *Hind*—then he's
through." She slid down into the dory.

14

I RETURNED TO the place where Atkins lay in his blood. I said
to Captain Parren: "Do I understand that your men refuse to
put him over? Just that? Or do they also refuse to have him
buried off this vessel? If it's all right with your men, Captain,
I'll sew him up in his blanket and let him go. I've tipped a
death-board for a Jonah before now and I'll do it again."

"No, by God!" LeNotre said this. The added strain of this
pother over a wretched cadaver, and the stirring of secret
fears drove him into a frenzy. He cursed hard and long,
stamped his boots, and cursed himself so terribly that the
draggermen drew off a pace. I think a wiser man than I
(Parren, for instance) might have seen that Paul LeNotre had
no wish to live much longer, if life was still to be what it had
been up to now. He seemed like a man possessed. He was. I'll
say that, although I'm no lover of myths. He gave himself
the lash, raved with a violence that made me draw off, too, in
fear of a crazier action. In stepping away, my boot struck
against the fork that Atkins had driven through Corkery's
hand. I looked down at it. I recall that I saw, with displeasure,
that the tines hadn't been washed.

Captain LeNotre howled at the sight of the bloodied tines.
He sprang forward and seized the fork. He then committed
a frightful deed, which is matched in the records of the fleet

only by the events on the Schooner *Ilena* after the Ram Island Wreck, where an insane skipper did exactly the same thing. It is my opinion that LeNotre meant to do it; that he was looking for a fork when I kicked that one with my boot.

Before any hand could strike him down or block his way, he swung the fork back, lunged forward and drove the tines deep into Atkins' body. He bellowed in an inhuman way and, in a skilled sweep of arms and thighs together, heaved the body to the rail. The body bent and dangled. LeNotre heaved again. The corpse vaulted into the brilliant sea, arms outspread, ruined face beseeching. LeNotre sent a curse after the body and sent the fork after his blasphemy.

I can recall nothing more; because this last indignity to a man, even such a man, made me sick. World sick.

The next thing I remember was a cry of: "God have mercy on us!"

The cook's tardy piety, bleated in a quaver, rattled the men. They stumbled away. One began wailing with his arms flung up. Another draggerman, whose head had been lately shaved down to baldness, ran to the rail and uttered a series of low cries, or phrases, either to the sea or to the body or to some god or other. A dory-length away from him, LeNotre half-fell against the rail. He also cried out, a pitiful sound. As before (that is, when he had lost his ivory knife) he held his hands out, stared briefly at them in wonderment, and then reeled toward the pilot-house.

Parren had words of scorn and hate ready: "There's whis-key there!" He then gave me a primary lesson in hardihood. He put on a smile of sadness, took it briskly off and at once became the draggerman again. "That's that!" He raised his hand. The helmsman blew the horn and the *Doubloon* steered toward the *Hind*, whose splendor filled the night to leeward.

She was under way; and I longed to be on her sweet deck again and sailing hard for our chance at the halibut on Misaine. Yet Parren's qualities made me resolve that I'd not rile him again; not until I faced him on land.

Parren walked calmly to the winch, threw out the clutch, released the brakes. The cables began to grind inboard. He left the winch and came to me. "Cowards, Captain Bannon! One and all! I was glad to see how you behaved. Fine! Wasn't poor Billy dead? And gone? This Jonah talk! Ah!" He spat. "Your captain's the worst of all. He worries me at times. But think nothing of it, lad. Think nothing of it. There's fish to be hauled. Why not? That's all there is to it. Work! Sure!"

I said: "I'll take him back to the *Hind*, Captain. He's in need of care and we've got to go fishing."

"Right! The moment the bag's in, my boy." He loudened his voice. "Wire-steerers! Tony! Buck! Tumble up now!"

One man came up.

"Ah, Tony! That's the good boy!" Parren gave him a taste of geniality. Rare and short rations, though. "Where's your chum?"

"He's sick."

"Poor fellow! Shouldn't have shaved his head." Parren spoke in the same breath to me; and used the same oil. "John, I know you don't like me and you don't like my style of fishing. But do me a favor, will you?"

"Yes!" I was so eager to get off that cursed vessel with the captain that I'd have done anything within reason. "Yes, I will, Captain."

He said: " 'Tis nothing! Just watch that bag for me. Pull her knot when she comes in, eh?"

I answered: "All right. But get that man into his dory, will you? Drunk or sober, get him in." While I spoke, I looked toward the pilot-house. There I saw LeNotre's face; even saw the muscles of it working in a jerky motion.

"Presently! Presently, my boy!" Parren examined his cables and the good strain on them. This cheered him. His love of the easy dollar cheered him, even then.

Another man came forward with a crowbar and took over a wire. Two more went to the gallows.

The bag burst through the lighted waves. It was a good one. Yet nobody gave a cheer for it. The studded doors clattered against the hull and slambanged into the gallows. The bag followed. It hoisted poorly and almost got out of hand because the men were so stricken that they wouldn't shout the usual signals. Had odd ideas, I guess, as to who might answer.

I bent down and crept under the cod-end, which was a job I'd done lots of times. I had some difficulty in finding the slip-rope, which had been poorly knotted. No doubt by Corkery. I gave it a jerk. It didn't slip. I took another purchase on it and put such a strain there that the knot parted violently. I lost balance and sprawled. I shouted a warning, then: "Help! Help!"

The sea of fish smothered my cry. I went down under the blow, my knees cracking against her plates. I tried to cry out again. Slime and blood and salt choked my tongue. I fought hard to stay on my knees. I let my head go down so that my arms might protect my mouth. The vast weight—tons of fish—pressed against me and under me. I felt the frantic blows of big cod, heard the uproar and the whispers of their dying. I heaved my shoulders against that writhing mass.

Twice the fall of fish defeated me. I then joined my hands over my head and drove them up to divide the flow. My third try did it. I sucked in air and pushed forward an inch. By this time, the cod-end had loosed most of the catch. The force upon me grew less. I shouted again and tried once more to go ahead. I guess I was as strong as any man in the fleet, yet this was a job that sapped me quickly. I had to go on my knees and heave from that position. I couldn't get the fish away, couldn't stay down. There, in one last effort, I thrust out my hands to break through to the mesh, where I could breathe free. I can remember well that, while I fought, my stifling heart cried out: "How I have been tricked!" It was to Parren and LeNotre I laid this fate. A wild thought. Wild!

Anger and loathing at such a death roused me up. I struck out savagely with my hands. At one and the same instant, both hands closed on a man's throat, stiffly straining against me in the suffocating dark. Certain now that I'd been hood-winked by men who meant to murder me and make the murder seem an accident, I laid my hands on that windpipe. I put all that I had left in me to press the strangle. Nothing yielded. The neck didn't bend. The man did not cry out. Nor did he fight. I roared at him. He gave me no answer. I felt a hand fumbling at my chest. The cod slipped away suddenly. Free of that burden, I drove my attack forward in a lunge. Not until I had beaten that silent thing down upon the deck, not until I lay sprawled upon it, did I understand that I had fought against a dead man.

"The Jonah!" This from a voice far away. Mine? I don't know.

In the hurly-burly of my outward fall, this shaking knowledge stayed my hands. Once I'd filled my mouth with air, I began to think again. I spat out the salt and gulped. I pulled my right hand away from the unyielding flesh, drew the hand swiftly down the nape, searching with fingers outspread. My fingers stopped on the hilt of a knife. I put all my strength into the wrenching draw. I pulled the knife clear of the wound, pitched away, roared for help. I slid the knife under my jacket and lay upon it; for I knew that knife, could feel the turned ivory of its gargoyle head. I knew I had the one thing that would hang both LeNotre and Parren. The two things: the dead man and the knife that had made him dead.

"The Jonah! The Jonah!" I heard the shouts of frightened draggermen. In that blaze of light and wonderful flow of fresh air, I struggled to my knees and dashed the slime and scales from my filthy head. I saw men running. Another man cursed and wailed: "He's back in the bag! Oh, by Christ! we're done for now!"

I rolled over and crawled away from Corkery's body. When I had gained the shelter of the forecastle hatchway, I thrust LeNotre's knife into my boot and tucked the trouser-end over it. I then staggered out into the rift of fish and flung up my hands. "'Tis Corkery! Corkery washed overboard! No Jonah! Ah, no!"

Parren and LeNotre came together from the pilot-house. LeNotre had been at the bottle. Yet he had balance enough left in him to shout: "Atkins? Atkins?"

Captain Parren cried: "What's that you say, Bannon?"

"Corkery! 'Tis Dan Corkery! Washed overboard and into the bag. What in blue hell is the matter with you, Parren? Haven't ye ever dragged up a dead man before?"

The word that then passed from Parren to LeNotre was a short one. And a savage one, uttered in freedom because the draggermen had fled. Even without actually hearing it, I knew the order that Parren had given to his dog. He had told LeNotre that the wide bag had taken from the sea a thing that nets had taken before: a dead man. A thing from which the cod fled; that the salt should clean and destroy. This time there was a difference. There lay a dead man with their knife and their knife-wound in his back. And a hangman's noose in his hands for them. Hands that were frozen in a gesture of supplication; and yet had mortal power.

Weak beyond all saying, I nevertheless realized that I couldn't withstand one blow. Had I taken the *Hind's* revolver from Nora, had it been lying in my pocket instead of in hers, I'd have killed Parren and LeNotre before they took another step. (And this is the time and the place and the dreadful circumstances I had in mind when I said at the beginning: "I did not kill Captain LeNotre, but I would have done so . . .") Guile was my only resource. My clearing brain shouted a warning to me: "You're alone here, chum! Alone!"

I fell back toward the forecastle and bent down. I filled my hot lungs again and shouted: "Tumble up! Below! Below! Lively now! Cook! a mug of coffee!"

An answer circled up dolefully. "What say? What say?"

"All hands! All hands! Lively now!" I looked to Parren.

The two captains had reached the body. Its face, barren of all that had once made the thing a man, stopped them there, and by its ghostly force enthralled them, chilled their hearts as its own heart had been chilled by death and the wintry deep. The half-open mouth accused them, offered up an indictment that they must answer. And there could only be one answer to this unuttered cry of "murder!" That answer was the same word, the same act.

LeNotre came around the body. Parren stepped over it. Their hands clenched and unclenched. Each face showed yellow under its brim; eyes round as coins and brighter. Mouths open also, to take in air for hearts awake to daring.

I said quietly: "I'm all right. All I want is a mug of coffee to get the taste out of my mouth. I slipped. Why in hell don't you teach those bums how to knot a slip-rope?" I sagged and let my right hand fall to my boot and I said to myself: "I'll rip LeNotre and gut the other one! One more step and I'll take them."

They didn't take the step.

In time, the *Doubloon's* cook came teetering out of the companionway, a pitcher of coffee in one hand and a mug slung on his little finger. He said: "You call for coffee, Captain?"

He saw dead Corkery and squealed, hunched up like a doll of a man. He took half a step backward. I caught him by the arm and roared in laughter. I snatched the pitcher out of his hand and kicked him briskly on the behind. " 'Tis nothing, you lousy greenhorn! 'Tis only poor Dan Corkery. Go take a look at him!"

Another draggerman came up. I laughed again in my relief and joy; for I knew these to be cowards, men of base ignorance. I said: "It's not the Jonah come back. Only poor Corkery. Washed overboard, he was. Throw something over that face or it'll drive you all mad."

I poured a mug of coffee and dumped it into my mouth, shook the hot drink back and forth and spewed it. I poured another and let it wash down. Did it again and my belly began again to sing out in the old strain. I stepped forward, filled the mug once more, and held it out to Captain LeNotre. "Drink up, Paul! It'll do you good."

LeNotre didn't have a knot left in him. His heart was out. He had fallen into that queer listlessness. Deeper this time, a trance. He said something in a toneless voice, a dead voice. Like a child bidden by his father, he drank. It's incredible, yet it's true, that it almost broke my heart to watch him swallow! Why? Ah, who can tell? I hated and feared him, yet that plain, natural act of drinking, there on the cursed deck, filled me with a pity so powerful that I had to turn my eyes away from him.

I then took the mug and handed it and the pitcher to the cook. I turned back to the body. A grey blanket flapped out and then settled over it. I said loudly: "Well, here's one drowned man who won't rest easy until he has the old earth over him. He'll not feed the salt." I bent over and heaved the body to my shoulder. There it lay like a man of ice. "One man who'll get what he wants—Christian burial!" I gazed at Parren over the blowing blanket. "Poor, drowned Corkery!" I let this repeated lie give them what present comfort there was in it. I then added: "I came here for him alive. I take him home dead. This here is my old friend, my father's dorymate. I'll kill the man who stands in my way!"

I swung around toward the rail, where the painter of LeNotre's dory was fast to the chains. I said gently: "Come along, Captain. Come along home and take a good kink."

LeNotre stumbled after me. "Why!" he said in a meek and sleepy voice, "I do need a sleep at that. Yes, I do. That is, if I—if I can—" He stumbled forward.

Captain Parren held out his arm. But LeNotre, unseeing and beyond all caring, pitched past that barrier. Pitched past? Aye! he did so. Yet I take it that it was neither drink nor weakness that made him take his steps. What decision had he made in thus turning from Parren? Rich and strong and wise Parren? Did Captain LeNotre know, even then, whither he was bound? I choose to think so.

15

BEFORE I had taken ten strokes on the oars, the *Doubloon's* deck went dark.

A sea lifted the dory, rolled away; and she pitched into a trough so deep that, for a little while, I had nothing but darkness to live in. I swung hard and drove up. I saw the sea break over the dragger and hide her. Before I ran deep again, I made out her port light. It pierced the spray; and seemed a bloodshot eye searching for me. Thus far I had gone in my fancy— to think that of a light! The dragger was under way, and following me toward the golden pool in which the *Hind* sailed. It was no surprise to me that Captain Parren should pursue me. I knew that the body under the thwarts could only be a lodestone to his heart. No matter what other course he might wish to steer, the true needle in his heart must point him in the *Hind's* wake to follow her relentlessly; because the *Hind* could not only enrich him now: she could also rob him of his very breath, once the body of Corkery was aboard her and safe in a guarded pen. To Parren, and to the man slouched in the stern-sheets, the knife in Corkery's back was a mortal tell-tale. I made up this opinion: that Parren now pursued me in order to stay with the *Hind* until the captain could strike upon an action that would free him. That action had already been chosen by Captain LeNotre.

I lifted the stroke a peg. The dragger's lights rose and fell steadily on my course. I rowed without speaking to the captain. At times, I thought he had fallen asleep. He kept the same pose: his bare, carroty head hanging forward, his hands slack between his knees. I sang out to him once, fearing he might be cold. He made no answer. I took little for granted, and kept his knife handy in my boot; for I'd had all I could take of his artfulness, his treachery. And didn't put it past him to attack me then and there, kill me, and pull the dory plug, thus washing all away.

I drove the dory through a tide rip, which sent up a dewy curl of light. This increase showed me a change in the captain. His eyes were open. The light gave to one of them a moonstone hue. He seemed to be staring directly at me.

I spoke up in a cheerful tone; having become, by now, a liar of some skill. I said: "Feeling O. K., Captain?"

His reply startled me. "Vessel on fire!"

I glanced hastily, warily, over my shoulder. I saw the yellow blaze heaving to the northward. At first, the flames seemed miles away. I turned again to take a leeward look, where there was less spray. The fire was much nearer than I had first judged. As I gazed, the blaze divided into two parts, then into three and four; and each became smaller, candlelike, except that they moved onward lightly, making a dance of it such as fireflies make in the gloom under apple trees.

I said to myself: "He's far gone to say 'Vessel on fire!'" And to him: "No, Captain. It's no fire. They're at work on the *Hind*, rigging trawl again. And she's bearing down. Soon we'll be aboard. Soon you'll sleep."

To this, he said nothing. His head sagged once more.

I changed course to answer the sweet rush of the *Hind* toward me. My longing for her deck grew to a pain. The green light of the *Doubloon* swung up and down, where she changed also. I soon made out the *Hind* in full. All her torches were going. Their long handles held the flames high, so that a shower of light filled her deck and flowed over her bow. The sea shimmered there, and turned, at last, into a moon-glade, through which she glided handsomely.

I gave her a hail. "Ahoy the *Hind!* A dory! Dory!"

She was too far off. I waited until I could make out the men bending over their trawl tubs and wielding gangin boards. I hailed again. This time, the bow-watch answered. I saw him run by the gleaming jib. I heard his loud "Wur-oo-oo!"

I came up to leeward of her and flung my painter into the silent throng at her rail. I heard one calling to Nora Doonan. She came to the rail. A doryman put a strain on the painter; another drew in the stern with a hook.

I said: "Give the captain a hand, chum."

My words cast a slowness into their actions. There was a standstill. What had they expected? I don't know.

I said in a sharper tone: "Look lively there!"

LeNotre rose and tried to go up by himself. I heard Nora say a word. A pair of hands reached down and drew the captain up. He sprawled on the rail, looking downward, as if his head were too heavy for him. He said nothing; only swung in and went down the deck.

I slipped the hooks into the dory-straps and waved the dory up. I jumped out and, with no word concerning my other passenger, guided the dory to the nest. It was top dory, of course. I climbed into it again and there fumbled about a bit, in a pretense of tending gear. Pulling the plug, maybe. I looked down at the staring throng, eyeballs straining and gleaming, bronze and brassy flashes coming off their jaws in the torch-light. They expected something.

The watch aloft yelled: "Wu-wu-ree-ee!" and: "Dragger coming up! Hey, below! On deck! On deck!"

So set were they in expectation that they kept their gaze on me. Here and there I saw a lip lift up and teeth shine for hate and anger. The man aloft shouted, this time with much indignation: "Dragger, I say! Is that well? Is that well?"

I turned my face upward and cried: "Oh, aye! 'Tis well!" And to those below the nest I said: "He follows us, just the same." I heard men in the outer rank murmur: "Follows us! Follows us!" And all shifted in uneasiness and wonderment.

Not wishing that they should know, right then, what had befallen me and what a strange haul I bore, I sent them back to their trawls by saying: "You, Clem! You, Terry! Stand by here." The grey man and the Lisbon came out of the ranks; and the others fell backward to their tubs.

I beckoned to the two and to Nora and called them to my side. I pointed to Corkery's body and said: "I've another passenger under the thwarts. The body of Dan Corkery!"

"What's that you say, John Bannon?" Her words came up on a sigh.

The Lisbon crossed himself.

Old Clem said: "Eh, my lad? What's that you say, Johnnie?"

" 'Tis so!" I told them all that had happened to me on the *Doubloon*, and when I spoke of the fish near drowning me, they stretched out their hands. Aye! and when I told them how I had strangled the dead, she bowed in anguish, tho' it was the least terrible of all the deeds she must hear. Surely, no doryman ever recounted a stranger and sadder tale to his mates. A tragic tale, and one that set up a stir in souls, as it did, on first telling, in my own; so that I could hardly credit my own words. Because foreboding gave forewarning to them and to me, making their looks of horror change to looks of beseech-ment, sent from one pair of swimming eyes to another, thence to mine.

The Lisbon cried: "Holy Virgin! the law! the law! Lest he run us under!"

Old Clem said: "Out all lights, Johnnie! Drive for Tor Bay! Rockets for the law to stand by."

I hadn't the will to pay them heed. No! nor hardly the strength to listen at all, because of my weariness. This she saw and closed her hand over mine, clenched on a thole-pin. I gazed at her; and found her almost unknown to me. Hard to remember then that I had once considered her mouth a beauty of my world; because the way we'd gone had racked it until all sweetness fled. She had grown old, gaunt, and a smear of torch oil lay across her cheek, like a disfiguring birthmark. The visored cap, pulled down over her braids, made her seem like a young sea captain, worn beyond youthful strength by running before a gale in a sea not known. Nevertheless, the torchlight, flowing in waves of splendor a-down the foresail, revealed her purposeful eyes, made them shine golden under curled lashes, left them beautiful. Before she spoke, her eyes told me the story: that she hadn't flung down her gaff. No, nor her gobstick, either.

The helmsman cried: "Hard alee! Hard alee!"

"Hard alee!"

"Hard alee!"

And: "Topmastmen! Topmastmen!"

"Ha! Ha!" and: "Gorry! he'll punish her. Lively now, chum!"

"Topsails?" I said. "Topsails on a night like this?" I looked aloft to measure the clouds blowing past the stars.

"Leave be, lad! Leave be!"

I turned and fixed upon the Pole Star, toward which we sped; and at this turn away from light a shadow fell upon my face; or some portion of my inner dark shadowed me. For I had murder in my heart again; and lost my little joy thereby. Which she, in her wisdom, perceived; and we were joined, she and I, in that hour as we had not been since three seasons past.

The *Hind* had been sailing to windward. Now the helmsman brought her up and shouted. The dorymen answered loudly and they hauled. Booms and sails crossed in turn. The *Hind* fell onto the new tack and lifted her pace.

Amidst the cracking and clanking of sails and gear, I heard Nora cry out to us: "No!"

So I said: "No! A-fishing we must go"; and I pulled the ivory-handled knife out of my boot, laid it on the palm of my hand so that they might see the Miquelon gargoyle of its hilt and the stare of the gargoyle, queer and thirsty crone. Yes, thirsty still. "From now on, you Clem, and Terry here, are to know all that we know. All that I know especially. Because if I tell Nora something in your presence, it's proper evidence for the court of inquiry. For it's to the court we're all going in the end, if we're smart enough to keep out of harm's way." I held my hand out farther. "You know this knife?"

"The captain's!"

"She told you that Billy Atkins was killed? And how?"

"Aye!"

"And that we saw LeNotre kill Dan Corkery?"

"She did. To us alone, she said it."

"This knife did it! In the captain's hand. At Parren's word and his blow. Bear it in mind now! I took this knife out of Dan Corkery's heart and I hid it from them. Bear that in mind."

"We will bear it, Johnnie."

I kicked up the thwart and folded the blanket back. I then turned the body until the back showed and the rip in the slicker. I said: "It's there the knife went in and it's the wound this knife made—and our word—that will hang his murderers. But say to the others now that he was drowned. This must be watched over and kept secure until we get home. Or find the law. I'll keep the knife. Put the body into canvas and slide it into Number Three pen. There's no fish there yet. Lash it. Don't sew it."

I jumped down to the deck, where I said to them: "For the time being, we'll keep this to ourselves. Every man must show all respect to the captain and watch him hard. And they won't do that if they know what we know. They'd iron him and give it away—because—mind you!—he's sure we know nothing. And a growl would put him wise."

The old men called others from the tubs and talked to them and said that Dan Corkery had been drowned. I heard a doryman cry out: "Dan, too?" and another said in amazement: "Brought up in the bag? God help us!" After this, they took down their shipmate's body and set to work on the canvas and lashing for it.

I said to Nora: "I'll turn in now. In the forecastle. Let me sleep long as I can. I couldn't sleep aft with him near me. I'll take Atkins' bunk." This made me shiver a little; couldn't help it. I laughed poorly and said: "Hope the Jonah's ghost don't board us." I took up her hand in my hands and found it cold. I asked: "Can you sleep, my girl? You need it."

"I tried to, John, while we were waiting for you. I'll try again. But before you sleep, you'll have to come aft with me. I can't face him alone. I've waited long enough to do this. I waited because Ambrose told me to. And the Lisbon. And you. Whatever fate Paul LeNotre meets, he'll not meet it as captain of the *Hind*. He's through. A prisoner aboard the vessel." This was hard for her to say; and she had an even more difficult word to utter. She took some time to make it ready and, as she spoke, kept her eyes fixed sombrely on the shimmering flood that we drew along with us. "John, you came on here as a doryman. I know now why you came. You are here—and you suffer—because you have always loved me. And you have loved the *Hind*. You must do one thing more for both of us."

"Say it!"

"You are skipper of the *Hind* from now on."

"All right!"

"Then call the watch. Call all hands."

The dorymen came to where we stood. She said: "I speak to you as the owner of the *Hind*. In order that everything shall be done properly. John Bannon becomes captain of this vessel now. Mark the time, you Clem. Hour and day."

"I will, Miss."

"Mark the reason. Captain LeNotre is unfit for duty. Clem and Terry and you, John, come with me and hear me tell him that he's no longer captain of my vessel. I'll say little of my reasons to him. But for you all—keep this in mind!—he's a prisoner and must be watched as one."

No word or gesture came from the throng. I heard a loud murmur rise amongst them when her voice thinned at the end and she thrust her hand against her lips to keep them from saying more.

She passed by the ranks and we followed.

The captain lay sprawled in his bunk. At her command, he came out and stood before us, his eyes passing dumbly from one face to another. Nora said: "Captain LeNotre, I speak to you as the sole owner of this vessel. You are relieved of its command. These men will bear witness to my order."

He swayed in his place. His right hand rose in the familiar gesture and beat back strands of yellow hair. His lips moved once without success. He gazed at her, at her alone; and, at last, whispered: "Why?"

"Because you are unfit for duty." I saw that he was hardly listening to her. His eyes stayed upon her, yet he seemed to be watching other things, things too terrible to be looked at long. She said: "Captain Bannon is in command. You will obey his orders as he obeyed yours."

He crawled back into his bunk.

We climbed up the companionway steps. She went forward to stand in her accustomed place. I stayed by the helm and then, in order to mark the beginning of my captaincy, I said to the helmsman: "I am now in command, chum. I'll take over." He stepped from the wheel and I laid my hands on the spokes. "Pass the word along. No orders are to be taken from LeNotre. He's not to leave the vessel or to speak one. Unless I say so. He's to be watched while on deck. I fear for him."

"All right, John."

I said: "Take in the torches. Begin forward and take them in. The work's done. There's no need of them now."

He went forward, presently returned and said: "Captain, Miss Nora asks—as a favor—can she have the torches for a time longer?" He came closer to my ear and spoke in some concern for her. "She seems to like them there, she does. Does, indeed!"

"She can have them then." Before he turned away, I said: "Clew up topsails. We won't carry them in this."

I said no more of the matter of torches burning; for I had no wish to cross her. Besides, it did me good, in my uneasy fancy, to live for a time in such a wealth of light. When the watch changed, I went into the forecastle and slept in Atkins' bunk, having left orders that I should called be if the wind changed.

16

THE *Hind* sped through the night with a wind that was fair for her most of the time. I took my sleep, hours of it, before the wind began to haul to the northward a little and kicked up something of a sea. I was called. I stayed below for a mug-up because I seemed weak with famine. But it was a famine not of the belly.

I found Nora on deck, standing by the helmsman. She had gone down into the cabin to take a kink, but got no more than a Gloucesterman's forty winks. The sight of LeNotre, stretched out lifelessly in his bunk, filled her with more than sorrow. Yet she was glad that he would never again give an order on the *Hind*; and she was glad (as I was) that he was aboard; for she was certain that if she had driven him off the vessel, as she once had wished, his presence on the *Doubloon* might lead to another joining of cunning minds. One that would produce a newer and more violent plan against the schooner. Such thoughts as these, and her new hopes for fish, kept her awake. Once while on the edge of sleep, she heard the watch hail a vessel. She hurried on deck and saw the lights of a Canadian schooner. She told the watch to ask if the sou'wester had struck him.

The voice came wryly back from the other's slanted deck: "Cost me two days' work and some gear, my friend."

The Canadian sailed off. We spoke another vessel half an hour later, just as I came up. This proved to us that the schooners which had run before the gale were now retracing the courses into which they had been forced. The second hail was the *Coralie*, a Nova Scotian long-liner. Her watch told us that she had been fishing on the eastern edge of Canso Bank when the gale caught them and drove them clear over Misaine before it blew out.

"Big sweep," I said.

Nora shouted to the Canadian: "You speak any Gloucester vessels back there?"

The watch, who was little taken aback by a woman's voice coming off our deck, laughed and said: "Nary a one, ma'am! Spoke the *Caliban* of Lockport last night. She's all right now."

"She's a jump ahead of you, Captain. All well aboard!"

"Ah, thank you!" The schooner went on.

Since it was full day, I sent a watch aloft with orders to speak any vessel in sight, even if our course had to be altered to do so. The exception being, of course, the *Doubloon*, which lay a mile or so astern, the sun flashing off her hull.

About this time, the *Doubloon* drew a little closer; which gave us the thought that she had once given up her pursuit and had changed again. Just as if the dragger captain had a strange communication over LeNotre, which could call him even from drunken sleep, he came up out of the cabin. He gazed at the *Doubloon* for a considerable time; and without any particular expression on his face. He then went forward, greeting us in an offhand manner, and went down into the galley for his breakfast. He didn't take much. He came on deck again, where he behaved just like a doryman. He did it with much grace; even joined in the patching of an old trawl that Ernie Wagner found in a locker. He talked of fishing, talked in such calmness that Nora and I looked at each other, wondering at the fathoms of his guile. Old Clem told him that we were going to make a set on Misaine for halibut.

LeNotre said: "It's worth trying if Ambrose's chart says so. Though I've never killed halibut on Misaine to any extent. Still, it's a wandering fish, the halibut. And must have gone somewhere from the Grand Bank."

I learned quite soon that he secretly sought amongst the the fishermen for their account of his removal. They were good to him, yet gave him no hint that they knew of his deeds ashore and aboard the vessels. By agreement, it was left to Clem to quit LeNotre's suspicion and stop his guesswork. Clem spoke sternly to him of the sin of taking whiskey aboard the *Hind*. He made such a fatherly sermon of it that LeNotre, I think, soon accepted this as Nora's chief reason. This must have seemed reasonable to him because of the words she used in discharging him . . . "unfit for duty . . ." Perhaps this deceit was an error on my part; and it might have been better to at least hint that there was something else on our minds; for our way of doing things left his mind free for the deed he resolved upon.

About noontime, I again had the helm. I had just repeated the course after the helmsman when a man aloft sang out. Another man, going up to relieve the watch, stopped in the shrouds and sang out for something, too. Both held their arms to the eastward and held them so until they heard my: "Hard alee!" I swung her over onto the other tack. The bow-watch then sent back word that a capsized dory had been sighted. In ten minutes, the *Hind* came up to it. I brought her into the wind.

The Lisbon thrust down a boathook and caught the dory where its bottom-boards had been stove in. He leaned over and examined her sides. He spoke briefly to the Nova Scotian hand, who was standing by. Ernie nodded and said: "Yes. That's right."

The Lisbon shouted to me: "Shelburne dory, Captain. Name of the *Caliban*. What you say?"

"Let her go!"

The Lisbon twisted the hook out and the dory whirled into our wake. The Lisbon stayed at the rail alone. He gazed after the dory thoughtfully; then drifted aft and stood there, his eyes fixed on the wreckage. He was watching something else, too: the tenacious *Doubloon* standing on our course. He saw something that made him murmur. The *Doubloon* came up to the dory, hooked it as he had, examined it closely, and let it go. She then came on at a faster clip and shortened the distance between vessels. The Lisbon reported this to me. I could make nothing of it, at the time.

Hour after hour, the *Golden Hind* sped on her course. At times, she logged over thirteen knots because the wind freshened and stayed fair for her and we had put on all her muslin. In the afternoon, I judged that we were not far from the edge of the Bank. I went down to look at the old chart and came on deck with the order: "Bait up!"

I kept the schooner under jib and jumbo for the slow sailing of the set. And I can remember that all of us became livelier as the time for fishing came nigh. For myself, I considered the venture a questionable chance. I said something to the effect; and hardly had the words out of my mouth before I spied a thing that made me change my tune. I whooped and pointed to the edge of a tide-rip to leeward. For a time, no other man could make out what I had seen; then a grey shape flashed out of a curl of foam, which had hidden it, and hurtled across the black rip. It was a halibut, in such good spirits and so hungry that he had chased cod to the surface. The men saw him thrash and dive back to where he belonged.

One shouted: "There goes twenty dollars!" Another: "And here we go after him!"

I waved my hand. "Buoy away!" The dories dropped off. I watched them anxiously. To the southward of them, the *Doubloon* lingered. The sea lay flat between us; and, it being slack water, the dories moved easily through the set. There was no great margin of time before nightfall. Therefore, I had told the dories not to return after hauling. One by one, I saw them finish. Sail after sail rose on the blue until all of them were on the way back to the inner buoys. There they tied up to wait for the fishing signal. The men lay down in the dories to keep out of the wind, so that their dories seemed unmanned and whirling adrift.

I gave the fish two hours to feed. At last, I brought the *Hind* around and began the passage down the line. Half-way down, I blew the signal. No sooner had the dories taken in their buoys than a piercing blast from a conch horn blew over the water from a dory in the middle.

"Hey!" cried the cook.

"Wait a minute!" I listened. The horn stayed silent; then a chorus began, a good clamor that sent the news from dory to dory and onward to us, anxious on our deck.

"They've struck in!" The cook danced a step to mark his joy. "Halibut! By the Lord Harry! we're all rich men. All of us!" He patted the *Hind's* rail fondly and said: "You found them, my girl."

"True!" said I. "Struck in all right! But is it halibut?" I added a dampener for him: "Can't be, chum! They'd be a long way from home." And yet I wanted it to be so; because the price of halibut was not much lower than the price of gold.

I kept my eyes set on that dory in the middle. Presently I saw an arm raised. A doryman bent in the gaffing blow and leaned far over the gunwale to handle his fish. A flat, grey shape came up against the sideboards. I shifted my gaze. I saw the same picture again and again: the gaff upraised, the strain, and a big fish thrashing against black dory-sides.

I said: "Cook, it's halibut. Never thought I'd live to see the day."

I sent him below to give the story to Nora.

We hadn't long to wait for proof of luck. A sail appeared, another drew behind it, and a third and fourth followed. The dories rode deep. Sometimes, in the long slide over rollers, the dories cantered a bit and showed the grey fish gleaming in rich piles. They came alongside and, without a word to say for themselves, began forking the halibut, great and small, into the checkers. There were fish that weighed two hundred pounds, others of a hundred; and doryloads of chicken. There were fine steaker cod, too, fit to lie alongside the halibut.

The cook began big talk about thousands of dollars; and the men, as they came aboard, sang out the praises of old Ambrose and of Nora for remembering his word. They had her bring up the chart, which he had left for us, and they read the legend written on Misaine long before she and I were born. "Halibut here—60,000 in two days" and, in a less legible scrawl: "Told nobody at home."

"Neither will we!"

We cleared the checkers, iced down the fish, ate, and dropped the dories for a second set. This was a harder one, because the tide was running the other way; and we didn't finish until the moon had risen and the north had filled with stars. There was much light, yet not enough, of course, for our knives. Therefore, the torches were set up as before.

Our luck held; our skill matched the luck. One by one, the dories sailed homeward and again the pitchforks whirled and tossed in the torchlight. On either hand, the dories came in; two at first, then three, then the sixth and seventh, until all but one were in the nests or were unloading. This late dory gave me some concern; because the fishermen in it were reckless loaders, who had laughed and sworn that they'd come home standing on fish. Good enough to say so, but there's a danger in over-loading, especially in late season fishing. For myself, I'd let fish go, rather than sail a dory made cranky by too much.

I said to Nora: "Give him a wind of the horn." She whirled the crank a few times. I sent her into the swifters to see if she could make the dory out in the moon-glade, which was where I judged it should be fishing. I couldn't help a creepy uneasiness, because the *Doubloon* was lying in that direction.

To Clem I said angrily: "There'll be a sermon preached when they do come in. And you know the text! What the devil's wrong with Ernie?"

Clem replied: "Johnnie, they've been hungry a long time and they're thinking of dollars for home."

A curious thing happened then.

So far, the *Doubloon* had kept her position astern. She began to close up in the moonlight, her port light showing. This change in her position was marked by my men. I should say: marked with anger. This didn't rise out of fear of losing fish. They had a wonderful stock aboard, money in the bank for all; and no dragger could rob them of the fish on the bottom; for there was never a net made that could handle big

halibut. I knew the course of their thought. It was mine also.
I said to myself: "Hey! I've got enough of that tramp. I'll
board him and knock his block off. I'll teach him to hang
around my vessel."

I called a doryman. "Keep that last dory down. I'll be needing it."

The Lisbon, who had the helm, heard me and sang out:
"What say, Captain?"

I hadn't time to answer. The *Doubloon* had come up so
close that I thought she meant to speak the *Hind*. Our torchlight beat upon the faces of men standing between her pilot-
house and winch. I saw at once that they weren't giving us
their attention. No, they were all looking beyond us and into
the moon-glade. I mulled this over and couldn't make head
nor tail of it. The men suddenly scattered. The *Doubloon*
swung sharply to port. I heard her gong beat for full speed.
Her engine loudened and she plugged off into the northeast.
Her lights went out. She smashed into the moon-glade, cut
a wide swath there, and became a part of the darkness beyond.

This pitch-poling business left my men amazed; and me
up the same old tree. I knew that in Parren I had a cunning
man to deal with; and one that been a notable seaman in his
days of sail. This knowledge and my instinct made me say
aloud: "He's out-smarted me!"

"How's that, Captain?"

I didn't answer. A foul thought had come uppermost: "Has
he killed my dory?"

Not so. It wasn't that.

We put our heads together; that is, Nora and four or five
men stood by me. All silent.

A man at the dory-nest broke into it: "Want we should

haul up on this one, Captain John?" He meant the dory I'd
ordered for the boarding party.

I said: "Haul up!"

I stood baffled; and hated to be so. The blazing torches left
my face an open book. To my shame, I didn't like it to be
read. Yet this was simply newness of command, a natural
thing. I looked from one face to another and said nothing.

This was the moment when Nora heard (or thought she
heard) a faraway cry drifting over the water. She moved to
the lee rail and leaned out, trying to search out that cry above
the noise of the tide.

This stirred me up. I asked: "You hear anything?"

"I'm not sure."

Old Clem said: "I heard a gull crying."

"No!" I don't know who said that.

Then, right up under our weather rail (the starboard), a
voice said quite calmly: "Hey! Take a painter, will you?"
This was Ernie Wagner and his mate. They had sailed up
without being seen; because we were all intent on the hail
(if it was that) which had come from leeward.

Someone took the painter and in a hushed voice said to
Ernie: "Shut up! Stand by!"

"Oh, aye!"

A yell burst out of our bow. An old hand on watch there
shouted: "Sail ho! A sail! A sail!"

"Where away? Where away, Tom?"

He came stumbling aft, crying out and pointing into the
darkness beyond the tide-rip, which is to say at about the
position where the *Doubloon* had jumped out of sight.

A silence swept the *Hind* like hail. And this speechlessness
at the sighting of a sail, drawn to us by our torches, showed
me that Nora's secret hope, held in silence before and now,

had become their hope. When it became mine, I cannot say; because of a crowded memory on which a hard strain has been put.

A shadow beyond became a gleam. The gleam changed into a curl of foam under the bow of a dory; and a grey slant above the bow turned into a rag of sail. And all along the gunwale other gleams appeared and became brighter where the oars were feebly dipping, barely touching the stream, and lifting feebly again.

Now I heard the wail; this time stronger; and it seemed to be a question uttered in a pleading voice. I wished to speak. I couldn't. Nor could the others. We gazed enthralled at that dory, gazed at the men bent on her thwarts, and at the festoons of frost glittering there.

The oars ceased. The voice of an old, old man cried out: "Ahoy the schooner! Ahoy! Be that you, the *Golden Hind*?"

All I could say was: "Come in, the dory!"

The oars struck again, harder this time. A sea pushed the dory onward until she glided near. An oar slipped and rattled in thole-pins; and the same old voice sang out cheerily: "Easy does it! You know that, my good man!"

A painter came looping over our rail. In silence yet (the silence now of too great happiness), the *Hind*'s people reached over, holding out their hands.

I saw a yellow glove flash in the spray. I saw a hand, clad in the yellow glove, reach up and close upon the Lisbon's arm. The Lisbon heaved, bent backward and said in a choked voice: "Madre de Deus!" He heaved around and there! there, at last, he stood before me: huge, frosted, indomitable—the Yankee conqueror of the gale!

I couldn't break my lips apart. My heart shouted: "Live forever, Cameronian!"

The hero took one little step. He struck his gloved hand against his mouth and cried out: "Ah!" and "Hem!" and: "Salubrious, is it not, my dear friends? I refer, of course, to—" The pocket compass slipped from his hand, rolled to my feet. His head dropped, yet never marred its nobleness.

The dorymen heaved again, and again. Four heroes came over the rail and stood behind the first, their heads bowed, their eyes staring at the solid deck.

A man amidships cried harshly: "Are ye ghosts there? Or men?"

Old Ambrose took a step toward Nora. He struck the icy sou'wester from his head. It rolled on an unbending rim and stopped against the compass at my feet.

He brought his silvery head up high. "In a manner of speaking, sir," he replied, with gold-lighted eyes fixed upon her pitiful face, "in a manner of speaking—men!"

Even then, when the old hero had taken her heart forever as he had mine long since, she had no word for him. She made a step forward and tried to lift her arms. Her lips opened in a poor whisper. He made the step and lifted his arms, so that she could move into them; and thus they embraced: saved and savior. She pressed her lips into the bristle of his hollow cheek. It was this reality of meeting, their coming together, that loosed her words. She cried: "Ambrose! And he —he said I'd drowned you on that hulk!"

He opened his lips to answer. His mouth seemed ready to laugh. No laughter came. Instead he whispered: "Torches!" and then he uttered the *Hind's* old rally: "Hard alee! Hard alee, Cap'n Nora! Don't cry, Cap'n! Get it on her!" He groaned and his head fell sideways sharply. "North-by-east! Scatari Shoal!" His legs shook under him. He slipped from her arms, stayed on his knees. "The *Western Star*!" He sprawled. "Couldn't stay on her. Afloat in shoal water. Mark-buoy! Rigged it myself." With these words, he keeled over and lay still.

She wailed above him. "What! Now?"

I knelt by the hero, touched his mouth, and shook away her fear of death. "Sound asleep, my girl! Trust him! He knows what to do."

I lifted him and laid him on the arms of my dorymen; and they turned, shouting with joy, and bore him and his companions to the warmth and food of the forecastle.

She seized my arm. "You heard that course!"

"Aye!"

Her eyes shone fiercely and the hand on my arm trembled with such violence that all of her seemed to shudder. "Ten thousand dollars' worth of fish iced down. A sixteen-thousand-dollar keel beyond!" She struck her other hand against the rail. "She's saved!"

I stepped back and flung up my hand to the watching topmastmen. I said to her: "Yonder keel's a loose-fish! Belongs to the first man that sets foot on her." The main-sheet men jumped to their stations; and I shouted: "I'll be that man! Or never kill cod again!"

The rally cry went booming fore and aft, into the forecastle, aloft, and down again into the cabin, where that one lay, waiting for the turn. "All hands! All hands! Tumble up! Oh, lively now!"

They swung the main-boom out of its crotch and fell upon the sail. I gave it to them! Hey! I yelled for sweat to show. "The *Doubloon!* Lay alongside that dog before daybreak and you're in the money!"

They roared again and hauled; and the topmastmen ran up to the stars and lay to it. I put my hands on the spokes and shouted to them again: "Sixteen thousand dollars in prime lead on Scatari Shoal! Shares for all! The old sixty-forty lay, chums. Heave!"

"Heave! Hey! Oh, gorry! Pile it on her!"

I heard old Clem shriek amidst the gang. "Hey! Hey! We'll punish her this night!"

The mainsail hammered over, filled hard and made her jump. The *Hind* trembled and splashed a little.

"Ease her! Ease her, chum!"

The foresail took hold. The *Hind* ceased her splashing and plugged away. Now we spread all that she had: topsails, staysail, jib and jumbo. And trimmed her well until she lay over and drank the Atlantic up, running as she had run in her old days of racing. She sank the moon and tossed her spray against the last of the stars. All her gear sang out shrilly or sang out hoarsely. A booming came up from her hold and marked swift time for the headlong passage. I punished her all right, but she was the one who could take it, high seas or low; and when she hit the long swell, left by the sou'wester, she lifted her pace until the men roared again in pleasure at her famous qualities.

17

I SET THE racing watches and ordered the lifelines rigged; for I swore I'd spread cook's shirt and let the *Hind* go until the sticks jumped out of her. We took down the torches. They had done their work; and more. I also took in our own lights, which was a risky thing to do, but I had no wish to light the *Doubloon* after us in case we overhauled her or she lost her meagre bearings and waited for us. Anyway, our lights would have been of doubtful service in the first hours, because a squall or two kept us blind. And the squalls left a thick vapor after them, through which we sped, our horn bawling.

I must confess that I couldn't stand the pace. I wasn't the sailing-master I had been. Nor the chance-taker. I shot off my mouth too much at the opening of the race; had set up too bold a pattern, especially for a man who had been out of sail for so many seasons. Well, I'm free to say that I didn't know the *Hind* any too well. Vessels age well and Yankee handiwork improves with age. Men grow cautious. As I did. I don't know that I was to be blamed.

I stood it as long as I could. The schooner ran dark as a whale through the thickening night. Give you my word! I could scarcely see my hand when I struck the salt out of my eyes. Toward midnight, the schooner ran out of the swell and struck into another squall. I could tell there was nothing much to it, but I pretended that it seemed hard to me. I made it count.

I said: "We'll get rid of topsails now."

This was done with the best will and speed; and the *Hind* was the better for it.

About this time, old Clem worked his way aft and shouted into my ear: "What's she got in the way of knots—that *Doubloon?* Night like this?"

I expressed my doubts. "Ten or eleven. With eighty thousand pounds in her pens—I don't know. She'll do well enough."

"We're doing that much now," he said.

"And can do better with light."

One or two others joined us. We put our heads together; for this question of the *Doubloon's* qualities (if the word is properly applied) left us baffled. There was the matter of her head-start. Were we evenly matched, that half hour or so for the *Doubloon's* three hundred horses might settle the race before it had well begun. I agreed with the Lisbon that it wasn't really a matter of one hundred miles. Ambrose had told him that was the distance we had to go. Our best opinion was that the *Western Star* lay considerably nearer; that there was hardly a degree of latitude between us and the prize. (Say, roughly, 45′ to 46′). The best of men, which Ambrose was, if fighting for his life in a dory, would tend to overestimate the distance he had sailed, especially if the sailing had been marked by squalls and ice making, which had been the case with him. Just the same, it was clear to us that for the present there was nothing to do except let the *Hind* plug along. This we did.

Nora Doonan had stayed a long time with Ambrose and his men. They told her certain things concerning the dory which had to wait for another time for retelling, but she did give me Ambrose's words concerning the *Western Star*.

She said: "She's full of water and barely afloat. But Ambrose thinks she'll not founder. It wasn't her hull. The sou'-wester smashed in her aft companionway and ripped off the main hatch. The seas poured into her. They stayed with her until she was awash. All lashed to the wheel. Then she ran into shoal water and they had to leave her because every sea passed clear over her. No food. No water. Lucky, he says, to get oars and a bit of sail to handle the dory—and almost lost Peter Lord doing that much. When the gale blew out, they steered this way. He figured that his best chance of getting picked up was to steer for the place he left us."

"What was the matter with Cape Breton Land?"

"I asked him that, John. He couldn't explain. When the whole story's known, we'll find they meant to get onto our course, no matter what the cost."

I asked: "Did Ambrose sight us when the *Star* was running before the gale?"

"Yes! And he said to me just now: 'It was plain to us that you'd come along after the *Star*, if you could, and that's why we came along and kept looking for you with hope.'" She halted over her next words and then, with some little pride, added: "They saw our torches night before last—"

"Night before last!"

"Aye! and steered for them, but they were so weak from hunger that they couldn't fight it out. Squalls—one after the other—drove them back again. But it was our torches that kept them going. They knew what they were for!"

I said nothing on that score, for the plain reason that there was no great credit in it for me; and I stood in need of some, just then.

She told me that, at the very end, Ambrose had picked up the glare of our torches again and, a little later, had made out the *Doubloon* passing the schooner. Ambrose knew the part that Parren and his vessel had been playing at the beginning of the voyage. When he saw the *Doubloon* plug off so suddenly, he had guessed that Parren had figured out where the *Western Star* had been abandoned and that the keel was his if he could get a man aboard before we did. This seemed reasonable enough to me, because Parren had as much knowledge as we did of the *Star's* position.

Nora asked: "Isn't the keel ours, just the same? Is it a loose-fish, as you called it?"

I shook my head. "I'm no sea lawyer, but, at the least, it's a salvage job for him, if he gets there first. But you know he won't bother with the long tow home. What's sixteen thousand dollars to him in such a case? To us—it's life. To him— just a few bags of fish. He'll ram the *Star* just to keep her out of our hands."

We talked then of the probable ending of the race. Our minds met on one thing: that Parren had no way of knowing how far the *Western Star* lay to the northward. He was as skilled as any man in adding two and two. In this case, he hadn't the two's to add.

"Unless," said Nora, "his friend in our cabin had some way of giving him the news. Which isn't possible."

Yet this queer turn of our thought made us both realize how profound our fear of LeNotre's cunning had become; and, at the same time, how much wisdom we had gathered up. For we were wise enough not to slight our enemy's strength of purpose. Certainly it was unreasonable for us to fancy that a man, asleep in the cabin of a flying schooner, could manage a communication with a vessel far ahead in the pitch of night. Just the same, I called one of the watch and spoke to him.

Now, before I say what I told him, I would make it clear that the events which followed my words are described as carefully as I can do the job. I've told the story many times before (as I said earlier) and under varying circumstances, including the court of inquiry. Nevertheless, there are certain parts of it which couldn't be told because these were events that took place inside myself and had no place in the proceedings. Yet they are required if a true understanding of the events is desired.

I said to the watch: "Chum, go take a look at that lad below. See if he's in his bunk."

This order was an error by me. If I hadn't become skipper of the *Hind*, I might have gone below myself. In a way, the order was like sending a boy on a man's errand. However, I had been giving top orders for the first time in many months and the best part of my thought was intent on the vessel's behavior and her circumstances.

The actual error lay in the doryman's execution of my order. I've no doubt he understood its grave meaning. It isn't every crew that has to watch a man as they would a maniac; and their own captain, at that. In this case, the ancient way of doing things served us far from well. The old way of following orders was often a time-saver. This saving was sometimes accomplished by means of symbols and such devices. The glass was one. A glance at it might keep a man off the deck when ice was making. Sounds were also symbols to us. A constant, hollow booming when the empty *Hind* was going off the wind was usually a signal that she was doing all right.

A signal that passed into our sleep. A man's boots, for another instance, had become a symbol, one that lived always in the back of our minds. It was a risk of death to set unshod feet on that wintry deck. We were all sad acquaintances of Jack Frost. Taking away a doryman's cowhide boots, which protect him halfway to the knee, was like taking away a man's horse on the old frontier. Boots were always at the side of a man's bunk, ready to be pulled on before he had the mist out of his eyes.

After I had spoken, then, the watch pushed back the companionway slide and thrust his head down. He immediately closed the slide and said to me: "Sound asleep. Drunk again, I guess."

The actual truth was that he hadn't seen LeNotre at all. He had merely looked at his boots. These, as usual, were handy.

The watch's report satisfied Nora and me. I believe there must have been a certain apprehension existing; because the knowledge that LeNotre still lay there, not stirring, made us hungry. I guess because of the relief and pleasure. We went down into the galley for a mug-up. I first passed up to the peak, looking into the bunks on either hand. I found Ambrose and his men doubled up. They were breathing in new life and strength at a great rate. I paused by Ambrose a while; and then went into the galley. Nora took down a pair of mugs from the rack and poured tea. I made up a sandwich, cut it in two, and took out a platter of cake. We ate in silence and listened to the cracking noise of the *Hind's* flight.

I then said: "I'm going aloft to trouble the watch. You turn in. I'll call you if there's a break."

"It's too cold for a watch aloft," said Nora.

"Not yet it isn't. But that's what I'm going to settle. They'll come down if I can't stand it."

Nora went aft. The deck was dark, of course. There was only a slight glow out of the cabin skylight to guide her as she went along. I had given a strict order that a little light should be kept below.

I climbed into the main weather rigging and went up carefully, stopping now and then to scan the sails and to search for the gleam of a mark-buoy; for I had in mind the chance that the clockwise tide might seize the *Western Star* and carry her to meet the *Hind*. A few stars were coming out in the west. In the east, where the day was at hand, there were clouds.

I climbed to the cross-trees and struck the watch's boot. (This was the Nova Scotian hand.) He bent down from the sky.

I shouted: " 'Tisn't too cold, chum?"

"Not yet it ain't!"

"Come down when it is."

"I will that, John."

I then said: "I was thinking that the tide might have swung the *Star* westward. Might be nearer than the old boy figured."

"Slow work!"

"Aye! true for you."

The doryman straightened in his perch.

For a while, I lay there in the shrouds, rejoicing, as always, in the beauty of the hull below me. Even in that whirl of darkness, I could see flashes of color from her runways and her inner bulwarks. The glow in the skylight made it seem like a panel of jewels, there being frost and hail on the panes. The *Hind* swayed at her work and, now and then, gave me a good sway up and down. I locked a leg into the rigging and looked ahead. I saw the crest of a roller crease the black and come toward the schooner. I heard its bray. This sea was a gear-smasher. Its force and direction, which would bring it in on the weather bow, gave me a quick concern for the vessel. No reason for it. At the right moment, the helmsman gave the *Hind* a spoke and, answering easily, she split the sea in two and slammed through it with nothing more than a dainty shake which came up lightly to my hands.

I said: "Well done, the *Hind*!"

The boarding sea whitened her deck. She cleared herself and flew on.

A hand struck at my boot. I twisted down. It was Nora Doonan, shouting to me. Her face gave off such an icy gleam, beneath the brim of her sou'wester, that I knew she had grown pale with fear. I couldn't come down to her side. I shouted and thrust my boot out. She began to descend and I to follow. I slid from the swifters and stood by her side. She put both hands on my arm. I heard her cry out and I saw her eyes slowly turn upwards as if she had become too tired to speak properly. I then heard these words: "LeNotre! He's gone!"

My state of mind is clearly indicated by my response. I shouted: "Over?"

"I don't know! That damned doryman—"

"What!"

She placed her lips against my ear and said: "He never looked into the bunk. Saw the boots there. But he's gone!"

I said: "In the galley?"

"No!" (She had gone there at once.)

I drew her close and said: "He's killed himself! Over the side. Clem said he would one day. Parren feared it. Saw the noose—LeNotre did!"

She answered: "Not that one! Not while he has a chance left."

I then shouted: "The pen!" I should like to be able to say that I thought of this earlier, but I didn't. The reason? Not bright enough.

When I said that word, Nora said one that the wind snatched. I could tell that she had thought of the pen, too. She hadn't dared to face such an exploration alone.

I ran to the main hatch. It hadn't been touched since the men closed it over the tardy load of halibut. Yet this had no meaning. On the *Hind,* there was a second way of getting into the pens. This was from the cabin. There was a bulkhead leading from the cabin to the small after-hold and a second bulkhead which opened into a gangway between the pens. In other schooners, this after-hold had been made into an engine-room. The *Hind* kept it as a sort of lazaret. There was a sail locker there, too, and some accommodations left over from racing days. This inner bulkhead hadn't been opened for some time. Its chief use had been to send men into the pens when ice was making on her deck. In a way, that bulkhead served the same purpose as manholes on larger sailing vessels.

I opened the hatch, thrust my head down past the coaming and looked into the pens there. "All dark so far."

Nora Doonan then thrust the old revolver into my hand. As before (on the expedition to the *Doubloon*) I rejected it. I said: "I'd shoot myself. I'll take care of him with this!" I lifted my clenched hand. By saying this, I don't wish to put out of mind the suggestion that I had murder in my heart as I had earlier. This is exactly so. And it is absolutely true that I could kill a man with my fists, if need be.

She then said: "I'll keep it. I'll go, too."

I replied: "You must come. You must see and remember. Keep out of the way, that's all. Give me a whack at that buck. But kill him! Kill him, if you must. A slug in the belly!"

We then went down the steel rungs. Here, between Number One pen and Number Two, I could see the length of the hold. What we saw was enough to stop us! And did. The inner bulkhead wasn't particularly tight. I saw a film of yellow light playing under it. This light waxed and waned amidst a sort of vapor that came off the ice. A clearer ray of light, this time from an auger hole, shot down from the upper panel of the bulkhead. It was plain that somebody was at work on the after side of that bulkhead.

I asked: "You hear anything?"

"No!"

"He's not in here yet."

"No, John. Nearer. Get nearer."

We crept out of the pen and went into Number Four. It was partly filled with halibut, well iced-down. I pushed her up onto the layer of fish. She crouched there. I stayed by her side, my head held out into the passageway so that I could watch the bulkhead. Although we were only eight feet nearer to the light, I could now hear quite clearly the blows of a maul. At times, the booming of the schooner muffled the hammering. Once, when the helmsman was caught by a freakish sea, the *Hind* fell off and the light went out. I figured that it was a lantern and that it had jumped off a nail.

About ten minutes passed before the bulkhead opened. A considerable thickness of crushed ice had fallen against it. This ice delayed the full opening. At last, the ice fell back and the whole gangway filled with the light of a lantern, turned up full.

I drew back, and struck Nora lightly on the shoulder to warn her.

The wavering light grew brighter as its bearer approached. There was no hesitation on his part. The circle of light came right up to the pen in which we were hidden; then it turned into Number Three pen.

LeNotre rammed the lantern handle into a crack between two boards. He knelt by the body of Corkery and began to untie the trawl lines which had been lashed around the canvas. At the first untyings, his back was turned to me. Thus I could see only the rusty fingers flashing back and forth. When the lines fell away from the lower part of the body, LeNotre changed his position. He straddled the body. This gave us a full look at his face. It was broken up and twisted; that is to say, the lower lips sagged in a sort of dull, meaningless way, and the cheeks had no life to them at all, save for strange blotches of crimson and black. But the eyes! Ah, they were wonderful in the intensity of purpose, even under the half-dropped lids. Brassy gleams kept shooting from them as he followed the turns of his hands.

Corkery had been laid out on his back. The men hadn't been able to bend his hands. They were held upward in that same gesture of supplication. Nor had that unspeakable face changed. Nothing had been taken from the sorrowful indictment that it had sent up to its murderer before. The eyes gazed in unaltered, pitiful force. Few men could have withstood this spectre, which had persisted through death and icy seas and the *Doubloon's* crushing net, to make its accusation here again, in the mellow light of its old sea-home.

LeNotre withstood the gaze. He cursed! I saw his lips curve into a little "o."

The schooner lurched and his knees shifted on the layer of

ice. He waited until she had settled down. Before the booming began again, he struck at the dead mouth savagely and said
a sentence which I clearly heard because of the triumphant
loudness of his utterance. The words were strange: "The
heft, eh? Oh, you ―― ―― ―― ――!" And then: "Gabber!"
The last word was plain enough; the first I could never explain.

A certain feverishness then seized LeNotre, because he
began his search for the one thing that would save him and
Parren. He ripped the canvas away with sweeping blows.
He roughly turned the body over and ripped the slicker
and shirts away. Thus he laid clear the wound he had made
in Corkery's back, the wound where his own knife had found
the doryman's heart.

Again I heard his words clearly. They were: "Tonnere de
Dieu!" He swore another Miquelon oath and then cried out in
English: " 'Tis gone!" I was used, by now, to the swift changes
of that handsome face, but he now put on and took off his
masks in such ferocious style that I must again admit that I cannot be sure of my words; and again plead a crowded memory.
At his first oath, he frowned and sucked in his lower lip in a
gasping way. This was most certainly an expression of terror.
Instantly, his hope rescued him, and all that fearful dark vanished before a pour of happiness which gentled his mouth and
brought his head up into the angle of prayer, so that I clearly
saw that the light in his eyes had become mild as a candle
flame. Take my word for it, he became pious in his joy!
There's no doubt he supposed himself fully delivered from a
fate that he himself had decreed. He, the judge; he, the execu-
tioner.

I know exactly the thought that upheld him, made him so
boyish and sweet-tempered, where he rocked to the plunge

and pitch of the *Golden Hind*. This was it: he believed that his knife had been lost in the sea when the cod-end struck the drifting body and held onto it.

Almost at once, his brain rejected this idea; and the same fear wracked him in the same way. He bent his head and stared at the purple swath of the wound and the cold, sallow flesh. These meant nothing to him. He had come there for his Miquelon knife. He meant to destroy it and the body together.

He cursed again. He struck his clenched hands together in a woeful way. His mouth gaped and the beaming, black pupils of his eyes passed upward until nothing showed but the whites. He spent a little time in this awful posture and grieved aloud. He then looked down at the body, passed his hands under it and made ready to heave upward.

I drew the Miquelon knife out of my boot and strode into the pen. I shouted his name. "LeNotre!"

I do believe that he had lost his senses by that time. I had shouted loud enough to wake the dead. Yet he didn't look at me. No! He stared down at the dead mouth. He might well have wished that those lips had spoken and not mine. He sank to his knees again and then let his burden go. He looked at me.

I held the knife in the palm of my right hand. I said: "You looking for your knife?"

This time, the grotesque eye in the gargoyle's head gazed at LeNotre; and that stare, revealed plainly in the lantern's glow, seemed arch, mysterious. Even gay.

I needed some time for other words. I stepped backward to gain it.

LeNotre came up in a dreadful, slow straightening of his legs. He lifted his hands, in that same weary measure, to his throat, where the fingers began to fumble. At first his eyes sent a golden gaze over those fingers; then it changed into a redder hue, as if his blood had burst its vessels.

My opinion, at the time and now, is that he was insane.

I said to him: "Listen to me! This is your knife. Nora and I saw you murder Dan Corkery at Parren's word. Clem and the Lisbon know who made that wound. And what knife made it. I found the body in the *Doubloon's* bag and took this knife out of it. And hid it here!" I let my hand fall toward my boot. "Nora Doonan and Clem and the Lisbon know all this. Atkins told me that you and Parren had killed the Yarmouth woman. You and Parren will hang!"

LeNotre screamed like an animal and leaped over the body, his hands outstretched.

I flung the knife down and met his assault with a blow on the jaw that stood him up, big as he was. I took a step closer and drove both fists into his ribs until he screamed again and flung out his arms to drag me down. I stepped into the embrace, not fearing his strength. Just before the hands and arms closed on me, I struck against his jaw with my left hand. The jaw-bone broke. Blood spurted from his nostrils and flowed from his bitten lips. Yet that man (it cannot be denied!) had vast sums of courage and strength to bear him up and a terrible fate to drive him to his best. And he was a knife-fighter, full of island trickery. He yelled fearfully, in that fashion, and struck me in the belly with his right knee. The belly was hard, but not hard enough to take that blow without a flinching of the whole body. I did flinch and, in that expected change, LeNotre hurled his whole weight against me, heaved me against the side of the pen with unbeatable force.

I lifted my fists and my right knee. This was a mistake. I

knew that LeNotre had no taste for fighting with hands. He required steel; knew no other way. He kicked me lightly, then lurched sideways across the pen and, in the very act of whirling to attack again, he picked up his knife, so foolishly disdained by me.

He blew blood and vapor out and shouted: "Now! you son-of-a-whore!"

Bawling the Banker curse, LeNotre sprang, knife held in the outward sweep. He caught me standing on one foot. The foot gave way on the crackling ice. This brought me out of my poise and left me only one defense. I closed one hand on his knife-hand and the other on the fingers that now pressed against my windpipe. I couldn't bring my strength to bear against his strength because my thighs and legs helped me not at all. I could hold back the fingers at my throat only at the cost of letting the knife press nearer.

Thus we were locked in the death-lock and, amidst the booming of the *Hind's* passage, each of us strained to break the lock.

His knife-hand, mighty in its skill, slowly won the bloody see-saw. Nothing in me could halt its downward thrust, its approach to my throat, hairbreadth by hairbreadth. The cursing ceased. Only blood and foam and vapor came from our broken lips.

Neither did Nora Doonan speak. Nor cry out. She stood at the mouth of the pen. She took a short step forward, so that she was within four feet of LeNotre before she pressed the trigger. In that tiny space, the explosion was awful. Le-Notre screamed again, making an extraordinary noise for the mouth of a man. The knife fell from his hand, struck my right boot and glanced outward toward her. He took a step back-ward and there, in by far the worst sign of agony yet, he actually joined his hands and wrung them in the classic gesture! Stranger still, he gazed directly at me, as if he thought the revolver had been held in my hand all the time.

She pressed back the hammer and took another step forward. She held the revolver up awkwardly and, at the same time, bent down and seized the knife. She flung it behind her, flung it far into the other pen. She shouted a warning to him.

"Now are you for it?"

This time he looked at her. He howled, again in that beastly way. He fell back another step. He raised his hands to his face in a blinding gesture, meant to screen them from an image of himself that even he could not bear. He lifted his bare foot in a sort of dancing step and plunged forward. He staggered into the open passageway. There he paused, howled again; and the weird accent mingled with the hollow accent of the *Hind*. The vessel lurched in a tide-rip and struck at him. He fell and then rose again, loud in his grief and terror. He stumbled against the steel rungs of the hatchway and climbed to the deck, where the first green of dawn was striking the spray.

I followed. She came after, her hands striking against my boots. We reached the deck in time to see LeNotre, his hands still over his face, run howling to the rail. He flung himself over it. I saw his blond, shaggy head whirl brightly in the icy tide. A wreath of foam, laced with white and blue, struck his head. He vanished.

18

THERE HAD been light enough for the four men on deck to see LeNotre go to his death. The two on watch in the bow had heard his crying. They had seen him cross the deck. The helmsman hadn't heard the crying because of the wind. He had seen him go over. The doryman on watch amidships might have stopped LeNotre had he been a stride nearer. He was one of the elders, however, and had neither the strength nor the agility for such a task. There was also some question whether he would have saved LeNotre, had he been able. In his later testimony, he said that the expression on the captain's face was really terrifying. He used the phrase: "I was too froze to lift a hand." At that later time, too, he made an astonishing statement. He declared that Captain LeNotre was blind when he killed himself; that he actually could not see. The doryman was never able to explain this conviction. He merely repeated, quite stubbornly, that he knew a blind man when he saw one.

LeNotre hadn't been blinded by the bullet. This was a point on which entire satisfaction could never be obtained. I declared (and now declare again) that the bullet never struck him. This belief is based on a fact which seems quite reasonable to me, but its nature is such that it had little value at the later time. The fact is this: I believe that I would have felt the shock of the bullet if it had struck him. Bearing in mind that we were in a lock at the time, jaw to jaw, hand to hand, this belief must seem sound. The fact that the court of inquiry could not find the bullet in the *Hind's* timbers has little to do with this point. I should have been pleased to have it found. I can only say that even well-seasoned wood can swallow a bit of lead and leave no trace, especially in timbers that continually drink up oil and moisture.

I'll let it go with this: Paul LeNotre was a madman at that moment. He was mad with longing for the only haven left open to him.

For myself (as I stood at the rail watching in sadness), I had no strong desire to prevent the suicide. It would have been inhuman, even if there had been a chance of rescue. There was no such chance. The water was cold enough to paralyze a man. And LeNotre, of course, couldn't swim at all. On that score, his story had always been the old Gloucester one, the Corkery story: "Why learn? It just takes that much longer to drown!"

Nevertheless, on the chance that LeNotre might have struck a bit of wreckage, I brought the *Hind* around briskly and sailed two miles. I made the best search possible. I supposed that the court of inquiry would be gratified to hear of this action. Yet, in its wisdom, it seemed to take such an action for granted; which is all right with me.

I gave up the search, after asking the consent and approval of all hands. I swung the *Hind* back on the old course and gave the helm over to the watch. I asked the helmsman where Nora Doonan was. He pointed to the cabin companionway. I went below and found her there, stretched in her bunk, her eyes closed. She lay dressed in green.

I didn't speak to her, having in mind that the lost man had

been dear to her. I hung up her doryman's rig, where it could dry; and I put her boots away. In LeNotre's bunk, I found another drained bottle. Near it, the cocked revolver lay, where she had flung it. I let the hammer down and put it back into the little box. Paul's boots were on the locker. I put them out of sight and went on deck.

Of course, the sailing had required all hands, so that the story of LeNotre's death was known before the *Hind* had come about to make the search. Moreover, the watch had changed; thus the actual witnesses had been in the forecastle for a good while before I went there. The sleeping was over. Old Ambrose and his chums had rolled out and were listening with grieving eyes when my appearance put an end to the story-telling.

In this silence, I said: "Captain LeNotre has killed himself!" I then added: "Let the witnesses bear in mind what they saw. Those who hear us—well! let them remember what they hear." I told them all that had happened below; and gave the account which I give here. No doubt, there was greater detail in such matters as the circumstances in the pen, Le-Notre's lesser words and actions, etc. Generally speaking, it is the same story. Of course, in the telling I had to reveal the circumstances of Corkery's death on the dragger, which had been kept secret by us until that moment of its uselessness. I should say nothing of the words uttered by the *Hind's* people at this revelation.

When I had done, I asked: "Is there any man who wishes to question me?" No man spoke. I took a step forward and asked in an even louder voice: "Is there any man here who wishes to question me or Nora Doonan? If so, let him speak up."

Ambrose spoke. He repeated the epithet that LeNotre had

used in his cursing of me after he had regained his knife; and then he asked: "Was it clear to you, Captain Bannon, that he meant to take your life?"

"It was clear to me."

I could see the old man's intention well enough; and was glad for it.

I said: "Parren will be brought to justice." Receiving no spoken answer, I added: "I continue as captain. We'll proceed as before."

I went on deck.

The *Hind* had sailed on that course since the setting of the moon. It was now full sunrise and she still plugged along handsomely, although the wind had hauled into the west a bit more than she liked. It was possible to come to a judgment as to the good or bad of all this sailing. As the daylight spread, we searched the blue water ahead for a sign of the *Doubloon*. A vessel was sighted several miles to the northeast. She was made out to be either a warship or a Coast Guard cutter. Her course lay toward the *Hind*.

I said: "We'll speak her."

We laid the *Hind* over onto the other tack and drove along.

One of the topmastmen then sent down word: "Dragger astern!" A minute or so later, the watch aloft sent down the same word to which he added: "The *Doubloon*!"

I saw the dragger soon after this. The stern-chase had ended in the night, unbeknownst to us. Thus it proved that Parren didn't know where to search for the *Western Star*, and, therefore, had to give the *Hind* a chance to lead him to the position. He had slowed down with the intention of making a jump for the hull as soon as the *Hind* steered for it. I could tell by the rate at which he closed the gap between us that he was the faster, under these conditions. The wind was jumping around again. There was no telling what it might be doing when the hardest sailing should be called for.

It was old Clem who spoke against the plan of just barging ahead until the look-out found the *Western Star*. He had been watching the vessel in the northeast. He said: "My guess is that she's one of the old Coast Guard cutters."

The Lisbon, who had been in the bow, said this was right.

"Then," cried Clem, "there's the law and I want it!" He spoke to me again: "You'll speak that vessel, Johnnie?"

"We will."

"Fact is," he said, "I don't want to be alone with that one any more." He jerked his head backward.

"I have enough!" said the Lisbon sharply. "The law is good. The law is there!" He flung his hand out toward the cutter.

I said: "Take the wheel. Take over."

The Lisbon put his hands on the spokes.

I broke out a roll of signal flags and hoisted a signal on the halyard: "Stand by. We require assistance."

A doryman said: "What's that cutter doing up here, anyway? She's making knots." I said that she was probably going home from Iceland or from convoy work.

"Will she stand by then?"

I had to laugh at this. "Yes. They like the *Hind*. All of them. Wait till they make out our topsails. There's no others on the Banks today."

Both the cutter and the *Doubloon* changed courses slightly; and in such a way that they were steering to eastward of the *Hind*. The *Doubloon* was doing her best. The cutter seemed to have reduced speed. She was still so far away that nothing more than the general cut of her jib could be seen. The answer to the: "Now what?" which was uttered in different ways at the *Hind's* wheel, came from aloft in a shout by the look-out.

A man forward cried: "He's got it!"

I jumped to the lee rail. The lookout held his arm to the eastward. I saw the sea break on a deck far beyond. It was the *Western Star*. I gave the order for all hands and the "hard alee!" signal. The men ran to their stations. Ambrose had the helm. He brought the schooner into the wind. The topmast-men were ready. They shifted sail and the staysail went over after the main and fore. The *Hind* lingered only the right moment in the wind; then she went over smartly and began sailing. We trimmed her as she flew. She had been handy. Vessel and men had shown all their qualities in the manoeuvre. Yet the three hundred horses under the *Doubloon's* deck had been at work. She had the lead by half a mile.

Ambrose held the *Hind* to it firmly. Her lee rail went down until it vanished in a swirl. He eased her and she lifted her pace. The distance between her and the *Doubloon* began to lessen. The distance between the *Hind* and the cutter closed up faster.

A sea lifted the *Western Star*. I saw the mark-buoy just astern of her. The mainmast of the *Star* stood unharmed. Its stays had held. Nothing remained of her other spars, except a stump forward. She was flying some ribbons. At times, a dark sea gushed out of her main hatch. It seemed to me that there was life left in her. Her buoyancy had been built into her by the best Yankees that ever knocked a block away; and there was reason to hope that her great racing keel could yet be taken.

The cutter swung out a lifeboat. She was so close that I

could see her officers on the lee wing of her bridge. They were reading our signal flags.

I saw the door of the *Doubloon's* pilot-house open. A man, whom I judged to be Parren, came out. He looked ahead, then turned and looked at the *Hind*. The *Hind* was over-hauling him rapidly. He shouted an order. Four of the drag-germen climbed to the top of her pilot-house and went to work on the dory there.

I shouted: "Top dory! Lee side!"

The *Hind* buried her bow into a roller and coasted over it. She dived down the trough and flung herself upward again. She was talking to herself now, talking loud in an accent full of booms and shrill whistles and some laughter. She hit the spray so hard that she flung rainbows to her gaffs.

I said to the Lisbon: "Four men to that dory! Two to a thwart. You to steer."

He nodded.

"Take your gaffs," I said. "If you get aboard that vessel first, keep Parren off. If you lose, steer away and stand by."

He walked forward at a careful pace, striking this man and that on the shoulder as he went, and thus drew his oarsmen after him.

I said to a doryman: "Get up there and tell the Lisbon to take on buoys. Five of them. This is going to a flying set and a tough one."

The *Hind* burst through a succession of heavy seas and pitched headlong toward the *Western Star*. Again I saw the water pour up out of her hatch. This time it was green.

The cutter's lifeboat had been lowered, yet the Guardsmen kept their oars at ready and did not row. An officer, standing at the rail directly above the boat, kept her standing by with his upraised hand. Apparently they had figured out the meaning of the race and had no wish to interfere. Just the same, there was our signal to be considered. A set of flags fluttered on the cutter's signal halyard.

I said: "They understand. Haul down on that halyard."

The distance between the *Hind* and the *Doubloon* had now shrunk to nothing.

"To windward!" I jerked my hand. Ambrose brought the helm up lightly. The schooner closed up on the *Doubloon's* weather quarter and thrust her bowsprit beyond her chains. Inch by inch, she drew ahead.

I lifted my right hand and held it aloft until I caught the Lisbon's eye. I withheld the downward signal until I saw the *Doubloon* suddenly veer off and fling her dory down in the most skillful fashion. Parren himself stood in the stern-sheets, howling at his men. His dory struck so hard that, for a moment, it vanished; then it rose out of a trough and the draggermen gave way.

"Dory away!"

I brought my hand down sharply. The men at the tackle let the dory go. Others pushed her clear with boathooks. No man could tell thereafter what happened to our dory. The whole action was too fast. A sea spun out from under the *Hind's* bow. I think the stern of the dory lagged. Anyway, the dory turned over, spilled her five men and whirled bottom up into our wake.

A yell of triumph blew over the dragger's deck. The cutter's horn began to blow.

Ambrose shouted: "Cutter boat away!"

"Drive her! Drive her!" The *Hind* raced on, leaving the *Doubloon* and her dory astern.

Now the watch forward and aloft began to yell like madmen. They sent down their warnings and the men in the bow ran aft with hands waving to windward. "Hard over! Hard over!"

I saw the *Western Star* lying directly under our bow. I looked over my shoulder at the *Doubloon's* boat. It was racing alongside the *Hind's* wake. Farther astern, the cutter's boat was picking up our dorymen, who were riding their buoys. I saw Nora Doonan standing at the rail. She was gazing at me calmly.

I shouted: "Haul down!" The main-sheet gang were at station, but we had no time to get anything off her. Ambrose could give her only a spoke to take some of the drive out of her. In the next instant, the *Hind*, obeying my wish, crashed into the *Western Star* and slid onto that flowing deck. There the *Hind* reared, groaned, and lay quiet. A sea struck her. She leaned a little to leeward and lay quiet again, all her music over.

The moment the *Hind* careened, I went over the rail at the fore rigging. I sprawled on the *Western Star's* deck, which had now gone under at that point. I ran to her mainmast and thrust my arm through a hoop that lay there in tangle of rope yarn.

I shouted to Ambrose: "Rig the pump! Send a man into the peak. See how she took it!"

He answered: " 'Tis only a touch for her, Captain. 'Twasn't as bad as pan ice—no!"

I called to the bow-watch. They came down to the *Western Star's* deck. I said: "No man puts a foot aboard this vessel. Unless it's the Guard."

The men ranged themselves forward to meet Parren's dory. He stood up in it, a pretty sight with his blubbering and cursing. One of our people sang out: "Fit to be tied, ain't ye, Parren? Come aboard and I'll beat the daylights out of ye!"

Parren spoke to his men. They backed water. He said to me: "Where's your captain? Where's LeNotre?"

"For us to know," I answered, "and you to find out!"

Parren at once revealed that he understood LeNotre was dead. My reply hadn't guided him to that knowledge. No word of it had been said by our dorymen. Yet there were expressions on all our faces that could be added up by a shrewd man. Parren did the sum and slipped awkwardly back into his seat. I heard him say: "Boys, Paul LeNotre is dead. I thought he'd do it. Bible oath! I expected this."

None of them answered. A bow oar lifted. At this, I shouted: "Parren, you stand by!"

He repeated: "Stand by?"

"Aye! There's a word to be said to you. And not by me."

At this, Nora Doonan and Ambrose came over the *Hind's* rail and joined us. The cutter's boat came up. A grey-haired warrant officer stood in the stern-sheets. His men rowed up to the submerged deck and he came splashing aboard.

He said: "The *Hind's* captain?"

"There!" Nora pointed to me. He hadn't noticed that there was a girl amidst the throng. He touched his cap and asked: "And you, Miss?"

"The *Hind's* owner. Nora Doonan."

He faced me, recognized me, and held out his hand. (I had last seen him on the occasion of the foundering of the *Ebb* after she had been shelled.)

I said: "Glad to see you, Mr. Hanson."

He began the business at once. "What's the meaning of all this, Captain Bannon?"

"It's simple enough—"

"I hope so!" said he gravely.

"You're standing on the deck of the old *Western Star*—"

"What!" He looked down in amazement.

"Yes. And to make a long story short—for the time being —we've got sixteen thousand dollars' worth of racing keel under our boots. Metal that's much wanted at the Navy Yard."

A seaman with a notebook and pencil took his place close to the warrant officer and, just as if he was taking a letter down by a 'longshore bay-window, began writing down questions and answers. The officer waited until the notes caught up and then asked: "The *Western Star*? Who is her owner, Captain Bannon?"

"The owner of the *Hind*."

"Miss Doonan again?"

"Yes, sir."

"And the dragger?" he asked. "Where does she come in, Captain?"

One of our people laughed grimly and said: "Last!"

I then told Mr. Hanson how the *Western Star* had been bought by Nora, had been lost in the sou'wester and had been found. I added: "The question of the *Star* is to be settled by us, Mr. Hanson. We want the sixteen thousand dollars. The *Star's* papers are—"

"Here!" Nora struck her topcoat pocket.

The warrant officer asked: "What's the other question then, Captain Bannon? Not that we can put the *Star* aside so easily as that."

I replied: "The other question is one of murder and robbery and piracy!"

"Murder!"

I said: "The captain of the *Hind*—Paul LeNotre—is dead.

One of our hands, Daniel Corkery, was murdered on the *Doubloon* a while back. I saw it!"

It wasn't such an officer's part to show surprise, considering what his day's work can sometimes be, but I must say he showed himself a cool citizen. He even glanced at the seaman's moving pencil. He then asked: "Who killed the captain of the *Hind*?"

I answered: "He killed himself. I saw it."

"Who killed—what was the name of your hand?"

The seaman at once repeated: "Corkery, Daniel."

I said: "Two men killed him, Mr. Hanson. Captain LeNotre was one. Captain Parren"—I pointed to the *Doubloon's* boat —"was the other. I charge him—that man there!—with murder!"

Parren hid his mouth with his hand. He didn't hide his eyes, however.

Nora said: "I saw the murder, too. I'll make the same charge when the time comes."

"The time is now!" The warrant officer took a step toward the *Doubloon's* boat. "Captain Parren, you will go to the cutter."

Parren gave no answer. He stayed hunched in his place, his big head weakly held up. He tried to pump out a word, but nothing came out except his tongue. It licked back and forth. A Guardsman left his place and stepped into Parren's dory. The draggermen rowed away to meet the cutter, which was steaming up slowly to leeward of the *Western Star*.

The warrant officer, whose memory had been at work despite the job he had on his hands, spoke to Nora. "You are Captain Doonan's grand-daughter, aren't you?"

"Yes, Mr. Hanson."

He kindly asked: "And how is he? I sailed with him once

long ago. On her. As his guest." He nodded toward the *Hind*.

"He is all right, thank you."

"I'm glad to hear it, Miss. A great sailor in his day." He then struck his boot against the deck. "And this? How do you propose to handle her? She can't be left here, you know. If anything struck her—a destroyer, for example—" He flung out his hand.

"She's tight," said Nora quickly. "She's no worse off than when we first got her. I've already sold her at Boston. We'll deliver her!"

"How?"

"With that!" She pointed to the *Hind*'s slanted deck. The old hand-pump, which had been rigged in case the *Hind* had started something, was coming down again, and Ambrose was making ready to get it into a sling.

Mr. Hanson shook his head. "I'm afraid not. It would take you days at"—he shrewdly sized up the pump—"at two hundred strokes an hour." He walked over to the gushing hatch and returned. "You must be prepared for a disappointment, Miss Doonan." He then looked to me, as if he preferred to give the bad news to a man. "Captain Bannon, I'm afraid my captain will order a demolition charge for her. It's too bad. Especially with the metal needed. But she's dangerous. Very dangerous." He looked at his strap-watch and, half to himself, said: "Yet we've all day before us. And there's no weather. No weather."

I didn't answer. I knew my men and knew his service well. I caught Nora's eye and gave her a signal, which meant: "Make it lively, chum!" I then said: "Long cruise you've had, Mr. Hanson."

"Iceland and beyond."

"She looks it!"

"We all look it, I guess." He sighed and added: "On the way home, at last." This seemed to me a sign, natural in a man home from the wars, that an interruption of this kind was something of a burden. He spoke again. "Of course, I knew the *Western Star*. I've seen her race in the old days. Sixteen thousand dollars in metal, did you say, Miss Doonan?"

"Sixteen thousand! And more!—the way the market's going. But it isn't the sixteen thousand, Mr. Hanson. Not for itself, I mean. It's the money to take the old *Hind* out of pawn—that's what we fought and sailed for. Parren's money! And I'll fight it out now!" She pulled out the *Western Star's* papers. "She's no derelict, I tell you! Here's her papers and the transfer and the customs receipt out of Shelburne. Why! there's nothing but a little water in her!"

The officer burst into laughter, waved the papers aside and asked: "Who's the *Star's* skipper?"

She pointed to old Ambrose. The old campaigner had made ready for inspection. Arms folded, head flung back, he gravely returned the officer's look; and then saluted in answer to the upraised hand, did so with wonderful disregard of the queer position he was standing in.

"Mr. Hanson, sir!" The hail came down loudly from the cutter's bridge. She had now worked up quite close. Her engines were holding her against the tide. It was her captain speaking. He repeated the officer's name and asked: "How long will you linger on that wreck? What's the matter with the *Hind*? Her captain crazy?"

Mr. Hanson crossed the *Star's* slanted deck and braced himself. He shouted: "The *Hind's* owner is aboard here, sir, and she sends you her compliments and—"

"She? What are you giving us, Hanson? She? She? What she?"

"I tell you, sir, it's a girl! The owner!"

I gave a nod to Nora and she stepped away from the ranks of men. She held up her hand to the bridge and waved it solemnly.

The captain shook his fist and roared again. "Do you mean to tell me, Mr. Hanson, that there's a woman on that derelict? Take her off this instant, sir. Hurry now!"

The warrant officer spoke first to us in a low tone. "You leave this to me and I'll get the whole kit and caboodle into Gloucester before Sunday!" He said to the captain: "She's the captain and owner of this vessel, sir. The old *Western Star*. Taking a sixteen-thousand-dollar racing keel to be melted down for the Navy Yard. She refuses to abandon and she demands assistance. She appeals to the tradition of the service, sir, and asks you to pull the *Hind* off and leave her alone!"

The cutter's skipper had his own hands full by this time. He asked: "The captain? She's the captain of what?"

"Captain of the *Western Star!* Out of Shelburne. Bound for Gloucester."

"What's her name, Mr. Hanson?"

"Nora Doonan, sir."

"Old Doonan's kid?"

"The same?"

"She's got more brass than her grandfather. And that's a lot!"

"So I gather, sir."

The cutter's captain turned to the officers at his elbow. With some thoughtful glances and head-shakings, they looked the *Star* up and down.

One of them cried out: "The *Hind* taking any water, Hanson?"

"She gave herself a rap, but she's sound. So is this!" He stamped his boot on the deck. "The hull, I mean."

The officers fell to talk again, which was interrupted by the captain's word to Nora: "Miss Doonan! You tell me yourself, please. What do you want that hulk for?"

She told him. When she had finished, one of the officers said: "I told you so!" in such a loud voice that we could hear him.

The matter was settled, right then and there, by the engineer officer of the cutter. According to the universal law which rules such matters, he was a Scot (or had been) and he spoke Scots. He cried out to the warrant:

"Lass wants yon hulk?"

"Lass do!" replied Mr. Hanson.

"Lass'll have her then!"

At this, he took a nod from his captain and went down to his black gang and his own pumping gear. The deck hands passed a hawser onto the *Hind* and the cutter eased her off. The *Western Star* came up a little. The Guardsmen rigged a ten-inch hose pipe, ran its nozzle down into the *Star's* main hatch, and the pumping began. Before moonrise, they had taken many tons of water out of her. The cutter passed the same hawser onto the *Western Star* and took her in tow, pumping as they plugged along. The *Hind*, under foresail and jib, ambled along to windward.

* * *

So ends, for us, the voyage of the *Golden Hind*. No need of my telling all that followed: the punishment of Captain Parren and the dragging days of the inquiry and the doubt and wonderment, now, I trust, dispelled forever. I will only say that I took my fish to Boston and sold the vessel through for thirty-eight cents a pound; and to the kindly inquiries of the dandies of the Boston fleet, I replied: "Halibut? Aye! plenty of them. I bought them off the *Flying Dutchman*. Go hail her!"

I stayed at Boston until the *Western Star's* business was done; and then I came back to the Doonan Wharf at Gloucester, where settlement was held, with nigh on thirty thousand dollars in the ship's box. I made the people of the *Hind* rich and sent them home rejoicing. I arranged that they should go as dragger pupils with certain skippers of my way of thinking. And, at last, I took my nets to the shipyard, where the *Hind* was to go when the ways were ready and a new engine and winch carted up from the railroad. I will say, further, that we did make our mark with my big-mesh nets and showed the fisheries, here and abroad, how big fish can be killed and little ones spared. (An odd thing: The *Doubloon*, under Captain Larsen, was the first to follow us in the change, first to give up the small mesh that was destroying our future.) Yes, a great future began for us, vessel and men. One hundred and thirty thousand pounds of cod and haddock the first trip; two hundred and ten, the second. Pens full and no shame in them.

Let me tell you, at the last, of the night I brought the *Hind* in from Boston; and furled those beautiful sails forever, and hauled her dories into the wharf-shed to let them lie there for mice to nest in or boys to buy. The old *Hind* was through with the past; and it was at my wish that her owner had said so. I knew how well and long the *Hind* would yet labor in the fisheries. I knew, more than others, that the change was inevitable, that it is surely in the great course of Nature to lighten men's labor, on the sea as well as on the land. Nevertheless, as I turned away from her and left her sighing in her old haven, I couldn't bar her sweetness from my heart; for I was full of understanding of the service she and her like had done for the Republic. They were nurses of men, the *Golden Hind* and all the Yankee sisterhood. Good-bye to them.

To the greatest of her captains, I now went, taking my time in the quiet of a frosty Sunday evening. I came to the house. She met me at the door and took me to him, where he sat, drowsing by the fire, as on the night I had left him. As before, venerable; indeed, the equal in beauty and dignity of the hero, Ambrose Cameron.

How wise old men are! His lids were closed when I came to his side. He lifted them at the touch of her hand. He cast a lead deep into me and said: "Captain, you have suffered!"

I said: "We have all suffered, sir."

He opened the fingers of his right hand so that I might lay my hand in his. Gently as my son's fingers now close on mine after long absence, his fingers closed. He said: "No more. 'Tis over. Change, Captain Bannon. Change her."

His lids drooped. I left him and stood by her side at the great window, where the generations, nourished by the *Hind*, had watched her go, strong and beautiful, to the Grand Banks; and had waited there for her return, always knowing that her strength and beauty and her crowded sails would bring their captain home, rich or poor. I held the curtain back. We saw the shipyards and the wharves. Beyond the town and under it, the ways gleamed under rows of lights. Night forges glowed and men passed to and fro upon her deck, slanting to the sky. Even while I watched, my hand in Nora's, a steel hand reached down out of the sky and fumbled there. Nora murmured. I said nothing. The steel hand closed on the *Hind's* main-boom, swung it upward and away into the dark. She had no need of it now.

Nora Doonan looked over my shoulder at tne man drowsing by the fire. A cry came from her mouth; the tears came down her cheeks, and she cried, like a little girl who has lost something quite dear to her. I kissed her cheek and touched her forehead with my hand. I knew why she wept. She wept for one who fed the salt. Long, long I had to wait before her grief should pass, before she should stand there, on another night of winter, to await the beaming of a port light and the coming of the new captain of the new *Hind*. Trusting it would be so in good time, I went out into the snow, which was beginning to fall on the old town, on the roofs where my dorymen slept, and on my *Golden Hind*.